Charlotte has been writing from a young age, and has written several novels in both the science-fiction and fantasy genres, published internationally by Random House and Pan Macmillan. These include *Fury*, Book One of The Cure series and *Avery*, Book One of The Chronicles of Kaya.

She studied a Masters of Screenwriting at the Australian Film, Television and Radio School, and is the author of the Australian Writer's Guild award-winning screenplay *Fury* – adapted from her novel of the same name. She now lives in London, writing novels and working on both film and television projects, as well as the upcoming graphic novel *Skin*.

Also by Charlotte McConaghy

Fury: Book One of The Cure

Melancholy

Charlotte McConaghy

First published by Momentum in 2015
This edition published in 2015 by Momentum
Pan Macmillan Australia Pty Ltd
1 Market Street, Sydney 2000

A CIP record for this book is available at the National Library of Australia

Melancholy: Book Two of The Cure (Omnibus Edition)

EPUB format: 9781760082567
Mobi format: 9781760082574
Print on Demand format: 9781760082581

Edited by Jo Lyons
Proofread by Tara Goedjen
Cover design by Matt O'Keefe

Macmillan Digital Australia: www.macmillandigital.com.au

To report a typographical error, please visit momentumbooks.com.au/contact/

Visit www.momentumbooks.com.au to read more about all our books and to buy books online.
You will also find features, author interviews and news of any author events.

For my grandfather, Kevin

"The soulless have no need of melancholia."

– Vladimir Odoevsky

Chapter 1

Josephine

Sometimes when I sit here I feel like all the heat in the whole world has come to keep me company, cocooning the two of us in an inferno. It's so hot out here it makes it hard to breathe.

I imagine words, thousands of them, forming conversations and sentences we never said when you were awake. I imagine the things I will tell you when you open your eyes, if you ever do. I imagine a world of truth that never existed for us in the beginning.

They tell me that it's unlikely. That I shouldn't hope. Here in the west they know a lot about hope. They know how to ration it just as they do with food and water. They dole out hope in tiny pieces, clutching it in their hard, calloused hands, spreading it thin so that it lasts and lasts until its very edges, until they have wrung it dry. They recognize when it is real and when it is false. They know that to hope can mean to survive, but so too can it destroy you.

They tell me, every morning, that today will be your last. That today I should say my goodbyes, harden my heart, let you go. They have dispensed with any remnants of hope –there is none left for this, for us. You have been asleep for too long, they tell me. I must let you go.

They know a lot out here. They understand a lot.
But they do not understand you, Luke Townsend.
And they do not understand me.

*

September 18th, 2065

Josephine

Every fiber in my body has reached a state beyond exhaustion, but I can't let myself fall asleep. Instead I sit slouched in this sticky leather seat, watching the blackness rush past the window, rocked into a dull state of trance by the noisy hum of the train.

Luke's head lies in my lap, the rest of his big body draped over the seat next to me. There's no blood – he looks to be in perfect shape, and he's breathing normally. I don't really understand how a body could just shut down into this kind of sleep. With my finger I trace his lips carefully, wanting to memorize their shape.

"That's creepy."

I jerk my finger away and look up at the big blue eyes, so blue they're almost violet, somehow. The bolt through her nose glints, as does the sheen of her skull under the razor-short hair. Her name is Pace and she stalks this train night and day. She likes to swear and laugh in a hysterical, crazy way.

I think I like her.

"Why?"

Her eyebrows arch. "All you do is stare at him. Or touch him. Real slow like that. Does he know who you are? Or are you, like, his stalker?"

This makes me smile. "He's mine."

She blinks once, then pushes off the seat in front of me and strides away.

Next to jog down the aisle is Hal, the big, brutish-looking one with the white mohawk and tattoos on his arms. As he passes he winks at me and keeps going. It's their exercise, apparently. And it makes me tired just watching them. I don't want to think about why they need to be so fit or strong.

My eyes shift to the black of the tunnel outside. It's disorienting being underground so long, moving so fast but unable to judge how far we've come. I have no idea where we're headed because Pace won't tell me. I don't trust them, but I believe that all three know Luke well.

"He's real calm and contained," Pace told me last night when they carried him through the bush. "But, like, all trembly under the surface."

"That's his wild," Hal had chipped in. "His animal."

And then the little one, whose name is Will, added definitively, "He's sweet like honey to catch the flies."

Yep. They had Luke pegged.

Now, startling me, Will's head pops down from above – *outside* the train. He grins, swinging down to pry open the window and clambering inside like a little monkey.

"What are you doing?" I exclaim as he shuts it again, blocking out the loud rush of sound. "That's dangerous."

Will laughs, his smile wide and full of white teeth. We look surreptitiously at each other, trying to figure each other out. He can't be more than fourteen or fifteen; I think Pace is a little older.

"You're tired," he observes eventually.

"How far are we going?" Having had no luck with Pace, I quiz him instead.

"Pretty far."

"What's that in miles?"

"Dunno. Pretty far though."

"And what's at the end of pretty far?"

"The west."

I already know this. It does nothing to help the nerves under my skin. "Do you have doctors there?"

"One."

"How does this train run?" Now that I have someone sitting still long enough to answer questions, I'm going to take advantage of it.

"Ask Hal. He's the engineer."

"Hal's an engineer? He's a child."

"He's nineteen."

"And where did he get an engineering degree before nineteen?"

Will stares at me, his amusement patent. "You really are from the city, aren't ya? Jeez."

I don't know what he means, so I shrug.

Will's eyes drop to Luke and he shakes his head. "Can't think of much that'd knock that one out. What happened to him?"

I look at Luke's face. "I happened to him."

Eventually I sleep. I'm too sore and woozy not to. My dreams are haunted. Blood and teeth and poles in spines. I wake with tears on my cheeks and, seeing Hal sitting opposite, I brush them quickly away.

"You'll be okay in the west," he says with complete confidence.

"What's in the west?"

"We will be in about twenty minutes. I came to help you get your boy up."

In the end it takes Hal, Pace *and* Will to lift Luke, big as he is. I'm useless, trembling with pain and fatigue, so I follow at a stumble. The train slows as if of its own accord, but doesn't stop, so we have to sort of hop out onto a weird, crumbling set of stone steps as it speeds off. The steps take us up at an angle, through rock and earth, until we reach a wooden trapdoor and emerge into boiling sunlight.

My breath leaves me. It's unbearably hot, and I start to sweat with a dizzying sensation. A hand takes my arm – I think it belongs to Pace – and steers me into what seems to be a large town square. Squinting against the brightness, my first awareness is of the yellow-orange dust under my feet. Next comes the brilliant, endless sky above. Not a speck of green anywhere, but I never expected green. Not in the west.

There's an odd wash of salt in my nose, the kind of pungent scent you can't ignore. I can't for the life of me work out where it could be coming from.

Around us are low mud brick buildings full of open windows and doors, presumably to let the airflow help against the heat. Taller concrete and steel buildings, much older in appearance, are dotted throughout. And beyond the buildings, in every direction, is a mighty stone wall slicing right up into the sky, rimmed in rusting barbed wire. It makes the hairs on my arms stand on end, because my first thought is, of course, *prison*. I have been brought to a prison, and I'll never be able to get Luke out. My next thought is *not another one*. In the city we were too used to walls. Too used to cages. I didn't escape one just to wind up in a second.

"Where are we?" I rasp, but I don't think anyone hears me.

Pace yanks me into a small brick building, then down a different set of steps. It is blessedly cool down here, and the relief, unfortunately, distracts me from what is actually happening. I just trot along, dazed and sore, until Pace shoves me into a square concrete room and then locks the door behind me.

I blink, staring at her face through the small glass window. "Get comfortable, Dual," she tells me, her voice faint. Then her footsteps disappear back up the steps.

"Hey!" I shout. "What – ?"

She's trapped me here. What a bitch.

The room has a steel table that's been screwed to the floor, and a single steel-framed chair. It's clearly an interrogation room, or a prison cell.

Okay. Okay okay okay.

I mentally get my bearings. Possibly two days ago – it was very hard to keep track of time on the train – I escaped from the asylum on the hill with a recently drugged and unconscious Luke. I was picked up by three wild kids in the bush, who brought me on a train trip and then promptly locked me in this room. I don't know where I am, or who lives in this place, or who the kids really are. They said they were resistance, but I have no way to trust that. And I have no idea where they've taken Luke.

That's it. That's all I have to work with.

My feet are still bleeding and my broken elbow is aching. Instead of slumping into the chair like I'd really love to, I squat to the ground and study the bolts securing the table. They look strong, but the legs were welded to the bases a long time ago, so I might be able to pressurize them at the right angle and get them to break. This seems unlikely, though – I don't think I have ever been as undernourished or sickly as I am right now.

None of it turns out to be necessary as the door swings open and I stumble back. A man enters and shuts the door behind him. He is shorter than me, but very muscular through the chest and arms. He looks a bit like a bull terrier. Though his face is quite pretty, actually, beneath the boyish sandy hair.

"Hi," he says.

My eyebrows arch. "Hey."

"Sorry about this. Protocol." He gestures to the seat. "We'd just like to ask you some questions, if that's alright."

"And if I say no?"

He smiles and I am met abruptly with the reality of this friendly-looking man: he's dangerous. "Let's start with your name."

"How about we start with yours?"

Another smile. It's a kind smile, but there's an edge of something beneath it. "Sure. I'm Quinn."

"And you're the boss of the resistance?"

"Boss makes me sound like I'm a thousand years old." A wide grin and a shrug. It's the perfect gesture of self-deprecation – he's good at this. At seeming non-threatening. He's trying to make me comfortable.

"Sit down," Quinn insists. "You look unwell."

I sit.

"What's your name?"

I didn't tell the three kids my name; they never asked. Instead, Pace started calling me Dual because of my two-colored eyes. Now it hits me like an electric shock – I don't know why but I really, really don't want this man to know who I am. I can *feel* the danger in the room.

"Dual," I tell him.

"Dual. Unusual. Do you have a last name?"

"Not one I can remember."

He frowns a little, confused. "Really? Why's that?"

"I've been in a mental health facility most of my life. Electroshock therapy and a nice cocktail of medication is a great way to strip you of anything and everything, including your name."

"I'm sorry to hear it," he tells me. "That's where Luke found you?"

My mind starts working quickly. "The guy who saved me? Yep."

Quinn watches me, studying my face. "You don't know him, then?"

"Nope."

"You aren't cured."

"How perceptive you are."

"Why is that?"

I'm sure he can guess why, but I tell him anyway. "They never bother curing some of the looniest in the loony bins. It's funny, really, 'cause we might have been the ones most in need of fewer emotions."

This was what happened to my roommate Maria. She'd been in a catatonic state for most of her life so the government didn't waste their cure on her – they just locked her up and waited for her to die.

"You don't seem very loony right now," Quinn points out.

"Thanks, that's sweet."

There's a slight twitch in his jaw. I'm annoying him, I can tell. He smiles again, as if pulling the mask over his face. "How did you know to go to the tree?"

From my pocket I pull the instructions scrawled on the small piece of crumpled paper. "Found it on Luke."

Quinn takes it and gives a wry sigh. "Not too careful of him, was it?"

"You'll understand if I don't mind too much about carelessness that saved my life."

He nods. "'Course. What do you know of Luke's girlfriend? The one he went back to save."

I meet his eyes. "Josephine Luquet."

"That's her."

"She was my roommate."

"Where is she?"

"She died," I tell him simply. And just like that, I am reborn. Josephine Luquet, orphan and murderess, is dead.

With those words I see all the plotting and strategy go out of Quinn's eyes and he looks tired. "I'm sorry," he says, and this time I believe him.

Perhaps I overestimated the danger. Maybe I'm paranoid. Then he asks, "And are you a Blood spy, Dual?"

I blink. He's watching me very closely. "Do you really think I'd tell you if I was?"

He smiles a little, but I can see him looking at my pupils and my fingers, at the rise and fall of my chest. I wonder if he can spot a lie.

I lean forward, holding his eyes. "I'm not a Blood."

Quinn nods.

"Can I go now?"

"Soon," he assures me. "There are just a few things we have to check before we can welcome you to our community."

"Like what?"

"Nothing bad. Hair and blood samples."

"What? No fucking way."

He is surprised. "Why?"

"I've just spent my entire life getting pricked and prodded by asshole doctors and I came here to get away from that."

"It's just to make sure you aren't carrying anything that could infect my people," he says. "We have to maintain our health out here, Dual. Health means strength and strength means survival."

Then I must look the picture of weakness right now. But I like the words. I like the idea of strength, even if I don't have any of my own.

"One prick, that's it. Promise. Otherwise I can pop you on the train and you can be back within the city in a couple of days."

I shake my head. There's no way in hell he's letting me go back to the city knowing what I know. Stubbornness rears its head and I battle with it. "Fine," I grind out. I can see in his face that this isn't a fight I'll win.

"You should know, Dual," Quinn says. "The fact that you're uncured is the only reason I'm letting you into my home. It's one of our laws here. But if you do anything to harm my people, I'll kill you myself."

For some reason, the dire warning makes me feel a little better. It makes me feel less like I'm walking into some kind of trap. I nod.

"Hang tight," he says and disappears.

I wait at least an hour before the next visitor arrives. I'm growing more nervous by the minute. It's a shaggy blond guy, about thirty or so. He smiles awkwardly, reaching to shake my hand. "Dodge."

"Dual." I almost laugh at the ridiculousness of the names. Why did I lie? It now seems silly – I'm not Dual, in any way, shape or form.

Dodge clears his throat and fusses about for a few minutes before nervously taking my blood and hair.

"Have you done this before?"

"Sure, plenty."

So he's just awkward and nervous by nature then.

"You ... came with Luke?"

"Yep."

"He really missed you. Talked about you all the time."

"I'm not her," I tell him.

"Oh – *oh*. Sorry. I just assumed – "

"No worries." My tone forbids any further discussion and he shuts up. When he's done he tells me he'll let me know when the results are in.

"After you let Quinn know, right?"

Dodge blushes and shrugs. "He's in charge. I'm to take you to the infirmary now."

"Is there a bed there?"

"Loads."

"Sweet hallelujah, that's the best news I've heard in my whole life."

Dodge has to support my arm as we climb the steps back up into the hot sunlight. It's embarrassing to be such an invalid, but I can't do much about it. Each step on my cut feet is a victory, and my head starts to spin as the heat hits me. He helps me to a room that has been painted with a fresh coat of white. Light linen drapes hang still against the open windows; there's not even a hint of movement in the oppressive air. Beds line one wall and there, in one of them, lies Luke.

A striking Indian woman is fussing over him, saying his name a lot. He's hooked up to tubes and wires, and connected to a small machine that monitors his vitals. The woman doesn't even glance at me, so intent is she on Luke.

They all know him. It scares me because I can't fathom it. But then again, there's so much about Luke I never knew, an entire life he never even whispered about.

I sink onto the bed next to his and let my head hit the pillow.

There's a kind of fear in the Indian woman's voice, and it's a fear that only exists when you care deeply about a person and you think they're going to die. With this understanding, something inside me switches off and I fall into a deep sleep.

*

September 19th, 2065

Josephine

The heat wakes me. I am sticky with it, and the light sheet on my legs feels as though it's burning my skin. Kicking it off, I blink awake and slowly remember the bizarre and foreign place around me. The infirmary I lie in has a dozen beds, some rudimentary supplies and tools laid out on trays that have obviously been stolen from the city, plus a locked cabinet of medicine and a couple of blinking monitors. It feels spare and cool with the windows open.

She's watching me take it in, the Indian woman. Her eyes have tragedy in them. She wears nose rings too, but not a bolt like Pace's – a small red gem in each nostril. It's hard to tell her age – I think she might be in her forties, her skin still flawless, shape fit and slim.

"I'm Ranya," she tells me.

I stare at her, not wanting to turn my head and see that his bed has become empty. If I look and he's gone, and they have stripped off the sheets like they do in movies when someone dies, I will give up right now.

"I'm Dual, I guess."

She seems to find this amusing. "You're going to be fine."

"How is that?"

"Your injuries weren't too bad. You have a fractured elbow, some lacerations on your feet, a small amount of brain swelling, severe dehydration and a bad case of exhaustion, but that's all."

"Oh, that's all. Good."

She cracks a smile, flashing white teeth. "I've dealt with it all. You'll be fine if you take it easy." She pauses, sees that I don't seem inclined to relax, and adds, "Honestly. You're alright."

"I believe you."

"Then try to relax."

She's not getting it. "Is he … ?" I swallow, clearing my throat. My hands clench.

Ranya frowns, then realizes. "He's alive," she assures me.

So I turn my head. He's there, looking for all the world like he's sleeping peacefully. The relief is so immense that I lean over and vomit onto the floor.

Ranya is by my side in an instant, holding my long black hair. "It's alright. Shock and exhaustion, that's all."

I spit and sag back against the bed. "Sorry."

"*Gross!*" Sashaying into the hospital room is Pace, looking fresh in clean clothes. "Are you serious, Dual? Get a hold of yourself."

"I'll clean it up," I say quickly. I stand, but a wave of dizziness hits me so hard that I fall back onto the mattress.

"Weakling," Pace declares. "She'll be worth nothing to us."

"Nice, Pace," Hal mutters, entering with a mop and bucket.

"How's Luke?" I ask Ranya.

"Bad. In some sort of coma," she says, not bothering to sugarcoat it, for which I love her. "I don't know how to wake him out of it, and I don't know if he has much chance of survival."

They all look at Luke, and then at me.

"She's green again," Pace warns. "Stand by for more chunks!"

"I'm fine."

"How do you know him?" Ranya asks me.

My eyes stray to his hand, lying on the bed at his side. It is as large and square as I remember it, a hand with big knuckles, a strong hand, made for hitting and breaking things. Not a hand for music, not delicate or slender. I know that hand as intimately as I

12

know my own. I know how it fits with mine, and all the differences between the two.

"I don't," I admit finally.

*

I sleep and wake again once the sun has gone down. The windows are still open but now there is a beautifully cool breeze ruffling the curtains. Luke and I are alone in the dark. I feel remarkably better now that the heat is gone from the air and I've slept properly. Sliding out of bed, I gingerly take one barefooted step to his side and gaze at him for a long, stretched moment.

Something brushes against my hand and I jerk in fright.

"Only me," Will says softly. He is so silent I didn't even hear him come in. "Time for your tour."

*

We stand atop the enormous wall, beneath only the silver smattering of stars, and here is what I now know.

This is a camp for the resistance, established and built twenty years ago in the remains of an abandoned prison – hence the wall. It's called The Inferno, not because of how hot it is, but because to the Ancient Romans this was the name of the Underworld, and in Quinn's settlement, this is where the city's dead come to be reborn. The metaphor's a bit belabored for my taste, but in any case The Inferno holds two-hundred-and-sixty-eight souls, each of whom works hard to keep the community running. Powered by several generators, the camp has only enough electricity for the important things – the medical machines, emergency lighting, food storage and the heating of just enough water for washing, cleaning and cooking. Most people live in the old cells, which I find disturbing, but Will assures me they're really homely, and not cell-like at all. There are also a bunch of newer mud brick houses for anyone too squeamish for the old prison building, and anyone with children.

The camp is hierarchical, and to get to the top you have to be strong. My new best pal Quinn is the leader, and according to Will everyone loves him because he's strong, kind and fair.

Every single person here spends time cooking, cleaning, building, repairing, gardening, tilling and, most importantly, hunting. I haven't asked what they hunt, but I assume it's food. Only injury or old age can exempt you from these tasks, and even then you have to find some other way to contribute. There are children, but only a few.

All two-hundred-and-sixty-eight are, without exception, uncured.

In the dark I look at the view. We are so far west that we have reached the coastline. Half an hour ago, Will brought me up here and I turned to behold what lay beyond, and I burst into tears. Because there before me was the ocean – a mighty expanse of it, so wild and unknowable, and I had never seen it before. The smell filled me up and the sound worked its way into the rhythm of my blood.

Now I watch it, having listened to Will speak for as long and in as much detail as he could about this new world I've stumbled into. Behind me is a different view. A forest of dead trees and scorched earth, skeletal fingers of wood that curl into the sky and obscure the moon. I can't see much down there, but I can see the faint shape of moving shadows.

"Why the wall?" I ask softly.

Will gazes down at the forest with a hard expression. "Because the only living creatures out there are Furies, and they're drawn to our scent."

I am no longer plagued by a virus that transforms me. I have found the resistance, as I've longed to for years. But the world of the beyond is more dangerous than I'd imagined. The man I loved betrayed me and now he is dying. I am broken and mended all at the same time.

Those are my facts. I'll hold onto them for as long as I can, because there's not much else that I know anymore.

*

September 19th, 2065

Raven

I wake from dreams I could never admit to with a hand on my cheek. It is Quinn, looking at me in the dim light. I blink, disoriented as the pleasant images slip from my mind.

"What?" I ask. Quinn's sandy hair and pale eyes make him seem angelic; it's the existence of his two halves living alongside each other that make me love him. Well, an approximation of love, at the very least.

I've always found myself drawn like a moth to a flame to those with cunning in their hearts.

"He's back."

And like that, a jackhammer in my chest.

"When?"

"Today."

"And you only just told me?" I fling the covers off and reach for some clothes.

"He's in a coma he might not wake from."

"Then how did he get here?"

"A girl."

We look at each other. "*His* girl?"

"She says she's not. But it's hard to imagine otherwise. She's uncured."

"She could be the one, then."

"She could be. She's weak, and a child."

I feel a slow, cold smile curl the edges of my lips. "The better to use her, my dear."

Quinn's smile appears innocently amused. But swift plans are forming behind his eyes; they look like shadows passing through his soul. I can't help it. I take the hem of his shirt and lift it over his chest. His teeth flash white with his grin and his hands go to my hips, lifting me onto the dresser. "The devil's got a hold of you, girl."

"He's got a hold of us all," I whisper as he moves inside me and I gasp aloud. My dream crashes back into my mind, the dream I dream every night, the dream of Luke, my Luke, of him kissing every inch of my body and of his girl, the one he left me for, watching us as the moon grows full and explodes over each one of us.

Chapter 2

January 20th, 2065

Luke

Harley hands me a can of baked beans and then goes back to his computer. I sigh, watching him in exasperation, although I can't complain because he's working this madly for me. "Anything?"

"I'll tell you when I have something," he snaps.

I head to his small kitchen and use the can-opener to attack my eighteenth meal of baked beans in four days. It tastes like ass.

"Dude, I know you're hard at it, but I need some real fucking food."

"While you're in hiding, you don't get to be a foodie."

"It's not being a foodie! I'm being a living human who needs more than baked beans to survive. I'm getting malnourished as we speak. These muscles don't get to be so big without a little help."

He rolls his eyes. "I'll go shopping tomorrow, beauty queen."

I nosedive onto the couch and cover my head with a pillow. I'm going slowly insane. It's been four months since I dropped Josi off at the asylum on the hill, and I haven't spoken a single word to her since.

It feels anatomically wrong, like the make-up of my body no longer works without her nearness.

I have Harley looking for something, and he tells me every day that he's close, that he's nearly hacked her system. He tells me every day, but every day he doesn't hack anything.

It isn't until eleven o'clock that he wakes me, looking wide-eyed and crazy. "I got it! I fucking got it!"

And I damn well love the man.

*

Being in charge of the Bloods and in the back pocket of the Minister, Jean Gueye – my ex-boss – has the highest level of security clearance in the world, and hidden within about 'a thousand mother-fucking firewalls', as Harley put it, is all her information on the whereabouts of the resistance.

*

January 21st, 2065

Luke

Harley and I stay up all night looking at the contents of Jean's illegally hacked hard drive. As morning rises my stomach can't take it anymore and I yell at Harley to go and get me some food, since I can't risk leaving the safety of his protected apartment.

While he is out buying me a celebratory meal, my best friend Harley is murdered by Bloods who traced the hack on Jean's computer. And I only discover this when I turn on the television and see his brutalized corpse plastered over the news, proclaimed a traitor to his people.

January 30th, 2065

Luke

I've waited nine days to move. Nine days of sleeping and scraping through the bottoms of empty tins for food. Nine days of *I want to die I want to die I want to fucking die.* Nine days of trying to drum up the courage and the energy to do this. To go.

There is a train line at the very bottom of one of the old, unused subway tunnels. This tunnel supposedly leads all the way out west, to the resistance camp. There's no running train, of course, but the line itself is like a direct path.

The Bloods don't follow it straight to the resistance because the one rule we obey above any in this city is the rule of never going beyond the wall.

Nine days, I tell myself, is long enough. I immediately feel nauseous at the thought of a time limitation on grief, but I forbid myself to sink down that black-hole again. Enough. I have something left to fight for, so I must fight.

With a last look at Harley's computer monitors all aglow with shimmering wasp wings, I say simply, "I'm sorry, I love you, I will make this right."

And then I set off. West.

*

The problem is going to be food and water. Wearing a pair of Harley's heavy-duty microscopic lenses, I head for the supermarkets. I can't see for shit, but at least no random retinal scanners will pick me up. Gathering enough to supply me for a month, I pile it all into a shopping trolley and walk straight out without paying. No one stops me – they don't care. No drone would steal. It wouldn't occur to them.

I've already stolen and reprogrammed the smallest and most manoeuvrable car I could find so that it won't send any alerts of my fingerprints back to the Blood base. I pack the mini tight, adding extra canisters of mind-numbingly expensive petrol, and away I go.

It isn't quite that easy, actually. The Bloods pick me up before I reach the subway. I see them before they expect me to, which gives me the tiniest advantage. Gunning the engine, I steer into a one-way street. The cars approaching are all fitted with motion sensors that steer them smoothly out of my way, so I just shoot straight down the middle of the road.

Up ahead I can see the gated entrance to the old train station. Accelerating as fast as the car will go, I am about to bust through the chains when shots are fired and my back right tire explodes.

The car skids sideways, hits the gate at an angle, bursts through the flimsy chains and tilts down the wide concrete steps. A grunt of shock leaves me as the car flips over and *rolls* down into the subway, miraculously landing upright with a bone-shuddering impact.

My teeth hurt. Every joint in my body aches. My head feels like it might rupture.

I turn the key and listen to the engine groan and splutter and then – amazingly – whir to life. "Holy shit," I breathe. "You are one hell of a car."

Behind me the Blood vehicles, which are practically tanks, can't fit down the staircase. I speed forward, bracing myself as I launch the tiny car onto the train tracks. My windscreen shatters over me and I feel glass slice a thousand miniature cuts into my face. But I keep driving straight down the train tunnel.

*

February 3rd, 2065

Luke

I've been driving only a few days when it happens.

I've burned through two full tanks of petrol and I'm starting to get seriously worried that I'll be walking most of the way, which means running out of food. Every eight hours or so I stop to get an hour's sleep. I look forward to these hours like a maniac, because this trip is, without exaggeration, one of the worst experiences of my life. It's bloody freezing with the windscreen smashed open, I can hardly see two yards in front of the car, the engine is noisy as hell and driving on the tracks means the mini bounces and skids over every single piece of rock, causing my spine to jar and my head to crack the roof. The suspension is shot, and I'm astonished the car's still driving at all.

So it's with a pretty solid dose of trepidation that I feel the vibrations in the ground. Which can mean only one, ludicrous thing.

There's a train coming.

What. The. Hell.

Sure enough, behind me approaches a soft, distant thrum of noise, and just the faintest hint of light.

Think, my mind screams at me. Right. Every mile or so there's a safety alcove to the side of the tracks. I have no idea if the car will fit in one, but it's my only hope. If that train is going to the resistance camp, I need to get on it. And I need to get the car out of the way.

I roar the engine and speed the mini forward as quickly as it'll go. The train is getting steadily closer; it's bearing down on me. I have to get out and jump for it. I'm not going to make it. The car's done for.

The light blinds me.

The swell of noise envelops the mini.

My spine is shattering.

But I don't get out, I –

– yank the wheel sideways and plough the car straight into the safety alcove. I hit the wall nose-first and feel the impact pummel the mini like it's made of tinfoil and has just been compacted in a rubbish heap.

Whoosh goes the train, taking a chunk of the car's tail with it.

Wind slams me sideways, but I don't have time to hesitate. Swinging out my window, I scramble on top of the smashed car. The train's moving too damn fast. I have to time it perfectly.

Peering sideways, there's just enough room for me to see the end of the train approach. Taking a deep breath, I throw myself out just as the silver metal flashes past and grab hold of something – anything. It's the ladder, and as my hands clench around the steel pole I feel the velocity of the train's momentum wrench me into space and yank my shoulder out of its socket.

A scream leaves my mouth but I don't let go.

Grasping the ladder with both hands, I manage to scrabble for a foothold. With shuddering breaths I rest my face against the back of the train and try to block out the pain. My training as a Blood means I can do it, but the toll of the last week or so on my mind and body makes it a slower process than usual.

When my brain seems to be functioning with a semblance of clarity, I pry open the back door and squeeze inside. Relief surges as the world falls blessedly quiet. I hadn't realized how unsettling it was to have noise pounding through your skull for days without respite.

I move into the first carriage and perch on one of the seats. I have no idea who I'll find on this train, so I need to prepare. Closing my eyes, I take my right hand and twist the arm hard, fast and up. Pain splices through my shoulder as it crunches back into place.

Moving my wrist to rest over my chest, I get to my feet and start searching the train. It's not until I reach the very front engine room that I believe – it's miraculously empty. It must run on some kind of continuous loop.

Sagging onto one of the seats, I settle in for a long journey with no food or water.

*

February 4th 2065

Luke

Pain lances through my head. It joins the rest of the pain in my body, accumulating and storing itself away so that I'll be able to really enjoy it later. My left eye is swollen shut and there's blood trickling into the right, but I can still see well enough to look at my torturer.

He is a tall man, lean but very strong through his wiry limbs. There's something familiar about his demeanor, about the set of his shoulders and the way his gaze turns dark before he punches me. His skin is tanned and leathery from having spent many hours under the sun. I judge him to be in his fifties, and he hasn't said a single word to me all day. I wonder if perhaps he doesn't understand the purpose of torture, but disregard the thought immediately – this is a man who knows exactly what he's doing. He took the measure of me straight away, and knows I won't speak unless I want to. So he's working me a bit, and enjoying himself in the process.

There's another who comes in and out to check on the progress. He asks questions, a crapload of them. Says his name is Quinn, and he doesn't understand that I'm not going to tell him shit until they stop beating me.

"Anything yet?" Quinn asks as he enters the small room for the fifth time today.

The torturer shakes his head.

Quinn, who is short but stocky, with sun-bleached hair and honest blue eyes, paces around the chair I'm tied to. "I'm going to ask you one more time, and then I'm going to kill you. Who are you?"

"I've already told you," I mumble through a mouthful of blood. "My name is Luke Townsend."

"But why are you here, Luke? How did you find us?"

"I'll tell you when you untie me. I'm no threat to you or any of your people."

Tall Guy punches me in the arm and it goes well and truly dead.

"Why the hell would we untie you?" Quinn asks. "The only possible way you could have found our train line is if you're a Blood. And I'd rather cut off my own limbs than set you free among my family."

Quinn stalks out and I stare at Tall Guy. He is as expressionless as he's been all day. His dark, dark eyes find a way inside me, but not even those eyes know how stubborn I can be.

I got off the train this morning and walked straight into the middle of the camp, hands up, unarmed. It took them all of ten seconds to surround me, take me captive and bring me to this dark little room for 'questioning'.

"How long are we going to do this?" the man asks suddenly, the first time he's spoken. His voice is surprisingly rough, as if he rarely uses it.

"You tell me, big guy."

He shrugs. "I'll keep hitting you until you admit that you untied your ropes hours ago."

I smile and let my hands drop to my sides.

Taking me by the arm, he pulls me to my feet and marches me out of the room. The night is cooling considerably. There is a cluster of people standing around in the dust and they turn as one to look at me.

"Did he speak?" Quinn asks.

My torturer doesn't say anything, and I realize that this is my moment.

"Like I said, my name's Luke Townsend. I was a Blood once, but not anymore. I'm here to help you destroy them."

September 21st, 2065

Josephine

After my tour they let me sleep for two nights and a day, and when I wake I feel more human. My elbow is still broken and my feet are still cut, but I'm otherwise alright. My teeth and fingernails don't ache like they wish to be free. My skin doesn't feel like it's been scoured. A miracle, given the blood moon has only just passed.

Pace is sent to start me on my first day of work, fitting me out in tough work clothes and heavy work boots. She doesn't look happy about it, eyeing me up and down and pointing out every physical flaw she can spot. "You're hobbling like an old gran," she says as we cut behind a water silo to find a huge field of wheat. It's like magic to my eyes to see things actually growing out here. "And your hands are soft like a baby's."

I don't know what she expects me to say.

Pace leads me to where a row of people hack away at the stems of wheat. They're all tanned and strong, and they look at me curiously until Pace shoves a massive sickle into my hand and turns to leave.

"Wait! What do I do?"

She glances back at me with irritation. "Are you daft? Cut low to the stem and tie it into piles."

I turn to my row of wheat, spying on the people on either side of me. As I try to copy their confident actions, I find my back aching and my hands getting cut. After about an hour I'm about to pass out, and slump to the ground for a break.

"No stopping yet," an old fat woman says as she breezes by me, cutting away like she was born to it. "Three more hours, then lunch, then four more hours."

I sigh in sheer disbelief. "I can't. I'm still weak."

She grunts in agreement and moves on.

Removing my work boots, I see that my feet have bled through the bandaging. Hobbling back toward the end of the row, I emerge to find Hal and Will passing by with massive machetes on their backs.

"Hey!" I shout.

They spot me and head over. "How's day one?" Will asks.

"I can't – my feet," I tell them, showing the blood.

Both the boys peer at me. "You have to," Hal says simply. "*Look.*"

"Ranya cleared you for work, so you have to work."

My mouth falls open. "But I *can't.*"

"Sure you can," Will grins as they turn to leave. "Gumption, girl! Gumption."

*

I jerk awake and blink several times to get my bearings. Pace's blue eyes glare at me from within a canopy of wheat. The sky behind her is golden and pink.

"You've got to be kidding me."

I sit up, not in the mood to get reamed. "Back off, Pace."

She shoves me hard in the shoulder.

"What are you *doing*? You gonna beat me up because I fell asleep?"

"You have no idea what you've got yourself into, do you?" she asks. Hauling me to my sore feet, she tugs me back toward the houses. "How many hours did you do today?"

I shrug. It was one. If that.

"How much time did you waste feeling sorry for yourself?"

Angrily I wrench my arm out of her grip. "What I do with my time is none of your business."

Her lip curls. "You think you own your time? Your life? Well you don't. You went to our tree and you accepted our help, and

26

you followed us here so now you and your whole life belong to The Inferno. Hurry up."

I watch her walk away. I'm exhausted and sore and I could really use a shower. Besides which, I'm desperate to get back to Luke. But in the end I have no idea where I am or where the hospital is, so I follow the cow.

She takes me to the biggest building in the camp – it's wide and flat, and has no windows that I can see. Inside is a massive dining hall, with huge handcrafted tables and an enormous kitchen at the back. Every inch of space is full of people chatting and laughing and arguing. I stop at the entrance, overwhelmed by the sight.

Only once before have I seen so many people in the same place – that was at the illegal warehouse party I took Luke to, and that was a nightmare of crazy drones. This is different. This is *wonderful*.

Loud, rowdy music is played by a band in the corner and a few men have erupted into an alarmingly rough wrestle-fight that no one seems remotely bothered by – in fact, those nearby are cheering them on.

Pace glances at me and grins. "Welcome to the Den." I can barely hear her over the ruckus.

She takes me to the serving line and hands me a plate. My eyes travel over the faces before me, so many that they start to blend into a sea of dirty happy angry *alive*. At the head of one of the tables is Quinn, wearing his easy, infectious smile. I watch him for a moment, wondering about how he came to be the leader of this place.

Another argument breaks out in the food line and a woman's plate is sent flying through the air to splatter over everyone nearby, including Pace and me. I blink, then realize they're all laughing.

I'm so disoriented that Pace has to nudge me to hold my plate out for a big slop of veggie stew and a chunky piece of damper. It smells delicious and my mouth waters. I'm looking around for a quiet corner when Pace drags me to the front of the room.

Quinn stands. He takes my hand and lifts it high. "Ho!" he booms and everyone gives a mighty cheer in response.

Jesus, they're all staring at me. In the city I was completely invisible. I never thought I'd long for those days.

"This is Dual. She's uncured and filled with the fury she was born with. Welcome the newest member of the uncured!"

Everyone rises to their feet to cheer and clap. It's a wall of sound and movement, and I feel heat rise to my cheeks. 'Uncured and filled with the fury she was born with' sounded like an intonation – I wonder if it's their motto.

"She's also brought our Luke back to us, and for that she has our gratitude."

This time there's an even bigger cheer. I wince. They all need to chill the hell out.

To me Quinn says, "Your blood's clean, kid. So I'm formally welcoming you to The Inferno."

A warm feeling fills my chest. But just like that, the kind smile is gone. "But you spend another day like you did today and you'll be asked to leave. Understood, Dual?"

A large section of the room seems to have fallen quiet around us, waiting for my response. I feel outraged, fire seething beneath my surface. It might also be embarrassment. "I don't take orders," I tell Quinn. "I'll work, but I'll do it when my injuries are healed."

An eruption of laughter bursts from the crowd.

Quinn tilts his head to better study me. I don't let my eyes leave his. "Is that so?" He cracks his knuckles; it's obviously to intimidate. "You've been medically vetted, so you work. I hope that's clear enough for you. Enjoy your meal and get a good sleep tonight. We're very happy to have you here."

I'm about to argue when Pace pinches my arm hard enough to make my eyes water. She leads me further down the table to where Hal and Will are sitting, both of whom laugh hysterically at me.

"What?" I snap.

"How the hell did you ever pass for a drone?" Will asks.

"Your animal lives at the surface," Hal agrees.

"What does that mean?"

Hal tears a huge hunk of bread free and puts the whole thing in his mouth, then takes about two seconds to chew and swallow. "Your animal. Your *wild*. We all have it. If yours is a strong animal, it'll be harder to control. If your wild is vast, you'll live deeper inside it and find it harder to come out."

I stare at him.

"He's nuts," Pace says with a roll of her eyes. But she smiles sideways at him, and while I'm not particularly good at interpreting his stuff, I'm fairly sure they're more than friends.

There's a movement in the corner of my eye, a flash of color, of something fluid, and when I look up the breath catches in my throat. A goddess has just walked into the hall. She's curved in a perfect hourglass figure, her hair is fire-engine red, and she moves like a dancer who can hear music in every step. I can't drag my eyes away.

"Oh lord," Pace sighs. "It's the evil queen."

"Avoid that one," Will agrees. "Devil incarnate."

"What's her name?"

"Raven."

I watch as Raven leans down to kiss Quinn on the lips, then slides into a seat beside him. She looks incredibly self-satisfied.

"Dual," Pace says sharply. "Listen to me. Stay away from her. You won't have any idea what she's thinking, and if she's nice to you, she's probably, like, about to scratch your eyes out with her talons."

I nod, but I want to know where her name comes from.

After dinner Hal walks me to my new accommodation. He and Will live in the cells, but I've been put in with Pace, who's in one of the mud brick houses but disappeared without a word after dinner. The house is small and simple, and just what I need. My room has a bed and a dresser, along with a cupboard that's stocked with clothes and shoes. Apart from my room and Pace's, the house has a small living room with a single couch, and a bathroom. No need for a kitchen, apparently, because everyone eats together in the dining hall.

I love the simplicity of it, even though it doesn't have one of my favorite things: a bathtub. I have never had a home so nice. Except for the one I shared with Luke, the one filled with lies.

"Why's there a room free?"

"Pace's roommate died last week."

"What? Shit. That's awful. How?"

"How everyone dies here – killed by the Furies while she was hunting. You gonna be alright?"

I nod, sinking onto my bed. My feet hurt so much I'm dizzy. "Why did I get a medical clearance if I can barely walk? I also don't think scything wheat is great for a broken elbow."

"Look," Hal says kindly. "The only thing anyone cares about here is fortitude. You earn their respect, you'll earn their loyalty. You act like a coward and they'll despise you."

When he's gone all I want to do is sleep, even though everything in this room clearly belongs to a dead girl. Instead I walk back out into the dark, quiet streets of the camp, and I find my way painstakingly to the hospital so that I can spend the night sitting beside Luke's bed.

*

September 22nd, 2065

Josephine

I wake in a chair, stiff and sore and more tired than I was last night. No one disturbs us as the sun rears its head and turns the room gold. The heat is already seeping into the day.

Ranya arrives to check on Luke.

"Why did you clear me for work?" I ask.

"Because you're ready. Pad your feet up and use your right arm, you'll be right."

"I'm still injured."

"You can do anything you put your mind to."

"Oh, Jesus. Can't I work somewhere else? Why does it have to be in the field?"

"Prove yourself and they might move you." She pauses, then smirks. "You think the field is bad? Wait till they start you in training."

"Training? For what?"

She doesn't reply, just laughs as she leaves. I sigh, placing a hand on Luke's forehead. "Everyone here is crazy." I wait for him to wake and tell me I'm just being stubborn, but he doesn't, so I keep waiting.

*

October 1st, 2065

Josephine

On Sunday everyone gets a day off for the tournament. I have absolutely no idea what this is until I follow Will to the central square and realize the entire population has crowded around two men, and as we squeeze through to the front, they launch at each other and start fighting. Like, *real* fighting. Scary, crazy, lunatic fighting. Soldier fighting. *Warrior* fighting.

My mouth falls open. Part of me finds it disturbing, but a bigger part is thrilled and fascinated with the athleticism in the blows and movements. It doesn't end until one of the men is on the ground and taps out.

The fights go on all afternoon, the winners moving on to fight someone else until they reach the top of the ladder and have to face the best. The best being, of course, Quinn. And it's not just the guys – the women fight too, and are equally ferocious.

I watch as Quinn's quick, flashy moves destroy his opponent in no time, and he bows to the cheers of the crowd.

"Does this happen every Sunday?"

"Yep."

"Do people volunteer?"

Will looks at me and laughs. "Oh lord, you are funny sometimes, Dual. Everyone fights. Once a month. I'm next week. You'll be entered as soon as you finish your first round of training."

I nearly pee my pants. "*What?*"

"It's how we stay strong," Will says. "How we survive."

"By beating each other?"

He doesn't reply. I follow his gaze to the crumpled figure on the ground, having made it all the way to the top only to be beaten by The Inferno's leader. "Does anyone beat Quinn?"

Will gives me a funny look. "Once. There was one."

"Only one?"

"Only one."

*

October 23rd, 2065

Josephine

I haven't yet made it to the end of a full day of work. I usually find somewhere to hide and sleep for the afternoon, and have trained myself to wake up before sundown when people will notice. I'm pretty much ignored for the most part. People don't like me, but that's not a new thing in my life.

I'm crawling out from under a row of wheat when I see her. She is waiting at the edge of the field as I approach, and gives me a wide smile. "There you are."

My mouth opens but nothing comes out.

"I'm Raven. But you already know that, don't you?"

I nod.

"You're the one with the dual eyes."

We look at each other. I have absolutely no idea what to say, but I do finally understand her name. It's the blackness of her eyes; they are chilling and bottomless.

"You came with Luke."

I give her another nod.

"You saved his life."

"No."

"I wanted to thank you for that. I don't know what I'd do without him."

And with that, all sense of wonder at her beauty vanishes. Instead my hackles rise.

Raven tilts her head, her smile growing wider. "Shall we go and see him?"

We fall into step side by side. "How long was he here?" I ask calmly.

"Several months."

I can't believe Luke dumped me in a loony bin and went to have an adventure with the resistance. It's been pissing me off since I got here – *I* was the one who always wanted to find them. And now they all know and love him, as of course they would because everyone always does, and it just makes me feel like even more of an outsider.

He sleeps, and I wait, and everyone here no doubt compares the two of us and can't fathom how a man like Luke could ever come to know a woman like me. I haven't told them that I'm a science experiment and a murderer because I can't say the words out loud. I haven't told them that Luke pretended to love me because I was a danger to humanity – it's too humiliating. I haven't told them how I killed my therapist with a stool leg in his spine. I haven't told them anything, because all the words I have to say are poison.

I realize as we walk the real reason I lied and told them my name was Dual. It's because I don't want to be Josephine Luquet anymore.

"How's the harvest going? Or should I say, how is the sleeping?"

I falter.

"Don't worry," Raven grins. "I won't tell anyone. You're tired and you've clearly never done a day of labor in your life – it's not your fault."

I am instantly outraged, wanting to tell her that I *could* do a day of work if I wanted to, but then I realize how bratty that sounds and start to feel embarrassed.

Raven stalls me at the door with a cool hand on my arm. "Do you speak, Dual?"

I remember all my words, all the thousands of them, spoken to Luke and then Anthony. Those days I spent talking and laughing, the hours in the therapy office, staring out the window and recounting incorrect versions of the truth. I meet Raven's eyes. "I used to."

Ranya is sponging Luke down when we go inside. His shirt is off and her strong, thin hands move with a mother's tenderness as they dribble water over his smooth skin. He looks pale, and there is bruising on his torso that scares me dark inside.

"What's that from?" I demand.

"It's internal bleeding, love," Ranya says softly.

"So fix it."

She doesn't say anything, because there's nothing for her to say. She's not a surgeon. She can't fix it.

The sun is sinking and the air has a chill to it. I want to cover Luke's body so he won't feel the bite, but I don't move; I stand frozen, watching as Raven calmly takes the sponge and starts dabbing his chest. As if she always does it. The image is scoured into my brain and for some irrational reason I can't look away. They are beautiful, the two of them. She is so at ease in her body, in her interactions with his body. Did he and I ever look like that together?

A hand takes mine and I realize belatedly that Ranya is leading me outside. "Dual? Are you listening?"

I nod dumbly. "Is she a nurse or something? Does she normally do that?"

Ranya looks at me and I see pity in her eyes. Pity. Jesus, I know what's coming. I know what she's about to say – it's all there in her gaze.

"He's dying, love. His organs are shutting down. He won't survive much longer."

I swallow, then shake my head. "You're wrong."

"Dual, listen to me – "

I turn and run. I don't feel the wounds in my feet or the jerking of my broken elbow, I don't feel anything at all but the wind against my face and the thump of my heart. Ranya is wrong.

And I am wrong – I have *been* wrong. Luke would be disgusted at the way I've behaved, cowering in fields and sleeping when I should have been helping. Avoiding people and skipping meals so I don't have to be in the hall under Quinn's probing eyes.

I plunge through the field until I find my discarded scythe, and then I start working on my row, the one bloody row I should have finished weeks ago. I bend my back and I hack at the wheat, cutting and dividing and tying it into piles that I carry on my back. And when the sun has gone down, I keep going. I don't stop, even when the pain in my body is unbearable, when my back aches and my feet ache and my elbow and hands and head all ache. I keep working, because my life has been a series of nightmares and throughout it all I have kept going. I kept going until I got here, and then I stopped, and I don't know why. I don't know why I suddenly became a coward – perhaps I have always been one, and reality has finally caught up with me.

"Dual!" a voice shouts late into the night. I ignore it and keep going, lost in the rhythm and the pounding of my head.

I am further into the field than I have ever gone. In the dark it all looks the same, but above me I can see the emaciated fingers of wasted branches snaking up to obscure the moon. For a disoriented moment I think I am beyond the wall. In the wild. My heart jams out of beat and I sway.

The next thing I know, I am staring up at the inky black sky, where the stars are the same as they have always been, but brighter and clearer. And now there are hands on me, lifting me, and I go to tell the hands that I'm fine, but no sound comes from my mouth. It is Hal, I think, from the white of his hair in the moonlight.

"Let me keep working," I manage.

His eyes are enormous and so pitying that I start to struggle. I can't bear the expression they all wear. I *hate* pity.

"It's alright," he says gently. But he's just a child, and Luke is dying. There will be no alright.

Chapter 3

February 4th, 2065

Luke

I've never been so thirsty in my life. There's dry blood on my cracked lips and my eye seems to be swollen shut, meaning my peripheral vision sucks. This is making itself apparent because each time I slyly want to take note of the people watching me, I have to really obviously twist my head the whole way around.

Quinn sits opposite, hands folded on the table, watching me calmly. We are the only ones seated in the large dining hall. Stationed around the room are several resistance fighters, all armed and very wary of me. My hands have been tied again, and the fact irritates me.

"Well go on," I say. "Ask me whatever you want."

"How did you know about us?"

"I hacked my boss' hard drive."

"Who's your boss?"

"Jean Gueye."

"Bullshit."

"Would you like me to forward you a resume? She might not have a particularly glowing reference for me though – "

"No, it's bullshit that you hacked her drive."

I shrug. "And yet here I am. Can I have a drink? It's hot out here."

Nobody moves. I sigh.

"Why did you come here?" Quinn asks.

I run my swollen tongue over my teeth. "Few reasons."

"Which are?"

"The first is my girlfriend."

His frown deepens and I see disappointment set in. Someone in a corner sniggers.

"The government's been torturing her."

"Revenge, then?"

"Of sorts. And redemption."

"For what?"

"For having spent the last thirteen years working for them. I can't take that back, but I can use it to take them down."

He considers this. "How can you prove you aren't a spy?"

"I guess I can't. Not until Jean's dead and the cure's been destroyed."

"What you're talking about is a lot bigger than Jean Gueye," he warns me. "She's practically a pawn."

"Good. Means she'll be easy to destroy."

"And the king?"

"Falon Shay, Prime Minister of the regime. He needs to be taken out, along with the other eleven Ministers."

"And when they're gone, we're still left with a city of drones."

"Not for long," I murmur. "I have an ally in the city."

"Who could possibly – "

"Ben Collingsworth." The inventor of the cure. I let that sink in for a moment. "He's already working on the antidote as we speak. If we can find a way to take control, we can make everyone human again. Which is why I came to you. I need fighters."

Quinn falls silent, eyeing me closely. Finally he smiles. "You're intriguing, Luke Townsend. I'll give you that."

"Can you also give me a glass of water?"

Quinn nods and someone brings me a cup, lifting it to my lips for me. It dribbles down my chin, making me look like a fucking infant.

"I'll make you a deal, Luke," Quinn says. "You stay here and we see what you're made of. If you can make it through a few months, and convince us of your loyalty, I may just believe you. Then we can start talking about working together."

I nod but all I can think to myself is that a few months better not turn into more than that, because Josephine is in an asylum waiting for the blood moon, and if I don't get back there in time to save her from the transformation then I might as well keel over and die right now.

*

Raven

Hal and Will are guarding the dining hall doors. "Move," I order.

"Sorry, Raven," Hal says nervously. "Quinn said it's private."

"Would you rather deal with him or me?" I ask sweetly.

The boys hesitate, then stand aside. I push into the hall to find Quinn alone at a table with a man I have never seen. The prisoner everyone's been talking about. Rumour has it he's a Blood. I stride over and slide into a seat next to Quinn's.

Quinn sighs. "Luke, this is Raven. Raven, Luke."

I extend a delicate hand to him. He's a large man, broad and muscular even when slouched in his chair. There are bruises over most of the skin I can see, and he has a bad black eye and split lips. But when he turns his one good eye to me, I see a forest of green and a world of cunning, and I know that if I don't make this man belong to me I will die.

"My hands are tied," he points out as if I'm an idiot.

I withdraw my hand. "A pleasure."

"Luke's decided to join our cause," Quinn informs me casually.

"And is it true that Luke is a Blood?"

"It is."

"*Was*," the man grunts.

I tilt my head, studying him more closely, but his attention has already gone back to Quinn. Which is unusual. I learned at an early age that whether I want them to or not, people stare. My father used to stare, before Quinn gutted him for it. So now I use the stares, and I like them.

They pick up their conversation. Luke is listing names of other Blood agents, a whole host of them, along with their security codes. He finishes by saying, "I want a vow that we'll stop the sadness cures before they're administered next year."

A bubble of laughter leaves me. "And how do you propose we do that?"

"With planning and courage," he answers me flatly.

"City folk are always foolish when they arrive here," I remark. "Full of heroic ideas. But as they settle in, they always see."

"See what?"

"The futility of fighting."

Luke leans forward in his seat, eyeing me closely for the first time. "What the hell are you doing out here then?"

"Surviving."

He stands without having been dismissed by either Quinn or me, which is a punishable offence for a prisoner, and says, "That's not enough anymore. Show me to where I'll be sleeping. I've had a rough few days."

*

October 24th, 2065

Josephine

They let me sleep. I am ashamed, but I let them let me sleep, again and again. I stay in bed for the entire next day, letting the world wash away from me, my soul beginning to ready itself for a vast, unnameable grief.

I wonder, in my dreams, if I will keep going once he's dead. Or if my soul will simply drift away, untethered.

As sundown nears I am assailed with an abrupt desire to see the ocean. And not just from atop the wall – but from the sand of the beach. I have always loved being immersed in water; it suddenly seems imperative that I have my first swim in the sea.

I rise stiffly from bed and hobble through the streets to the gate. Guards above peer down at me. "You alright, kid?" one of them calls to me.

"Can I go out for a bit? I just wanna see the beach."

The guard snorts. "No way in hell. You're untrained and unarmed. Who do you think'll give you permission?"

"You?" I ask hopefully. "There's a rock cliff protecting the beach – I'll see them coming from a mile away. There's never anything out there anyway."

He whistles. "You are green, aren't you, kid?"

"Look, whatever," I snap, growing frustrated. "I'm opening that gate and I'm walking through it, because this isn't a prison anymore, and it sure as hell isn't the city."

"You open that gate without permission," the guard says clearly, "and I'll shoot you where you stand."

It causes something in me to go cold. Without warning a very large, dark-haired man appears silently beside me and I lurch in fright.

"Jesus," I gasp. "Don't do that."

He glares at me with eyes of coal and he has a *bow and arrows* strapped to his back. Without a word he signals to the guard on the wall.

"Training?" the guard asks, and the dark-haired man nods. He then unlocks the gate's heavy iron bolt and walks out into the shadows, long and lanky and utterly silent.

He pauses only very briefly to glance at me and say, "Come."

It's a bit like déjà vu of the morning Luke first appeared as a tall stranger. I followed him, too. I must be the kind of person who's incapable of learning a lesson.

Moving through the dusky night out here in the beyond, it's quiet enough to be creepy. The air has grown cool but remains thick as always.

I've lost sight of him. "Hey!"

A hand clamps over my mouth and I gasp. "Shh," he utters. "Be silent or we die."

Fear curls within my gut. I follow him into the dead, moonlit forest, trying to remain as quiet as possible, but I'm breathing fast and there's dry earth crumbling under my feet. If we weren't heading in the direction of the ocean I'd be bolting back inside the walls by now. My earlier bravado is gone, replaced instead by an instinctive awareness of danger. I think, over and over, of Pace's last roommate, and how she died.

We walk for about fifteen minutes or so. The man leads me past ghostly white trees until we come to a ridge. He motions for me to flatten myself to the ground and then we crawl up to the lip of earth. I'm not sure what to expect, but it certainly isn't what I see.

There, down in a ravine that leads directly to the sea cliff, are dozens of people grouped around campfires.

"What the hell? Who are they?" I whisper.

The man doesn't reply, and I find myself looking more closely. They're people, yes, but they're … strange. Distant sounds drift up to me on the wind and I hear not words, but the animal noises of breathing and snarling and growling. It's unnerving, and the back of my neck prickles. The creatures down in the ravine, even from such a distance, are *wild*, and as I realize this I know what they are. "Furies."

"That's the path to the sea," he tells me softly. "We're upwind now, but if they knew we were here we'd be dead."

"Why did you bring me?" I ask him, even though I know the answer. It is my lesson for wanting out, for wanting free.

He doesn't reply, and I can't help but murmur, "They look just like us. It seems … civilized, the way they're grouped around the fires. The children's stories describe them as mindless."

I think, inevitably, of my first encounter with the fabled creatures. Luke and I were in an abandoned building when we were set upon by Furies, and I heard four words that changed everything I knew about them. *Hold. I smell flesh.*

But however intelligent they are, they still wanted to devour us. I remember that just as clearly as I remember the fact that they could speak.

"What's your name?" I ask the man beside me.

"Shadow."

"Shadow. Really? Okay. What are they, Shadow? Where do they come from? What makes them like this?"

He shakes his head slowly. He doesn't know.

"But you kill them."

He nods.

"And if they're still human?"

Shadow looks at me for what feels like the first time. "They are human."

The moon is almost full. I can see the ocean in the far distance, reaching up to meet the inky horizon. The night is undeniably beautiful, but whatever we're doing here suddenly feels ugly.

I crawl my way back down the incline and head for the compound, even though walling myself in is the last thing I feel like doing.

"Your last name?" Shadow asks, moving silently alongside me.

"I can't remember it. Why?"

"What happened to your parents?"

"No idea."

"And Townsend?"

I glance at Shadow. He's probably in his late forties or so, leathery skin, wiry muscle in his limbs and a completely unknowable darkness in his gaze. "I met him for an hour. Then he went into a coma," I lie bluntly.

I am angry with him, I realize. For teaching me this lesson, for teaching me how caged I am.

That's when a soft, whispered shuffle sounds from our left. Shadow doesn't have time to ready his bow before something snakes into a shaft of moonlight slicing between the trees.

It is a man, or the approximation of one. It runs at us and in this moment I see the savagery in its face and I hear the rabid snarl torn from its bleeding mouth. Shadow manages to unsheathe a long hunting knife and intercept the Fury as it lunges at me. The blade takes it awkwardly through the cheek but doesn't send it entirely off course – it still barrels into me and I hit the hard earth.

The air leaves my lungs in a *whoosh*.

I'm unable to do anything except blink up at the bleeding gaze and snapping teeth of the thing that is trying to kill me, for every second up until the moment Shadow inserts his knife into its skull. It dies atop me, looking at me, and I can't look away from its soulless eyes, because actually its eyes don't seem so soulless in death.

Shadow rolls the body off me and helps me to stand; I do so shakily and then wrench away from him. "Don't touch me."

He makes a wary, calming gesture with his hands, as though *I* am the wild thing. "They'll smell the blood," he tells me quietly. "We should run."

So we run, and the moon seems to be swimming above, and I try to breathe through the images in my head. Because in with the macabre carcass with its overflowing eyes is a pole erupting through a spine and blood spilling from lips, and ravens circling overhead.

*

October 25th, 2065

Josephine

Pace's fist lands squarely on my cheek and my brain explodes. I hit the mats and lie still, groaning in pain.

"Come on, you big baby. Get up."

"You just sucker-punched me."

"No, a sucker punch is when you can't see me coming. I just hit you from the front, so slowly and lightly that my drone grandma could have dodged it."

I clench my teeth and drag myself to my feet. Hal and Will are wrestling on the mats beside us, and there are teams of other people scattered around the training room, practicing under the tutelage of Shadow, who runs the training of the hunters. He hasn't said one word to me since last night when he led me outside to get attacked by a Fury. And now everyone seems to just expect me to know how to fight.

"Get your hands up," Pace orders.

I lift my fists into the spot she showed me earlier.

"Protect your face. Get your elbows in. Not that tight. Try to be ready but relaxed. Loosen your shoulders."

"It's really relaxing knowing you're about to get creamed."

"If you put half as much energy into training as you did into whining, you'd be the best damn fighter here."

"Hilarious."

She attacks me, punching at my face again; this time I manage to leave my arms in place to block her. But this just means that her punch takes me in the forearms, and it *hurts*. "Ow!" I yowl, retreating backwards and out of the line of fire.

"I give up," Pace announces. "Shadow! This is bullshit! She won't participate!"

"I *am*!" I hiss. "You've been whacking me all morning!"

Shadow arrives in time to hear Pace say, "You're not even trying."

He looks me up and down, taking in my pathetic weakling body and wounded expression. Then says to Pace, "She can run."

He walks away.

"Why don't you tell me yourself?" I shout at him.

"Ooh, you've done it now," Pace sighs. "He doesn't even think you're worth training. Means you're gonna have a really fun time in the tournaments."

My mouth falls open. "I still have to compete even if he won't prepare me?"

"Yep."

I storm after Shadow, grabbing his arm and wrenching him to a halt. Everyone stops what they're doing to watch. "Don't walk away from me," I snap. "You're here to train me, so train me."

He looks at me with those black eyes of his, and they practically drip with scorn. "You're too weak."

"Then I'll lift some weights!"

"You're weak of spirit," he clarifies simply.

I feel myself shrivel into a tiny ball of shame. I dash from the room and run all the way back to my house. Slamming the door behind me, I crawl into bed and squeeze my eyes shut.

My fingers find the wooden bedframe, using the sensation to try to calm me. My pinky finds a groove, suddenly, an unusual one. Tracing it, I realize it's rough as if it's been carved. Sitting up to peer at it, my heart stutters with astonishment. There are two words cut secretly into the wood.

Josephine Luquet.

*

At the dining hall, Quinn arrives at my side just as I am lined up for dinner. "Hi, Dual."

"Hey," I mumble.

"I've been led to believe that you didn't show up for field duty today."

"I had training …"

"This morning. Which you departed from halfway through, and neglected to then go to your work shift."

I stare at him. He can't be serious. Training and then work in one day?

"Therefore you haven't earned your food for the day." He gently removes the plate from my hand.

People are staring and I feel my cheeks flame. Raven is sitting in her usual spot at the head of one of the tables, and as she looks my way I see the faint hint of a smile at her lips. I bolt out of the dining hall.

Outside in the warm night I kick the dirt in rage and humiliation, letting out a small and rather pathetic scream of frustration.

Stalking to the hospital wing, I slump into the chair beside Luke's bed. "This isn't working," I tell his comatose form. "I don't fit in here."

I imagine him rolling his eyes.

"There are hardly any books and no coffee!" I rant. "My brain's bored and my body keeps getting beaten up. Plus everyone here is a total *jerk*."

"Ouch," says Ranya from behind me.

I jump in fright and then clutch at my racing heart. "Jesus. Don't do that."

She moves quietly into the room and sits on the other side of the bed. I wish she would leave us alone. "I didn't mean you," I mutter. "Even though you did clear me for work when I still have severe injuries."

Ranya smiles. "They're far from severe. Come here and let me check them for you."

I hop onto the bed and let her unwrap the bandages around my feet. She looks surprised. "These are healed, Dual." Next she takes my arm and gently manoeuvres my elbow in different directions. "Does that hurt?"

"No," I admit. "But Pace spent the morning hitting me. And no matter how much scything I do, my back still aches."

"Keep at it. Your body will grow stronger."

"Apparently I'm weak of spirit, so it hardly matters does it?"

She doesn't respond to that, which is not exactly a shining vote of approval. When she sits back down it's clear she's not going anywhere, and I don't feel like sharing Luke tonight, so I head for the door.

"If someone called me weak of spirit," I hear her say, "I'd be doing everything in my power to prove him wrong."

"That's because you're easily manipulated," I tell her, and leave.

*

Back home I find Pace, Hal and Will sitting on the floor of the living room playing a board game. I walk past them to my room.

"Don't you dare cower in there like a loser," Pace orders.

"I thought I was the town leper."

"As long as you're not contagious we don't mind lepers," Will replies cheerfully.

They're playing Trivial Pursuit, and I grin slowly. "Oh dear. You three are *really* going to regret including me."

Hal smiles. And I proceed to answer every question correctly.

"What is the scientific name for a rabbit's tail?"

"A scut."

"What is the minimum number of masts on a schooner?"

"What's a schooner?" Will asks.

"A beer glass," Pace tells him.

"Two," I answer. "And in this case it's a boat."

"What eye-catching device was invented in the 17th century by Anton van Leeuwenhoek?"

"The microscope."

"What is the first name of the New Zealand poet Tuwhare?"

"Hone."

"What amphibian did Pliny the Elder suggest be tied to the jaw to make teeth firmer?"

"A frog."

"Who on earth is Pliny the Elder?"

"Ancient Roman philosopher."

"How the hell are you doing this, you freak?" Pace demands after a couple of hours of this.

"She's gotta be cheating," Will agrees, grabbing my sleeves and lifting them up to see if I have the answers written there. I laugh and push him away.

"I'm clean, boys and girls."

"Then how?"

"I've played this game before."

"So what? We've all played it a million times."

"Yeah, but you don't have photographic memories."

They stare at me.

"Really?" Hal asks.

"Really really."

"Prove it," Pace says.

"I thought I just did."

"Do something better."

"Okay ... Umm, have you got a deck of cards?"

They grab me a deck and I throw the cards onto the floor, mushing them around until they're in a complete mess. "You pile them together and then hand them to me."

Will pounces on the pile excitedly, scurrying to gather them up and pass them over. I make sure I show them what I'm doing, flipping through each one and glancing at the cards for half a second each. Then I pass the cards back to Will.

"I'm gonna tell you what order the cards are in, so check as I go."

"What – *all* of them?"

"King of diamonds, four of clubs, two of clubs, nine of hearts, ace of spades, queen of hearts, jack of clubs ..."

"Holy shit," Hal breathes when I've done the whole pack. Pace has been checking every single one suspiciously.

"How come you can't be this cool all the time?" she agrees reluctantly.

"Kind of a veiled insult there but okay."

"What else can you do?"

"I'm not a circus freak," I say, and they fall awkwardly silent. "Just kidding. Go get that book and I'll show you something cool."

So we spend the whole night being entertained by my wacky memory as it helps me recite any page of text they ask for, and I have to say – it feels good to have maybe-possibly-pseudo friends for the first time in my life.

*

October 26th, 2065

Raven

The girl would be beautiful if she didn't look so thin and sickly. That was my impression when I first saw Dual. I haven't had reason to think much more of her since then, frankly. She is underwhelming at best. Which means I'm fairly certain she isn't the girl Luke went off to find, his ex-lover, the girl he spoke of as the strongest creature he'd ever met.

Therefore she isn't immune to the cure. Which means she isn't the one Quinn and I want.

I stroke my hand down the back of his neck because I know it drives him crazy. "Not now, love," Quinn says.

"Yes now."

"The girl will be here any second."

"So? Let her wait." I climb onto his lap and kiss him hard, finding his lip with my teeth. But there's a knock on the door and before I can call for her to wait, Quinn has plonked me unceremoniously on the couch beside him. "Come in."

An eruption of dark fury in my chest.

Dual trails in. We are waiting for her in the living room, candles lit, wine poured: the perfect place to entertain. She looks bedraggled, as usual. Her shoulders are slumped, fingers fidgeting.

"Hey. I …" She clocks the romantic setting. "I can come back another time … ?"

"Sit down please, Dual," Quinn says kindly, handing her a glass of wine.

She sits awkwardly on the floor and looks at us. "So what's up? Am I here for another scolding?"

"Not at all. I'm told you were present at your duties all day today."

"Like a good little girl scout." She salutes with a mocking smile. Then turns her two-colored eyes to me, and I am suddenly aware of where all the bratty behavior is coming from: Dual is burning from the inside out, alight with as much fury as me. The realization strikes me and I find both my dislike and my fascination for her increase tenfold.

"We thought since you've been here a little while now that we should have you over for drinks and chat. Get to know each other better."

"And get to know what I know about the Bloods and the cure?" she surmises.

"Of course," Quinn replies, no less smoothly. "We're a resistance group after all."

"Are you?" she queries. "I haven't heard of anyone going on a mission to the city since I got here."

"Missions are dangerous and require a lot of planning. But they do happen when we need supplies."

She studies him.

"Perhaps you could start by explaining how you know Luke?" Quinn asks.

"Funny, I could have sworn I already told you that during my questioning."

"Not quite, no. You said you were Josephine Luquet's roommate. That explains nothing about Luke."

She takes an elegant sip of her wine, then plays with the stem of the glass between her slender fingers. It's a stall if ever I've seen one. She launches into the story, sounding bored. "As you already know, I was in the asylum when Luke came. Josi was unwell. Something weird was going on with her. Luke broke us out of our room and took us to one of the labs. She ... lost it. Went bat-shit crazy. Killed our doctor. Hurt Luke so bad he passed out. Then she died. Just slumped onto the ground and didn't wake up again. Luke saved me from my cell, and from Josi, so I wanted to repay the favor. I got him out, and followed the instructions I found in his pocket." She pauses, licking her lips and smiling crookedly. "He came for his girlfriend but he got me instead. Lucky Luke, huh?"

Quinn and I watch her. There's nothing flawed in her performance, nothing unbelievable in the detachment she speaks with. There's also absolutely no reason for her to lie to us, as far as I know. And yet I *feel* the untruth of it in my pores.

"You've spent an awful lot of time sitting at the bedside of a man you barely know," I point out softly.

"Like I said. He saved my life. I owe him his."

"Why were you in the asylum in the first place?"

"I go on murderous rampages." We stare at her and she dissolves into a soft laugh. "I get depressed, okay? It's not something I love talking about." Dual shakes her head, the smile fading. "But that place ... it's a waking nightmare. I couldn't stand it for one second longer, and I saw my chance to escape. I feel bad for Luke, and Josi – I do. I liked her. But I don't regret what it's meant for me."

"And what's that?"

"Freedom."

Quinn nods, sitting back against the couch. And it hits me. The reason I don't believe her. It's because I know how to recognize cunning and subtlety. I've spent my whole life attuning myself to them, learning to note even the faintest hints. And this girl is drowning in both.

"Well, wonderful," Quinn says, clinking his glass to hers. "Cheers. To new beginnings. And to our gain."

She hesitates, then nods. With a quick, wry smile, she murmurs, "You're certainly gaining a lot, with a girl who can't work or fight for more than five minutes at a time."

Quinn chuckles, and I smile, realizing I'm supposed to.

"But I do plan to try," she says reluctantly. "I'll work hard at being better."

When she's gone, Quinn turns to me. "Well, I guess we have our answer. She's just a normal girl."

All I'm thinking is that Dual is quite the little actress. "You're too trusting," I tell him.

"What – you think she's lying?"

I shrug, unwilling to admit it yet; Quinn's always telling me I'm too hard on our people. He sees the best in everyone, while I see only the worst. It's why they hate me, every one of them. But what they don't get is that my mistrust keeps us safer than Quinn's kindness does.

So for him, and for all of us, I'll have Dual's lies and her truths from her, and if I have to I'll use them to destroy her. Because I'm one of the few who was born out here in the lonely west, and I'm not foolish enough to pretend it isn't exactly that brutal.

*

Josephine

I walk from their house with my skin crawling. I'm not sure why I keep lying, but I know that I don't trust either of them as far as I can throw them.

Chapter 4

Luke

I walk from my house and into the dusty street. It's empty; I am alone.

Until … There.

An old, aching thing awakens inside me and I walk toward her. She is standing in the middle of the road, her bare feet in the dust. She's wearing a simple white dress, the hem of which is covered in dirt and blood. Her long dark hair is tangled but sweet, somehow.

And her face. She is looking at me like she did in that moment. That moment when she first said her *I love you*. With a kind of life-altering certainty, one she was brave enough to find before I did. Her eyes, the dark and the light, look at me as though I was made for her, born for her, have lived every breath of my life for her.

"Luke."

"Josephine."

Then she says, "I love you, I adore you, I need you."

And I know the dream from reality. Because beyond the dream realm she will never again say such things to me: I'm not sure how I'll ever deserve them.

*

October 28th, 2065

Josephine

It is Sunday. The day of my first tournament. I wake with fingers tracing my name and my head full of ravens. All of these people are waiting to see me fail. See me beaten to within an inch of my life. It'll amuse them, because they know how weak I am. I have to ready myself for humiliation. And pain.

After showering and dressing, I head for the hospital to sit with Luke. No one else is up yet, so I enjoy the quiet with him. His breathing is very slow, skin pale. The bruising on his abdomen is bad.

Stroking his fingers, I hum a song under my breath, my lips close to his ear.

"The world will be very sad to lose you," I whisper.

I have the sense that with him gone I will cease to be known. No one else has ever understood the truth of me. Anthony knew pieces, but he's gone. Now Luke is the only other person who *knows* me.

But it's more than that. It's bigger. It is the *waste* that hurts so much. Because the truth is that I don't want him to wake for me, to be with me. I am still too bruised by all the things that lie in our past. I want him to wake for the world, to be in it once more, I want for life to recognize the unforgivable waste of a man who is brave and skilled and funny and complicated. How could such a person be stolen when there is so little beauty left?

"Wake up," I order.

Then, "You were meant to do great things. Magnificent things. You were always supposed to outlive me and change the world, Luke Townsend."

*

At the tournament, I get ready with dull numbness. Everything has vanished from me. Any sense of shame or fear or anger. I'm an empty shell. Let them beat me. Let them humiliate me. What do I care about shame or agony? I can barely imagine it touching me in this state.

Pace says something to me but I can't hear her. I'm herded into the ring of sand, surrounded by people in silent frenzied movement around me. Distantly, I realize I'm facing Raven. I'm not supposed to be, so she's obviously requested the fight. She dances on the balls of her feet and looks like a glorious angel as she eyes me coldly.

I raise my hands to the position Pace showed me, but there are ravens circling me, flying all around my head, making it impossible to see the fist that collides with my cheek. I hit the ground, vision black. It seems an odd coincidence that I should be plagued by imaginary ravens and faced with a real one. When I force my eyes open there are thousands of black, feathered wings flapping against my skin, around my face, screeching and attacking me in a way that is a million times worse than anything Raven can do to me. I gasp and try to shield myself, but they don't abate, and then I feel a boot slam into my ribs, smashing pain up through my middle.

This is hell, I think suddenly. A hell I have earned. This is where I have been brought by Anthony Harwood. And by every other innocent person I have murdered. I'm a monster, and this is what I deserve, for all of eternity.

She keeps kicking me, and the crows keep screeching and flapping and scraping. I curl into a ball, squeezing my eyes shut and willing it all away.

Darkness overwhelms me and abruptly it's all gone. I'm alone within a world of shadow.

Until I see him, my Doc. He looks like he always did, medium height, on the thin side, prematurely graying at the temples. He peers at me with a reproachful gaze and simply says, *"You're so strong. So resilient. You changed my life."*

Words he said to me on that last night before he died. What a joke. "I'm not," I tell him. "I'm the weakest person in this whole place."

"You're also an excellent liar," he snaps. "You've never once been a coward, Josephine Luquet, and I didn't die so you could become one. *Stand up and fight.*"

And it hits me. The truth. If Luke won't be here to change the world, then I'll have to do it for him.

Reality collides with me, snapping me awake in a flurry of pain and noise and light and movement. My mouth tastes of blood and my ribs are broken, but I understand what the ravens are here for – not to attack me, but to help me rise.

On trembling legs, I drag myself up and gaze around. No one in the crowd is screaming anymore, they're all just watching with pity. I glimpse Pace yelling at Quinn, but he's ignoring her, and then I don't have time for anything else, because Raven is attacking me again.

I jerk my hands up but still take the punch. She hits me again and again, and each time I fall down I force myself back up. I think I've swallowed about a pint of blood, and my vision is blurry, but I demand myself to remain standing. I must be the most pathetic sight they have ever seen, but I don't care, because this is a deal I have made inside my own soul. A deal with myself to be *better*.

A high kick lances into my shoulder, dislocating it from its socket. My arm hangs limply to my side as I groan through the pain and sway on my feet. This chick is one nasty bitch.

"Submit!" Pace screeches from the sideline. "For pity's sake, Dual, *submit!*"

Never, I think, spitting blood from my mouth and moving forward into the oncoming punch. It hits me in the chest, sucking the air from me, and I swing wildly in the same moment. Raven dances backward with ease, and I swing a few more times until she sinks a fist into my guts.

I bend over in agony, wheezing. She takes the moment to smash her elbow into my spine, and I fall to my knees. That's it. This woman is going to pay for this, one way or another. I have never in my life submitted willingly, and I'm not about to start now. Lachlan's brand on my hip is evidence of that. I rise slowly.

Our eyes meet and I see reluctant admiration, and something much darker. "Just submit," she tells me.

"You'll have to kill me first," I say, and mean it.

"Fine," she retorts, and comes at me again.

"*Enough!*" a loud voice slices into the melee. Quinn strides to take both our hands. He's practically the only thing holding me up at this point. He raises Raven's arm into the air and there's a very reluctant smattering of applause.

Through blurry eyes I see that she's furious at the interruption.

Suddenly everyone is moving, and I'm surprised to feel many sets of hands supporting me – Pace and Hal and Will are here, but there are others too. A whole bunch of people trying to help me. It's the last thought I have, and a smile, before I finally lose consciousness.

*

Raven

I hate to even think it – and I mean *hate* – but the kid is made of harder stuff than I thought. I beat her to a bloody pulp, and she didn't land one single hit, but damn. She kept coming back for more.

And though it pains me deeply to acknowledge, there's a part of me that can't help but respect her. Indeed, everyone in the whole bloody crowd now respects her for the undeniable strength of will. It leaves a sour taste in my mouth.

*

November 27th, 2065

Josephine

I watch Luke as the needles pierce my back. The feeling is certainly not as bad as I was expecting. But I have hours more of this before it's done. Hal is bent over my bare back, tongue poking out the corner of his mouth as he wields the tattoo gun. Pace and Will are draped over other hospital beds, lazily watching the process.

"How bad is it?" Will asks at one point when I wince.

I shrug, which makes Hal whack me over the back of the head. "Stay still!"

"Alright – Jesus," I mutter, holding still.

"I don't get it," Pace drawls. "Why this?"

"Long story."

"Got nothin' but time."

I can't say it aloud, not yet, and probably not ever. My shame and my love, both of which I'll now wear on my body forever.

"Why do you always stare at him?" Pace asks next, noticing the way my eyes rest inevitably on Luke.

"I owe him."

She runs her tongue over her teeth. From here, the metal in her face glints and she's had her head shaved again so I can see her skull. "You've been telling everyone you barely know him, but I reckon it's bullshit. I saw the way you were touching him on the train."

I meet her purplish eyes. "Shock. Fear."

Pace shakes her head slowly. "You don't trust us."

"I do," I start. But I don't. I'll never trust anyone again.

"No. Not if you keep lying."

"Leave her be, Pace," Hal tells her from behind me.

Pace stalks out, shooting me a look of disgust. It makes me feel like shit, but if Quinn and Raven were to find out who I am, I have a feeling in my gut that it would be a very bad day for me. Which means keeping it a secret from everyone here. I'm the outsider; they're the family. I know where loyalties lie.

"You're in for it now," Will announces as he does a handstand on one of the beds. It's quite a feat.

Hours later, when the sun has disappeared and the room has gone cool with night, Hal finally sits back. I don't know where he learned to wield the tattoo gun, but apparently he does all the inking for the resistance.

"Done?" I ask.

He grunts. Grabs a hand mirror so I can see the fresh tattoos. A flock of black crows circle my back, wings stretched in a graceful twist up my spine. The sight makes my eyes prickle and fills a dark hole inside me.

"Thank you. They're perfect."

Anthony's birds, the birds he drew and saw and dreamed of for his dead daughter, Marley. The ones I promised him I would get tattooed on my body, as a way to remember that he is the reason I'm no longer a servant to the blood moon.

*

Back at our house I find Pace lying on her bed, twirling a knife. She looks at me with a surly glare.

"What's going on?" I ask, perched in the doorway. "Why are you so mad?"

"You're a liar."

True. But it gets under my skin that she knows it. "We're all liars," I snap.

"I'm not."

"Well good for you." I turn to leave.

"I know you love him."

Pausing, I can't quite bring myself to face her. "Who?"

"Oh please."

"I don't even know him, Pace. How do you love someone you don't know?"

"The same way you love someone you do know."

I turn and look at her, surprised by the insight. "Is this about Hal?" The look on her face is so murderous I'm instantly afraid for my life. "Alright, alright, it's not!"

"Do me the damn courtesy of answering me one single question truthfully," she says.

"What's the question?"

"Is he your person?"

I frown. "What does that mean?"

"Is he your person?"

I chew on my lip, drumming up the courage to find her a response. I barely understand the question, except that I guess I sort of do. "Luke's even more of a liar than I am."

"So what?"

I shake my head. "He hurt me."

"I thought you were past being a coward."

"Ha!"

"Where's the girl from the tournament? The toughest person I've ever seen? You know everyone's been calling you the Iron Queen?"

"That's dumb. And it's different."

"It's not."

"Fine. You want the truth? He doesn't love *me* and he never did. That's the fact of it." As soon as the words escape I want to die of shame.

Pace considers. Eventually she says, "Well that's a different story then."

I watch her continue to twirl the knife. "I really need you to stay quiet about Luke and me. Seriously – "

"What do you think I am?" she snarls. "Some kind of back-stabbing scumbag?"

I blink.

"You and I are blood now. I don't narc on blood – I'd die first. You idiot."

It's so astonishing to me that I'm speechless. I just gape at her.

"Get going," she orders. "Shadow's decided he wants you for training after all."

*

February 20th, 2065

Luke

I watch from the side of the mats as pairs wrestle and grapple with impressive severity. They really take their training seriously here. Shadow arrives at my side as I watch a young girl take a massive punch to the eye.

I wince. "Jesus." Glance at the big man. "If it isn't the torturer. How are we today? Come for some more blood? A pound of flesh?"

He doesn't bother replying. He's clearly in charge of the sparring matches, despite the fact that he rarely opens his mouth. A gaze or a gesture seems to be enough for the students to understand his orders. Sometimes he whacks them on the back of their heads and they concentrate harder.

And I have to hand it to him. He's done a good job with them. They're rough and they lack technique, but they're as ferocious as any army I could hope for. I plan on getting them into shape myself, because fighting Furies is a breeze compared to fighting Bloods, but first I'll need permission to take control of the training. Which, at a hunch, is going to be tough because it means going through the big fella beside me.

"Where'd you learn to fight?" I ask him.

There's a long silence before he mutters, "In the wild."

Meaning he just figured it out for himself, on the run and trying to survive.

"You're still sore about the beating. You face me in the ring. Otherwise we leave it in that room."

I crack my knuckles and smile. "Name the day."

"Tournament on Sunday."

"It's a date." I nod at his soldiers as I turn to leave. "They could use some real training." Just to piss him off.

*

February 23rd 2065

Raven

He has to beat five men before he reaches Shadow. That's the way it works here. The better you are, the fewer bouts you fight, the closer you are to the top. Luke will have to fight his way up, but it's hard to improve your rank because the more you fight, the more wounded and weary you grow until there's no way you can keep going.

People make bets around me. The camp's been talking about it for days now – the agreed bout between the Blood and our very own number two. Quinn is at my side, watching cheerfully. I have never been so curious. A Blood. And not just a Blood, but a *Gray*. Even if the rumors are true, Luke has a very slim chance of making it to Shadow.

"Your guess?" I ask Quinn.

"Reckon he can win three. I'll be worried for the Bloods if he can't."

"Three's a lot," I point out. Because of the savagery and the speed at which you have to move on. I remember when I was first fighting my way through the ranks. It was horrible. Took me years to reach the top. You have to be at the peak of your physical strength and fitness, or you don't have a chance. Now I'm number one for the women, third overall. The only two people in The Inferno that I can't take down are Shadow and Quinn. And it really gets under my skin.

The whistle's blown and Luke's first fight begins amid hushed excitement.

The mood shifts within moments and as we see Luke fight, there's a kind of stunned awe – we freeze as one, fall silent as one, feel our hearts ratchet up with astonishment as one. Because we like fighters here in the west. We like strength and guts and souls made of steel.

This man is different. He's *more*. We all know it, together, immediately.

His first opponent takes a hammering blow to the jaw and is dropped. Luke waits for him to get back up, then smashes him again, and this time the boy stays down. It happens like that for all five bouts. Luke's iron fists tear flesh and smash through bone. He's too fast and much too strong. No one gets a single hit on him.

My soul feels like a dark place as I watch. The desire for him that has been building inside me is surprising, and I don't know if I'll be able to keep ignoring it after this, regardless of the rules.

Shadow enters the ring and by this point everyone in the entire camp has come to watch. Luke's barely broken a sweat. He gives the taller man a salute, then begins.

Shadow's a lot older than Luke, but the man has always been the toughest among us. He can take a lot before giving in, and that being said, the only person he's given in to is our leader, because Quinn's unbeatable.

Luke ducks low and takes the man's chin in a mighty uppercut, snapping Shadow's head back. Without waiting, he hammers the older man in the chest, sending him flying onto the sand.

Shadow gets swiftly to his feet, but Luke spins and cracks him across the head with his boot. I'm struggling to remain expressionless as I watch one, two, three quick jabs slam into Shadow's nose.

Blood sprays. As he takes a moment to wipe it away, Luke looks straight at Quinn.

And with a cool, sly smirk, he says, "I don't want to incapacitate your best hunter too badly. You need him."

Shadow lunges forward, taking Luke in the chest and tackling him to the ground. The older man manages to get in a few body blows before Luke's elbow takes him in the face and he's rolled off. Now Luke's on top, pinning him.

"Submit yet?"

Shadow looks up at his assailant, and we all see him ... smile. I blink – in all my life I have never seen Shadow smile. But he smiles now, and *chuckles* a little. "I submit, you cocky young shit."

Luke grins, helping the man up and clapping him on the back. "You nearly had me there for a minute, mate."

"Bullshit."

The cheering erupts and that's all it takes, really. You fight hard and you win our loyalty. He has them now; I can feel it in the air.

Everyone looks to Quinn. I stiffen, unable to predict what he'll do. He hasn't prepared for a fight, but ...

"Rules are rules," Quinn grins. "He has the right to face me for number one."

"I don't want numbers," Luke says. "I want a deal."

"Is that right, Blood?"

Luke's smile vanishes and I see, with cold fingers clutching my heart, the steel of his soul shining through his eyes. "Firstly, my name is Luke. No one here will refer to me as a Blood again. And secondly, if I win, I own the right to command your soldiers when the time comes."

Silence falls.

"You won't win," Quinn informs him.

Luke shrugs. "Then what's the problem?"

"Alright," Quinn says, obviously realizing he can't back out of this without looking like a coward. "You win and my soldiers are yours for the war. If I win, you do double time here before we agree to swear you into our ranks."

Luke and Quinn shake hands and then move into the ring.

I thought he was impossible before. But now for the first time in my life I feel dwarfed by someone. By what they are, and what they're capable of. It's as if he was not born but created for this very purpose, made with a soul carved in blood and iron. Forged by an ancient Viking god of old and brought here, into this cold world to show us children how they fight in Valhalla.

When it's over and Quinn's bleeding badly on the ground, there's no smirking or laughing. Everyone in the crowd is a little stunned, a little freaked. Luke is breathing heavily, a bruise on his cheek, some blood on his fists. He offers a hand to Quinn, who takes it, and when they're facing each other once more, Quinn says, "They're yours to train. Be worthy of them."

Luke searches the shorter man's face. "They're *yours*. But I'll guide you through the storm and try to be worthy."

"We're honored to have you here, Luke Townsend."

"Thank you." He pauses, glancing at me again, and then at Shadow. "You have spirit, all of you," he says, looking around at his opponents. "It humbles me, having come from a place full of the soulless. I see you and I have real hope for the first time in my life."

The cheering begins, and this time it's an ocean tide washing over us. It's contagious, his hope.

*

With the moon high I hurry through the night to his door. I knock once and wait. He opens it and I brush past him before he can say anything.

"Lock the door."

"No thanks."

I don't like his tone. I unbutton my coat to show him my naked body. His expression doesn't change.

"What are you doing, Raven?"

"Offering you a gift."

"You can keep it. You're with Quinn. And I have a girlfriend."

"The one you left behind? She's long dead by now, Luke."

"No," he says, and I'm discomfited to see a smile curl his lips. "I guarantee you, she's not."

"How could you possibly know?"

"Because I know her. Surviving is what she does best."

I consider this, tilting my head and moving closer. "It's another world out here. We do what we can to enjoy ourselves. She wouldn't mind. And she wouldn't know."

He hesitates, and I know I have him.

But then I realize his hesitation is simply so he can figure out how best to put it. "Listen to me, Raven. I'm not remotely interested in fucking you. Don't come back here again."

Under the moon once more I am humiliated.

*

March 20th, 2065

Luke

I work in the fields and train with Shadow in the evenings. He's started taking me out on hunts and I'm learning to use a bow and arrow, which is spectacularly fun. There's no shortage of Furies to kill. We don't go near their camp – not with only two of us – but there are plenty of the things roaming the dead forest beyond it. Shadow doesn't talk much, but what I've managed to extract from him is the fact that apparently the monsters roam the country all the way to the city.

"How do you know?" I ask him quietly tonight. "That they're everywhere?"

We have wordlessly decided that we're competing for who can kill the most Furies.

Shadow shoots one in the eye, and we cross to where it dropped. I don't know why we do this, but we always do. It's like he needs to look down at the creature he killed before being able to move on from it.

I figure he won't answer my question, but then he says, "I walked."

"Walked where?" It hits me. "From the city? To *here*? Holy shit, man." That is a hell of a long way to travel above ground. I foolishly thought that maybe I could walk a part of it in the tunnel, but I know now it would have been harrowing. And if above is full of Furies, I can't imagine how Shadow survived it.

"When was this?"

"About twenty years ago."

"*Why?*"

Another long silence as we walk and drag, walk and drag.

"Heard there was a resistance out here."

"The cures hadn't been administered twenty years ago. What were you resisting?"

A long silence. "There was a wall around the city," he says simply.

The man is hardcore, you have to give him that. "There's a wall around The Inferno," I point out.

"But we can walk through it," comes his measured response.

It's the most he's said to me in one go since I met him, and it occurs to me how incredibly *right* he is, how utterly messed up it is that they caged us and wouldn't let us leave. I can't count the number of people I stopped from escaping through the wall when I was a Blood. I caught them and escorted them to be cured, like a good little lapdog, and it was sick.

"So the Furies have been around that long," I muse. "Reckon they came from the plague?"

He shrugs. Fair enough. Chat time's over.

We hunt and kill over a dozen Furies before turning back for the night. Inside the wall, after I've bid Shadow an unreciprocated goodnight, I procure three very enthusiastic followers who've apparently been waiting for me to return.

I have never seen Pace, Hal and Will separated from each other in the two months I've been here. And each time they spot me they accost me with questions. *How many people have you killed? How long were you a Blood? Who recruited you? What did you have to do? What are you good at? What are the rules? How many of you are there? How did you escape the city? Are you a good liar?*

It's exhausting, but I can't help warming to them.

They also want to know about life in the city, life for the drones. All three of them were brought here by their parents before they were old enough to be cured – more than ten years ago. And all three of them lost their parents to the Furies.

Tonight Hal asks, "I heard someone say you have a girlfriend in the city." There's a measure of wistfulness in his voice; he's a romantic, bless him.

"Yeah."

"What's her name?"

"Josephine."

"Why did you leave her?" Pace asks me bluntly. I can hear in her voice the desire to deny the existence of love, bitterness extending down to her bones.

"Because she's sick."

"How caring of you," she replies, deadpan.

"I didn't know if I'd make it here, or how difficult it would be, and I was pretty sure she'd died on the journey." I swallow, feeling heartsick. "She was very weak by the time I left her."

"So she's dead now?" Will asked.

"No."

"How do you know?"

"I just do."

All three of them think about this for a while. We're headed to the Den for food. Pace asks, sort of angrily, "How could you love a drone? Do they lobotomize you when you join the Bloods?"

I smile at her. She's an interesting creature. "Almost. She's uncured."

They all stop and stare at me in shock.

"And you left her there?" Hal is incredulous.

"I told you – "

"You can't leave an uncured in the city on her own! No matter how sick she is! What if they find her?"

I get it. The uncured are a rare commodity these days. I try to explain. "She's not like the other uncured."

"How?" Pace demands.

"Can you all just chill out?" I shake my head. "She's immune."

"Bullshit," Pace says flatly.

I shrug, walking on. My stomach is grumbling.

"Come with me, Blood," she says suddenly.

"Don't call me that," I warn.

"Come with me, *Luke.*"

"Are you going toward food? Because otherwise I'm not going anywhere with you."

"You're gonna wanna see this."

I sigh hungrily, following her as she cuts through several streets to reach a narrow demountable I haven't entered before. Inside is what can only be described as a science lab. When Pace switches on the lights I see long tables filled with lab equipment. Staring into a microscope down the end is a man I haven't met. He's been sitting here in the dark. Weird.

Pace leads me to his side. "This is Dodge."

"G'day, Dodge."

Dodge is blond and looks like he'd be more at home on a surfboard than in this lab. He looks up at me and his glasses remind me, unbearably, of Harley. I glance away, feeling my blood quicken with an all too familiar anguish.

"Luke says he has a girlfriend who's immune to the cure," Pace tells the man.

"Not possible."

I look around at all the stuff. What strikes me are the vials of blood. There must be hundreds of them.

"Why do you think that?" Dodge asks me.

"She was given one of the first test rounds of the drug, before it became the cure. It didn't work. And now she's immune to the current anger cure."

"What was the earlier drug made of?"

"I dunno, mate. You'd have to ask my friend Ben."

"But what you're saying is that if we gave this initial drug to people, they would be immune to the cure?"

I turn to face him. Dodge and Pace are both filled with such excitement that I feel bad for them. I shake my head tiredly, murmuring "No. Not unless you want a population of mass murderers."

As I walk through the night in search of dinner I really, really miss my girlfriend. In my mind I hear her playing the cello.

Chapter 5

January 8th, 2066

Josephine

I am perusing the painfully crummy selection of books in the 'library' – there are, like, twenty books – when my eyes catch on one that must have just been returned, since I'm in here every day waiting for anything new. Something inside me leaps with joy. *Brave New World.* One of my favorites, in that way that favorite books cause something inside your chest to hurt.

I pull it reverently from the shelf and open it slowly, taking a deep breath of its ancient pages. It took me years as a teenager to find a real, print copy of it, having read it a thousand times digitally but wanting something physical to keep with me always. It got banned eventually, and all copies were burnt or erased. I kept mine though, hoarded it like treasure.

"*If one's different, one's bound to be lonely,*" says a voice from behind me and I turn to see Dodge and his bespectacled eyes.

"*I like being myself,*" I answer him. "*Myself and nasty.*"

We smile at each other.

"You returned it?" I surmise.

He nods. "I came ... I need to speak with you."

"Am I in trouble?"

"Oh, no! I ... I'm sorry, I – "

"Relax, I was kidding. Sort of. Lead the way."

I sign the book out and Dodge takes me to his lab, which is very dark and bizarrely as one would imagine a science lab to look like. Beakers and microscopes and vials of blood.

"I know who you are," he says bluntly, without his usual preamble.

My eyebrows arch. "That sounds creepy."

"I mean ... I know. I know the truth."

I frown, watching his handsome face. "What truth, Dodge?"

"I know your name is Josephine Luquet and that you're immune to the cure."

There is a heavy silence between us. My guts feel liquefied.

"I won't tell them," he murmurs fervently.

"There's nothing to tell."

"Raven would have you cut into a thousand pieces for experimentation."

A cold finger trails down my spine. "What makes you think you know what you know?"

"Luke told me he had a girlfriend immune to the cure. Your blood looked normal at first, but when I studied it I realized it had strange properties that fought off all number of afflictions."

"What do you mean?"

"You were given an initial experimental phase of the cure, right?"

I nod, giving up the pretence.

"It triggered all kinds of things in your blood. It remains."

"Remains? What do you mean remains?"

"I gather you were given a secondary drug at some point?"

"An antidote to what the Zetemaphine was doing. A blocker."

"Right. Well a blocker doesn't erase. It ... blocks."

This is not sounding good.

"Dodge, just tell me what's going on."

"You have properties in your blood that have stemmed from neurotoxins created by the combination of the Zetemaphine and its blocker. They have resulted in an extremely high rate of regeneration in your cells."

"Meaning healing?"

"Right." He smiles awkwardly.

"So I heal fast?"

"It seems that way. Have you noticed anything?"

I shrug, thinking about it. I feel like I'm constantly being beaten and battered, and recovering from some injury or another, but if I think back, my beating from Raven – which broke bones and bruised tissue and dislocated joints – only took me a couple of days to heal from. Ranya's made a few comments about how well I heal, but I didn't think anything of it – I just assumed all my injuries felt worse than they were because I'm such a wuss.

"Well ... Christ. That's good, right?"

"It needs to be monitored, because if one of the two drugs in your system was to unbalance the other then you could find yourself seriously ill. Or ... dead."

"Oh. Great."

"That's not all. I've been studying samples of Luke's blood since you returned him to us."

And just like that, I feel a terrible ache build in my chest. Because there it is again, right there in his eyes – the pity. "What?"

"His cells are morphing too rapidly for him to survive it."

I shake my head. "That's what everyone says. All the time. But he's still alive."

"I understand that, but the samples I took from him yesterday are drastically evolved."

"So what – he's changing?"

"Grossly. He won't last much longer, that I can guarantee." Dodge swallows and drops his eyes. "I debated telling you, but knowing what I know about your relationship, I felt you deserved to know the truth with … enough time to say goodbye."

I take a breath. "How long?"

"At this rate, a day. Maybe two."

"Use my blood. It'll heal him. Take as much as you want."

"I'm afraid I already tried that. It seems the properties in your system aren't contagious after having been combined with your blood. They become indivisible from each other."

"So what – you're telling me there's nothing you can do?"

"I can't even begin to understand the composition of the synthetic inside his brain and tissue. I …"

I turn and walk away from him. I need Ben. I have spent the last months sitting around here and doing absolutely nothing except bitching and moaning when I could have been retrieving the scientist from the city.

"Josephine!" Dodge calls and I pause, unable to even face him, or to believe he has used my name so brazenly. "You said you wanted to be yourself, yourself and nasty. So why do you hide behind another name and another life?"

I give a soft, bitter laugh. "It's a fucking quote, Dodge. Grow up."

*

January 9th, 2066

Josephine

My back aches and my neck is twisted. The chair beside his bed is uncomfortable, but we have a love–hate relationship, me and this damn chair. When first I sit in it, I love it with every fiber of my being.

After a hard day's work, this chair is my best friend. After a few hours I begin to loathe it with all the fire of hell.

I have been sitting in it, watching him sleep, for four months. For four months Ranya has told me that he has only days, if that, left to live. But every day he does not die.

They don't understand Luke Townsend. But I do. He has an iron will.

I have been here since yesterday morning. I am in trouble, because I have missed two training sessions and two work shifts. I've had Pace, Hal, Will, Ranya, Quinn and even Raven in here telling me to leave, to get back to whatever commitment I'm supposed to be fulfilling. But I can't look at any of them, and I can't leave.

I don't care anymore if they know I love him.

I don't care about anything.

Ranya, Quinn and Dodge arrive and move to surround Luke's bed. I sit up, not liking the way they're looking at him.

"What's ... ?"

Quinn looks at me sadly. "We've come to a difficult decision, Dual. We can no longer sustain the power it takes to keep Luke's vitals monitored and attended to. We're going to have to switch off the machine."

I feel my heart pick up speed. Remaining calm, I rise to my feet. "He's not hooked up to anything important, though, right? He hasn't needed help breathing or anything."

"No but I've been giving him medicine to help his body heal while he sleeps," Ranya tells me gently. "Without this, and without the means to monitor his heart-rate, he'll die."

I shake my head. Blind disbelief fills me. "No. You can't ... "

Ranya reaches for the cords linking the machines to the generator and I lose it. Something wild comes over me and I lunge at her, tackling her away from the cord.

She gives a yelp of surprise and then Quinn is hauling me off her. "Don't touch me!" I snarl, struggling fiercely against his hold.

He starts dragging me toward the door and I give a scream of fury. "Don't you dare! Get the fuck away from him! Dodge – do something! Tell them you can solve this!"

Dodge shakes his head helplessly and I buck savagely against Quinn's arms, wanting to tear them from his body if it means I can get to Luke and stop Ranya but she's reaching for those cords again and I'm shouting and struggling and I can't get free and she's really about to do it –

"Stop," comes a blunt voice from the door, and we all swivel to see Raven. She is expressionless as she takes in the scene. Her eyes move to rest on her boyfriend. "Let her go, Quinn."

Quinn hesitates, then does so. I wrench myself away from him and try to catch my breath. If Raven stops this, then I will forget every bad thought I've ever had about her.

But, still completely wooden, Raven says, "Let her say goodbye first."

And hope dies in my chest. I look between them all helplessly, but there's no changing their minds.

"We'll be just outside," Quinn warns, and they troop out.

I turn back to Luke, unable to believe that this is really happening. Until yesterday I thought I would sit here and wait forever. I knew I wouldn't give up. I knew I might walk heavy with longing every day. I might feel sad in every movement of my limbs as I scythed the wheat and learned to fight, but I wouldn't give up. I thought I would teach The Inferno something about hope.

But this is what I think now: *He's really going.*

And I have to find some way to say goodbye to him.

Impossible. Brutally, unforgivably impossible.

I climb onto the bed beside him and I press my face against his cheek. My tears slide over his skin. "Darling," I whisper. "How am supposed to do this? I can't say goodbye. I can't."

I start to cry, holding him as tightly as I can.

"I wish I knew you better," I tell him. "I wish so many things, but even if it meant I could never see you again, I would still wish for you to be alive." And then the truest thing of all: "Luke. I'm so angry with you. But I would still trade places with you. I'd give anything to be the one dying, if it meant you'd live."

He doesn't stir, and I rise slowly from the bed, watching his face. *This is it. This is the last time you will see his eyes, his nose, his cheeks, his lips. This is the last time you will ever touch his skin.*

I kiss his mouth so gently our lips barely touch. I'm trembling. I whisper, "Bye, darling."

And then I walk away. My ribs are cracking open and my heart is being shredded. It hurts and I can't breathe and I'm crying and in this moment as I walk away I decide a very dark thing: the only way I'm going to be able to get through never seeing him again is to take the sadness cure.

*

There's so much screaming inside me that I almost don't hear it.

It's a sound, the whisper of a sound, the ghost of one. Drifting past my ears. Making me freeze at the door. A sigh, almost.

I feel strange, parts of me knowing, other parts refusing to believe. *Don't you dare turn back*, I tell myself. *Don't allow yourself even the barest sliver of hope. It will kill you.* But I do. I turn back slowly. My heart is exhausted from the force of my longing and my grief and my farewell.

But the hope is real. On the bed, Luke is moving.

I draw a sudden, shocked breath. He makes another sound, an uncomfortable groan. In a moment he will open his eyes and see me here, because he is conscious at long last, just as I have wished every second of every day for the last two thousand, seven hundred and thirty-six hours.

Abrupt terror strikes. Now that it's happening I am completely unprepared for it. What will be in his eyes when he looks at me? What will be *missing* from his eyes?

I study all the sharp, lovely lines of his face. He stirs more, his hands clenching on the sheets. I watch his throat move as he swallows. I watch the flicker of his eyelids, and then I see them open.

Dashing from the room, I sprint past three bewildered people as fast as I can, as fast as my tired muscles will allow me, running and running and running, because I don't know how to do anything else. Behind me is a life I said goodbye to, a version of myself I am not ready to face. And no matter what is or isn't still in his eyes when he sees me, I'm scared it will have the power to turn me once more into the girl who was foolish enough to trust when she shouldn't have.

*

Luke

I wake numb.

Blinking against the brightness of the light, I peer around the room. People are entering, but they are blurred and slow-moving and silent. The two women have familiar faces. I open my mouth but only a rasping sound comes forth.

Someone puts a cup of water to my lips and I drink gratefully. "Josephine?" I manage.

Neither of them answers.

"Where is she?" I ask, trying to lift myself. They push me back down and I'm so weak I can't resist. "Is she alright?"

"Luke, just rest."

The only thing I remember is that fucking lab. The drugs and the blood and Anthony. Oh shit. Oh, Anthony.

"Where?" I groan, but no one will answer me. "Where am I?"

"You're at The Inferno, Luke."

I stare in shock. It's Ranya, I realize suddenly. Ranya and Raven. "*How?*"

"Calm down, Luke. We'll explain it all when you're well." They're pumping me with a sedative. I can feel it filling my veins and making me squishy.

"Please," I whisper. "*Please* just tell me where Josephine is."

It's Raven who finally tells me. "She's dead, Luke. She died in the lab."

The room around me vanishes, the women above me blinking out of existence.

It's so clear to me, suddenly. The white and gray room with the flickering lights and the cold, shiny surfaces. Anthony lying dead in a pool of his own blood. Josi trying to kill Ben and me intercepting her. I can see her face, with the red eyes and the blood smeared over her skin.

That was the last time I saw her. It will be the only time I ever see her again, in this macabre memory.

My brother finds me, suddenly. Dave had the best smile, lots of slightly crooked teeth that were full of character and eyes so sharp they rivalled Josi's. "Little brother."

"I couldn't save you," I tell him from within the waste that is my heart. "I can't save anyone."

My mother is here next, and my father. Then Harley, my Harley.

I'm spinning in this impossible limbo and everywhere I look I see the lost. There are too many of them, too many for one life.

Because last is Josi. She's my dream Josi, standing in the middle of the road in a blood-smeared dress, telling me she loves and adores me. But then she is the Josi from real life, licking mango off my chin and grinning wickedly. She's the Josi playing cello and rolling her eyes and throwing food at me. The Josi who lies in the bath and watches day turn to night, the Josi who complains and nags and sings terribly, the Josi who laughs like it must hurt her guts and looks at me as though I am a real person, a valid, worthy man who is meant for more than he is.

It is too much. I have been ripped out of my own skin. Ripped out of my soul. I try to endure but some part of me switches off and it all fades, blissfully, to black.

*

I wake what could be a few hours later. Or maybe it's days. Ranya and Pace fuss over me, then I get Hal and Will in to see me, then Quinn, of course – bursting with excitement. Last is Raven again, strolling in with that devilish look in her eyes and a clear determination to extract or gain something from me. She is a carrion bird, come to pick at my remains.

I tell her to leave and she does so, outraged as she always seems to be. I used to marvel over her ability to be angry with anything and everything – it's quite a skill. But now I hate her with an irrational hatred, purely because she was the one to tell me, and she did it without an ounce of compassion.

I lie quietly, gazing out the window.

Ranya makes her way to the chair by my bed. "You've been here nearly four months, Luke."

I can't summon any feelings about it. So many days of my life stolen. But really, they were days saved from the reality of having to deal with Josi's death. I'd rather be back in the coma. I'd rather be dead, actually. I think my brain is preparing itself for that. To die. I think I will, soon. The knowledge occurs to me in a weird, mathematical way, as though I am solving the problem of my life, and the only solution is no life at all.

"Rest," Ranya insists. "You've been in a coma, Luke."

As if I am unaware of it.

The three musketeers troop back in. Pace, Hal and Will all flock around my bed, reclining next to me or in the chair. "So what the hell happened to you, Townsend?" Pace asks.

I shrug, incapable of more.

"We got pieces of it from Dual, but it's bound to be a good story."

"Pace," Hal admonishes, as though the girl has just murdered a kitten.

"Sorry," she mumbles.

"We're really sorry about Josephine," Hal says. His sympathy makes my skin crawl. I hate it and I want them away from me. "But you saved one life, at least."

It occurs to me belatedly. "How did I get here?"

"Dual brought you."

"Who's Dual?"

"Someone who found you at the asylum," Hal explains. "You don't remember?"

"I can't remember shit." Except Josi's blood-smeared face.

"She's surly," Pace comments with approval.

"And kinda brilliant," Hal adds.

"Tough," Will offers. "Like a big old piece of stubborn rock."

"I really couldn't care less," I say frankly. "How did Josi die?"

"Dual didn't say much about it."

"Well what *did* she say?"

"You deaf? *Not much.*"

I feel it like a blow, her callousness. She doesn't give a shit that I've just lost the love of my life. I am abruptly without a body, without a soul, without anything. I can't grasp hold of anything. Can't *feel* anything.

"Get out," I mutter. "Just get out." It's a poor effort, but I really don't care.

They watch me pityingly.

My stomach bottoms out in a moment of profound terror, profound disbelief. I have had many of these moments since waking up. A part of me says *no, it's not true*, and then my mind flails wildly, having to deal with the reality anew each time.

Ranya returns and shoos the three kids away, telling them I need rest. Hal pauses a moment alone with me to say, "We missed you."

I can't even return the compliment; I'm a voiceless shell.

"They've told you about the girl who brought you here?" Ranya asks casually when the kids are gone.

"Not really."

"She saved your life." Ranya's acting weird. She studies me and I meet her eyes. That's how you lie. You look into people's eyes. They never spot it if you do that. Especially now that everyone is so uncomfortable with intimacy.

Ranya looks away, unable to hold my gaze. Interesting. "I'm sure she'll be in to visit you – she's been anxiously awaiting your recovery." She packs up a few things and leaves me for the night. This is a woman who has done nothing but look after me as a mother would since the moment I got here last year. Am I going mad, thinking she's hiding something from me?

If I was stronger, I'd get the hell out of this place. I can't even retreat to sleep and even if I could, I'm too terrified of my dreams.

Sometime during the night a figure moves in the doorway.

"Only me, lover boy." Shadow moves into the room and for the first time I manage a faint smile. The ghost of a smile.

"If it isn't my torturer."

He stops by my bed and shakes my hand. I see the faint curve of his lips, which means he must be extremely happy to see me. "Thought you'd got yourself killed, boy."

"Nah. Not yet."

He sits in a chair and we share a moment of silence.

"Anything to report here?" I haven't asked anyone else because I trust them all, of course, but Shadow is the only one I *trust*.

"June and Grill died. Hunting."

"Oh. Sorry." I don't even know who they were, really.

"And there's the new girl." I look at his face in the dark. Lines of it are illuminated from the window. He is expressionless, as usual. "She yours?"

I feel a rupture of grief. "No. Mine's dead."

Shadow sits quietly for a long time, and I try not to cry for every second that passes. I haven't cried yet. And I don't intend to. It would be like admitting the truth to my heart.

"I'm going back to the city," I tell him.

"Why?"

"I need to know where they buried her. I need to say goodbye."

His head lowers a little, then he nods. "I'll go with you."

The tears build in my throat. Shadow doesn't go to the city, ever. "Thank you."

He meets my eyes, and there's something rawer in him than I've ever seen in a human. "I left my wife and child to die. I understand, son."

"How do you do it, then?"

He knows what I mean: all of it. Everything. Anything. Shadow sighs heavily. Shakes his head with a weariness I always saw in him but never recognized for what it was: grief. "I don't know, kid. You just do."

*

January 10th, 2066

Josephine

I am hiding in my room, lying on my bed, reliving the absolute mortification of my relationship with Luke. Now that he is alive, I no longer fear for his safety and am instead filled with a bewildering, overwhelming rage. I relive with perfect clarity all the moments we spent together, all the words he said to me, and as I do I see it all so differently. I see the lies. The deception, the *falseness* of it. How fucking imbecilic I was. How cruel his secrets were. I lie here and my skin burns with embarrassment as I think of the kisses and touches, of the incredible intimacies we shared and the way he used to make love to me. I am humiliated by my own blind, limitless love, and by my inability to see the truth.

Ranya comes a-knocking and Pace brings the doctor to my bedroom. I stare at her blankly. "Yes?"

"Luke's awake," she says with a breath of such joy.

"And?" *What is wrong with you? I ask myself. You are the coldest monster on this planet.*

She falters, confused. "Don't you want to come and see him?"

"No. Why would I want to do that?"

"Because you've been asking after him for the last four months."

"Well, now he's awake, it's all good. I don't actually know him."

Ranya and Pace both stare at me.

"Just fuck off, alright?" I snap. I can feel a dark shadow taking root in my heart. I want to scream. *Stop looking at me. Stop looking at me.*

But they keep looking at me.

"What are you so angry about?" Ranya asks me suddenly.

I sit up. Is she serious?

"Life's beautiful," she declares.

My mouth falls open. I feel a deep, resounding incredulity fill me. "Oh my god. You unbelievably naïve idiot," I tell her, looking into her chocolate eyes. "Go and live in the city and then tell me life's beautiful. Life is *struggle*."

"You're not in the city. You're here, and you're free."

"I'm not free," I utter. "Not from anything that matters. Get out of my room."

They leave, and I realize it is the first time I have ever been cruel of my own volition. I thought the blood moon had rid herself of me, but now I'm not so sure. Perhaps she left a little something in my heart, a fragment of her ugliness.

Or perhaps I was a monster all along, even before the moon.

*

January 11th, 2066

Luke

For two days I've drifted in and out of sleep, torn to shreds by nightmares. I don't know how to make it stop, but I know enough's enough. Pulling the drip out of my arm, I search through the infirmary for some clothes and pull them on. Then I walk out into the street.

In my blood there is something different. Something darker. It's the virus, I know. But I am barely rational enough to be aware of that. Instead I am full of fury. It feels unnatural, but it also feels completely welcome, like an old lover I've had to ignore for years. It fills me up, seductive and sinister.

Will appears in the dark. "Luke! What are you – ?"

I walk past him. I don't know where I'm going or what I'm doing. I just want to destroy something.

I find myself at the Den. Shadow sees me first, as he is perched near the door. He looks me up and down. It seems like I should be in bed. Seems like I should be weak, but the truth is I'm not. I feel strong. I don't know where I'm trying to get to but I know I'll inflict a world of pain on anyone who stands in my way.

Shadow recognizes this in me, for he says, "Take a breath. Go home."

"Home?" I let out a choked laugh. "*Home.*"

"It's alright, son," he tells me, reaching for my arm, but I shove him away and stride into the hall.

I can smell things. And they're causing colors and shapes and textures to burst to life in my head. Every smell and every sound makes a color in my mind and it's blindly disorienting.

A man approaches but I can barely see his face. I slam him in the chest and he falls backwards, out of my path. Chaos is unfolding around me; I can feel it. The unrest and the fear. The fear. I can smell the fear.

I swallow, moving forward until –

Everything stops. Everything inside me, everything around me, everything in the entire universe. My heart is pounding shuddering uncertain wild. It is made of Anthony's feathered wings it is aching and impossible and desperately yearning because –

"Luke," a voice says.

*

Raven

I am watching as it happens, and it's as if the whole thing is in slow motion. Quinn's hand is on my knee, the smell of rich wine is in my nose, the sound of strumming guitars in my ears. I am aware of all of this as Luke strides into the hall. A thrill finds me to see him awake and on his feet. But it's clear all too quickly that he is taken by some kind of fever, for he sends Blue flying from his feet with a single blow.

I lurch to my feet, as does Quinn.

Luke looks crazed, almost *beastly*. It is grief, I am abruptly reminded. And it hits me suddenly how much he must have felt for the invisible girl from the city. He spoke of it so often I began to dismiss it. But now I am faced with the reality of someone who has lost the person they love most in the world. It is undeniable.

Luke storms into the room and people make way for him as though they can instinctively sense the danger in the air.

And then someone says his name; he stops. He stops and he stares.

My eyes search through the crowd around Luke and find, at the very back, a single figure.

The girl with the dual eyes and the dark tangle of hair gazes at Luke through the people, and he gazes at her.

He gives an abrupt laugh. It sounds slightly mad in the silent, echoing hall. And that's when we all watch him drop to his knees and begin to cry. This huge thing overcomes him and he drops his head and just ... weeps.

When I look back to Dual, she has vanished.

*

Josephine

My feet pound until my hands rest on the rough bark of a tree – one of a small copse of trees that survived within the wall. I am haunted by his face in my mind, the dreadful brokenness of it.

Out in the night air I try to steady my heavy breathing. I can't seem to stop running away from everything.

But I hear the thud of footsteps behind me, and I know that what I've been running from this whole time has caught up to me at last.

A low, rough voice says, "Hello, beautiful."

I close my eyes. I can feel the wind moving through the trees and brushing against my skin. I can hear it lift and move every blade of grass. I can taste it on my lips, repeating those two words over and over again – the first words he ever spoke to me in a stupid, stupid bar.

He moves nearer and I try to prepare myself, but I can't – I'm stuck in this one tortuous moment, with him alive and breathing the same air as me. Tears are slipping beneath my lashes and sliding over my face.

"Did it work?" he asks, pleading.

I don't understand.

"The moon," he says. "The curse. The antidote."

My heart lurches and I spin to face him. "Yes, yes, it worked."

He breathes out, like a dam wall has burst. An enormous weight seems to lift from him and he gives another laugh, this time in sheer relief. And then his hands touch me, big and warm, first at my hips and then sliding around my waist, pulling me against his chest. His lips duck to the curve of my neck to kiss me there, then move up to my jaw, trailing over all the tears on my cheeks, edging toward my mouth. It feels dreamlike, it feels in slow motion.

"Josi," he says, and then he is touching his lips to mine. I open my mouth against his and taste him. Taste his tears, allowing him to hold me against his body just as I have imagined for months. He is here, really here, bigger than I remember, alive and real, and I can't clutch onto any of the things I know. All my certainties are gone and all that's left is Luke Townsend.

He feels like he always used to, but so too is he different now with the weight of truth. At least, *I* am different. I feel him with different skin, taste him with different lips, touch him with different hands. It is this realization that brings me back to reality, back to the world we live in, ripping me out of this fantasy.

We were not real people when we loved each other, we were pretend.

"Luke," I breathe against his mouth. He rests his forehead to mine. I allow myself this last moment – just this one – to let him sink into my bones again, the guiltiest of all pleasures, and then I push him away gently, my hands trembling.

"Josi," he says. His eyes are so green and so feverish that they make me want to take his hand and run into the dead forest beyond and stay there with him forever.

I swallow. My tears have ceased, and I clench my hands to stop them shaking. I have lived through a lot of things in my life, a lot of very bad things. I can live through this. I draw a cloak of iron around my shoulders, using it to protect me, to make me certain and strong. "I'm glad you're okay."

Luke flinches slightly at the sound of my flat voice, drawing further away and peering into my face. He is confused, I see now. And very tired. His skin is pale and he has deep hollows under his eyes. I banish an urge to stroke his hair from his forehead.

"I'm fine, girl," he says. "Are you?"

"I'm fine too," I nod stiffly.

"Then what – ?"

"Luke, stop. You have to stop."

He stares at me, uncomprehending. "Why?"

"Because we're not … together anymore."

"What?"

"We're not – "

"Since when?"

"Since you told me the truth."

"You're still angry."

I meet his eyes.

Luke frowns and I can see the understanding start to form behind his gaze. He shakes his head. There's panic building there. "But I – "

"I'm happy you're awake," I tell him, "And I'll help find an antidote to the virus in your blood. But that's it."

He stares at me, and then suddenly: "*What?*" The word rushes from him, an eruption of disbelief. "That's it? After everything we've been through?"

I stare at him. Here before me is a hurricane of fury, where before I only ever knew him to be calm, deathly calm. The forest is closing in around us, turning itself into a jungle of vines and trappings, a living thing that throbs and aches. I can feel it, every breath of it; it's inside my head.

"You're not ending this," Luke snarls, grabbing me and pushing me against the tree. "Not now."

I am ashamed of how thrilled I feel. I want his clothes to be gone, and mine too, and I want him to push me harder against the tree and shout and yell until his voice is hoarse. But none of that can happen, so I fuel my desire into the next best thing. It becomes fury, my dearest, oldest friend.

"You want a fight?" I snap, my face only inches from his. "Easy. I don't know who you are. You *tricked* me into loving you. All I have from our life together are false memories. I have nothing real, nothing honest, nothing I can hold in my hands and *feel*."

"And what's this?" he snarls, shaking me. "What's *this*? You can feel me and you can hold onto me for as long as you want, for the rest of our lives, so don't fucking pretend you have nothing – I've given you *everything*!"

"Lies," I say. "You've given me lies."

"This is no lie," Luke growls, pressing his mouth to mine. It's rough and desperate but I can't, I can't – I shove him away as hard as I can and storm past him. He grabs my hand and tugs me back. "The only lies being told now are yours."

"Fuck off," I whisper. "I hate you."

"If you do this," he says bluntly, "if you leave me here after everything we've been through, then I'll hate you too."

Good. In my head I say the word a hundred times, a thousand. *Good good good.* If he hates me it will make this easier. I open my mouth to say it, to say *good*. But nothing comes out because I can't bear it, the thought that he might hate me. The word doesn't come. I don't think I'll ever be able to say it.

And that's when he sinks to his knees and I am stunned by the sudden disappearance of all rage, of everything except a world-weary despair. "You let me think you were dead," he whispers, broken. "How could you let me think that?"

A throbbing pain starts in my chest and I drop to my knees before him. "I didn't mean to. I'm sorry. I swear, I never wanted you to think that ..."

He pulls me to him and rests his face in the curve of my neck. His fingers move to thread through my hair. We stay like that for a long time. I can feel his heartbeat; I feel as though the very essence of his life is against my body, moving inside me. I'm cradling within my arms a precious thing.

But it isn't mine, this precious thing. It doesn't belong to me. Not anymore, and maybe it never did.

I stand and extricate myself from his arms. He holds my hand until I have to pull it forcibly from his grip. "*Don't,*" he pleads.

I turn and walk away.

As I reach the outskirts of the enclosure I hear a howl behind me, something raw and everything I always wanted Luke to be – this scream is alive and full of emotion. But as it strikes inside me I feel cold cold cold because I am frightened of what I have unleashed and all I want is to go back there and scream with him until I can't anymore.

Chapter 6

January 12th, 2066

Luke

I'm still sleeping in the infirmary until they can work out where I'll be living, and because Ranya is adamant that I'm not discharged. She hasn't cleared me for work or training, even though I feel fine – I feel great, actually. You know, apart from thinking I'm constantly about to stroke out from rage.

I've spent the day wandering around, visiting all my old haunts – the training rooms to see how Shadow's been going with his soldiers, the fields to say hi to all my old planting and scything pals, the lab to check in on Pace and Dodge, and the kitchen, my favorite place of all. I haven't seen Josi anywhere, so she's probably avoiding me.

I have to keep reminding myself that this pain at her rejection is nothing – *nothing* – to how I felt when I thought she was dead. I just have to get over this initial hump and then I'll be fine. I always knew it was coming. I knew she'd never forgive me when she found out the truth. So now I have to deal with it. Plus she's not going to turn under the blood moon or kill herself, which has been the whole point of our lives for the last few years. It's just hard to believe we can't enjoy the victory together.

As the sun sets I head for Quinn and Raven's house. I haven't been able to sit still all day. Nervous energy thrums through my body and makes me jittery. I want to run.

"Luke!" Quinn grins, letting me in.

"Hey, man."

"How are you feeling?"

"Fine, bro. You?"

"Always good, brother." He hands me a home-brewed beer from the small fridge only his house is allowed. We clink the bottles together and take a long drink. It's the best thing I've ever tasted and it helps to calm my nerves.

"We were worried about you for a while there," he says gently.

"Things got a bit hectic in the city."

"I was truly sorry to hear about your girlfriend."

I swallow and nod. I have no idea what the fuck is going on, or why Josi's lied about this, but she's obviously got a reason, and until I find out what that is I'm not about to give the game away. I look into Quinn's eyes: it's how you lie, and it's how you convince people you're not lying. I let a little of my all-too-real sadness into my expression. It satisfies him, even makes him a bit uncomfortable, for he drops his gaze and takes another gulp.

"But you're here with us now, where you belong."

"And we can get things started. I want to organize a mission to the city."

"For what purpose?"

"We need to start working out how to stop the sadness cures."

He considers this.

"I waited for you, man," I remind him. "All of last year. I was patient. But we had a deal. I have the use of your people to start attacking the Bloods and stop the cures."

Quinn tilts his head, running his fingers over the condensation on his bottle. "They're your people too, Luke."

"I appreciate that. Then it's settled."

"You need to re-gather your strength," he says with a kind smile. "When you're well again, we'll talk."

"I'm fine – "

"Dinner time!" He abruptly claps his hands together, then finishes his beer. "Let's go eat, brother. We need you strong and healthy. The others will be excited to see you when you're not so … delirious."

I watch him closely, wanting to give him the benefit of the doubt, but you'd have to be a moron not to notice his evasions. I hope he knows that this isn't up for debate. I hope he knows that I will die before I let my parents be given a cure for sadness – one that will surely mess them up even more than they already are.

I hope he knows that I will kill before I let that happen.

*

As we enter the Den there is an eruption of cheers so loud I'm surprised it doesn't take the roof off. My eyes widen when I realize it's for me. They're on their feet, clapping and cheering for *me*. It is completely surreal. I've done nothing at all to deserve it. In fact, last time I was here I attacked people. A few of them look a tad nervous, some seem excited. My eyes travel over their faces and spot one that is not smiling. She's not standing either. She's sitting with Pace, Hal and Will, and when she looks at me she rolls her eyes in that completely withering way of hers, and despite everything it makes my heart beat a little bit stronger and I can't help laughing with relief that she is here and alive and rolling her eyes in that perfect Josephine Luquet way.

Quinn perches me in a seat beside his and Raven comes from the kitchen to hand me a plate – I don't know why I'm suddenly being treated like royalty and it feels weird.

I spend the whole meal half-listening to the conversation around me, half-watching Josi at one of the far tables. She doesn't look at me once. People keep patting me on the back and refilling my cup.

Raven is asking me something. I blink, looking at her expectant face. Those dark eyes probe me and I can see she is very close to getting royally pissed off.

"Pardon?"

Her jaw clenches. "I asked you what happened."

"When?"

"You're addled from the coma, I can see. When you went to the city."

I shrugged. "I failed. Excuse me." Leaving my unfinished plate – I have no appetite whatsoever – I make my way to Josi's table.

"Hello, children."

Hal and Will happily shove over to make room for me, and I find myself sitting opposite Josi and Pace. Josi ignores me completely.

"You're a medical marvel," Pace tells me.

"Everyone's talking about it," Will agrees.

"It's amazing what stolen government medicine can do," I reply, looking at Josi. She's eating away, seemingly unbothered. "Don't you think, *Dual*? It's Dual, right?"

"I wouldn't know, Luke," she replies mildly without taking the bait. "But why don't you explain it to us, since you were a government man yourself, weren't you?"

"He was a Blood," Pace supplies.

"Pretty impressive," Josi goes on more softly. This time she looks up, meeting my eyes with her blue and brown gaze. "You'd have to be skilled to get that job, wouldn't you? Patriotic, ruthless ... Someone told me once that the Bloods are more robotic than drones. So how many people did you cure in your time? How many did you stop from escaping the wall?"

We stare at each other for a long, stretched-out moment. I say, "Too many to count."

"Amazing," she breathes. "You must have been good at your job."

"Yeah. I was good at it. I was the best, actually. Which is why they would never have let me quit."

"Did they teach you how to lie? Or were you born a liar?"

This is starting to hurt. She's so emotionless. I spread my hands, giving a shake of my head. "Which answer would be better?"

And like that, she is ice-cold. "How about the truth?"

"Okay, fine. Truth is I've always been good at lying."

She smiles a completely empty smile. Then goes back to eating.

"Uh … would you two like to be alone for this inappropriately intense conversation?" Pace asks.

"No need," Josi replies with a warmer smile for her. "I'm done." And so saying, she stands and carries her plate to the wash-up area and then leaves the Den. I watch her the whole way.

"Dude," Hal says.

"What?"

"If you and Dual are meant to be a secret you should probably try not to be so obvious."

I blink, following his pointed gaze. Quinn and Raven are both watching me.

"There is no me and Dual," I tell Hal.

*

Josephine

On my way out of the dining hall I find myself intercepted by Raven, who walks me out into the night. She doesn't seem intent on speaking, so I clear my throat awkwardly. "I wanted to thank you."

"For what?"

"For sticking up for me in the infirmary. Why'd you do that? It's pretty obvious you don't like me."

She stops walking and I do the same. "I have no tolerance for men laying hands on women," she says bluntly, and I remember the way Quinn was roughly detaining me.

I'm impressed, abruptly, by this insight into Raven's integrity. Then she says, with a smile, "But make no mistake. I'm not as gullible as the rest of them. I know you're lying, Dual. So don't get too comfortable here."

She strides off into the night, and I watch her confident, sensual walk with a sick feeling in my stomach.

I go to the training room and start hitting a punching bag. No one else is here. I haven't bothered to put gloves on, which is stupid as it's really hurting my hands.

"More from your center," a voice comes from the door and I look over to see Shadow.

"What does that mean?"

He doesn't bother explaining. Just hands me some gloves and helps me lace them.

"Your arms are weak," he comments.

"How is that helpful?" I snap, frustrated. "I *know* I'm weak. You tell me every damn day."

"You shouldn't train when you're in a bad mood."

"Oh, piss off, would you?"

He shrugs and leaves. I keep punching. I know I don't have the right technique, and that my punches are wildly unskilled, hurting my shoulders and wrists. But my stupid trainer isn't *training* me.

A loud scream of frustration leaves me as I punch the bag as hard as I can and feel pain shoot through my elbow.

"Pretty sure he's into you."

I turn to find Pace this time. "Who? Shadow?"

She laughs. "You said he doesn't love you. I'm not sure that's true, given the torture we were just forced to endure."

"He's just feeling guilty," I mutter, spinning to whack the bag ineffectively with my left fist. "And have I ever given you cause to believe I want to talk about my personal life?"

"That was the worst punch I've ever seen," she observes.

"I know," I reply through gritted teeth. "I don't know how to do it better."

"Use the weight from your center."

"What does that *mean*?" I exclaim.

Pace gives me a wave. "You're in a bitchy mood. I'm out."

My shoulders slump and I stand alone on the mats.

I don't know what I'm doing, or what I want. I wanted to find the resistance so I could do something about the world, but nobody here seems to be doing anything about it, and so I'm just … existing. I have only ever known a life of survival, of running and hiding and fighting the blood moon. I was a woman whose entire life revolved around one thing and now that thing is gone. So what do I do? Pretend I can throw a punch and pick some wheat.

I don't know what the point of anything is. I'm not a good enough person to just exist. I'm not *worth* just existing.

So what do I do?

*

January 13th, 2066

Luke

I wait.

I try to wait. I feel wrung out and empty. The anger has waned somewhat but not completely. Now I'm hurting all the way through and I don't know what's going on.

Sitting up in my hospital bed, I peer through the darkness and see Ranya sleeping in the chair. As quietly as I can manage, I creep from the bed and pad for the door.

"You haven't been discharged," Ranya murmurs sleepily.

"Where's Dual staying? I gotta ask her something about the city."

She hesitates, then sighs. "Your old room."

So I make my way through the quiet settlement, the moon bright above me and clear as cut glass. I feel a trembling in my spine, a kind of unsettled restlessness. My heart is racing ahead of me to find her before I do.

At the door I pause. It's dark inside. I stalk quietly around to the back window. She's in bed, not moving except for the soft rise and fall of her chest. I try to draw a breath but find that I barely exist. Am suddenly just ... this boneless, fleshless *thing*, made of fear and yearning and guilt.

I tap on the window.

She wakes immediately; was sleeping only lightly. She spots me and this look of pain fills her. Warily she climbs out of bed, wearing a t-shirt and undies and looking like a creature leapt straight from my dreams. She's healthier than I've ever seen her as she walks to the window, looks down at me. Places her hand on the glass. Moves her lips close. Our eyes meet, search.

I reach up to place my hand against hers.

"I love you," I say softly, and she sees the shape of my words without hearing them. I wait, not knowing if she'll let me in. After a long, terrible moment, she reaches down and slides the window open. I climb through.

"What are you doing?" she whispers.

"Following you. Forever."

Josi sits on the edge of the bed and rests her head in her hands. "I told you – "

"I know." I sit beside her and we lie back on the mattress together, staring at the ceiling.

"What's going on?" I ask her. "Why are we lying to them? And why do they all think your name is Dual?"

"Pace called me that and I just … let her. I don't trust them."

"Josi, they're good people. I – "

"Luke," she says, and I know the voice. I know it very well. It's her frightened voice; her brave one. "I told them I was a mistake. That you saved me by accident."

"But *why*?"

She sits up. "You told them the girl you went back for was immune to the cure, didn't you?"

"Yeah."

"They want me for something. Because of that. And I can't let them have me."

"I know them – "

"You know them and you trust them. I get it. But listen to me." She holds my gaze fiercely. "They don't own me and I don't owe them anything. They have their own agendas, and I don't want to be studied or experimented on anymore. I just want to be left alone."

Josi licks her lips in that way of hers. "I need you to trust me. Even if you don't believe me, I just need you to help me."

She doesn't say *you owe me*. Which she could. And even though have spent months with these people, and they've shown me a home and a cause that I never thought to hope for, gave me a place to belong, something to fight for … even then, I say, "Always."

Because she is everything, and more than everything, and forever.

"Thank you," she says, and then opens the window.

I climb halfway out before pausing to look at her. Josi averts her eyes from me. She's really serious about this break-up and I can' believe it, except that I can. The notion of her hating me was bad enough, but the reality of it is excruciating.

Extreme weariness overtakes me. I let my eyes drift shut and I rest my forehead on the side of the window. "I dreamt of you. The whole time, I think."

There is a long silence. Then she murmurs, "Dream of something else now."

I climb out and she closes the window behind me.

Chapter 7

January 17th, 2066

Josephine

We are at dinner. I am sitting with my friends, and the idiot comes over even though he is completely not invited. Which is exactly what I tell him.

"Of course he's invited," Hal says quickly, flashing Luke an apologetic smile.

Luke sits down, shooting me a smug look.

"You're right," I admit. I take a purposeful bite of my sandwich, chew thirty times and then swallow. "We can learn a lot from Luke. Tell me. How did you get these three to like you?"

He frowns.

"Which tricks did it take? A Blood knows he can't seduce anyone without his tricks and lies and performances. So which ones did you use?"

"What are you talking about?" Pace snaps.

I don't look away from Luke; he says nothing. I let my voice drop. "Did you tell them about a dead family member? I've heard Bloods do that to gain empathy."

He goes rigid. He told me once that his brother, Dave, killed himself after having been given the cure. But I don't even know if that story was true. That was the same night I first played him the song I wrote for him. Remembering that song is brutal embarrassment.

I lean forward, holding Luke's eyes. "Did you make them love you for all the pain you were in?"

"You're so cold," he tells me abruptly.

"Yes."

"I was never cold with you."

"You were worse." I don't care anymore if Hal and Will know about us. I'm sure Pace has told them anyway.

Luke's mouth twists into a grimace.

"Get it together," Pace suddenly orders, and I look up to see Raven coming this way.

I take a last look at Luke and see disappointment in his eyes, but I don't care. I can't live like this. Anger eats me from the inside.

Raven invites the two of us for drinks as though we are a couple. I *hate* it. It's like listening to fingernails on a chalkboard. It takes everything I have not to tell her that I hate Luke Townsend and she can shove her fucking drinks up her ass.

*

Raven

I watch them. Now that he's awake and my heart has remembered how to beat, I watch them. Some nights they eat together with the children. They don't talk much, they mostly listen to Pace, Hal and Will chatting incessantly. Luke was always prone to bouts of reticence though, and I don't know Dual well enough to know if her silence is unusual. She was in a mental asylum for most of her life, so I suppose it would be unusual for her to act too normally. Their eyes dart often to each other, though, and I want to know why, and what

105

is in those looks. Is it simply fascination, after having gone through whatever they did together? Gratitude for having saved each other? Or something more?

Thick, heavy tar clogs my arteries when I think it might be this last.

Tonight I cross to their table. "Hello, you two."

The conversation ceases and they all look up at me. "I'll take a stab in the dark at which two you're talking to," Pace mutters and I ignore her.

"Raven," Luke says with a smile. It doesn't reach his eyes.

Dual goes back to her sandwich without saying anything.

"I wanted to invite you both for drinks tonight. After dinner. See you at my place." I leave before they can answer. Quinn is hunting tonight, which is why I invited them. If he was home he'd make it too hard for me to really investigate them. Plus he'd be disappointed in my suspicion.

At home I pour wine for the three of us and plug my tablet into the ancient speakers. Luke, I remember, used to love cello music, so I had Hal steal me some tracks when he was last in the city. It'll be a nice surprise. Once the low notes are plucking through the living room I sit down to wait.

They are very late. When I open the door it's to find them both leaning lazily against either side of the doorframe, looking equally uninterested in each other and in being here. Actually they both look a bit like surly teenagers.

And as I take them in I know. They are in love.

It's the effortless familiarity. The startling similarity. The bristling animosity that only comes from some serious feelings. If they are not in love then they know each other very well.

It causes a sharp pain inside me. "You're late."

"Did you specify a time?" Dual asks.

I stand aside and they traipse in. They both sit on cushions on the floor and reach for a glass of wine, not bothering to wait for me before drinking thirstily.

I sink onto the couch. "Cheers."

"Sorry." Luke grins, clinking his glass to mine. Dual does the same but doesn't apologize. "Quinn hunting?"

I nod, meeting his eyes. "I thought it'd be a good chance for us to catch up."

"Might be easier for you to catch up without me here," Dual suggests.

"Stay," I murmur. "I want us to be friends, Dual eyes."

"How about we start by not calling me Dual eyes?"

"I like it," Luke comments, and she rolls those dual eyes of hers. It grates at me that they are the most beautiful eyes I have ever seen.

"So why the turnaround?" she asks me mildly. "The last time you and I spoke you had a slightly different perspective on the matter." And she smiles. It takes me aback – I'm the one who's supposed to be relaxed and in control.

I shrug, matching her manner. "Quinn had words with me. I do tend to be on the suspicious side."

Dual holds my eyes for a few seconds too long – I refuse to look away. "Ah," she says eventually, nodding and taking another sip. She turns to Luke, who's looking between us curiously.

"What's your Inferno name?" she asks him.

He shrugs. "Didn't get one. They used to just call me Blood."

She doesn't react at all. She knew already, then. "You two have been getting to know each other," I point out.

Luke nods. "Over the last few dinners." He scratches his arm absently; he hasn't stopped moving since he sat down. He used to be deeply still.

"Sounds like Luke's certainly had an adventurous life," Dual offers with a wan smile.

"Unlike life in the asylum?"

She shakes her head, her smile widening slightly. "You know what life in the asylum is? Boring." Then she gives a breath of laughter and meets my eyes and I believe her, I really, really believe her.

"Hanging around uncured people can't have been that boring."

"You'd be surprised at how much more insane people become *after* being given the cure. I was the only uncured in there most of the time."

"Until Luke's girlfriend, right?" I ask, watching for her reaction.

Dual nods, not missing a beat. "That's right. She didn't talk much though. And she was separated from most people."

"But not you."

She shrugs, smiling again. "Guess they thought we could do our worst to each other and it wouldn't matter."

"Why was she separated from the others, then?"

"They were cured and she was dangerous."

I lean forward. "How so?"

Dual and Luke share a quick look. She turns back to me and shrugs

"Was it the immunity to the cure you told Dodge about?"

They both nod. Dual finishes her wine and gets up to pour us some more.

"How was she killed?"

"Her last transformation killed her, as Ben told me it would," Luke replies flatly.

"What a shame. We could have learned a lot from her blood."

"Yeah, that was my main concern when she died," he snaps, and can see the anger kindling beneath his surface.

"Seems she wasn't a survivor after all." I can't resist needling him.

He doesn't look away from my face, his gaze hard. "You already know how she died," he points out. "Dual told me you discussed it So why are you bringing it up?"

I shrug, sitting back. "Curiosity."

"Of course," he laughs bitterly.

Dual puts Luke's refilled glass in his hand. It does not escape my notice that she touches his fingers deliberately, and that he is promptly distracted from his anger as she must have intended.

"Interesting taste in music," she says, changing the subject.

"Cello is Luke's favorite."

"Really? Why is that, Luke?" she asks.

His eyes dart to her as he shrugs.

"It's a bit slow for me," she admits. "I like stuff with a beat."

You would. Cretin.

Luke smothers a laugh by taking a long gulp.

"Before we put the subject to bed, I will say one more thing on the matter of immunity to the cure."

They look at me.

"I'm going to suggest a mission into the city to retrieve blood samples from the girl."

Dual frowns. "She's dead."

"The Bloods will have her samples. From the first round of testing they did."

"So you want someone to break into a Blood facility?" she clarifies. "That's suicide."

"Not for someone who knows what he's doing," I reply, looking at Luke.

"I'm not a Blood anymore. I don't have any clearances."

"If you'd managed to get her out then none of this would be a problem," I say. There's a long pause. "Didn't you want to organize a mission to the city anyway? To stop the sadness cures? This is an opportunity to gain the blood that could immunize us against it."

He frowns, searching my face. "You don't want to inject yourself with whatever was in her blood," he tells me finally. "Trust me."

"But we can study it. Tweak it. Find a way to make the resistance members immune, so there's never any threat of us being cured."

"And find a way to return the cured in the city to normal," Dual adds.

I shrug, swirling my wine.

"Right?" she presses.

"Something on that scale would be impossible."

"We can try, at least."

"Why?"

She stares at me. "Because they're people."

"They're ruined. It's too late for them."

"No." Dual shakes her head. "I thought that once. But I was wrong. They feel as much as we do. They're still capable of love and grief."

"Their brains are mush," I say. "We would do better to wipe them all out and start afresh here, with a new civilization in which people are free."

She stares at me, shocked. "Their neural pathways have been re-circuited and numbed, but it's far from irreversible. And even if it was, there's enough remaining in them that they're worth saving. If there was only one emotion left, it would be worth saving."

She stands and I can see she's throbbing with indignation.

"If there were *no* emotions left," Dual declares softly, "Not a single one, they would still be worth fighting for, because they are people, no matter what they're capable of feeling."

She walks to the door.

"Where are you going?" I demand. "I haven't dismissed you."

"Dismissed me?" Her look is so cutting it makes my cheeks flush. "Your ignorance is boring me," the girl says and leaves.

I stare at the door, stunned.

Luke calmly finishes his wine.

"She's a stupid child," I manage. "A person without emotion is a soulless monster."

"Why?"

I blink, looking at him. "They're an empty shell."

"So they deserve to die?" He stands up. "I think she's right. The ones who deserve to die are the ones emptying the shells." He pauses at the door too. "And she's not a stupid child – she cottoned on to the truth before either one of us did."

When he's gone I feel embarrassed and small – and angry. It's the way Luke Townsend makes me feel just about every time he and I are in the same room.

*

Josephine

A terrible, aching sadness fills me up and I run. I run and run until I reach the wall, and I climb the steps until I am standing atop it and gazing out at the violent forest of teeth and hands, and I let myself shatter into a thousand tiny pieces and sob and sob.

Because Anthony was a drone but he loved me and I killed him. Because I killed many people, normal people with families and jobs and people to love. People with no choice about what they had become, who did not deserve to die.

Those people. Those people I have spent the last ten years calling soulless. They aren't. They deserve life. Not to be treated as animals. Not to be discarded by the real monsters of the world – the ones like Raven who have no love in their hearts.

Oh god, my whole body hurts as I cry and cry. I am a worse monster than Raven. A worse monster than anyone left in this world. It floods me. Crashes through the wall I have built around my heart, a wall that is the only reason I am a functioning human being and not a guilt-ridden madwoman.

I should have killed myself. Instead I am drowning in the deaths I caused, the murders I committed, all those poor people I can't even remember. It is vile; *I* am vile.

Footsteps sound and I moan because I can't bear for anyone to see me like this but I also can't stop crying. It's Pace, and she stares at me in the dark for a few moments before crouching to drag me against her body. I sob hysterically and try to shove her away but she is much stronger than me and eventually I stop fighting and allow her to hold me. Her heartbeat against my cheek is a steady, calming thing.

By the time I fall asleep I think I have cried an entire ocean's worth of tears. I'm a dried-up husk. A girl with skin coated in salt.

*

January 20th, 2066

Luke

Josi has been asleep for three days. Though I look otherwise, I am scared. She is swallowed whole by her guilt and her grief over Anthony and the people she killed. She loved him, I think. And now the depression is worse than I have ever seen it. It was the conversation with Raven that triggered it, and the woman's brutal, callous dismissal of drones.

Pace came to find me on the second day, uncomfortable.

"What's wrong?" I asked.

"Dual's ... There's something wrong with her."

"What is it?"

"She won't get out of bed."

Something in my heart broke at the words. Some part of me had hoped now that the virus was gone from her blood that she would be healthy again, and no slave to the moon. I hoped that her depression wouldn't follow her anymore. It was a stupid hope. It isn't something that just goes away.

I followed Pace back to their house and checked on Josi. She was dead to the world, and when I tried to get her up she woke briefly and said, "I need the sadness cure."

It was the worst thing she'd ever said and it scared me stiff.

I left it a day, trying to wake her at intervals. I tried tough love, gentle coaxing, shaking her awake, but nothing worked.

Today I carried her to the infirmary so that Ranya could attach her to a drip because she still wouldn't get out of bed or move or speak. Ranya didn't want to do it – she said that Dual needed an incentive to wake up. But I told her that Dual was more likely to let herself die. Ranya didn't ask how I knew that, she just hooked up the drip.

I try to act like the concerned friend I supposedly am, but obviously I feel like a lunatic inside a body. I hate seeing her like this.

My mother once told me that passion and melancholy are two sides of the same coin. But what she didn't tell me was how to flip the coin.

I meet Shadow at the wall and we go hunting. I am rusty with the bow, as I was only starting to get good when I left. There's so much movement in my body now that I have trouble aiming.

"You shouldn't have come," Shadow tells me.

"Why?"

"You're unfocused."

I sigh, sliding the arrow back into the quill and letting him fire the shot that takes the Fury through the eye. Two more see this and run at us, so I draw knives from my belt and cut them both down before they get anywhere near Shadow.

Wiping the blades on my pants, I sheathe them and we take a moment with the corpses.

"I don't know how to help her," I say abruptly.

There is a long silence.

"Melancholy," Shadow replies, "is an unconscious yearning for something lost, something that can't be named and can never be had."

My mouth falls open. It's literally the last thing I ever expected Shadow to say. Before I can think of any kind of response, he strides back for the wall.

I keep watch as we return quietly through the dead forest. We reach the wall and wave to the guards on duty, then Shadow places a big hand on my shoulder and gives me a look that manages to bolster my strength.

"But what do I do?" I ask him. He doesn't answer.

113

Inside we part ways and I go straight to the hospital. Raven is there, watching Josephine. She glances at me with distaste. "It's becoming clearer why they stuck her in a loony bin."

"Get out," I order, and I'm so angry I'm scared I'll hurt her. Raven looks smug as she leaves.

Grabbing one of the books from the shelf, I sit beside Josi's sleeping form and start reading to her. There are a couple of other patients here tonight, both with injuries from training. I see their eyes in the dark as they listen to me read. But Josi doesn't open hers even though I read to her all night, trying to imagine of all the things she might be yearning for.

*

January 21st, 2066

Josephine

I dream of birds and blood. But I dream of gentler things too. Smiles and touches and clipboards and reading glasses. Words spoken in a deep, poetic voice. I dream of Anthony's daughter Marley.

I feel so heavy. I am barely able to breathe I am so heavy.

*

Something is warm and bright against my face. It takes me a long while to become conscious enough to be annoyed at this and groan. It also doesn't feel like I'm on a bed. It feels … gritty.

Dragging my eyes open, I am startled to realize I'm outside. The sun beats down and my hands move through … sand? Jerking upright, all the air is stolen from my lungs.

Because I am sitting beyond the wall, on the beach. And before me is the sea.

Luke Townsend is standing further down the sand, writing something with a stick. My heart thumps. Oh, god. To be outside. *To be free.*

I stand and walk to him, looking at the words.

a bright thing, the brightest thing of all

Words I spoke to him a million years ago. Luke looks into my face and he smiles. I feel that smile of his fill me up, and then I turn and look at the ocean. It glitters silver in the sunlight. There are tears in my throat, but it is not because inside I'm black and ugly and rotten, it is because I am overflowing with the sudden beauty of it, the aching beauty, and when I walk into the water and let the salt swell of it wash over me I am laughing.

*

We swim for hours. I love this ocean. Love it like I was born to it.

"Seaborn," Luke agrees when I try to explain. We are floating on our backs and looking at the clouds.

"Have you been to the beach before?"

"Last year. I snuck out a few times to come here."

"Before that." This is the first question I've asked him about his life since the Big Reveal. I am very aware of it.

"How would I have gone to the beach? They're all beyond the wall."

"I thought … maybe Bloods were allowed outside."

"No one's allowed outside."

We fall silent. No one has been in the ocean for decades, is what that means. It seems tragic. I can see a fisherman's hook in the clouds. And what I imagine to be a mermaid tail. I move my hands through the salty water. The waves are calm, and I'm getting sunburnt but I don't care.

"Seaborn," I murmur, liking the sound of it.

"There were people who lived in the sea, once upon a time," Luke says in his deep storyteller's voice. "The souls of the drowned. Sometimes taking the form of a seal, sometimes shedding their sealskin to become human. They were bound to the ocean, tethered to it by their souls."

I want to shed my skin. I want to take a different form, one that lives in the sea. I want my soul to be tethered to something. In this moment, I want it more than anything.

"It sounds lonely though," Luke murmurs.

Not to me.

"How long did I sleep?" I ask eventually.

"Four days."

I breathe out slowly. "You carried me here?"

He doesn't answer, which means yes.

"How did you get through the Furies?"

"Came south."

Right. Meaning Shadow lied to me when he said that north of the camp was the only way to reach the beach – when he was trying to scare the shit out of me. "Will they find us here?"

"Hope not."

I can't help smiling at his blasé manner. It's a nice change from all the dour terror everyone else has of the Furies, despite it also being blatantly reckless. "I'm gonna get in so much trouble for not going to work."

"Yep."

"Think Ranya'll write me a note?"

"No."

"She's a battle-axe."

We both start laughing.

"She made Hal work after he'd had a ruptured testicle," Luke tells me. "He waddled around like he had a cactus up his ass for days." This sends us both into hysterics. The sound of our laughter drifts up into the sky.

Eventually we wade onto the sand to dry off, our skin wrinkled like prunes. I lie in the warm sand, feeling the coarseness of it all over my body. It is these moments, these tiny moments, which remind me how wonderful it is to be alive.

"You said you wanted the sadness cure," Luke tells me. He sounds betrayed.

"I don't want to be powerless anymore. I don't want to feel all this sadness."

"Josi, you've been through some seriously, seriously bad shit. It's normal for you to be sad, just like it's normal for you to be angry: you're uncured."

And then when Luke sits up and starts moving his hands as though he's wielding a bow against the strings of a cello, and when he hums the notes of 'The Swan' as if they are coming from his imaginary instrument, I realize that my soul *is* tethered to something after all. It is tethered to his.

I feel more tears spill out of my eyes and I laugh, and then I join in, pretending to play the cello while we hum along together.

Chapter 8

January 21st, 2066

Josephine

There are people waiting for us inside the wall. Quinn, Raven, Shadow and a couple of guards I don't know. Luke tenses beside me, and I know something's very wrong.

"It was an emergency," Luke says automatically.

"What kind?" Quinn asks.

"Dual hasn't been well – "

"Ranya says there's nothing wrong with her," Raven interrupts.

"You didn't clear it with anyone before leaving the walls," Quinn goes on. "You both know it's illegal. On top of which, Dual hasn't shown up for her shifts or training for the past three days."

"Okay, yes, I'll own that," I say, "and I'm sorry, but – "

"You're both to be punished."

Great – no meal tonight. And right when I'm finally hungry again. Except that Shadow isn't meeting my eyes. And Luke seems too still. And Raven is way too smug.

Quinn studies us both with a look of regret. "You *have* to follow the rules. We all do, or this place falls apart."

I'm starting to get nervous now. It's his tone.

"Ten lashings for each rule broken, which makes it ten for Luke and twenty for Dual. You'll receive them at sundown."

"*Lashings?*" I repeat. "Is that a joke?"

"I volunteer to take Dual's punishment as well as my own," Luke says immediately.

There's a momentary hesitation, a rustle of surprise.

"Very well." Quinn shrugs.

"He can't!" Raven protests.

"It's within his rights," Quinn replies.

"It's my right to take them, so I'm taking them," Luke agrees firmly. "It was my fault she was beyond the wall anyway. I wasn't thinking – I should have cleared it."

"Hang on ..." I am staring between them all, still convinced this is some kind of practical joke. A queasy sensation uncurls in my guts. "You're honestly telling me that you punish people with physical torture? Did I just step back into the Dark fucking Ages?"

There is a momentary silence as everyone stares at me.

"What? Am I not allowed to argue now?" I demand. "Is that illegal too? What kind of dictatorship are you running here, Quinn? Am I about to have my mouth sewn shut for speaking an independent thought?"

He still doesn't answer, and I step towards him. "*Surely* you can see the hypocrisy of not letting people outside the walls."

"It's different," Raven says flatly. "The wall here keeps you alive, it doesn't imprison you."

"What's the fucking difference?" I ask her. I am so angry it's a struggle not to scream.

"You broke the rules of The Inferno, which exist only to keep you safe," Quinn says finally. "We punish in order to teach a simple fact: *that to break rules in the west can mean your death.* It's a very dangerous world out here. One day you'll thank me for instilling a sense of caution in your careless spirit. Be in the square at sundown."

"He can challenge it," Shadow says and everyone looks at him. "He has the right to challenge his accuser to a bout."

Quinn's eyes narrow. "That's right."

"Who's my accuser?" Luke asks.

"I am," the leader of The Inferno says.

Luke considers him, then shakes his head. "You go down a second time and you irreparably damage the respect your people have for their leader. Not good for anyone."

Quinn's mouth opens then closes again. I watch a shadow chase through his eyes. He nods once and they disperse, leaving us standing in the sun. Shadow is last to walk away and he does so with a guarded look I can't read.

My head is spinning. "You're not taking my lashings," I tell Luke.

"Actually," he replies, "I am."

"It's not your choice."

He spins to face me, taking my upper arms urgently. "*Listen to me.* If you were healthy and strong I would let you take your punishment because you seem hell-bent on it, but you're *not*. You're sickly and weak. You haven't eaten in four days. Severe blood loss and pain could *kill* you, Josephine."

I stare at him, ashamed. "It's not your choice," I repeat faintly, my voice scratchy.

"I don't care."

*

At sundown Luke's arms are tied to a wooden pole on either side of him. His shirt is removed.

120

I've spent the afternoon arguing with Quinn, trying to volunteer to take my own lashings back, as well as Luke's, even though I know Luke's right and it'd probably kill me. The principle of the matter remains the same: I don't need or want a man to take my punishment for me. Neither of us should be punished in the first place – not like this, anyway – but if we have to be then I ought to have the same right to volunteer as Luke does.

There's no budging the leader of the resistance on this one though. Because of my reaction to all of this, he's taken it into his head that seeing Luke punished for me will actually be a better lesson than having my own back lashed.

"Your own suffering suddenly doesn't seem to bother you all that much," he pointed out.

So now here we stand, all two-hundred-and-sixty-nine of us, even the children. Nobody looks happy, but nobody looks outraged or incredulous, like I am. Which means it's happened before.

Will, Pace and Hal are beside me. Will holds my hand, knowing somehow. Or perhaps he is the one looking for comfort. I have none to give. I feel hollow.

Quinn and Raven watch from near the poles. Shadow steps up with a whip made of knotted rope. It has been made wet so it's heavier.

"Breaking the laws of The Inferno is not to be tolerated. No one is above our rules. Fifty lashings."

There's an intake of breath. Murmurs of unease and outright denial. Fifty is too many.

"You said thirty!" I shout.

Quinn ignores me. Shadow looks paler than I have ever seen him. He leans close to Luke's ear and says something too soft for anyone else to hear. Luke nods.

The whipping begins. The first blow slaps out with a resounding *whack*. I flinch; my whole body recoils as though *it* has been whipped. Luke's jaw clenches and he squeezes his eyes shut. The second lash makes him flinch a little more. The third a little more. But he remains silent. Even when he has been whipped ten times, twenty, thirty.

Blood is streaming down his legs and pooling on the sand.

Shadow looks wretched as he keeps going. It seems to last forever.

By the time we reach forty-five Luke is weary with pain. His face is twisted, his shoulders bowed. Each time he is whipped his legs give out and he falls against the bindings around his wrists. Each time he stands once more, and Shadow waits for him to regain his footing.

The Vikings of ancient times used to blood eagle each other, flaying open the backs of their enemies and removing the lungs to place over the shoulders like bloodied wings. If the victim could withstand this torture in silence, he would be admitted to Valhalla when he died. I don't know if that's what Luke is thinking of now, or of all the other foolish people who've believed throughout the ages that pain must be endured in silence, but I wish that he wouldn't. I wish he would scream. In rage or pain or anything. Because whatever heroic role he is playing in this quiet evening seems like madness.

*

Luke

Getting flayed hurts like a bitch. At first it feels fine and delicate, an intimate kind of pain. By the end it's heavy, brutal, a dull hammer.

"Can we hurry this along?" I growl.

"Quiet," Ranya chides me as she cleans and dresses my back.

I'm sitting backwards on a chair in the infirmary while she tends to my wounds. We've gone through an impressive amount of whisky, as she pours it over my wounds and I drink it in equal measure. I'm having trouble holding my head up, woozy from pain or alcohol or both.

Hal hurries in. "You okay, man?"

"Peachy."

"That was brutal. What'd you do?"

I shake my head, barely able to string a sentence together. I'm drunk and in excruciating pain.

"Brought you more supplies," he says, offering me another bottle of booze.

I take a few gulps and feel it make its warm path through my body. It's dulling the fire needles jabbing through my raw skin nicely.

"Have you seen Dual?" I ask him.

"She's outside yelling at Quinn."

"Oh god," I groan. "Get out there and stop her, will you?"

"No way." He smiles. "I'm not getting in the firing line."

"Stop moving!" Ranya orders me and I try to hold still.

When she's finally finished bandaging she helps me to lie face down on one of the beds for a sleep. Lying down is nice. Quite … squishy. My eyes fall closed and I struggle to get them open again. The lids are extremely heavy. And my back … Ah, my back. Sleep might be a nice way to make it stop burning.

Time passes, I think. I dream of cellos. And my brother.

Voices interrupt like softly floating leaves on the wind. I don't open my eyes because I'm not sure that I can, but I think there are two people somewhere nearby, speaking in low tones.

"… don't believe that do you?"

"It's not about that."

"Why did you do it then?"

"Because I was ordered to. And if I hadn't, someone else would have."

"That's the kind of attitude that winds up causing genocide."

A silence. It's Josi and Shadow.

"Lazy, weak soldiers doing as their masters command them to, even when they know it's wrong."

"You are very comfortable passing judgments."

"Yep. You shouldn't have done it." She sounds so stubborn in the quiet night. It makes me smile, or at least think about smiling.

"You think him incapable of enduring it?"

"That's not even close to the point and you know it."

Another silence.

"What did you whisper to him at the start?"

"I told him that pain isn't real."

She pauses, maybe thinking about that for a while. "Why does Quinn have more power than you anyway?"

"Someone has to be at the top."

"He hasn't built an army," Josi points out. "There's no need for military law if he won't even fight. Instead he's made a community of people. It should be a democracy."

The conversation goes on like this while I drift in and out of consciousness.

I wake again and it's still night. This time I feel a little more lucid, which means the pain has returned. Groaning, I slowly realize that once again I'm not alone. This time it's a solitary figure standing by the window.

Josi turns and in the moonlight I can see how bleak her expression is. One of her eyes seems to glow, the pale one. The dark one looks almost too black to see. Like a demon eye in the night. She brings me more painkillers, helps me to swallow them and then returns to the window.

"Go back to sleep," she tells me.

"You okay?"

I can see a storm within her. "Don't ever do that again," Josephine tells me softly.

I close my eyes. My neck is sore from sleeping on my stomach, so I turn my head the other way.

"Don't ever take something that belongs to me."

"Not even pain?"

"Not even that."

I've ruined her, I realize. I've taken all her softness and left her with mistrust and anger. Her heart is impenetrable. She thinks she has to do everything alone again.

"This is why I didn't tell you the truth straight away," I murmur. "Because I knew it would make you like this."

"Like what?"

"Cold."

There's a long silence.

Eventually she says, "Guess you were right." And I hear her walk out.

It hurts more than the whipping.

*

February 1st, 2066

Luke

I've been putting off visiting Dodge for weeks now. Mostly because I've been in the infirmary, partly because I know what he's going to say. I'm also reminded of Harley each time I see him. But in the end I just grit my teeth and go in for testing. I explain that I have the same thing in my blood that Dual was injected with, and that I need him to come up with a way to block it. He knows who Josi is, apparently, but I tell him I don't want him using her – he'll just have to start from scratch.

He shakes his head as he gazes into the microscope at the tiny pieces of me. "It'll be a miracle if I come up with anything. Honestly. The man you need is the one who developed this in the first place."

"Yeah, well, he's in a city surrounded by walls and Bloods with guns who have orders to kill me."

I head out into the night; above me is a crescent moon that hardly sheds any light. As I walk slowly toward my little house, I consider Ben Collingsworth and where he's likely to be right now. Josi and I apparently left him in the lab, waiting for Jean and the Bloods to break in and find him. Which means there's every possibility that he was killed for his crimes.

Someone's sitting on my front doorstep. "What have you been sneaking out to do?" she asks me.

"I wasn't aware there's a curfew."

"No curfew, surprisingly. Nothing interesting to do either."

"Are you coming in?"

Josi shakes her head. "I want to go back to the city."

"*What?*"

"Not to live. Just to get Ben."

"Oh." I clutch a hand to my heart. That really scared me for a second I study her – it's bizarre that I have just been thinking about Ben and here she is, bringing him up. "He's … Jose, I'd say he's probably dead."

She nods. "Yeah. But maybe not."

I consider her outline; I can't see much else of her. Her scrawny legs are drawn up to her chest and she's resting her chin on her knees. We've barely spoken since the whipping. I haven't been in much of a state to talk to anyone really, dosed up on pain meds and alcohol. My back's healing slowly, but I'll always have brutal scars the result of only having access to medical treatment that belongs in the Medieval Ages.

"It'll be like walking straight back into the lion's den," I warn her. She nods again.

"If it's because you want him to help me – "

"It is. But it's also because I owe Ben my life, and he doesn't deserve to be left there, and because he might be able to help us reverse the cure."

The last thing I want is for Josi to be anywhere near that city. But I'm not her boyfriend; it's not my decision what she does with her life and I learned the hard way that she doesn't want me protecting her.

So I just say, "Okay."

*

February 5th, 2066

Josephine

Luke is given permission for the op. Ostensibly it's to retrieve Ben and the blood of the dead immune chick, aka me. But aside from that Luke and I are in agreement that what we really need to do is reconnaissance on the sadness cures. Where the government is manufacturing the drug, how they're distributing it, what their plans for injection are, how they're advertising it, what the date for administering it is, and so on. He says the more information we have, the more it will help us to make a proper hit later this year.

He was allowed to choose his team, and he wanted to keep it small so he picked Hal, Pace and Will – explaining that they work so well together they're like having six people – plus Shadow. And ... me. Because I gave him no choice in the matter. It was then a case of convincing Quinn and Raven that I should be allowed to go, given how useless I am, but Luke gave them a whole song and dance about how I know the asylum inside out, which is where we'll be starting our search for Ben, and how I still have retinas and prints that might not have been updated in the security system. This sounds far-fetched to me, but they bought it.

So now the six of us are spread out in the fifth carriage of the train, watching the tunnel walls flash by.

Why *did* I insist on coming? I can't be of any real help. I'll probably be a liability. But I guess I just can't stand hanging around at the settlement, farming and running around the wall. It feels so utterly useless. And wasn't the whole reason I came here so that I could try to make some kind of difference to the messed-up world? That's probably overestimating my capacity as a person, but I have to at least *try*. And regardless, I'm starting to feel excited just to be doing something.

Luke has me dismantling, cleaning and refitting guns of all different sizes. He says the only time my hands shouldn't be loading and unloading weapons is when I eat. It's dull as hell, and I don't get to be included in any of the card games the rest of them are raucously enjoying, but I definitely feel more comfortable holding and aiming guns now that I know how they're built and how they function.

"How's it going?" he asks, sliding into the seat opposite.

"Like a children's sweatshop!" I reply. "Why can't I just take this little one here? *These* ones seem fit to annihilate whole towns."

He has a whole array of semi-automatic rifles and machine guns laid out for me to practice with and most of them are intimidatingly large.

"Giving you a pistol would be like giving you nothing."

"Why?"

"You'd never be able to hit anything with it."

"Why?"

"They have terrible scope and they kick all around the place. You'd struggle to hit a wall directly in front of you."

I frown, lifting the pistol to my eye and pointing it at his face. "Reckon I could probably hit you if I tried."

He grabs the gun and wrenches it out of my hand. "Don't joke around with weapons!"

"It's not even loaded!"

"*I don't care.* They're not toys. You need to respect the damage they do."

"Fine. Sor-ry."

He sits back, looking out the window. A long, awkward moment passes before he mutters, "I hate guns."

I wonder how many people he has shot. "I think I hate them too."

"You'll be fine as long as you try not to fire yours."

"What if someone's shooting at me?"

"Take cover."

"What if there is no cover?"

"*I'll* cover you."

"What if you're not there?"

"I will be."

"But what if you're not?"

"Well *then* you can return fire. But if someone's shooting at you and there's nothing between you and them, and you're alone ... then you're in trouble, girl."

I'm suddenly not so excited about this mission.

"Are we really going to the asylum?" I ask.

Luke shakes his head. "No point. We'll start at Ben's house. He might have a computer system I can hack into."

"Wouldn't it have been disabled when he was taken in?"

"Probably."

"What's the likelihood that he's not in custody? Or dead?"

Luke breathes out, shaking his head. "If they believe he helped us of his own free will he would have been either executed or incarcerated. We'll hope for the latter. We'll then tackle how to get him out of a high security prison. If he managed to convince Jean he helped us under duress there's a slim possibility she might have put him under house arrest, expecting that I'd return for him at some point."

"So we could be walking straight into a trap."

"Yep. But cured folks ain't too good at lying, so he's probably dead."

"He wasn't cured," I say.

Luke frowns. "Yes he was."

"Trust me. He wasn't. He was cleared of having to be because of his contribution to society. He was one of the inner circle."

Luke scratches his jaw, where stubble is growing. "Why didn't I know about that?"

"They covered it up, obviously. Not good for business if the guy who makes the cure doesn't have to take it."

"Yeah but how do you know?"

"He told me." I clip a magazine into the loading mechanism of a huge semi-automatic rifle. It hurts my palm.

"Get your finger away from the trigger," Luke snaps.

"Can you stop talking to me like you're my drill sergeant?"

"Can you stop handling deadly weapons like you're a child?"

"Not all of us were trained for combat when we were fifteen."

"That's becoming painfully obvious."

"You were *not* this much of a jerk when we lived together."

"I was just pretending not to be."

"Enough of the bickering!" Pace hollers back at us from a few rows ahead. "I'm about to blow my own brains out just so I don't have to hear it."

Luke and I stare at each other and our lips twitch at the same time. I look away from him so I don't laugh. I'm over the whipping debacle. I was angry with him for weeks, especially watching him in so much pain, but I don't have the energy for it anymore. I also don't want to look beneath the anger to what's really there.

The trip feels a lot shorter than it did on the way out west. But I'd been nearly catatonic with exhaustion and blood loss then. And now I feel fit as a fiddle. Apart from the shiner Pace gave me yesterday in training.

She keeps shooting me dour looks and I know she's pissed I'm here. I put the guns down and stand up.

"You'd better be going to the toilet and coming straight back," Luke warns.

"Bite me."

I go and sit next to Pace and Hal. Will is jogging up and down the aisle.

"Are you going to say it?" I ask Pace eventually.

Her eyes narrow and she peers sideways at me. "Okay. You should be at home having your nappy changed."

"Pace," Hal admonishes.

"It's fine, Hal," I tell him. "Let her get it out of her system."

"You'll endanger the rest of us. He knows that, and the only reason he let you come along is because you batted your pretty dual eyes at him."

Actually, I'm fairly sure it's because of his guilt. "I'll stay out of the way," I promise.

"And that's half the problem! You don't get it! On an op you have to be able to trust your team. You have to know they're strong enough to have your back. You're not strong enough to have shit."

"You said I was tough," I reply feebly.

"Once. And it musta been one hell of a fluke, 'cause before and since that day you've spent about ninety percent of your time in bed." She leans in close, her purplish eyes holding mine fiercely. Her voice drops, and she goes in for the kill. "It's not just the world that's too difficult for you, Dual. It's existing itself. And that's too pathetic for words."

I remain forcibly expressionless. I don't look at Hal, whose eyes are burning holes in the side of my face. Carefully I stand and walk down the aisle to the next carriage. I sit by myself and watch the black walls flash by.

Will speeds past, a never-ending ball of energy. He hesitates by me, considering stopping.

"Keep moving," I tell him, so he does. I am not sulking. I'm not. I'm just trying to work out if what she said is true.

An hour or two later it's Shadow who comes to find me, and I'm grateful it isn't Luke – I don't want him to see me feeling vulnerable and take advantage of it.

The older man stalks toward me, his legs lanky and graceful. Silently he sinks into the seat across the aisle from mine and copies my stare out the window. Twenty minutes – I count them – pass before I can't stand the quiet any longer. "How long has it been since you've been back to the city?"

A pause. Don't ever try to have a quick conversation with Shadow. "Twenty years."

Jesus. Before the cure. He must have been one of those who built The Inferno. "It's changed a lot since then."

He doesn't reply. There's nothing to say.

"Did you have a family?" I ask.

No answer. I surreptitiously watch the side of his face. It is severe and blank as always. "Yes," he says at last.

I lick my lips, an old habit left over from when they used to get dry and cracked after the blood moon. "They're dead, aren't they?" I say softly.

No answer.

I lean my face on the glass and feel the cool of it against my cheek. He is an orphan just like me. A loner. I know now why he spends his days and nights alone, stalking the dead forest. It is because he had people, and he lost them, and he doesn't want new ones. You can't want new ones.

I wonder if I ever had people. If, in those two short years before I was dumped on the side of a highway, I had people who loved me. It is a particular kind of sweetness, being loved. A very rare thing that combines both complete safety with absolute risk.

But then again, I don't even know how it feels to be loved, do I? Not honestly, if at all. I can't believe that love could exist in someone's heart when everything else is a lie. I can't. Every single thing I know about love is truth.

"She's right," Shadow grunts.

"Who?"

"Skinhead."

I blink. "Right, thanks. I know how useless I am. You can piss off now."

He does. I sit alone for another few hours, counting the safety alcoves because if I don't keep my mind focused on something I will go mad. Maybe I'll just stay on the train when they get off and ride it all the way home. It'd be safer for them. I get up to announce my new plan, but stop when I reach the open carriage door. I can see them all sitting together, and it's quiet enough that their voices drift back to me.

"... nicer scope," Hal says.

"Nah, it's too short range," Luke argues.

"We don't do a lot of sniper-ing," Pace says witheringly. She's still in a foul mood.

"Longer range means better aim," he replies mildly.

They continue talking about stupid weapons and I feel better about my decision – let them enjoy their happy little gun-wielding gang of psycopaths.

Then Pace asks moodily, "She having a cry?"

"You don't have to be such a cow," Hal tells her.

"You gonna ream me for having a go at her?" she asks, and I realize she's talking to Luke.

"No. I know why you said it."

"Oh yeah?"

"Same reason Shadow just went and made her feel even worse, I'm betting," he says. "She's tougher when she's angry."

Abruptly I am furious. I'm so mad I feel like running over there and punching the lot of them in their smug little faces. That'll learn 'em for manipulating me.

Instead I wait a few minutes and then return to my seat to dismantle the guns. I will clean them until my fingers bleed, and then I'll clean them some more, even though I know it's playing right into their game. I refuse to be useless.

*

February 7th, 2066

Josephine

It is mid-afternoon when the train approaches our station. It isn't going to stop, so we have to jump. I haven't spoken a word to any of them in about thirty-six hours. It's not because I'm pissed at them – it's more because I'm trying to maintain a general level of pissed-ness. Basically, they're right. My anger formed so much of me over the last ten years of my life, and that wasn't healthy. But it did focus me to the sharpest edge of a knifepoint, it did make me strong enough to endure almost anything, and most of all it made me wily enough to stay hidden from the Bloods and the cops and the child protection services. Which is exactly what I'll need to be for the next few days.

So they might think I'm being a brat. Let them. What I'm trying to be is tough.

Everyone starts to weapon up, and wordlessly Luke helps me to arm myself with as many weapons as I can conspicuously carry under my coat. Two knives in my shoes, two sewn into the sleeves of my jacket. A pistol in the waistband of my tights, held firm against my lower back. And in my pocket, funnily enough, a canister of pepper spray, since apparently it's the best way for someone like me to quickly incapacitate someone and get away. The larger weapons go in our backpacks. We are dressed as though coming from the gym, as this is just about the only thing you're allowed to carry a proper bag for these days. It won't hold up if we're searched or scanned, so we have to hope we're inconspicuous enough to avoid that. I managed to avoid being scanned and searched for about six years, but I was never traveling with five wanted fugitives.

"Wait for it!" Pace shouts as we line up at the doors and hang out, ready to leap onto the steadily approaching platform. "The second that platform comes level with the start of the train, we jump," she orders, and I know it's for my benefit as I'm the only one who hasn't done the jump before. And Shadow, who's as much of a novice as I am when it comes to city missions.

Whoosh goes the opening of the platform and I don't think – I throw myself forward and try to roll.

I land hard on my feet and one of my ankles twists painfully with the impact. The next thing I know I'm crashing sideways onto my head and shoulders, tumbling furiously and scraping raw the skin all down my right side.

With a groan I feel myself come to a stop, and then struggle dizzily to my feet. "*Ow.*"

"Can't even get off a train." Pace grins. The rest of them are all upright and unharmed, looking at me. Of course. I give her the finger, which only makes her smile widen.

"Let's go," Luke murmurs and we turn for the tunnel.

As agreed in the train, we wait at the bottom of the stairwell while Luke jogs up to make sure the coast is clear.

Hal is looking very burly in his jogging gear, while Will seems like a tiny aerobics instructor. Shadow is just hilarious and weird in his exercise shorts – I'm so used to seeing him in black combat gear that this is like a sudden intimacy akin to seeing someone in their underwear.

A soft whistle comes from above and we climb the stairs into the sunshine. I blink until my eyes adjust. The afternoon is quiet. A few drones walk past, heading home from work. All are impeccably dressed and look either distracted or completely zoned out of reality. The buildings that line the roads are all tall, gray and perfectly matching. I never noticed before how *gray* everything is. Gray is calming, in the right shades. Too dark, and it conjures thoughts of storms. Too pale and it hints at white, which most associate with illness. Everything in this place is designed for calm.

Too bad most of its inhabitants are anything but.

We split into our pairs. Shadow and Will, Blue team, head forward and cross to the next block over. Their cover, if asked, is father and son. Behind us Hal and Pace, Red team, move to the other side of the street. Pace has taken the bolt from her nose and donned a blond wig, which actually makes her look pretty in a depressing, *Stepford Wives* way. Hal's mohawk has been combed down and he looks like a dapper young sportsman. They are brother and sister for the next few days, which I know Luke decided just to mess with Pace – she was clearly repulsed by the disguise but too embarrassed to say so. It was very amusing. But now I can hardly stand to look at them in their perfect little city outfits. They are colorless, characterless, *lifeless*.

Luke and I continue straight together. I didn't want to be in his team, but he said there was no way under the sun that he was letting me out of his sight for this entire mission. And since he's the team leader that apparently means he gets to do whatever he pleases. He's wearing a simple navy hoodie and tracksuit pants, he's cut his hair to regulation military length, and he looks so relaxed I can't believe it, until I remember it's his job to look relaxed when he isn't.

I've just pulled my black hair into a ponytail and put glasses on so anyone who looks at my face will be distracted from my noticeable eyes. Just a few years ago I would have been able to find colored contact lenses to help me blend in, but now they don't exist – retinal scanners need to be able to pick up your real eyes at any point. I wonder if the drones care. I wonder if the desire for material accessories and vanity exist as they once did. Motivations have become simpler: eat, sleep, work, fuck.

One day they will cure us of vanity. I have no doubt they will cure desire, too. Ambition, shame. Amusement. Maybe they will start matching people in a lottery, or matching them depending on their vocation. Maybe people will be assigned vocations. Maybe there will be drugs designed to make us fuck each other and reproduce, like cattle manipulated to breed the best spawn. Maybe.

It's what I'd do if I wanted to rule over a city of obedient ghosts.

We walk past a shopping center. There are a whole lot of drones here, bustling about with almost robotic calmness. They must look pretty freaky to Shadow, who would remember this city very differently. Above us is a moving hologram of the words CALM, HEALTH AND PREVENTION WITH THE CURE.

It flips to an image of a happy family, grinning from ear to ear and playfully wrestling into the shot. The words beneath them read: *Soon there will be no need for sadness. Soon we will be free to love without boundaries ... Soon we will be the best versions of ourselves.*

The mother says, out loud over the entire city block, "*We've never been so connected to each other. There's no space in our hearts anymore for regret or fear – we're just happy.*"

It is so vile I want to vomit.

When we're free of the emerging shoppers I shake my head. "It seems like madness, this blanket belief that everyone has to be happy all the time."

"What do you mean?"

"It's just such a misfire. If we have a right to pursue happiness then we should also have a right to frustration – to understanding what we're deprived of. And then there's the subjectivity of the notion that they don't bother taking into account – for some people happiness is caused by cruelty or immorality or perversion or power or masochism or transgression – a million different things they don't consider valid! And what about our right to *unhappiness?* To melancholy? Who the hell decided that removing those would result in happiness? It's this fucking '*we know what's best for you*' attitude. I can't stand it."

The street feels abruptly quiet. I need to chill out.

"You're being quite intimidating right now," Luke comments and I laugh. "Maybe you should take your own advice, Miss I Want the Sadness Cure."

This wipes the smile from my lips.

"They seem to reckon they can make complicated things simple with brute force," Luke adds more gently.

"You got it," I mutter. "Thanks to the esteemed Harold Connolly, author of the handbook on anger."

"Aw, I love that book."

"Yeah it's my favorite."

At the time when all this started, people were too frightened of the epidemic that had wiped out most of the world. They didn't care about mental health or psychology. They wanted safety from the outside, from beyond the wall and the disease that was running rampant. They wanted physical health, and when the inoculation came with calm and an end to anger, they ate it up. They didn't know they were being silenced, controlled, caged. Now we are free of disease, and steadily becoming free of our feelings.

"Have you met any of them?" I ask. "The Ministers?" The ones who decided to take advantage of six billion deaths and live like kings with dominion over the survivors.

He nods. "Once. They limit contact with outsiders. They have their own little society with their spouses and children and their pretty little dogs. They do the unfortunate business of dealing with the drones through Jean and her Bloods."

"So how did you meet them?"

He doesn't seem to want to tell me, exuding unease. "At an award ceremony."

"What kind of award?"

"The medal of honor."

"Who got that?"

"I did."

I stare at him, eyebrows arched. "What did you do?"

"Don't ask questions you don't want the answers to, Josephine."

"Tell me," I insist.

He breathes out, shaking his head. "I took out a cell of resistors who were trying to free a holding facility of uncured teenagers."

The air leaves my chest quickly.

"I was promoted to Gray for it – the highest rank of Blood there is. It's rare enough that they had a ceremony for it. And I met them all, including Prime Minister Falon Shay."

Luke looks at me. I don't know how to respond, but he speaks again, forestalling me. There's a very violent thing in his voice as he says, "I didn't know it then, but I know it now. I'm going to kill him before I die."

We walk in silence from then on, and I think about how deeply you have to hate someone to truly want them dead.

*

At the end of Ben's street our pairs reconvene. It is dusk, and the sky is deepening to an inky blue. The shadows are long and every noise I hear causes me to jump. Being in the city makes me miss Anthony with an unbearable pang, even though I mostly hated the guy while I was here. All that time we spent together ... we wasted so much of it distrusting each other.

Crouching in the bushes feels silly to me, but we do it anyway.

"Shadow and Will, scout the back of the block," Luke says. "There's an alley that runs behind his house. Take positions there. Hal and Pace, you two keep watch out here. I want intermittent scouts of this whole street, and I want you to keep eyes in every window of every house that has a possible view of our point of entry."

They all nod and head off to do their jobs.

Luke turns to me. "We're looking for anything out of the ordinary. Trip wires, sensors, alarm triggers, explosives. We don't go in until we have the all-clear from both Red and Blue teams that there's no one inside."

"I'm coming in with you?"

"I told you I'm not letting you out of my sight. You're a walking hazard."

Amazing. He's really letting me partake in the most dangerous part of the job! Along with a pretty hefty insult there, but whatever. I'm still chuffed.

"What if there are people in there?"

"Then we don't go in."

"But we need to go in."

"So we'd better hope it's empty."

He's infuriatingly logical, as usual.

In his hand is the walkie-talkie. Will – who is surprisingly technically skilled – wired it to make sure it's invisible to the Blood radio network and can't be interfered with.

About half an hour later it crackles and Hal's voice comes through. *"All clear. No visible movement from within, no visible signs of surveillance. Over."*

"Copy, Red. Report, Blue. Over," Luke says.

"No visible movement from within, no visible signs of surveillance. Over," says Will cheerfully. Then adds, *"This is fun, over."*

"Hood up," Luke tells me, and we draw our hoods. "Weapons check."

I reach down to check my knives, then I remove my pistol and check that it's loaded and the safety is turned on, then I make sure they're all covered up. "Done!"

"Sweet. Calm and normal, got it?"

"Calm and normal."

We walk to the front door. My heart is pounding as Luke rings the bell. My eyes scan for anything out of the ordinary. It's a small, red-brick house with curtained and barred windows. The security door is heavy iron, with multiple padlocks. Ben Collingsworth was a man who endured a hell of a lot of attacks in the days when people still protested the cure.

"Above me," Luke says softly, "are two small cameras. Stay where you are and don't look at them." He edges casually sideways until he is out of view, then reaches up and pulls free the tiny, tiny little black dots that have been placed in the gutter. How the *hell* did he spot them?

Luke removes his kit from his waistband and starts to work the locks on the door, while I block him from view. He has to unpick them physically as well as digitally – and overriding the PNR security system is no easy feat.

"There were so many clues," I say faintly. "That first day you picked my lock to get into my apartment."

"That was not an apartment," he mutters. "That was a bubonic-plague-infested hovel."

"And when we stole from the police – how did I honestly think you were doing that? No one normal can do that. I don't even know how I explained it to myself. I was really blind, wasn't I?"

"No. I was good at my job. There's no shame in being fooled by a professional liar." He picks away, moving onto the second lock. "And the big factor to remember, as I have told you a thousand times, is that you never would have suspected the lie because I buried it in truth."

I swallow and lick my lips. "You've never told me that."

"Jose," he says softly, gently, "I need to concentrate."

I shut my mouth with a snap.

It's being back in the city, I think. I'm pondering and philosophizing and reasoning and trying to understand things. I'm *questioning* again, and I feel alive for the first time since last September, since the day before the blood moon.

Never stop questioning. Anthony told me that once, in a rare moment of truth. I remember thinking it a miracle, and I remember perfectly the look that passed through his eyes, as if he had shocked himself most of all. I remember it because I remember everything. And in this moment I wish I could forget him. I think killing him has made me into an entirely new person. One who doesn't question, who doesn't smile or laugh, one who is lazy and morose and sees the worst in everyone and everything. I think killing Anthony Harwood has cured me, as the cure cannot.

"We're in," Luke says and I turn around, banishing it all and forcing myself to concentrate.

He peers into the dark hallway without stepping over the threshold. The care he takes is impressive and I find myself taking more notice of everything. My eyes move down over the carpet, the walls of the hallway, trying to pick out anything unusual in the darkness.

"Any visual indiscretions?" he asks me.

"Nope."

"Me neither. I'll enter. You wait sixty seconds before following me."

He steps inside and goes still again, measuring his weight on the floor. We wait the sixty seconds, but nothing happens, and he nods for me to enter. Scanning the ceilings and skirting boards for any more cameras or alarms, we move through the dark house. When we've determined that it's all clear we go to Ben's computer.

"It's probably got an alarm set to trigger if this turns on," Luke warns.

"Do we have any choice?"

"Nope." He turns it on. The enormous clear screen powers up and then Ben's computer is projected over the wall of his living room. Luke touches and flicks the images and words around until he has a blank screen that fills with coding. It's full computer-nerd time, so I wander around the room, looking at all the little knick-knacks that belonged to the man who decided to experiment on me as a child and ruin my life.

A secret part of me whispers that maybe what he actually did was save it.

Ben has photos all over the mantelpiece, framed moving images of him and his wife, who died many years before he did. I look at the young couple. It is a rare moment of perfection because the captured video footage is not like the disgustingly 'perfect' family with their boundless love and free, happy hearts – instead Ben and his wife Adele are utterly awkward in front of the camera. They fidget uncomfortably and then glance at each other, and when they laugh it's not the carefree laugh of the actors, it is the embarrassed laugh of normal people who don't particularly want to be filmed.

Goodbye, Josephine. I'm sorry for everything.

Goodbye, Ben. Thank you for everything.

Goodbye, Ben, you visionary idiot. You well-meaning moron. You kind-hearted fool who destroyed the world.

I turn and see that Luke is hacking away for his life. "That all looks very impressive," I tell him.

"I'm no Harley," he replies, and I can hear the tension in him, see it all through his back.

"You're doing well," I encourage. The mission needs him to not tense up and ruin everything. The mission needs him relaxed and working well, so I rub his shoulders, and I feel immediately like I have betrayed myself.

"There are so many firewalls," he mutters distractedly. "But Ben is alive. I'm tracing his movement from the night in the lab. So far I know he was admitted to the hospital and fitted with a pace-maker. Then he was moved."

I knead the knots in his back.

"Josi? That's distracting me way more than it's helping me."

I recoil from his body. "Sorry."

"No, it's cool. I mean it's sweet of you, I just …"

"It's fine, get back to work," I all but shout, then stride into the kitchen and look around carefully.

I cross to the fridge and open it to find a whole lot of rancid food, the stench of which hits me in the face. "Woah."

"What is it?" Luke shouts from the other room.

"Nothing!"

I go into Ben's bedroom and check all the cupboards; his clothes smell like moths and mold. He has a whole bathroom shelf of medicines and I read every label. Several have been prescribed to

me, several I have stolen to ease the pain of my transformations
and several I have never heard of, which immediately interest me.
study these closely and realize that some are medications for a hear
condition, meaning Ben's heart was faulty before he endured tha
nightmarish night in the lab and I left him to die of heart failure. Som
are very mysterious, all of which were prescribed to Adele and seen
to be for symptoms such as paranoia, irritability and disassociation
There are mood stabilizers, anti-psychotics and tranquilizers. It's ver
full-on stuff. I gather the bottles and shove them into my backpack
wondering what Dodge will make of them and imagining that Ber
might also be able to explain it when we get him home. After furthe
thought I grab the entire contents of the shelf, because if Ben is taker
out west with us, he's going to need his medication.

"Josi!"

I track back into the computer room. "What's up?"

"I can't transfer this – can you look at it for me?"

I scan the image on the wall. It's a blueprint. I let every detail tak
its place in the picture in my mind. "Got it."

"Sweet, let's roll." He heads for the back door and check
it carefully.

I'm about to ask him why we're going out the back when my eye
trace over the inside of the doorjamb and catch on something. Ther
is a small black screw on either side of the doorway. Which isn'
weird, except that ...

"Wait!" I hiss.

He freezes. But it's half a second too late – his foot is sitting or
something that makes a very soft *click*.

Luke and I look at each other. "That's not what I think it is ..
is it?"

He nods. Breathes out. "Sorry, girl."

"For what?"

"You'd better run for it."

I shake my head. "You really are a heartless bastard if you think I'm doing that. Tell me what to do."

He scratches his chin, peering at the screws. "It's a spring-loaded sensor that's probably connected to a small detonator."

"Probably?"

"Want me to step off and find out?"

I glare at him. "Is it like a mine?"

"More advanced, but yeah. Theoretically we'd have to disconnect the wires within it, but they're tricky things and it can't be done while I'm standing on it."

I remove the radio from his pocket and click it on. "Will. We have a problem." I talk Will through the situation and he tells me to hang tight. When the crackling cuts off there is silence.

Luke looks at me. "Fool's hope."

"Just shut up, Luke."

"I don't want you to die in here, Josi," he says, and he sounds angry. "This is a bullshit ending to it all."

"I agree," I reply bluntly.

Will and Shadow arrive, and after searching the shed out the back of the house they manage to find a power tool that allows them to cut through the floorboards around Luke's feet. He hasn't moved once – he is the picture of still calm, and I am reminded of life before I Found Out. This was what he was: still calm.

It's a strange understanding – like a tingling in my chest, this return of the man I knew.

"Just go," he says tiredly, like a sigh.

We ignore him. Shadow has burrowed beneath the ground and found the mine, and now Will is working on it with tweezers and pliers. My nerves are shot – I'm expecting an explosion any second.

"Josi," Luke says suddenly.

I look at him. I'm standing apart, but still here, still in the vicinity, just as Shadow is. Will is brave enough to work on the

145

mine, and Luke is brave enough to be so still, so we will stand here with them.

"Do you really hate me?" he asks.

And there's a world in my heart, one in which I used to live. This world was where I lived before I met him, and after he took me to the asylum: it's a world of longing for something I can't have.

I'm brutally alive with it, with the longing for something that used to be, something that can never be again. And with the longing comes the stark understanding of the beauty of what we shared, like the tension has finally snapped on the rubber band of my heart. I cross the floor to him.

"It was special, wasn't it?" I murmur, not caring if Shadow and Will hear me. "And too real."

He struggles to speak, and then says, "Go. *Please*, go."

I hold his eyes, remembering everything.

And that's when Will says, "No need. It's disconnected."

*

As we leave, Luke radios the other team and tells them to head to the rendezvous point. When he and I reach the safe house the resistance have been using for years, he spots surveillance and radios the others not to enter. We circle around and meet a few blocks away in an underground parking garage to figure out what to do. We aren't ready to go straight for Ben – we'll need time to work out a plan. So we need a place to stay for the night.

"What do we do now?" Pace demands. She, Hal and Will all look rattled to have lost the safe house – they've obviously counted on it more than once.

"We need a new place to hide out for the night," Luke says calmly.

A dark thing uncurls inside me and I don't know how to name it, but I certainly recognize it. It's there because I'm realizing that we don't have any other choice but the one I never wanted to reveal.

"I have a place," I say flatly.

"Run me through it," Luke implores.

"Apartment block on the east side. Run by dealers, but I know them and they used to let me stay in one of the apartments. It'll be safe for a night."

Luke frowns, searching my face. I silently beg him not to ask me. *Don't ask why they let me stay.* He doesn't – he trusts me enough to let me lead the way.

*

Luke

We illegally catch two different trains and then walk for about two hours to get to the other side of the city. The atmosphere changes drastically. This is poverty, I think, and I remember it well because I grew up about five blocks north of here. I can't offer for us to stay at my parents' house though – after what happened to Harley I would rather die than lead the Bloods to Mom and Dad.

Josi takes us into the heart of the drug-using populace, larger and more rampant now than it has ever been. It's no surprise that people who feel alienated from themselves and terrified of their confusing behavior would find solace in drugs. I came here a thousand times as a Blood, back when I was a Red. And I even did a few rounds here as a kid before I was recruited. Which is why I know how rough it is, how cruel, how unforgiving. And which is why I feel sick to my stomach to know that Josephine lived here. How many times have I wanted to change her adolescence? How many times have I wanted to smash the skulls of the heinous pigs that hurt her?

I feel a raw, aching fury find its home in my skin as I follow her into a dilapidated building. It scares me, how much more anger I feel since being injected with the same shit that made Josi a bloodthirsty killer. It scares me to imagine what it's doing to me.

"Get your wig off," she tells Pace, who happily wrenches the blond wig off to reveal her shaved head. "Try to look less ... preppy," she tells the rest of us.

Hal takes his jumper off to show his tattoos and messes up his hair a bit. The rest of us can't do much but try not to look like complete pushovers. It's quite unfortunate that Will is wearing spandex tights.

The lift takes us up toward the top floor. It's hideously bright in the way only elevators are.

"He's going to call me by my real name," Josi says suddenly, not looking at any of us. "I'm sorry I never told you the truth. But I didn't want to be me anymore."

Before anyone can reply the doors open and we are met by half a dozen men. They are all wraith-like, with gaunt features and detached-looking eyes.

"Take me to John," Josi says softly, and I am stunned by the sudden coldness that has descended upon her.

"Who are you?" one of them asks.

"A runner."

"And who are they?" the guy asks of the rest of us. He looks particularly concerned by Shadow, who is having a hard time concealing his complete disgust at this situation, and is also a lot older than the rest of us.

"Recruits."

After his eyes land on Pace appreciatively he takes us down the hall. The room at the very end has a group of people sitting around on old, torn-up couches that smell like shit. A hologram plays in the corner, some old sitcom with people flailing their arms around.

The people in the room look up as our delivery boy clears his throat. "Runner and recruits." The guy bolts before the sentence is even finished.

"Holy shit," says a scratchy voice.

A man stands from within a throng of women who all look doped out of their minds. I see one of them using a needle to inject another. The man is tall, very thin and very muscular, with a face that would be handsome if it weren't covered in disfiguring scars. They are scars that can be made only by serrated knives, and I know abruptly who he is.

John Smith. Lord of the east-end drug cartel.

"Josephine Luquet," John says, moving to eye her up and down with an undeniable smirk.

My friends barely react at all to her name being spoken aloud for the first time, but to me it is obvious. Hal and Will both baulk, frown and then manage to cover it. Pace smiles a little. And Shadow goes more still than I have ever known him to be, if that's possible.

"John Smith," Josi says calmly, softly. There is the slightest edge of a purr in her voice. "If that is your real name."

It's obviously a shared joke, for he smiles in a nostalgic way. And then he leans in and kisses her on the mouth, and I think I might kill him where he stands.

A hand takes my wrist and I look to see Shadow holding onto me. His grip calms my racing blood. Fury: she's a seductive companion. She wants me to tear this fool's head off, and I want her to help me do it. Instead I watch as John kisses Josi and then pulls away to rake his eyes over her body. She has not moved an inch. Has not kissed him back, has not reacted at all.

Until she says, so softly I almost miss it, "Touch me again, with any part of your body, and I will make sure that part is torn free and fed to you."

John stares at her and then he smiles. "I've missed you, rabid heart."

"My friends and I need a room for the night."

"Your friends. You've never had any friends before. I'm curious. Shall I show them my party trick?" He considers us respectively. Looks first at Hal. "Pretender."

Hal frowns, a bit confused.

John looks at Will and says, "Desperate." Will's eyes drop, embarrassed.

John's inventory shifts to Pace with a smirk. "Frightened."

Her lip curls savagely, but Josi places a calming hand on her shoulder.

Next John moves his eyes to evaluate Shadow. He is enjoying his power. Knows he's good at reading people and their insecurities. Takes pleasure in what this ability affords him, and the discomfort of others. It is the behavior of a small, weak man to make himself seem stronger.

Quietly John says, "Ashamed."

I see Shadow's face tense fractionally. Not enough for most to notice. But John does, smiling a little and then moving on to me.

I meet his eyes.

The smile spreads in this astonished, delighted way. "J, who's this one?"

Josi glances at me. Doesn't say a word.

I haven't moved. Haven't given him a single thought or feeling or expression. But he shakes his head, laughing a little. "You, big fella, stand at the very edge of it all." He spins back to Josi. "And all of them uncured. You are my favorite person in the world, Josephine Luquet. But then I guess you always were."

"The room, John?"

"The room's yours for tonight for a vial of blood from each of them."

"What for?"

John considers us again, but he's too smug not to tell us. "Like I said, they're uncured. I've got people looking at the difference between cured and uncured blood."

"So you can come up with an antidote?" Josi asks, and the mockery drips from her voice.

150

John takes her throat in his hand. "Careful," he breathes over her mouth. "You're my favorite, but no one is exempt from manners." It's not that he's angry. It's simply that he must follow a set of rules, and she's stepped outside of them. And I don't care why he's touching her like that, because I'm going to kill him either way.

"Easy," Shadow tells me.

John's eyes lift to me and he smiles again, at the height of his amusement. "Yes, *easy*." To Josi he laughs, "You should leash your beast. Did you know he covets you?"

"Covets?" she repeats coldly. "Goodness, he must be a heretic then. Shall we burn him?"

John laughs again, but I can see a dead quality come into his eyes. His brain is telling him he should be angry at the mockery but instead it is short-circuiting to something else and his whole body is revolting against the unnatural interference. He must go through this daily, as an angry creature by nature. Which probably means he's mostly mad.

His brain rewires and an abrupt, unexpected desire blooms inside him. It comes from a similar, primal center. Rage, fear, desire. The three big ones. I watch the lust cross his face. He reaches for Josi's breasts and ass, pulling her against him, and it is a single second, less than a second, in which I am about to hammer the shit out of him when instead Josi removes the pepper spray from her jacket and sprays him in the eyes.

John howls in pain, falling to his knees and clawing at his burnt eyes.

Josi smiles a little. Glances at us. "That was fun. Not quite as fun as it would be if he could get annoyed by it, but fun nonetheless." To John, she says, "I told you not to touch me, didn't I? Which room is ours?"

"Eight-thirteen," he gasps in pain.

"A key?"

John gestures and some kid passes her a key.

"We're going into room eight-thirteen and locking the door. Deliver a syringe and vials, and I'll leave our blood on the sink. You'll make sure no one bothers us tonight, or you'll get a lot worse than this spray. Agreed?"

He nods, his eyes streaming with tears.

*

Once we're all locked inside room eight-thirteen there is a general exhalation of breath.

"Christ!" Hal announces.

"Badass!" Will compliments Josi.

"What the bloody hell are you doing with degenerates like that, Dual?" Pace hisses. "Or should I say *Josephine*?"

Josi slumps onto a ratty old couch. "What did you find on Ben's computer?" she asks me.

"In the morning. We need sleep now."

Will runs into one of the bedrooms and excitedly bounces on the bed. "There's a TV in here!"

"Bet you ten bucks it doesn't work," Josi mutters.

"Get some rest, guys," I say.

Shadow insists on taking first watch. Hal, Pace and Will then insist on the king bed in the main room, leaving Josi and I with the double in the second room. It's an obvious ploy, but I wish they could read the room and see that Josephine – yes, the girlfriend I mooned over all last year – would currently rather murder me in my sleep than stumble into a romantic tryst in a shared bed.

She looks at me. "I'll sleep on the couch."

"In the bed. Now. Tomorrow's gonna suck."

And it's a measure of how hopeless she feels that she walks straight to the bed and collapses.

I cross to Shadow at the door. "Wake me up in a couple of hours. I mean it." Then I trip my way to the couch and nosedive onto it, falling asleep instantly.

*

When Shadow shakes me awake it feels like five seconds later, but three hours have passed. He takes my place on the couch and falls asleep almost as quickly as I did. I head into the main bedroom and peer at the three sleeping bodies curled around each other like puppies. It's actually kind of adorable.

Reluctantly I shake Pace and Hal awake. "One of you on watch duty, just for half an hour."

They frown sleepily, but don't question me on the odd time frame. "I'll go," Pace says, and as she gets up Hal slumps back to sleep. "What are you doing?" she asks me.

"Lock the door behind me and don't say anything to the others," I order her, and slip into the hallway.

Moving quickly, I feel for the knives sheathed at both of my hips. There are two guys out the front of John's room.

"Hey – "

I drop the first with a quick punch to the jaw. Calmly I spin to block the second guy's fist, gripping his wrist and pulling him into my chest. My knife is at his throat, nicking the skin.

"Open the door," I say, and he does so with a few dopey blinks. He's high as a kite, struggling with the electric key.

Inside I tell him to take a seat and relax. I find John in bed with a woman who's having a nightmare or a bad trip or something, moaning and shifting on the dirty sheet. John is sitting with his back turned to ignore her, and he's bent over a tablet featuring a photo of Josephine from a few years ago. She looks young and thin, and as much like a drug addict as the rest of these poor people.

"Hey, mate," I say softly.

John twists in alarm and clutches at his chest. "Jesus. Scared the shit out of me, beast." His eyes are horribly red and puffy.

"She alright?" I ask, nodding to the girl in bed.

"Dream enhancers," John sighs. "You never know what they're gonna do to your head. She likes the nightmares, you know. Doesn't like to be woken out of them."

Live like humans, dream like savages. The dream enhancer slogan.

I crouch before him and look up into his scarred face. "You really do like her, don't you?"

He glances at the picture of Josi again.

"How many guys have you sent to detain her in the morning?"

John's lips twist in humor. "Six."

"Do they have orders to kill the rest of us if we get in the way?"

"Of course."

I hold his brown eyes. "And did you really think six men would be enough?"

The smile disappears. "I let her go once. It's not happening again."

"Who do you give your orders to?" I ask him. "Can that bloke out the front relay directions from you?"

He looks surprised at the very idea that I would expect him to answer.

"I'm going to assume he can," I say. Into the other room, I call, "Kid, come in here."

The guy on guard duty stumbles in, looking at us blankly.

"Orders for the morning have changed. No one is to attack Josephine and her friends."

John laughs. "You're audacious, aren't ya?"

I turn, draw my knives and swiftly slice through both his wrists, long slashes that open up the length of his arteries.

John stares in shock for a moment, and then the blood swells out of him. A strangled scream erupts from his throat.

"Calm down," I murmur. "You'll be alright. There's a hospital right down the road."

"Why did you – ?" He is going into shock. The color has left his face. A lot of blood is gushing at this point. I reach down and pull the bed sheet out from under the dreaming girl; she doesn't wake despite the sudden chaos in the room.

"Would you like me to wrap your wounds?" I ask John.

He nods dumbly.

"No problem. First you tell this man here to change the orders."

"Do it," John urges, and the guy dashes out, glad to be away from this nightmare.

"You won't give Josephine another thought, will you?"

John shakes his head quickly. I tear the sheet and wrap it around his two slashed wrists, then help him to the door.

The first guard I knocked out is coming around.

"You can take your boss to the hospital," I tell him, and watch the two of them stumble down the hallway, dripping blood.

An idea occurs to me and I go back to the bedroom, grabbing John's discarded tablet. Before it locks itself I change the passcode.

The poor girl is still thrashing wildly and I feel as though I should wake her, but in the end there's something too chilling about it. Whether it's my own cowardice at the thought of what I would be faced with if she woke, or whether I'm simply afraid of seeing the remnants of the nightmares in her eyes, I leave her.

Pace lets me into our room and I tell her to go back to bed. There is blood on my hands and she looks at it, then at my face, and seems to re-evaluate what she knows about me.

First I stash the tablet in my pack. Then I go to the bathroom and without turning on the light I wash my hands. Someone moves in the doorway and I look to see Josi. Standing in the spill of light from the lamp in her bedroom, she gazes at the blood trickling down the sink in a swirl of water.

"Is he dead?" she asks. Her voice still sounds cold: the person she has to be when in this building.

I shake my head. Not yet, anyway.

And the scary thing is that I don't feel bad. Nor do I care if he makes it to the hospital before he bleeds out. I could have killed him; he's scum. But for all the lives I've taken in combat or on missions, I have never murdered anyone.

"But you hurt him?"

I nod.

She rests her head against the doorframe. "I wanted to hurt him."

"You did – pepper spray's a bitch."

"I wanted to *really* hurt him."

"You're not a violent person, Josi."

Her lips pull into an incredulous smile. "What world are you living in, Luke Townsend?"

"The one in which you're so horrified at the thought of harming anyone that you go into a state of complete catatonia and sleep for three days straight," I reply bluntly. "So don't tell me that you're a violent person, because you're not."

She gazes at me in the dark. I can *feel* her longing for what we once had on my skin; I am saturated in it. "Are you a violent person?"

I don't answer. We both look at the blood as it swirls down the drain.

Josi sighs and heads back to bed. I finish washing up and take my position at the door.

Chapter 9

February 8th, 2066

Josephine

"Ben's in a medical research lab," Luke tells us as the sun rises and we get our stuff together. He's taking us through the info he hacked into on Ben's computer.

"Where?" Hal asks.

"Two suburbs north. We'll walk it."

"Why's he in a medical research lab?" I ask.

Luke shrugs.

"Doesn't that seem weird to you?"

"I guess." He contemplates, but there's not really an answer. "We need supplies first."

"How are we meant to get those?" Pace asks. "We can't buy anything."

"I've got a bunch of untraceable credit cards," I say.

"Where?"

"Locker at the bus station."

So that's where we head. Nobody tries to stop us in the apartment building and we don't leave a single vial of blood behind. I'd rather cut off my own hand than leave my blood for John, and I'm pretty sure the others feel the same as it doesn't come up once.

It takes us about an hour to get to the bus station and thankfully my locker is still intact. I pull out the duffel from within and search through it for the cards. They don't have all that much credit on them, but at least they can't be traced to me. Luke's illegal cash may have worked on the outskirts of town last year, but we won't be able to use cash in the middle of the city – it'd be way too obvious.

There's a spare t-shirt in my bag, which I grab, but nothing else of any use. It strikes me how little I actually *own*. Everything else I carted around with me is long gone now – left in Luke's swanky apartment, no doubt pilfered by the Bloods. I took pains to carry my books wherever I went, but losing them is hardly the end of the world. I had a few items of clothing, two pairs of shoes, some toiletries and that's about it.

The only thing I have ever cared about owning, *really* cared about, was my cello.

"Got 'em," I say, stashing the bag back in the locker.

We stay spread out in our little pairs to travel, but maintain visuals of each other as much as possible. Our next stop is a huge shopping center, where there will be too many people for us to stand out. None of them look at us, just as they don't look at each other.

We head to the hardware section. I push the trolley and Luke piles in items like coils of rope, hammers and nails, measuring tape and gas masks. The blueprint takes shape in my mind and I'm starting to see what his plan might be.

"Get a flashlight," I tell him.

He grabs two. When we've stocked up we all reconvene in the parking garage, finding a blind spot where none of the security cameras will catch us. Luke has bought a sheet of poster-sized paper and a pencil, and he pops me down in front of it. "Recreate, Rain Man."

I start drawing the blueprint from Ben's computer.

"Freak," Pace calls me, but I ignore her and make sure I get every angle, door, window and staircase perfect.

"This is the lab, provided by our resident savant Josi," Luke says when I'm done. "First-floor entrances, security check points, stairwells, levels two, three and four." He points out each element. "These here are the underground levels, and this bottom one, six floors below ground, is where Ben was being kept until yesterday, and hopefully still is."

"Oh Lord," Hal sighs.

"At least we don't have to find Josephine Luquet's blood!" Will exclaims cheerfully, winking at me.

"Yep, we've got only one objective."

We all study the map together. I know Luke already has a plan, but he obviously wants us to get our bearings before piling on.

"Elevator shaft," I eventually say. It's the only way to move down through the levels without being noticed.

"Yep."

"Not me," Hal says immediately. "I *hate* heights."

"You're right, mate," Luke tells him. "It'll be me and Josi."

My eyes widen. "*Me?*"

"You go where I go. That was the deal when I agreed to let you come." I can hear the note of warning in his voice that reminds me how seriously he takes his job. "Our three teams will split up and enter from different points around the building. We go in through the vents. Josi and I will drop down through the shaft. But here's where it gets tricky. These doors need the prints and retinal scans of one of the specified scientists. They can't be overridden."

"So we need to incapacitate a scientist and use his body," Pace surmises.

"Right. Once we've done that, we face multiple security points, at which there will be several Bloods."

"We can't take out multiple Bloods!"

159

"That's why we're gonna gas them with whatever Hal and Pace can steal from the storage supplies."

"And then feed it through the air-conditioning vents?" Hal ventures.

"Got it. When everyone's down, Josi and I'll go in and extract Ben."

"What gas are we using?" I query. "And won't it mess with the patients? We can't just gas innocent people if we don't know how it'll affect their treatments."

"There's a synthetic toxin that won't harm anyone, no matter what's in their system," Pace tells us. "It's just like going to sleep. Reckon the lab'll have some."

I'm impressed that she knows this. Guess Dodge isn't quite as useless a scientist as I gave him credit for after the Luke-nearly-dying debacle.

"So you'll need to go in dressed as Bloods," Luke tells them. "And then get out fast before you go to sleep."

"What about you two?"

I hold up the gas masks with a *Wheel of Fortune*-esque flourish of my fingers.

"What about me and Shadow?" Will asks.

"You guys need to disconnect the alarms, which you can do from this point, *before* we set off the gas – it only takes the push of a button and the whole thing could be screwed. Stay to the vents and head north. Then we need you to make sure we have a clear exit, 'cause we're gonna be lugging an unconscious old guy."

We change into our black combat gear, which will make us look like Bloods at a glance, then stuff our backpacks in a garbage bin ready to retrieve on the way out. We hunker down on the roof of the building opposite to wait for night, watching the building for the patterns of movement outside and within. Guards walk the perimeter with dogs, but they only pass by every hour.

As darkness descends Luke orders us to do a weapons check.

I have my knives and my pepper spray (which I now have complete respect for), as well as two handguns, an automatic rifle over my shoulder, and a sheath of extra magazines strapped to my chest. I'm also wearing a bulletproof vest underneath my shirt, have my gas mask clipped to the back of my belt, my backpack full of supplies and all of it together has ended up being so ludicrously heavy that I can barely walk.

"Walkies check."

Everyone checks their walkies, as well as their watches, and then we go for it.

There's no one around at this time of night. We've waited for most of the workers to go home for the day, and we've made sure to move only when the guards should be on the other side of the building. Luke and I identify the security cameras and skirt around them to find the exterior vent we need. A screwdriver makes quick work of the frame and Luke boosts me up into the metal duct. I have no hope of pulling him in after me, but luckily he hoists himself in without any trouble, replacing the vent behind us.

Crawling as silently as we can, we make our way forward and take two right turns, heading for the vent directly opposite the elevator shaft.

"Josi," Luke says softly, pausing in front of me. "Take a deep, slow breath."

I frown, then realize that I have been breathing very quickly, and my heart is pounding with nerves. "I'm fine," I whisper.

"I know you are. Humor me."

I draw a long, deep breath, then another and another, and slowly feel my heart rate moderate itself. "Okay."

We keep moving.

The walkie crackles and Will's voice sounds. "*Alarms are off, amigos. We ran into a few guards along the way but Shadow made quick work of 'em.*"

"Nice," Luke replies. "Make your way to the north vents and scope out our exit. Red team, how are you guys coming along with the gas?"

"We've found a lock-up of medical supplies, but we're just waiting for the ground to clear a bit before we make a move," Pace replies.

"Okay, take it easy – we can wait longer if it means you get in and out without being seen."

"Copy that."

"If the alarms are off why does it matter if they see us?" I ask Luke.

"They'll just put the lockdown protocol into place, and then we have no hope of getting in even with stolen prints and retinas. Plus you know – they'll, like, come and kill us."

"Oh. That was a dumb question."

"You're allowed one or two every blue moon," he consoles. "You doing okay?"

"Yep. You?"

"I'm having fun, actually."

"Sicko," I grin.

"I'd be having more fun if you weren't here," he admits, then stops and turns around with a wriggle so he can face me. He reaches out and starts to carefully remove the rifle. "Leave this one behind, kid. It's too heavy and it's making a whole bunch of noise."

"What about the fact that me only having a pistol would be like me having nothing?"

"Ah well, shit happens."

"Oh, great, Luke."

Still, as soon as the enormous weapon has been dumped in the vent I'm a lot more relaxed. Feeling as though you can't move properly is not how you want to go into a stealth mission.

"How many rounds are in each of your magazines?" he asks me.

"Ten. Why?"

"If you have to shoot your weapon, I want you to count the shots you take and stop at ten. Never fire your weapon with an empty magazine in place."

"Why?"

"Because a Blood will hear that clicking sound and he'll know he's got thirty seconds until you can reload, and he's sure as hell going to use those thirty seconds to kill you."

I breathe out, feeling a tad woozy. "Okay. Count my shots."

As we crawl Luke keeps talking and my mind latches onto his words. "Remember there are two types of fire. The first is when you have a target. You take your aim carefully and don't waste your bullets. The second kind of fire is to create cover, firing at any oncoming attack as hard and as fast as you can so that the opposition will be forced to take cover. I'll then use those moments to move positions, so I'll be out in the open and relying on you to keep heavy fire engaged, and vice versa if you need to move."

"Target and cover," I repeat. He told me all of this on the train but I'm more than happy to hear it again.

"The most important thing is to always remain calm and focused," he adds. "So the second you feel your breathing or heart rate speed up, you immediately stop and take very deep, slow breaths until you feel clarity return. You don't do shit if you're panicked. *Nothing*, Josi. Got it?"

"Yes."

We arrive at the vent. Through it I can see the elevator doors. There's no one in the corridor, but we sit quietly and survey the area for a while.

"It's not enough recon," Luke mutters suddenly. "I feel blind."

"How much would you normally do on a mission like this?"

"Weeks. I'd have people placed inside to tell me the movements and security protocols, I'd know every member of staff and what shifts they work, the escalator timing mechanisms and weights, and I'd have access to their radio frequencies."

"*God.*"

He shakes his head. Watching his face and the tense angle of his jaw is not helping me to feel confident. I take three deep breaths.

Luke unscrews the vents and swings out into the hallway. As I follow clumsily, he's already prying open the lift doors. They edge apart, spring-loaded to move more easily after the initial resistance.

Using his flashlight to peer up and down the shaft, he spots the elevator below us. It doesn't move without prints and retinal scans. We have to wait until it's above us before we can abseil down the shaft, which is a problem.

Into the walkie, he says, "Red team, elevator is below us so don't set off the gas until I give you the go-ahead."

"*No problem,*" Pace replies. "*We haven't even retrieved it yet. There's drones everywhere. Like rats.*"

"Why are there so many here this late?" I wonder aloud. Luke doesn't reply because he doesn't know the answer any better than I do.

Handing me the two coils of rope from over his shoulders, Luke lets me start tying the harness knots while he aims his weapon down the hallway. There's a silencer on the end of his long, sleek Glock, and his stance is relaxed as I fumble my way nervously through the knots.

I loop the ends around Luke's legs and hips, making sure the knots will tighten under pressure and allow him movement. I do the same for myself and then take the hammer and pins.

"Take it easy, we're not in a rush."

Amazingly, he doesn't sound sarcastic. The calm in his voice eases something inside me and I hammer the first pin into the metal grooves inside the shaft.

"It's not every day you have to make harnesses out of ropes."

"You're doing great."

That's when we both hear voices. I freeze, nearly dropping the hammer down the shaft. Luke keeps his gun aimed and, as two men round the corner, he takes out the first and then the second with two perfect shots to the head. They drop like lead weights.

My body goes numb.

"Keep going," Luke says, but I'm staring at the two dead men. "Josi."

I blink, dazed. Find his face.

"Long, deep breath."

He breathes in deeply, and I copy him, though I don't think breathing will do me any good at this point. There are pins and needles in my fingers and toes. "Okay, now turn around and keep attaching the harnesses. Now."

I turn with a jerking motion and wedge the second pin behind the steel brackets.

That's when the elevator starts moving up. "Shit. It's coming."

Luke motions for me to get out of the way. "Stay flat." I hold myself against the wall, not wanting to see any more shootings. My bottom jaw is trembling in this really weird way that's making my teeth chatter.

The elevator stops at our level. Fuck. Of course it does.

It pings and the doors slide open.

One, two, three shots from Luke's gun. A single yelp and then the heavy slump of bodies.

I squeeze my eyes shut as Luke climbs into the lift and uses one of the dead people to set the scanners to ascend.

"Wait," I say. "Why are we doing all this shit with the ridiculously dangerous homemade harnesses when we could just ride the lift down to the bottom?"

"It could stop at any of the other levels on the way."

"So? You're happy to shoot everyone anyway."

He looks at me, his eyes abruptly vacant. "I'd rather not shoot anyone, if it can be avoided," he says in this flat voice.

I swallow, feeling nauseous. "So why don't we climb on top of the carriage and ride it down?"

"And if someone presses for it to go up? We'd be crushed."

"I don't know if this will hold us," I try desperately. "I haven't tested the texture of the rope against the pins or what our weight and the movement of our descent will do to it – things have variables, Luke – anything might cause it to destabilize – "

"So we'll close our eyes and hope for the best."

With the lift set, he climbs out and we watch the doors slide shut and then disappear upwards.

"Someone's going to see all these dead bodies," I say through gritted teeth as I loop his rope through the pin and synch it with a hang knot.

"Yes. But hopefully not before we gas them."

"You hold this one," I tell him, passing him the rope. "You let the tension go like this when you want to descend. You grip it to stop."

He nods, taking the rope. I turn to attach mine.

"We just murdered five people," I say numbly.

"This is an op, which makes that collateral, and *we* didn't do anything – I did it."

"It's murder."

We pull our backpacks on, check our weapons, check the ropes again and then we walk backward over the edge of the shaft. There's sweat trickling down my neck. If this fails, it will be entirely my fault.

We're both wearing gloves, but as we hold and release the tension I can feel the burn of it all the way through the material. The first moment of weightlessness causes my stomach to bottom out and I nearly pee myself with fear. But after the second release, and the third and the fourth, I'm starting to feel that weightlessness move inside me – it's as though the fear is untethered and lifts free.

We have to make sure we don't swing too wildly, but keep the rope in the one spot, which is harder for me as I don't have as much weight to keep it steady as Luke does. It's all hard, actually – a lot harder than it seems when you read about it in a book. My hands and shoulders are starting to really ache, and the rope is cutting into the flesh of my thighs painfully.

"Ah shit," I gasp as my fingernail catches and rips off inside my glove. I scrabble to catch the rope but am flailing badly.

Luke reaches over and grabs my tension rope before I fall too far. I close my eyes and breathe through the pain before nodding for him to let go.

Above us something creaks and rumbles. We look up to see the elevator returning down the shaft.

I make a weird, strangled sound just as Luke shouts, "Go!"

We abseil as fast as we can – so fast we're almost free falling. I can feel my rope working against the pin and know it's about to come loose. I'm more concerned, however, about the elevator reaching where the ropes are connected, because as soon as that happens the pulley will unravel and we'll be done for.

You just have to get as close to the bottom as possible before that happens, I tell myself. *Minimize how far you fall.*

My hands are burning terribly and we're flying toward the ground, closer and closer to the bottom with every second –

The elevator hits the pins, knocking them free and all the tension goes out of the ropes –

I look once at Luke in the dark, our eyes meet, and –

We fall.

Chapter 10

May 20th, 2064

Josephine

"If you knew you were going to die," I say, "If you had a split second before it was going to happen, what would you do in that split second?"

Luke groans. "I don't wanna play this."

He's basting a chicken that must have cost him a fortune, and I'm watching him from the stool behind the kitchen bench. This is how we spend most of our lives: Luke cooking, me watching and thinking of stupid things to ask just to get a reaction out of him.

"Go on. Tell me."

"How could I possibly know?" he asks.

"Use your imagination."

"I'd stop myself from dying."

"No, that's not one of your options."

"Why? How am I meant to be dying?"

"That doesn't matter. It's inevitable."

"Nothing's inevitable."

"You're not playing properly," I whine. "It's a hypothetical."

He hides a smile. "A split second isn't enough time to *do* anything," he counters, holding out a teaspoon for me to taste his plum sauce.

"Mm, yummy. Okay, five seconds."

"Five seconds? What could I do in five seconds?"

"Okay, a minute."

He tilts his head, pausing to think about it. "One minute to live, huh? I'd eat crème brûlée."

I stare at him, smiling slowly. "You're a hopeless addict in need of an intervention."

He shrugs, smelling his chicken and giving a delighted sigh.

"I was going to say that I'd use my last split second or five seconds or minute or hour to kiss you."

He freezes. "Oh, shit. Wait. Can I change my answer?"

"Too late, pal. You value food over your girlfriend, and you can never take that back. Nev-er."

Luke rounds the kitchen counter and leans in for a kiss, but I dance out of his reach. "Go back to your cooking, crème brûlée boy."

He walks over to the tray with its beautifully basted and trimmed roast chicken, a creation that looks and smells so utterly mouth-watering that every time I take a breath my stomach grumbles. He lifts the whole tray and walks into the living room.

Confused, I follow.

And watch as he goes outside and throws the whole thing off the balcony.

Turning to me, he says, "I'd never throw *you* off a balcony."

I stare at him, utterly stunned. "How generous of you," I manage.

"Do you believe me now?"

"All I believe is that I'd much rather come in second to food if it means we get to eat dinner."

*

Josephine

That moment is what fills my head as I fall through the elevator shaft. Luke wanting crème brûlée in the split second before he dies, and me wanting to kiss him. That moment, and numbers.

One, two, three, I count before I feel my body smash into the ground.

Pain erupts through my hip and spine and head and wrist, my *wrist*. I moan loudly as I squeeze my eyes shut and roll over in agony. Tears stream beneath my lashes.

"Josi," I hear Luke grunt, and from some place within all the pain I am immensely relieved he's alive. It wasn't that far, really, but it felt far.

"Sit up," he orders. "Tell me what hurts."

"Everything," I moan.

"Stop being a baby and sit up."

What an *asshole*. I struggle upright, woozy with shock. I probably have a concussion. The elevator has stopped a few feet above us, trapping us in a small metal hole in the ground – we won't be able to get out of the shaft until it goes back up again, so we really need Pace and Hal *not* to gas everyone before that happens.

"Identify your injuries," he says. He has blood all over his face, dripping from what looks to be a cut on his scalp.

I close my eyes, trying to move my limbs. My legs are both fine, my back is alright, my hip feels badly bruised, my head is pounding and there's something definitely wrong with my left wrist.

"Think it's broken," I say, holding it gingerly.

Luke asks me if I can move it but pain slices through my arm and I yelp. "Yeah, it probably is broken," he agrees. "But pain isn't real, Jose. Concentrate on external stimuli to pinpoint your focus away from your pain receptors."

"Good job – the Blood-talk is aggravating enough to distract from the broken bone," I mutter and he gives a breath of laughter.

Luke searches in his pack for the med-kit and produces a bandage. Working quickly, he wraps my wrist and even though it hurts like hell, it feels a tad better when it can't flail around as much.

"Are you alright?"

"Four broken ribs and a superficial head wound," he replies promptly. I help him place a thick white patch over the cut and wipe the blood from his face – it's hard in the dark and we fumble awkwardly for a few minutes.

"What did you think of?" Luke asks me suddenly. "With your split second?"

I am amazed that he remembers, that he thought of it too.

"I knew I wasn't going to die," I lie. "It was only a few feet."

"I didn't think about crème brûlée," he admits, and that's all, and it's enough, because if he said anything else I think it might hurt inside my chest too much for me to ever climb out of this dark steel trap.

*

When the elevator finally moves up a few floors, we're able to stand and pry the lift doors open a crack. Luke peers through, gun at the ready, and then hoists himself into the hallway. When he reaches for me I have to give him my right hand only, and it feels as though he's about to pull my arm out of its socket.

We creep down the corridor, on the lookout. The vent we need is on the right and along another hallway.

Around a corner an armed Blood is standing outside a glass door. If we go for the vent he'll see us. We stop, and Luke motions for me to wait. Then he rounds and fires rapidly.

The Blood's weapon discharges in response and the noise is like a blow to the head. Peering around, I see that Luke and the Blood have sprinted toward each other and collided, both their guns sent flying clear.

Luke's weapon hits the wall and slides into my reach.

As he and the Blood punch and block and move too fast to believe, I grab the gun and aim it toward them.

"Luke!" I shout. "Hit the floor!"

"No!" he yells, but he flattens himself as I fire wildly.

I don't hit anything except the glass door, which is obviously bulletproof, for the bullet ricochets off into the vent, then embeds itself in the wall with a spray of plaster. The Blood uses the opportunity to kick Luke in his broken ribs while he's down, and I realize I have just made things a thousand times worse.

Luke sweeps his leg and takes down the Blood, rolls on top and crunches his elbow into the man's windpipe, then cracks him so hard across the jaw that he's out like a light.

Luke staggers to his feet and glares daggers at me.

Sheepishly I hand him the gun. "Sorry?"

"Get in the vent, Rambo."

*

This vent is wider than the last so Luke and I can crawl forward side by side.

"Move over," I whisper.

"*You* move over."

"You're twice the size of me!"

"And yet look who's taking up more space. Get your bony elbows away from my ribs."

"Get your shoulder out of my face! It keeps clacking my chin."

"You mean that huge mouth of yours?"

A grate below us comes into view and we both shut up, shuffling forward to peer into the room. As expected, we're above the labs.

I can't see anyone down there. Pace and Hal have retrieved the gas, so now we're just waiting for them to feed it into the vent before we can climb down.

"Want to talk about John Smith?" Luke asks me.

I glance at him. Light from the lab is shining up into his face so I can see it quite clearly. "Boring." There's no way I'm telling him about that period in my life.

I'm finding it hard to concentrate on counting the seconds. My wrist hurts and Luke's smell is familiar and too close in this confined space.

"Where'd you learn to fight?" I ask him to change the subject.

"Dad. I grew up in a madhouse. Mom threatened to move out just about every week 'cause we fought so much."

"So your dad really did teach you to fight? That wasn't a lie?"

He nods.

"What kind?"

"All kinds. I was a boxer though. Born and bred."

"As a kid?"

"Yeah. There's a league. And an illegal one."

"What's an illegal boxing league like?" I ask curiously.

"Bare-knuckle. No shirts, no shoes. You get thrown in and you don't come out again until someone's unconscious."

"And your father put you in this league when you were a kid?" I ask, disbelieving.

"Sure."

"How young?"

"'Bout nine, maybe."

"Jeez. How'd you do, then?"

"Champ at seventeen."

"Champ of what?"

"The city."

"In your age group?"

"Nope."

I stare at him, trying to work out what he's saying. "You were the boxing champion of the whole city when you were seventeen? Including grown men?"

He smiles again, and this time it has a cocky edge.

"I thought you were already a Blood by then."

"I used to sneak out. Met Dad and Dave for the fights. Nobody gives a shit what your job is when you're in the ring."

"Was Dave good too?"

"He was alright. Bit soft."

I lick my lips. "So … what's the secret?"

"To what?"

"Boxing."

Luke looks at me and grins. "You want to know the secret to boxing like it's a piece of information you can learn and then succeed at? It takes training, girl. Instincts, strength, speed … Things you develop over time and with discipline."

"Yeah yeah yeah. Just tell me. What's the secret?"

His smile shifts and he meets my eyes. He considers; it feels like forever. I want the moment to last until time ceases, the two of us in this vent with him looking at me like that. Luke leans toward me, close enough that he can brush his lips against my ear. His breath is warm.

"It's simple. You can't be afraid to get hurt."

I consider this, looking at his mouth.

"Train me," I say.

"You've got a trainer."

"He's taught me nothing."

"You haven't wanted to be taught."

"*Whatever*. Semantics."

What am I doing. Why am I saying this. The last thing I need is to be spending more time with him. But I know in my guts that

174

if there's any hope of me ever being able to defend myself, it'll be because of Luke.

"Want to make a deal?"

I tilt my head suspiciously. "What kind?"

"If I train you, you have to agree to something else."

I wait. There is a glint in his eyes.

"You have to ask me questions. One a day, every day. I give you one-hundred-percent true answers, no matter what the question."

My eyes narrow. "How does that benefit you?"

"It's a long game."

"It won't change how I feel about you."

He shrugs. "Great. Then agree."

"Deal." We shake on it. "I'll have no way to know if you're telling me the truth."

"It's called trust."

"Yeah, and it's long gone between us." It comes out harsher than I mean it to, and the smile is wiped off his face.

That's when the people appear below us. Two men and a woman, all wearing lab coats. Beside me Luke tenses. His eyes dart to one of the men, and then he leans very close to my ear again to whisper, "Falon Shay." The prime minister.

I lean to Luke's ear. "He's not our mission. Ben is."

Luke doesn't respond, and I'm pretty sure he's far more interested in revenge or whatever oath he's sworn to kill Shay than in rescuing Ben.

"… scheduled date can be moved forward," Shay is saying.

"Not realistically, at the rate of testing," replies the woman in a deep voice.

"Where are we?"

"It isn't ready," she says bluntly. "I need another round. Several, actually."

"There isn't time. Show me the subjects so far."

They continue further into the room and I can no longer see them. Their voices drift back to us. "Subject sixty-four, like many before her, shows bouts of unpredictable lethargy."

"Lethargy isn't productive," Shay snaps. "Fix it."

"Subject sixty-five, like many before him, shows hyper-sensitivity to light."

"And sixty-six? This one?"

"Severe anxiety attacks and paranoia."

"But no sadness for any of them?"

"No detectable sadness."

I close my eyes, head swimming with a bone-shattering fury. I'm completely aflame with it; my whole body is burning. Sixty-six people experimented on and ruined. I'm going down there. I'm going to kill all three of them and then I'm going to burn this whole fucking lab to the ground –

Rough, warm hands take my face and I jerk in alarm, so utterly lost within the rage that it takes me several seconds to realize that it is Luke with his hands pressed to my cheeks, looking into my eyes.

Breathe, he mouths, but I don't want to, I don't care about breathing or calm or panic or any of it I just want to kill them I want to torture them in the same way they tortured those poor people I want to watch the life fade from their eyes and I can't breathe or think or feel anything I just –

Lips press against mine.

Everything vanishes. The world, instead, is his mouth, the warmth and the softness, the ache of it and the perfect way it fits against mine.

When Luke pulls away he is feverish, and I am calm.

Falon Shay and the other man have left. Now there is only the female scientist below us. Belatedly we pull on our gas masks, because the gas is dispersing. We swing down from the vents (difficult with only one hand and a complete lack of coordination) and land in the lab.

The woman spins to face us in shock. She is pretty, with fine, sharp features and thick dark hair. "What – " But that's about all she manages to say because she is abruptly very sleepy. Stepping toward the disconnected alarm, she presses it before slumping almost gracefully to the floor and conking out.

Before us are several glass cages in which people sleep. Test subjects sixty-four, sixty-five and sixty-six. Two girls and a boy, all children around ten years old.

There's a pain in my chest at the sight of them, something nostalgic and cruel. Memories circle, faint, shadowy things unlike any of the precise memories that fill my brain. Discomfort and fear and a lab like this. Needles, cages, lab coats ...

"Josi!" Luke says, and I return to the world. There's no time to engage in whatever messed-up stuff lies in my ten-year-old brain. Luke scoops the scientist into his arms and we duck out of the lab, moving swiftly through the underground levels of the building. I find the woman's security tag in her pocket and read, Dr Meredith Shaw, Head Scientist and Medical Researcher, Collingsworth Institute.

I wonder how Ben feels to know this vile place has been named after him.

We creep past sleeping scientists and Bloods, all here late in the apparent rush to get the sadness cures ready for administering. We check every room and every bed, but Ben isn't to be found.

"Goddamnit," I moan in growing frustration.

We reach the final hallway and see a huge NO ENTRY sign out the front, as well as two sleeping Bloods. Praying that this is it, we prop Dr Shaw's eye up to the scanner and press her fingers against the pad.

With a hissing sound the door opens and a waft of very cold, disorienting air hits us. I go first, creeping slowly down the stairs and into a room even further underground. It's well lit, the bulbs almost painfully bright. And what's with how cold it is? My teeth are chattering.

"Weapon up," Luke orders me, and I draw my pistol with shaking fingers, even though he specifically told me I wouldn't be able to hit anything with it. Why did he tell me that? To freak me out? My gas mask is making my breathing louder in my ears.

Luke's close behind me, but because he's holding Dr Shaw he can't draw his own weapon. Which means it's all me this time: the girl who can't hit a grown man three paces in front of her.

A billow of what seems to be mist caused by the low temperature wafts aside and I am able to see the glass container. Inside it, lying asleep on the floor – without even a bed to lie on – is Ben Collingsworth.

Lowering my gun, I run to the glass. He looks older than I remember, his skin much paler, hair wispier. "Open it," I implore Luke quickly. I don't know why I feel so profoundly protective of this old man. Maybe it's simply because although I don't remember him experimenting on me, I do remember him saving my life last year.

Luke gets the door open and I rush in to squat beside Ben, rolling him over. There is blood in his mouth, and I lift his top lip to see that it's coming from his gums. His skin is freezing to the touch, and there is blood under his fingernails too. I can't help but look worriedly up at Luke. He wears a pensive expression that doesn't make me feel any better. Gathering the old man into his arms, he carries Ben up the stairs and out of the cold room.

"I want to take Dr Shaw with us," I tell him.

He considers quickly, eyes darting back to where he left the woman at the bottom of the stairs.

"We can find gurneys to carry them," I press. "Think how badly it'll mess up their schedule to lose their head scientist. And imagine what she'll be able to tell us."

With a quick breath, Luke nods. "Righto, wait here and keep your gun aimed down the hall."

He puts Ben on the ground and runs back down the steps to get Dr Shaw. That's one of the things I like about Luke, I realize. He's the one in charge, he knows a thousand percent more than I do about this stuff, but he's always open to suggestions and happy to listen to other people's ideas. It's a nice quality.

"He's a lot lighter than she is," Luke says when he returns with the scientist. "You'll have to get him in a fireman's hold."

"I carried you on my back for about two miles," I grunt wryly. "I think I can carry one old guy who looks like he's mostly made of paper."

"When did you carry me on your back?" Luke demands.

I pause to look at him. "To get you out of the asylum."

"*You carried me all the way from the asylum to the resistance tree?*"

"How else did you think we got away?" I ask, leaning to try to roll Ben over my shoulder. I don't really want to talk about it, to be honest. Leaving my pack and a bunch of the crap I've been hauling around, I instead try to get Ben over my shoulders. I have to stop, though, as my wrist feels like it might snap off.

"Uh, give me a hand here?"

Luke belatedly rushes to help me, lifting Ben over my shoulders and supporting our weight as I straighten my legs under the load. Despite my bravado, Ben is really heavy and incredibly awkward to carry. He keeps slipping and every time I catch him my wrist jerks and feels like it's breaking anew.

One of the rooms we saw held a few unused gurneys, so we backtrack and gratefully put the sleeping beauties down. Then we roll them back out to the elevator, which still has three dead bodies in it.

Dragging these out, I feel a pit in my stomach, along with a whole ocean's worth of guilt for having been excited about a mission during which we murdered five people. Doesn't matter that they're scientists in a clinic that essentially rapes innocent people of their personalities. It only matters that Luke shot them without batting an eyelid, and now they'll never again go home to their families.

179

I hate it all. I hate these people and their science, I hate Ben, I hate Dr Shaw, I hate Luke and I hate myself. And I am having some serious mood swings. Anthony would tell me it's due to stress. And normally I'd tell him how mood swings are my right, but in this moment I think I'd rather not feel anything at all.

We squeeze the gurneys into the elevator and ride it up to the ground floor, only to have the doors open on six mask-wearing police officers with their guns pointed straight at us.

"Freeze!" one shouts.

Oh dear.

"Get low," Luke orders me.

"Don't fire," I hiss, because I can suddenly see how this is going to play out. He's going to fire, and there's going to be a gunfight, and I'm going to have to watch him get mowed down by a hail of bullets and I can't do that –

Someone fires and my heart skips a beat, but I realize belatedly that it wasn't the officers or Luke – it came from behind the cops, wounding and dropping three of them.

Luke picks off one, two of the other men in quick succession.

The last cop is firing wildly, and then a few more of the wounded ones start to fire from the ground. Bullets go past my head, smash through walls and ding against the inside of the elevator. The doors start to close in front of us but Luke shoves them open and shoots the last cop.

I rise shakily and push Ben's gurney out into the hall behind Luke and Dr Shaw. Around the corner comes Will, panting in panic.

"Shadow's hit!" he shouts.

No. We sprint to Shadow's side and I see blood all over his abdomen and pooling onto the floor. He has his hand pressed into his stomach just beneath where his vest ends, and his face and lips look gray. It is a horrifying sight.

"Still here," he grunts.

"You're okay, mate," Luke says. "Will, get Ben's gurney." He picks up Shadow and runs with him toward the parking garage door. Will and I push the beds in a sprint down the hall, careening around corners and almost overturning them at one point.

Pressing through the heavy swing doors, we arrive in the garage to see a white patient transport van. In the driver's seat is Pace. Hal is already helping Luke get Shadow into the back, so we bring Ben and Dr Shaw to be loaded in next.

Once the three of them are laid out in the back, Luke, Will and I squeeze in, Hal jumps in the passenger seat and Pace roars us out of the garage and into the night.

"Where are we going?" she shouts.

We're all looking at Shadow, who is bleeding everywhere.

"We can't take him back to the train like this," I murmur. "He'll never make it."

"Can't take him to a hospital," Will points out.

"Head back toward the apartments," Luke calls.

"We can't go back to that shithole," I argue. "John's boys'll be out for blood."

"We're not," he replies, meeting my eyes. "We're going to my parents' house."

Chapter 11

February 8th, 2066

Luke

When my mother opens the front door she finds a gaggle of rough, bleeding soldiers carrying an unconscious woman, an unconscious elderly man, and a dying giant. She takes one look at us, sees me at the forefront, and bursts into laughter. I am reminded of how, after she was given the cure, she always laughed when something went wrong.

She is bent over double when Dad comes to the door behind her, spots the chaos on his front lawn and frowns.

"You'll be wanting to get that van into the garage, boy?"

"Thanks, Dad." To Mom I say, "We've got a gunshot wound to the stomach here."

Thankfully she sobers quickly and shepherds everyone inside. It takes us a few trips to get all the unconscious people in, but we manage to settle them on beds and put Shadow on the kitchen table for Mom to work on. Pace pulls the van into the garage.

Josephine looks spooked. She has imagined this house a million times, I know, and I never made it easy for her by giving her any details. I was so tight-lipped about my family that she probably started to think I'd made them up, but here she is in their living room.

It smells the same, and even though I am always transported into memory when I walk in the door of this house, now it is more than that – now I have this tingling sensation on my skin, and there are pictures in my mind so vibrant I feel like I'm having a seizure or a hallucination or something.

"You okay?" Josi asks me.

I blink, returning from a memory of Dave picking Mom's pot-planted flowers to give to her and being mystified when she screeched in horror at the sight. I nod quickly, trying to rid myself of the uncanny sensations. I shouldn't have brought danger here; I can taste the regret already. But what choice did I have? To let Shadow bleed to death on the train home?

Wanting them out of the way, I sit Hal, Pace and Will on the couch and tell them they have to either sleep or eat. "Mom's a trauma nurse," I assure them. "She'll sort him out."

I go back into the kitchen where Dad's helping Mom cut Shadow's shirt away. Shadow is still conscious, and I cross to his side to lay a hand on his shoulder.

"Rookie error," I tell him.

"Cocky little prick," he manages, and I grin. "Where's the girl?"

"I'm here," Josi says, moving to his other side.

He looks like he's about to say something to her, but instead just quietens down, her presence seeming to calm him.

Dad brings over a bottle of vodka and makes Shadow drink as much as he can, then he sluices the rest over the wound, causing the man to groan in pain.

"If you're staying, sweetheart," Mom says to Josi, "you'd better be ready to help."

"Yes, ma'am. What can I do?"

183

"Mop and bucket in the laundry. Make sure I don't slip on the blood. Get towels too – pack them and change them as needed."

Josie rushes off to get supplies, despite her broken wrist and the shock-after-shock-after-shock she has endured tonight. She's done really well, actually. Better than I imagined a complete novice could. Her presence alone focused me while on the job – surprising, given I'd thought she would be distracting.

I watch as Mom gets a pair of tweezers and starts digging around inside Shadow's stomach for the bullet. He screams then, a terrible sound that reverberates around the room and through the house.

Mom gets the bullet out, followed by the two fragments that have broken off in his stomach. Then she gets to work sewing the organ and tissue back together.

"I need blood," she says briskly at one point.

"I'll give it," Josi offers immediately.

"Not you," I say. "I can't either." Mom looks at me as though she's never been more disappointed. "Our blood's diseased," I explain. Or something to that effect.

"Take mine," Dad says, rolling up his sleeve.

"What type is he?" Mom asks.

"B negative," Shadow mutters.

"It's too rare," Mom sighs.

"You three – you got B negative blood?" Dad asks the three musketeers. They all reply no.

"I do," Josi says.

"Josi, we don't know what's in your blood."

"It's nothing that's transmittable, Luke," she argues. "The Zetemaphine has been blocked. Dodge well and truly discovered that when you were dying."

"You were dying?" Mom screeches at me.

"No, Mom." Of Josi I ask, "What if the blocker's done something weird?"

"Whatever it is at this point is better than Shadow bleeding out."

Dad starts setting Josi up to donate blood, but he's shaking so I guide him to a chair and take the blood myself. Mom makes sure I'm doing it right as I insert the needle and siphon the blood through the tube and into the bag. We used to joke that Mom needed to bring all this stuff home from work because Dave and I were always so badly injured. But I'm sure as shit glad about it now.

"How's your wrist?" I ask Josi softly as we watch her blood flow into the bag.

"Fine."

"I'll get you some painkillers once we've done this. Mom, how much?"

"Eight hundred mills," she says without looking over.

"That seems like a lot …" I hedge.

"It is, but we'll watch her."

"I don't think – "

"Do it," Josi snaps. "It's just blood, Luke."

So I measure the blood and pass it off to Mom, who hooks it up to Shadow's IV. I get Josi a loaf of bread and make her eat a few slices, as well as a sugary cup of tea. She looks pale, so I get her some painkillers too.

"I've repaired as much as I can, so now we wait," Mom says eventually. "If he gets an infection overnight there won't be much I can do for him unless you can find me some antibiotics."

I nod, mopping up the blood all over the floor and placing new towels around Shadow's abdomen.

Dad's setting up bedding for the three in the living room, placing down blow-up mattresses and sleeping bags. Ben is asleep in Dave's bed, and we've tied up Dr Shaw on the floor so she won't escape during the night, which I admit is kinda mean. But Pace assures us that the amount of gas they put through the vents is enough to keep both Ben and Dr Shaw out for at least twelve hours. We'll leave

Shadow on the table as he needs to be hooked up to the blood bag and the fluids, and he needs to keep his wound flat. The five of us will take turns monitoring him and if there's any change during the night, we'll wake Mom.

Which leaves Josi and me in my old room.

I show her in and tell her to take the bed, setting myself up on the floor. She's weary beyond any point of embarrassment because she turns her back to me and gets undressed down to her underpants. I'm about to turn away when I see her back.

Circling her bony spine and spreading out to her shoulder blades in an expression of emerging joy are dozens of small black birds in flight.

They're beautiful, beyond beautiful; they're poignant in a way I haven't recognized many times in my life. Like a whisper of truth, of freedom and memory. All I want is to touch them. Because I realize now as I look at these birds that Josi has grown so much since those years she and I spent together. There's something sad in the shift and tilt of her bones, but there's also something far more aware of the beauty in the world.

I wish she wouldn't swallow that awareness away so much, living instead in the misery and pain of existence.

"When did you get them done?" I ask her softly.

She looks over her shoulder at me. Seeing her like that is almost painful in its loveliness. "Couple of months ago. For Anthony."

"They're beautiful."

"They're sad."

I nod, moving closer in the dim rosy light from the bedside lamp. The space between us feels full of memories and longings.

"Your parents are wonderful," Josi says, and I can hear in her voice a need for family, a simple appreciation of love.

"They're so lost."

She's holding her arms in front of her breasts; I get her an old singlet out of my drawer. She has trouble putting it on with her broken wrist, so I take it and slide it over her head and shoulders, threading through her arms and pulling it down over her tummy. My fingers skim her warm, smooth skin and I feel delirious with the luxury of touching her. I pass her some shorts too.

"Do you have any pictures of Dave?"

I nod, going to my old dresser and feeling a pang to simply be here in the place I grew up. Here are all my old things, my stupid knick-knacks kept by my parents for so many years. My awards and trophies, my old books and toys and teddies and clothes. It's weird, actually, like stepping back in time to a very confronting period of my life that always seemed to be about finding a space for myself between poverty and skill, family and work. I don't have any real connection to these things, but the fact that Mom and Dad have kept them makes me feel more nostalgic than the items themselves.

I get an old photo album out of a drawer, and as I pass it to Josi and watch her flick through the pictures I feel a desperate ache for the fragile thing we once shared. In fact, everything I once enjoyed or experienced now seems fragile to me. "I look at all of this," I tell her softly, the truth spilling out unbidden, "and it's torturous to me that I threw it away so carelessly, when it was so painfully precious."

Josephine looks up from the photos and meets my eyes. The singlet and shorts she wears, once mine as a boy, show off her long, bony limbs, the limbs that are filling out more with each day. It is such a relief to me to see her gaining weight, to see her becoming a person again.

Her brown and blue eyes watch me and I feel so helpless, so vulnerable, standing here like the biggest idiot in the world. But it's in these moments, I think, when you have to be bravest of all.

So I say, "But you, my darling, were the most precious thing of all, the love between us the most fragile. I tried to cherish it, but I was clumsy. And for that I'll be sorry until the day I die."

Her eyelids fall shut, and I see tears slip beneath her lashes.

A soft, tender moment lies between us; my eyes follow the lines of her face as though trying to memorize them.

"I want to ask my first question," she tells me quietly. "You promised to answer me with complete honesty, no matter what."

"I did."

Josi opens her eyes. "If I ask you to hold me for tonight, will you be able to let me go in the morning?"

I feel a swelling inside my heart. "I don't know," I answer truthfully. "But I can try."

She swallows. "Try, then."

I cross to her and lift the singlet back over her head. We move to the bed and lie down, and then I duck my head to kiss the birds, smoothing my hands and my lips over each one of them. I am as careful as I would be if the creatures were alive or could shatter with one touch.

When I have kissed them all, every one of her ravens, I hold her against me and look into her face. Our legs entwine, hands clasp, gazes lock.

"I love you," I tell her.

She shakes her head a little. "Just for tonight."

"Why?"

"Because you're the only person on this planet who can destroy me."

"I would never."

"You already did."

My forehead rests against hers. "I didn't. You're stronger than you ever were. You just can't see it yet."

Josi smiles a little, moving her lips to the crook of my neck. With my free hand I stroke her dark hair.

"The lovely thing between us is gone now," she says quietly, breaking my heart, "but I'll miss it every day of my life."

*

February 9th, 2066

Josephine

Pace wakes me some time in the night and it's a measure of how tired Luke is that he doesn't stir even when I disentangle my limbs from his and get up to take Shadow-watch.

She walks with me to the kitchen, where I check the windows for any signs of police or Blood patrols and then sit beside the table. "Get some sleep," I tell her.

She nods, but doesn't go anywhere. "I didn't mean that stuff I said to you," she says suddenly. "I was just giving you a hard time because when you get pissy you get strong."

"I know."

"You're not helpless and you're not a freak."

"Are you in love with me or something?"

She snorts. "Shut up."

"I'm sorry I didn't tell you my real name."

Pace shrugs. "We all get to start over at The Inferno."

She heads into the living room and I sit with Shadow, reaching for his hand, which feels cool to the touch. The night is abruptly too quiet and too still. His unconscious breathing is too soft for me to hear and it makes me uncomfortable.

"You're not allowed to die," I say. "You're not meant to be killable." I lean my head on the table and press my cheek to his palm. "Not by a stupid drone cop with a stray bullet."

I can't help thinking of Luke in his bed, and me in his bed with him. I've always been so sure of how people should behave when betrayed or lied to or cheated on. I had this standard … I pitied women who forgave their lovers and fell back in love with them. In my head I urged them to be stronger, to respect themselves more. Lying, to my mind, was selfish and it was cruel.

But I hadn't yet understood the power of the thing that overtakes you when you fall in love, and what I feel in Luke's touch is not selfish or cruel. What I feel when he looks at me is neither. It is generous and kind, it's pleading and sorry and protective. I don't know how to marry those things that I feel with what I know to be true, which is the simple fact that liars lie and will keep lying.

I've no reason to believe anything good about people. They hurt each other, and that's fact. Love seems to invite betrayal. It implies heartbreak.

Even with everything he's done, with the impending pain he's sure to bring me were I to forgive him, it's the shame, I think, that feels worst of all. The shame of forgiveness. Of valuing myself so little as to yearn for the cruel love of someone who made a fool of me. I do yearn for it, of course I do. But I can't let myself give in to it.

"Are you a praying kind of person?" a voice asks and I see Luke's father emerge from the hallway.

"No," I murmur. "Are you?"

He shuffles in and pulls up a chair to sit beside me. He is a tall man, someone who obviously shared Luke's stature but now seems hunched and smaller than he once was.

"I used to know the answer to that adamantly," he says. "I was sure that anyone who put faith or belief in something that couldn't help or be proved was foolish."

"I don't see what the point is," I agree.

"Nor do I. I suppose I've simply come to question things a little more than I used to."

"And does it help you to wonder if there's a god?"

"No." He smiles.

"I don't wonder," I admit. "If there is, then he's a cruel God to make us endure a world like this."

Mr Townsend rises to pour us both a glass of whisky. I watch him, watch his hands shake almost to the point where he can't

190

pour the drink. I don't offer to help – I think that would offend him, somehow.

When he hands it to me I look up into his aging face. He is a handsome man, the lines around his eyes and mouth making him no less attractive. He looks like Luke, a little. "Parkinson's," he explains with a sad smile.

I sip the whisky, feeling the burn of it go down my throat.

"I don't know your name," I say abruptly. "I'm so sorry."

"Tobias. And you're Josephine."

"You taught Luke to box," I murmur.

"If I hadn't, someone else would have," he replies. "He was so restless. Heartbreaking for a parent to watch."

"What did he want?"

"I don't think I'll ever know. I'm not sure *he* does."

"But you loved him anyhow." It is a question, not framed as one.

"Sweetheart," he murmurs, and what it really means is *of course*.

I swallow. "And Dave?"

Tobias stops a while, swirling his whisky. Eventually he says, like the weariest of all sighs, "My Dave. He was sweet and funny. He was the best of us all."

And I start to cry because it's too sad, and I am grieving, suddenly, for this invisible man I never knew, because I love more than anything the man who loved him more than anything.

Tobias takes my hand and gently sort of tugs me so that I'm resting my head on his knees, and he strokes my hair while I cry.

*

The sun is rising as we pack the van. We'd prefer to be taking a different car, but Claire and Tobias' vehicle is too small to fit all of us, and we don't want to split up.

Ben and Meredith are still unconscious, but Shadow has woken and according to Claire he hasn't yet got an infection, which is a great sign.

I feel bone-weary. Nothing actually happened between Luke and I, but even just lying in his arms sent my mind spinning so badly I was hardly able to sleep at all. My wrist aches, but what I haven't told anyone is that I think it's already healing itself. It itches in this maddening way and no longer feels as though the bone is snapped. Which for some reason embarrasses me.

"Must have just been sprained," Luke comments when he redoes my bandage. We are sitting in the kitchen while the three musketeers make sure everything is ready for the trip to the subway. Tobias has organized food and water for us, and Claire's set us up with a whole lot of painkillers and instructions for Shadow.

"How are your ribs?"

"Sugar, if you think a few broken ribs are enough to bother me you don't know Luke Townsend."

"And if Luke Townsend keeps referring to himself in the third person I might feel inclined to break a few more of his ribs."

He smiles as he pins the end of my bandage. "Done."

I use the hand to shake his. It's a very weird thing to do and I can only blame it on nerves. "Friends?" I ask.

He looks down at our handshake and then up at me. His eyebrows arch as if to point out how idiotic I am. "Sure. Friends. Are we also business partners?"

I wrench my hand from his and blush pink. "Let's go already."

I hear him laugh under his breath.

"Get a move on!" Pace shouts from the garage.

Claire and Tobias are waiting by the door for us. I hug them both quickly, wanting to give Luke a moment alone with them.

"Thank you so much," I say to Claire.

"It's my job, sweetheart. Well, actually it's not at all. It's illegal. But, you know, all in good fun."

I grin. To Tobias I murmur, "I think you're right to question. Don't stop."

"Only if you'll do the same," he smiles, kissing me on the cheek.

"Deal."

I climb into the back of the van with Will and Shadow, crammed in beside the sleeping Ben and Dr Shaw.

"What are we doing with this woman?" Hal asks from the passenger seat.

"Taking her with us," I shrug.

"So we're kidnapping people now?"

"Why not?"

Luke joins us and it takes me one glance to know he feels like absolute crap. There's a heaviness to his shoulders and mouth I've not seen in a long while. He rests his head against the side of the van and orders Pace to drive. She starts the van and begins reversing.

"Stop!" I shout suddenly. The van jerks to a halt halfway out of the garage.

"We have to go or we're not gonna make the train," Hal warns.

I open the back door and jump out. "Josi?" Luke calls but I run inside.

Claire and Tobias are hugging in the middle of the living room, but turn to me in surprise. "Did you – "

"Get in the van," I tell them. They stare at me blankly. "We're not leaving you behind," I say clearly. "It's ludicrous. Come to the west and be with your son."

They look at each other, then back at me.

I spread my hands. "What have you got to stay for?"

"We're cured," Claire states. "They won't take us!"

"Trust me. Parents of the second coming will be treated like bloody deities in that place."

"Can I bring a few things?"

"Yes," I laugh. "Just hurry up. Go go go!"

When we finally return to the van, I explain, "New recruits."

"If it's okay with you," Tobias hedges.

Luke stares at his parents, then at me, and finally he smiles the best smile I've seen him give in years.

Chapter 12

February 9th, 2066

Luke

It is selfish and stupid to take them with us. The west is dangerous, not to mention we could be caught by Bloods at any point on the way. I vowed never to bring them into the storm of my life, and here I am, sucking them right into the heart of it. I know this. But for the first time in years I feel like I can breathe. With the simple act of inviting them along, Josi has basically countered the secret fear I harbored that my parents were gone forever. To me, cured meant dead, essentially. Stripped of a soul, a personality, any kind of truth. Now I'm not sure what it means, but Josi is demanding that we at least explore the idea of life after the cure. With one simple act she has refused to believe that drones aren't real people, aren't worth loving or protecting.

She hated them once. As I have always done. Not because it's their fault. But because they are a product of our ruined world: the proof of humanity's worst traits. But it was spending a year with a cured psychiatrist that made Josephine understand the complexity of our remaining population.

Which all means, in essence, that I might have a family again.

*

We are stopped at a checkpoint. I refrain from pointing out how idiotic it is that Pace has just driven straight up to it.

"How was I supposed to know it was here?" she hisses.

"Calm down," I order crisply. "Mom, get in the driver's seat."

"What?"

"You're a nurse. You're taking supplies to the hospital. They'll want to check you're cured."

There are about a dozen cars in line before us, so Mom climbs into the front seat once Pace and Hal have joined us in the back.

"I don't even know how to drive this thing," she points out.

Dad takes that moment to start ripping through the sheet covering Meredith and Ben.

"What the hell are you doing?" I ask.

He doesn't respond, and when I catch sight of his face I know his brain's completely short-circuited. He tears violently through the sheet, his eyes vacant.

"Hold onto him," I snap at Hal. "Don't let him make any noise."

While Hal grabs hold of my dad's shaking hands I scramble to the front of the van and perch myself behind Mom, gun pointed out her window. There aren't any windows in the back so the cops won't spot me unless they open the doors, and if they do that the game is up anyway and I'll have to shoot them.

Mom starts giggling hysterically and it makes me feel queasy. I reach through the grill and squeeze her hand tightly. "Listen to my voice," I tell her. "Take a deep breath and think about rain falling on a tin roof."

It was always her favorite sound. When I was a kid she told me that it calmed her so deeply she felt like she could dissolve into a puddle on the floor.

Mom's laughter slowly peters out and soon she is breathing steadily.

"Drive us forward a little," I tell her gently. "But keep thinking about rain."

She revs too much and the car lurches into a bunny-hop. We can't turn the auto-drive on because it responds only to prints and is connected to the network, which means the Bloods would instantly be able to track the stolen car and Mom's presence in it.

"Easy," I soothe her. "You're doing great."

A glance behind tells me that Dad is wantonly trying to destroy anything he can get his hands on, giving small whimpers of grief. Hal has wrapped his arms around Dad's middle to limit his movement, and Josi is pinching his fingers. It's clever, because the physical pain will hopefully ground him in his body and stop his confused emotional centers from firing incorrect responses to stress.

We approach the blockade, only one car remaining in front of us.

Mom jolts the car forward and winds down her window.

"Print please, ma'am," the police officer says in a bored tone.

Mom lends him her hand so he can take her print, then a prick of her blood. When his tester blinks green he drawls, "Very good. What's in the van?"

"Medical supplies."

He reads the file projected from his tablet – Mom's info, along with the fact that she's a registered nurse.

"Says here your son's a fugitive," the cop frowns. Goddamnit.

"So I'm told."

"When did you last speak to him?"

"Is it really your job to be questioning me?" she replies calmly. 'You're a traffic cop. I answered every question I could about my son when the Bloods interviewed me last year."

He blinks, then nods. It might have offended him once upon a time, but now he simply understands the words as true. He considers her, long and slow.

Behind me, Dad tries to speak through Hal's hand.

The cop hears it and looks at the back of the van, frowning.

I hold my breath.

"I'll have to check the van in any case," he says apologetically.

"I'm in a rush – there was an emergency this morning and I need to get the blood supplies to the operating room."

"Won't take me a second, ma'am."

I sigh inwardly. He seems like a nice bloke. I squeeze the trigger and fire a bullet straight into his thigh. It takes him a few seconds to react, as he has no idea what's happened or where the sudden burst of pain has come from. Falling to the ground, the man wails.

"Drive," I tell Mom.

She revs so hard the engine roars, then takes her foot off the clutch way too fast and stalls the car.

"Move over," I say and she does so quickly.

I wriggle into the driver's seat and take us straight through the checkpoint, setting off an alarm in the process. The cop fires his gun six times and I feel one of the bullets hit our back tire.

Two police sirens whir behind us, but I'm not worried about cops. I'm worried about the fact that it won't be long before the Bloods join the party. Turning right, I feel the tire skid and lose some of its rubber. It'll be a miracle if it lasts until we get to the tunnel.

"Train's in ten minutes!" Hal shouts.

Uh-oh. I skid into oncoming traffic and then jump a median strip to get to the right side. A traffic cam takes a nice, blinding picture of us as we speed past. A third police car swerves to chase us, and I can feel the steering go because of the blown tire.

Thankfully the subway tunnel looms and as I approach it I spin the car to block its entrance, making sure the back door opens onto the stairs. I'm not about to roll my vehicle down these steps a second time.

"Will and I'll cover," I announce because Will's the best shot and makes the smallest target. "The rest of you get these bodies down into the tunnel."

From our windows Will and I start firing at the cop cars, fast as we can.

Hal has Ben over his shoulders, leaving Pace and Josi to carry Dr Shaw between them. Mom and Dad have managed to get Shadow below ground. It seems like we might just make it.

Until in the distance I see a sleek black car arrive and my heart sinks.

"Go, mate," I tell Will. "I got you."

Will ducks his head and sprints around the van for cover. I take out three policemen crouched behind their car doors who are too stupid not to keep popping back into my line of sight.

When Will is safely below I round the van, bullets raining over me. One takes me through the upper arm, another grazes my ear, a third ricochets into my big toe. I keep moving. There is no time for pain, there is time only to stop those Bloods from getting into the tunnel. I fire three rounds into the oxygen tanks in the back of the van, then another two into the engine.

It takes about four seconds to make a popping sound, then the car bursts into violent flames.

I am already sprinting down the steps. Here comes the tricky part. Getting two bodies onto a moving train. Josi and Will have decided they're going to jump on at one end and get the doors open wide. The rest of us will wait at the other end of the platform so that by the time the first carriage reaches us we can swing Ben and Dr Shaw straight in and then grab whichever carriage we can get a hold of.

It's impossible to count the number of things that could go wrong.

And that's when, of course, the two Bloods emerge onto the platform, having managed to get past the flaming van.

The moment slows as I take them both in. Everything inside me blisters; adrenalin pumps through my body and I reach calmly to harness its strength and speed within my limbs.

They raise their Glocks toward us and I am already firing two guns and two sets of bullets smash through their hands. Their respective weapons go flying and by the time I hear them clatter to the ground I have already shot one man through the neck and am approaching the second.

He's a Blue, more deadly than his Red companion. He reaches me before I can get off another shot and knocks the gun from my grip. My second fires wildly into the air but I allow my hand to let it go. This needs to be close and fast; I can hear the train approaching already.

I slam my fist into his face and feel his nose break. He doesn't react, instead lifting his knee and extending his foot in a beautiful kick that cracks straight into my broken ribs; I must have been favoring my right side. Pain splinters through me and I let him punch me once, twice in the cheek. Letting someone hit you does a couple of things. It can be an insult to mess with his head. Or it can be a trap. Because when he hits with his right you can hammer a heavy left into his unprotected kidney and drop him to the ground. Like I do now.

I turn in time to see that the train is rushing past. Josi and Will are already on and I catch a glimpse of the others all jumping or being hoisted on in a tangle of limbs.

They're going to make it.

But so is the first Blood, the Red I shot in the neck. He has his hand held to the wound, staunching bright spurts of blood, and he's launching himself onto the train.

I sprint after him, leaping onto the very end of the last carriage. As the train whooshes into the tunnel I stumble into the aisle and run after the Blood. I spot him up ahead, so with two fingers I whistle loudly and he turns. He's young, probably only about twenty or so. A new recruit.

"If I were you," I say, "I'd throw myself off this train right now."

"You can kill me," he replies, "but they're going to find you, one way or another."

"Not if I find them first."

I meet him in the section between the cars. The doors are still open and the noise of the tunnel is intense. He punches, a quick left jab. I dodge once, then again for his follow-up blow. Can feel myself smiling. "Who taught you to box?"

Instead of replying he comes at me again, right, left, right. I haven't yet raised my hands – it's rude of me.

"You try to hit me with your right, you're pretty much giving me a whole lot of time to dodge," I point out.

I swerve out of the way of another blow. He's trying to angle me toward the open doors, but it's simple enough to maneuver him around again.

"If *I* punch with my right it's a different story."

"Why's that?" he breathes.

"It's an insult, see? 'Cause I'm gonna hit you even with the extra warning."

And with that I swing a huge right, hammering it into his jaw, and even with all my words of caution it's still too fast for him to block. Blood spills from his mouth, along with several teeth. He's tough – he shakes it off and faces me once more, still bleeding from the bullet through the side of his neck. His blood loss will hit him in a second and he won't be able to keep fighting.

But I've lost all focus. My mind feels abruptly as though it's underwater; everything has become agonizingly slow. Because the smell ... the scent of his blood has caused something to erupt inside me. I can *feel* the smell on my skin, it's an electric prickling. My teeth ache and my mouth floods with saliva.

What the fuck is going on?

The boy hits me, a body blow to my chest and another to my shattered ribs. I don't feel the pain because I'm swimming and tingling and I can see the smell now, making thick heavy shapes in my head. It's dark and smooth, draping me in a veil or coating me like paint sinking through the levels of my brain.

I am on the ground, I realize abruptly. The sound of the train roaring through the tunnel is a drill in my skull and I can still smell the blood as the boy rolls me toward the opening. The blood smells so strong I think I'm going to gag it's taking up every inch of my body and permeating every one of my pores and I can't get rid of it I can't and it's trickling down my spine –

And just like that the world drops out from under me.

*

Josephine

"Where is he?" I demand. "Where's Luke?"

Everyone in their various states of dishevelment looks around. There is no Luke.

"The Bloods," Shadow wheezes. "He was fighting two."

I turn and sprint down the train. I saw him fighting, but I also saw him run toward the train and jump. He must have made it. I will find him down the end. I will.

But what I find instead is a black-clad man between the carriages, his back to me. I draw my gun and aim at him. "Hey!"

He twists quickly, spots me and raises his hands. My feet carry me closer, but I can't get too close in case he has any ideas about snatching the gun from me.

A merciless creature lurks in my chest. She is graceless. My mind is an ocean of roaring hungry teeth and all I can think is *where where where where.*

"Where's Luke?" I try to keep the trembling from my voice.

The Blood is young. He has a baby face, and no hair in sight on his chin. His lips are split and swollen, and there is blood trickling from his mouth and neck.

"*Where?*"

"He's dead," the guy says tonelessly.

"Bullshit."

"Rolled him right out the door."

The creature in my chest screams, wild and abruptly free. I take two steps closer, raise the gun and shoot the boy in the head.

Turns out I *can* hit a man three feet in front of me. His skull splatters over the wall behind him and he drops.

My ears ring painfully and all other sound warps into a rushing hiss. Lowering the gun, I am no longer trembling. I walk forward and stand over the body. His eyes stare sightlessly at the ceiling; they are cold and empty but they are not as cold as my body and they are not as empty as my soul.

I don't know what makes me turn my head. But I do, and so I see four fingers clutching onto the edge of the train carriage.

In an instant I'm at the side and there I see him. Hanging from the exterior door handle with one hand. His grip is like iron when I reach for his wrist.

"Luke!" I scream.

He can't talk, hammered as he is by the oncoming rush of wind and the gravity dragging him backwards. I have no choice but to offer him my left hand, the one with the broken wrist, as I need my right to grab hold of the railing inside the carriage.

"Reach for me!" I shout.

He swings his free hand toward my outstretched one, misses once, twice, three times. His arm drops and I can see his fingers slipping on the handle.

"Keep trying!"

With one mighty effort he hauls his arm forward and grabs my hand. It snaps my wrist instantly, the bones too brittle from only just having healed. Pain eclipses all else and I feel nausea roar through my guts. A shriek is torn from me and I cut it off by biting down on my tongue so hard that I taste blood.

He starts to let go – I can feel him.

"Don't you dare!" I yell. "Hold on!"

I am woozily trying to work out how I can pull his weight inside when I feel hands take hold of me and wrench me backwards. Luke is hauled inside and crumples on top of me.

Spots dance before my eyelids. There's a howling in my wrist and a flood of darkness.

"Josi?" Hal and Pace are staring down at me. I don't know how long I have been lying here.

They help me to sit up and I look at Luke, sprawled against the wall. He's holding his side uncomfortably and the second I meet his eyes I get a fright. "There's something wrong with me," he says.

It sends a chill over my skin because I have never seen him look so scared.

In the corner of my vision I can see the body of a dead boy.

*

We are quiet on the train ride home. Claire has set and bandaged my wrist, which hurt so much that I vomited and we had to move carriages to get away from the smell. Now we're all sprawled together in the one carriage, nursing our wounds and injuries, and sinking into an exhausted stupor.

Luke is staring vacantly out the window, and I can see how spooked he is by whatever happened at the end of the train.

I'm too numb to be spooked.

When Dr Shaw finally stirs I realize we haven't discussed what we're going to do with her. She's tied at wrists and feet, and she struggles groggily. "What ... Where am I?"

Luke's still off in his own world so I guess it falls to me to explain since I was the one who wanted to kidnap her in the first place. move to crouch beside her. Claire is giving her water and trying to soothe her.

"You're on a train going west," I tell her.

"*West*? Then you're …"

"Yes."

"I've been kidnapped by the resistance?"

"Yes."

She slumps back down, looking a bit defeated. That's when she clocks Ben lying not far from her. Dr Shaw lurches up, her eyes widening in terror. "What's he doing here? Why did you bring him?"

I glance at the others, but they look as confused as I feel. "We rescued him from you," I say, thinking it obvious.

"Tie him up!" she cries, scrambling away from him. "Quickly!"

"He'our friend," I point out. "Not to mention a sickly old man."

Ben starts to wake. He moves a little, groans feebly.

Dr Shaw looks straight at me and whispers, "You stupid girl. You have no idea what you've done."

And it hits me the second before he opens his eyes: the bleeding gums and fingernails I noticed when we found him. The paper-white skin. The nagging fact that he was in a research facility.

Ben Collingsworth looks at me, and his eyes are the deep, blood red of a Fury. I know it in the moment before he lunges at me with a rabid snarl of hunger.

Chapter 13

February 12th, 2066

Josephine

I have never been to a zoo. They don't exist anymore; most animals are dead, and all the birds extinct. But I have imagined them, seen them on television, read about them. Which is how I know that what we have in the dark science lab on the very east edge of the settlement is a caged animal.

I stand on the other side of the glass and I watch him in there. Pacing his cage back and forth, gazing pitilessly out at me. There doesn't seem to be any humanity left in his red eyes. Is Ben Collingsworth still inside that body somewhere? If we have souls, then what has happened to his? Did it flicker out when this was done to him? Or did it shift into something else entirely?

Quinn, Raven and Dodge all arrive to join me at the glass. Last to enter is Luke, who's had his superficial gunshot wounds tended to at the infirmary; I had to have my wrist re-set and cast this morning too, despite the fact that I can feel it healing on its own. We gaze in at the beast, who is really just a very old man dying of heart failure.

"I'd like to study it," Dodge says. He sounds excited. "The implications are many."

"The implications are – " Luke starts.

"We don't discuss implications," Quinn interrupts him. "We discuss facts."

There is a long silence as we watch Ben's lips curl to reveal his sharp teeth and bleeding gums.

"We'll have to feed it," Raven points out. "If you want to study it."

"It eats human flesh," Quinn points out.

"He's not an 'it'," I snap. "He's a man."

"He *was* a man," Raven replies.

Ben screams abruptly, throwing himself against the glass as if to break it with his body. I flinch and try not to look away but it's too awful.

"*That's* no man," Raven murmurs.

I wish I could disagree with her, but I can't. The creature in that cage is an animal or a monster, or something in between.

And when I look at him there is an all too familiar reflection gazing back at me.

*

Quinn asks Raven and Luke to go and question Dr Shaw and find us some of those facts he's so keen on. He stands with me for a while after they've gone, and we watch Ben in silence. For the first time I feel curious about what this man thinks. It seems odd to me, suddenly. Quinn is the leader of the resistance and I don't know what he believes about anything. Except corporal punishment.

"When did you leave the city?" I ask.

"Twenty years ago."

"Why?"

He takes a moment to consider the question, arms folded over his thick chest. "I was grieving," he shrugs. "Sixteen years old when my parents died in the first wave of sickness. The second wave took my four younger sisters. The wall was built but I didn't know how it was supposed to fix anything. You can't build a wall against death."

He turns to face me, his blue eyes sharp.

"I came out here to die," he admits simply. "Instead I found Shadow, and then we found a prison, and we both decided to just ... live a little longer." Quinn pauses, remembering. "It was a graveyard out here. So many dead. An Underworld."

"How did the others come?"

"I went back for them," he replies, "when the cure was first announced."

It strikes me as incredibly brave, being the first of a kind. The first to save himself, and then to go back to save more. And at only sixteen years old.

"And the resistance?" I ask. "When did the fighting start?"

"Do you know who gets named 'resistance'? Those who disagree." Quinn shakes his head. "I never chose that name for us. I never wanted to fight. I wanted to escape. I wanted the fury I deserved when life took everyone I'd ever loved from me. It was Shadow who wanted to fight. He had a different kind of grief in his heart, a different kind of fury."

"But he never went back."

"He couldn't."

"Why?"

"Too many ghosts there. So I went for him, and I looked for people we'd known. Then I just looked for anyone at all who wanted to be freed."

"*Wanted* to be freed?" I repeat. "Didn't they all?"

"Most people don't want to be angry, Dual. They don't *want* to be sad."

"Then what do they want?"

"To surrender."

*

Raven

Luke and I look through the small window. Dr Shaw is quietly staring at the wall of the interrogation room, as though her thoughts are a million miles away. She looks exhausted.

I reach for the handle.

"You ever questioned a drone?" Luke asks me.

"No. You?"

"You can't assume they'll respond like a normal person would," he counsels.

"So what do you do then?"

"Well, for starters, don't try to make her angry."

I roll my eyes. "You're a fount of wisdom."

"When you question people you always use the same tactic, Raven."

"I do not!"

"You do."

"Fine, which tactic should I be using?"

He shrugs, looking back at Dr Shaw. "She's a scientist, and she's cured. So reason with her."

"Why don't you show me how it's done?" I hand him a tablet and Luke enters the room to sit opposite the doctor.

"Sorry to keep you waiting, Dr Shaw. I'm Luke Townsend. Do you need some water?"

She shakes her head.

Luke flashes her a smile – his painfully gorgeous one – and says, "You must be tough if you can stand this heat without a drop. I was panting like a dog the day I arrived."

No response, but I can see her shifting in her seat as though to re-evaluate what's about to happen. She was not expecting warmth.

"We've taken you in order to retrieve certain information," he begins. "So I'll be asking you some questions and if you could answer them that would really make my day. Can I call you Meredith?"

She nods.

"Cool. You work as the lead scientist in the Collingsworth research facility, right?"

Another nod.

"Which project are you currently working on?"

"The sadness cures. But you already know that."

"I do, yeah." He is watching her closely, the expression in his eyes intimate somehow. "How long have you been working for the facility, Meredith?"

"Four years. Since it was started."

"And the government? When did they recruit you?"

"Twenty-five years ago."

"Were you in any way involved in the development of the cure for anger?"

She says nothing, and that's how Luke knows where her marker is. She's hiding something.

"It's okay, I know you're legally obliged not to discuss employment with anyone," he says gently. "I signed all the same contracts when was working for the government. I won't make you talk about that i you don't want to."

Her hands fidget in her lap.

"It'd help me out a lot if you could give me some professiona opinions, though," Luke goes on. "What's the measure of success fo: the anger cure? For example, when it's administered, how do you know if it's worked correctly?"

"Side effects," she says simply.

"Which are?"

"We measure heart rate, response and reaction time, sensory reactions to light, olfactory stimulations, temperature regulation, organ function, blood cell count, blood clotting – I could go on, but it's all been published, and the fact remains that any physical side effects are very rare."

Luke nods. "I've read the papers."

"Then why ask?"

"There are some side effects that haven't been published. Those are the ones I'd like you to talk about."

"I don't know of any."

"Really. You've spoken about physical effects and tests, Meredith, but you haven't mentioned the rate of psychiatric testing. How do you judge if the cure has effectively erased a brain's ability to trigger an anger response?"

"That's exactly what it was designed to do, Mr Townsend. And it was designed by a mind far superior to any left in this world."

"Sure, but how do you *know*?"

She says nothing.

"You don't, do you? You give people the cure and then send them home with no real way to know if it's responded correctly."

"The test parameters were thorough. A drug isn't cleared for administration unless it passes certain checkpoints designed to protect against harm. Citizens are encouraged to monitor their health and report any symptoms."

"Right, but mental health hasn't exactly been a number-one priority for the government, has it?" He lets that hang in the air for a moment, then asks, "Do you experience any side effects, Meredith?"

"No."

"That's pretty lucky."

"No, that's statistically expected. The cure reacts positively in ninety percent of the populace, Mr Townsend. They're calmer, happier and healthier."

"So let's talk about the other ten percent. What happens to them?"

She sighs. "They can have unpredictable emotional responses to stress and stimuli."

"And do you think that's also a likely result of the sadness cure?"

"It isn't yet finished."

"But the test subjects have all shown such symptoms, haven't they?"

No response.

"How many have you tested so far?"

No response.

"I'm pretty sure I heard you say there were at least sixty-six, right?"

Her eyes are glued to her hands.

"Here's the thing, Meredith," he goes on softly. "There's a woman outside that door who's waiting to have her turn with you. She's not going to be as nice. In fact, I'm sometimes convinced the sole purpose of her life is to inflict pain. If you can tell me the names and ages of all sixty-six of your test subjects, I'll make sure she doesn't come in here."

Meredith's eyes dart up to Luke. She's starting to look frightened now, the idea of the pain seemingly worse than the pain itself. In a slow, small voice she begins to speak names. Sixty-six of them.

"Jennifer Soyles, fourteen years old. Ben O'Malley, twelve years old. Tony Lin, fourteen years old. Harry Rinks, ten years old. Liza Shircova, eleven years old ..."

And on and on.

Luke types each one of them into his tablet. It's the ideal strategy – he has read her perfectly. With each name Meredith falters a little more, her voice grows wearier and by the time she's finished remembering every child she has ruined, the doctor looks wretched with shame.

"Thank you," Luke says.

"It was to help the many," she says. "Harm the few to help the many."

"How many of these children died?"

She says a number and then has to clear her throat before she can be heard. "Forty."

"You're going to go through them and mark which ones." Luke hands her the tablet and she goes through the list, slowly checking them off.

"How long did you work for Dr Collingsworth in his lab before the anger cure was approved?" Luke asks when she's finished.

"Ten years," Meredith mutters, utterly defeated.

"During the initial test rounds, what did you do with the failed subjects?"

She opens her mouth but nothing comes out.

"Did you report them?"

She shakes her head.

"Did you ever see any with bleeding gums and burst blood vessels in their eyes? Did you ever inject a round of subjects with something that stole their humanity completely? Did they grow violent and aggressive? When you played god, Meredith, did you stumble and instead create monsters? What did you do with those monsters afterwards? Did they have to be killed? Or were they quarantined somewhere? Somewhere such as beyond an unbreachable wall?"

She clenches her hands tightly.

My heart is pounding.

Luke leans forward and tilts Meredith's chin up so that she is forced to look into his face. "Did you and Collingsworth create the Furies and then blame them on the plague?"

She stares at him, and then finally she whispers, "Yes."

I breathe out in a rush.

"Does the current version of the cure also cause certain patients to become Furies?"

"Yes."

"Is that what happened to Collingsworth?"

"Yes."

"Does Falon Shay know about this?"

"Yes. It was his idea to put them beyond the wall so no one would be able to leave the city."

Luke is so still it seems for a moment that he has turned to stone. Softly he murmurs, "Is the land beyond the wall diseased at all?"

"No. It's perfectly habitable. It's regenerating as we speak."

*

When Luke finally emerges he looks exhausted. "Let's get a drink," he suggests.

He follows me to the Den where we raid the pantry for the whisky selection. The people on kitchen duty are all happy to see Luke back from the mission and want to give him hugs and kisses, which he looks pleased about. They don't talk to me, but that's because they know I don't much like them. I don't much like anyone, really.

We sit in a corner table and watch the people on dinner duty setting up the meal for later tonight. Afterwards there's going to be a party to celebrate the homecoming of those who went to the city. We always celebrate when no one comes back dead.

Luke drinks his whisky in two large gulps then pours himself another. "My skin's crawling," he admits. "I wish we didn't have to tell anyone."

"We don't have to." He gives me a funny look. "Why? What difference will it make?"

"It's a big deal, Raven. People deserve to know the truth. The government created monsters and then built a wall to keep them out. If we can get rid of the monsters, we can get rid of the wall and be free."

I nurse my drink, sliding my fingers over the glass. He makes it sound very simple, but there are dangerous people who will kill to keep that wall up. "How did you know she'd react that way?"

Luke shrugs and takes another swig. "She has a chip on her shoulder. Has rules and standards to live by, and punishes herself if she can't live up to them. She compartmentalized the kids into numbers so she could deny their humanity. I just gave the kids their names back. Plus she was really tired. That always helps."

"How do you know that?"

"You get used to reading people when it's your job to lie to them. I'm only guessing anyway."

"What about me? What do you read in me?"

"Not a good idea, Raven." He shakes his head.

"Why not?"

"People don't like hearing the truth about themselves, and I get in trouble for telling it."

"I'm not *people*. Go on."

Sighing, he pours himself a third drink and considers me. "Your personality has been shaped by the deep knowledge that people respond to you or behave the way they do because of your beauty. It's intrinsically tied to your self-worth and your perspective. You expect to be desired and you hate it when people play into that expectation. You don't respect anyone because you don't respect yourself. You enjoy cruelty because it makes you feel strong. You hurt so you want others to hurt too. You take pains to make yourself feel in control of every situation. You're terrified that anyone will glimpse your terror."

Heat flares all over my skin and I think I might vomit.

"Don't freak out," he adds. "We all have our shit. You're also very smart and you care way more about this place than you let on.

I want to hurt him. I want to tear the skin from his perfect face with my fingernails and teeth. Instead I smile coldly. "You enjoyed that, didn't you? I wonder if you can look at yourself with such brutality."

"I didn't mean to be brutal. I'm sorry."

"Of course you did. You were trying to hurt me. Do you want to know why?" I pause, finishing my drink and feeling it burn down my throat. I look at him again, hiding the sudden inferno of hatred in my heart behind the words I know will most disturb him. "I might expect people to desire me, but that's only because I'm very good at reading when they do. And you, Luke Townsend, want me more than anyone in this whole fucking place. You're just too pathetic to admit it."

I leave the Den, my mind working quickly. I have to stop giving him power over me. I have to reclaim it.

*

Luke

Shiiiiiiiiiiiiit. I'm gonna pay for that one.

I follow her back to her house and enter uninvited. "Raven."

She turns and with one mighty swing socks me in the face. It hurts but not too badly given the whisky I just skulled.

"There. We're even."

"You think a punch hurts half as much as those words?" she exclaims.

I blink, surprised. She's never admitted to being hurt before, never admitted that anything can even touch her. "I really am sorry," I say again. "I'm not interested in fighting with you, or being your enemy. I want to be your friend."

"*Friend*?" She laughs. "You have enough friends. Everyone in this whole compound is your friend."

"Yeah, but you don't have any."

Her eyebrows arch. "This is the cruelest apology I've ever heard."

"You know it's true, Raven."

"I don't want friends!" she spits out. "I don't *need* friends!"

"Right." I head for the door, wishing I hadn't bothered.

She stops me, pushing me roughly against it. "Why can't you just admit that you want me?"

"Because I *don't*."

Her black eyes and red lips are very close to my face. "You're such a liar, Luke Townsend."

Abruptly I can smell her desire. It's red and thick like a cloud in my mind.

"Your girlfriend is dead," she says. "There's no reason to deny yourself."

"I'm not interested," I tell her again.

"Is it because you like someone else?"

I shake my head, frustrated. "Can I go?"

"The spoiled child with the dual eyes?" she asks. "I can't see how, Luke."

"Dual and I are friends, and I'm honestly *just not into you*."

"Then why did you come here?"

"To apologize. Even though you pushed me into saying what I did."

"You're desperate for everyone to love you. You lie and manipulate people into it."

Her nearness is starting to muddle my brain. I feel a weird tingling on the back of my neck and down my spine. Like on the train, I begin to experience things I shouldn't. Thoughts and sensations and images in my mind and the heavy scent of Raven and heat in my gut and pins and needles in my fingers and –

Lips against mine.

The kiss is soft and I feel myself leaning into it.

But confusion rushes me because it doesn't feel right, doesn't taste right, and so I open my eyes and see the wrong person –

I push Raven away and she smiles slowly as if I have walked into her trap. "You liked that. I felt it."

"Temporary insanity," I snarl. "Don't come near me again."

I wrench the door open to find Josi with her hand raised to knock. She blinks, looks at me, spots Raven looking smug. Her eyes narrow in on my lips and my heart pounds; I'm sure I look guilty too.

She's too smart not to join the dots, even though I have no fucking clue *how* I wound up kissing a woman I hate. My head feels on fire and I can't work out what to say.

Josi's gaze hardens and she laughs this clipped laugh. "I'm interrupting."

"Wait – "

"See you round."

I watch her stalk away and I feel as though I'm going insane.

*

So I tell Dodge. "I feel as though I'm going insane."

"Tell me about it," he implores gently, sitting me in his test-subject chair. But that's when I see Meredith. She is perched behind the workbench, handcuffed to her chair. Behind her in his cage is Ben, pacing back and forth.

"I'd rather not have a medical examination with the government pawn listening in," I say. "Who brought her here?"

"Don't mind her," Dodge says with a wave of his hand. "Quinn wants her working."

Meredith watches me, her expression unreadable.

"What are your symptoms?" Dodge asks.

I tilt my head, appraising Meredith. I have zero respect for her and everything she stands for, but it can't be said that she's irrational or unpredictable – she is calm. She is everything the cure was meant to be.

I'm too agitated to keep worrying that she's here, so I turn my eyes back to Dodge. "I see things. Smell things. Feel things. They don't make sense."

"What's the trigger?"

I shake my head, trying to work it out. "I don't know. Adrenalin? I get these rushes of confusion ..."

Dodge takes a vial of my blood and peers at it under his microscope. "Your cells are degenerating at a rapid rate."

"I know that. Can you maybe tell me something you haven't told me a million times before?"

"What exactly have you experienced?"

"I just lost all sense of reality for about thirty seconds. There were such intense sensations that I forgot where I was and who I was with."

Dodge seems stumped, staring at me helplessly.

Ben gives a cat-like yowl from his cage.

And then Meredith asks, "Do you have synesthesia, Mr Townsend?"

I blink, looking at her. "A mild case."

"Were you injected with Zetemaphine at any point in your life?"

I swallow. Can only manage to nod.

"It's intensifying your synesthesia, which is why you're experiencing sensory confusion each time your brain triggers a rush of adrenalin. Smells cause sights? Sights cause sounds? Sounds cause physical sensations? Hallucinations?"

I nod again.

"It's not fatal. Just very confusing. Avoid situations that cause your heart rate to rise and trigger adrenalin emissions and you'll reduce its effects."

"Oh, that'll be easy. What about the degeneration of cells?"

"That's unavoidable," she says. "I watched seventeen children die of rapid cell degeneration. There's no antidote for Zetemaphine."

"Actually," I say, standing up. "There is. Your boss worked it out. And I reckon if you want to remain unharmed you should start doing the same."

*

Josephine

I'm back in my chair. It's still sitting beside the same bed, but this time Shadow is the one sleeping in the infirmary. In my hands is a battered old copy of *Jane Eyre. It agitates me to pain that the skyline over there is ever our limit.*

I close my eyes, letting the book rest in my lap.

"What stirs that weary head of yours?"

I open my eyes to see Shadow watching me. "Dissatisfaction."

"With what?"

"This world and how it is."

"So rectify it."

I sit forward and take his hand with the one of mine that isn't in a cast. I feel the weathered lines of his, look at the dirty fingernails, the callouses on the edge of every finger. "Have you killed anyone?"

He searches my face. "Yes."

"Does it haunt you?"

"No."

"Why not?"

"Because I am haunted already, and there isn't enough space for that many ghosts."

"Who are you haunted by?"

"My wife and daughter."

"How did they die?"

"Plague."

My thumb moves over his thumb. "I used to change. I used to become a monster, and I used to kill people."

He watches me, waiting.

"The only thing that kept me sane, I think, was the fact that I didn't have a choice in it, and hardly any memories." I meet his eyes. "Three days ago I murdered someone in cold blood. I decided to do it and I did it, and now I remember every detail of it."

"Yes."

I stare at Shadow. "That's it?"

"What do you want me to say, kid? Do you want me to absolve you?"

"No."

"Do you want me to punish you?"

I swallow.

"I won't do either." He squeezes my hand painfully tight. Then he says, "Sometimes we are sweet. Sometimes we are brutal. Some days we will be gentle. Other days we will be ugly."

"But …" I swallow, my heart swollen and sluggish in my chest. "What's it supposed to mean?"

"Nothing. It's not supposed to mean anything."

"Is that grief talking?"

"I've believed that since the day I was born."

I rest my forehead against the back of his hand. "I'm glad you didn't die. Even though you're a cranky old thing and you make me punch the bag without telling me how."

He moves his hand to stroke through my hair.

"I'm getting a new trainer, by the way." I look up to see the corner of his mouth curve. "Are you offended?"

He shakes his head, smiling more fully.

"It's probably a mistake," I afford.

"Gravity," is all he says.

Kissing him quickly on the forehead, I walk for the door. "Parties to attend," I sigh. "People to charm. The glamorous life."

*

My next stop is to check in on Claire and Tobias in their new place. They were given the smallest one bedroom in the whole compound, which was a battle for Luke to achieve, given the resistors didn't like it one bit that we'd brought cured people into their camp. He had a very

221

good argument for their safety, though – one Quinn couldn't ignore. In the cells with everyone else, there's no telling what could happen.

Luke answers the door. "Hey, pal. Should I call you pal? How about buddy? Amigo? Comrade?"

I roll my eyes. "Your folks okay?"

He nods and gestures me in. I can feel how sheepish he is, but neither one of us brings up the fact that he was definitely making out with Raven the last time I saw him. I could throttle him for it, though I'd have no right to.

Luke's parents are sitting on the small couch in the living room, and I sink onto the floor opposite.

"Hi, sweetheart," Claire says.

"Hey. You guys alright?"

They both nod.

"Anyone giving you a hard time? 'Cause I'll get these babies lined up and ready." I kiss my knuckles, making Claire laugh. "But seriously, are they?"

"What do you think?" Luke slumps beside me and hands me a glass of wine.

"Who? What are they saying?"

Tobias grins. "I like you. Luke, didn't I already say that I like her?"

"Yes, Dad, you did. About eight times."

"Huh. I'm not usually likeable," I point out with a smile.

"I've dealt with the idiots who have an issue, and Quinn's on board," Luke assures me.

"Is Raven on board?" I ask.

"Don't know."

I bet he does know, the bastard. I really wish the thought of them together didn't make me feel so ill. Finding him with her lipstick on his mouth was like some kind of nightmare.

"Did Ranya get you set up in the infirmary?" I ask Claire. "I reckon she's probably desperate for some proper help."

"She did." Claire nods. "She was a bit worried about my capabilities."

"Emotional capabilities," Tobias elaborates.

I look at Luke's mother, at the well-kept hair and makeup, the ironed clothes and the eyes that still hold so much depth. "Well, all I know of you is that you laugh a lot, and I think we could all stand to laugh more."

Claire watches me scrupulously, and then slowly smiles.

"That's what I always say," Tobias agrees.

Luke's fingers shift over the wooden floor to touch my hand, but even though I know it's just a moment of gratitude I'm compelled to move out of his reach. "I should go," I say, getting to my feet. "See you both soon. If you need anything …"

"We know where to find you," Tobias assures me.

Luke walks me to the door, and then keeps on walking me home. "Me and Raven …" he starts.

"Don't," I say quickly.

"There's sort of an explanation, if you want it."

"I don't. We're friends, remember?"

"I remember."

People pass by and call out to Luke, or wave. He greets them all by name, and asks after them.

"How do you know them all so well?" I ask once we're walking alone again.

He shrugs. "I talk to them. I ask them things."

I feel abruptly sad. I spent so many years hating the fact that there was no one to talk to or connect with. Now I walk The Inferno as though I am still the only uncured person in the world, when in fact I am surrounded by them.

"I don't know how to do that," I say. "Why is it so hard for me and not for you?"

"I can think of a thousand reasons."

I swallow. His eyes are beautiful. This sadness I feel. This ache. When will it end? I hate it, and think, for the millionth time, about the sadness cure. Would it work on me? Or would I be immune to it too?

Stopping in the middle of the dusty road, I say, "Raven isn't right for you."

He stares at me.

"You look like you'd be perfect for each other. But she's ugly on the inside."

Luke walks a few steps closer, standing at least a foot taller than me. His outline is clear in the moonlight, the sharp, square features and broad shoulders. "Is this really what we're doing?" he asks. "Talking about other people?"

"Maybe we *should* be *seeing* other people," I reply. Inside my heart something screams *no no no* but I quell it.

"So that's what we're doing then?"

I clear my throat. "I think so. Yes."

"As you wish," he sighs, and I think, of course, of *The Princess Bride*, as any sane person would. *You thought I was answering 'as you wish' but that's only because you were hearing wrong. 'I love you' was what it was, but you never heard.*

"To celebrate this horrid agreement, here's a present." Out of his back pocket Luke pulls an old tablet and flicks it on. Tapping open an application, he passes it unceremoniously to me. "For you, my bestest pal. A thousand books. Most of them banned, just 'cause I know how naughty you like to be."

I stare at it and forget to breathe. My mind is full of questions like *how and when did you get this* – but then he says, "A thousand worlds for you to live in that aren't this one." Luke smiles a little crookedly, then walks down the dusty street.

I watch him go, wondering how he could be blind to the fact that I wouldn't live in any world, no matter how wondrous, if it did not include him.

Chapter 14

Luke

Before the Gathering I check on Shadow in the infirmary, armed with a bottle of whisky straight from the distillery. He's looking pretty uncomfortable, the poor guy. I'm surprised he's conscious, given he just got shot in the guts. He's made of tough metal. I pass him the drink and he swigs gratefully.

"You doing alright?"

He nods. "Don't you look pretty. Shouldn't you be off dancing with your dead girlfriend?"

I wince. "Sorry about that. When I said that I did actually think she was dead."

"How long have you known her?"

I'm surprised – Shadow doesn't usually do personal questions of any kind. I sink into the chair by his bed. There's no one else around because they've all gone to the Den already, so I sit here and I tell him everything, the whole sordid lot of it, like the big dumb idiot I am. Everything about Josi and me comes pouring out of my mouth and I've got no hope of stopping it – our relationship, our search for answers, the blood moon, my deceit and her eventual discovery of it.

"And now it's done," I finish breathlessly. It's probably way more than he wanted to hear.

Shadow watches me, his dark eyes shrewd. I feel naked and uncomfortable. "Why?" he asks finally.

"'Cause she told me. She specifically said the thing between us is gone."

He frowns, shakes his head like I'm a moron. "She's healing, boy," he says. "You gotta give it time. If she was detached, you'd be right to think it was over. But she's in pain, which means she's feeling the loss – just don't make her do it alone. Connect with her over your shared loss 'n she might eventually find her way back to connecting with *you*."

I stare at him, astonished. "How do you keep doing that?"

He shrugs impatiently.

"You a shrink or something?" I joke.

"Psych professor. In another life."

"You're joking!" I laugh, unable to believe it. "I sure as hell didn't see that one coming."

He hides a smile. "Get, ratbag."

"Yes, Professor." I grin as I leave, pausing briefly at the door to say, "Thanks, man. Really."

He ignores me, drinking his whisky instead.

*

Josephine

After Luke drops me at home I take a shower, holding my cast awkwardly out of the water. I think of all the time I'll spend reading the books he gave me and am giddy with excitement. Who needs sleep when you have books?

There's a knock on the door. "What?"

"You're taking forever!" Pace shouts.

"What's got you bent out of shape?" I climb out and wrap a towel around me. Pace pushes into the bathroom, shoves me out of it and then slams the door. Jeez. I head to my room to get dressed. All the clothes here are loose and comfy, much to my liking. They have that old-person cut, which is unflattering on *everyone*. Except Raven, who has found a way to look hot in everything she wears.

It comes to me again, the sight of her having kissed Luke, and that look in her eyes as she stood there behind him, knowing exactly how upset I'd be. Which essentially means that she knows there's something between Luke and me. Which essentially means she's dangerous. Luke and I spoke of seeing other people, and it hadn't occurred to me before tonight, but now I think it might be the only way to convince Raven that there's nothing between us.

Pace barges into my room wearing a clean shirt and slacks. That's the only word I have for them. They're not jeans or pants. They're old-lady slacks.

"What's going on?" I ask.

"Is that what you're wearing?"

I look down at my night shirt and shorts. "To bed? Yes, if that's okay with you."

"It's the Gathering!" she exclaims.

"What's the Gathering?"

"God, you're annoying. After the return of a mission there's like a ... dance. In the Den. Everyone goes to celebrate."

"Oh. Sorry for not intuiting that out of thin air."

"Just get dressed!"

"I really want to have an early night reading."

"Don't be daft," she sighs, as though I have made the most ridiculous statement of all time.

"Fine. I'll bring my reading then. As Lemony Snicket said, *'Never trust anyone who has not brought a book with them'*."

"La la la la," Pace sings loudly to drown me out, her hands covering her ears like she does every time I quote a book.

"Why are you so freaked out?" I follow her into her bedroom and watch as she fidgets before the mirror. She has a bunch of eyeliners stolen from the city, and she uses one to coat her eyes. "I'm missing something," I surmise.

She can't look at me. And she's being more weird than usual. I cross to sit on her bed.

"If you make a single sound or facial expression, I'm going to beat you black and blue," she warns.

"The *violence*," I sigh.

"Have you had sex?" It's flung into the air so bluntly – like a weapon fired – that my mind goes blank.

"*Oh*," I say. Pace angrily applies more eyeliner. "Yes," I tell her. "Have you?"

She gives a stiff shake of her head.

I watch her. "Give the eyeliner a rest," I say finally.

Her hand drops. She looks a bit defeated.

"I mean, hell, *I* don't know," I admit. "But you have the most amazing eyes I've ever seen. So don't put all that crap around them."

Pace looks unsure. She's very unused to going anywhere without a whole lot of eyeliner. Eyeliner like armor. But slowly she takes a tissue and starts to wipe her eyes clean. Then she reaches for the bolt through her nose.

"Don't you dare take that out."

She looks at me in the mirror, then smiles.

I head out to get dressed, saying, "If you want to have sex, have sex. If you don't, don't. There's no other rule."

"Not that simple, actually."

I look back at her. "Why?"

"It's illegal."

"What is?"

"Having unsanctioned sex."

I stare at her, my neck prickling with horror. "Tell me you're kidding."

"Couples have to apply for permission to have sex, because there's a risk of getting pregnant. It's how we control the birth rate here – we only have the means to support a particular population."

"That's the most disgusting thing I've ever heard!" I exclaim.

Pace shrugs as though it doesn't bother her all that much, but I can't believe it. It's just like I imagined would eventually happen in the city – the next step will be forcing people to breed with genetically compatible partners or something.

"All we have out here is endless space," I say. We should be *growing* our numbers.

"Not inside the walls," Pace replies, and to me this place starts to feel like the prison it once was.

*

The Den is rowdy tonight. People are dressed in their clean clothes, and miraculously look as though they've *washed*. Musicians are playing in the corner – guitars and violins, which will do in a pinch, but sadly no cellos. The tables have been shoved back and the floor is crowded with dancers. Everyone looks like they're having a great time, wild and free and full of all the good stuff.

I watch Pace cross to Hal, but because Will isn't with them right now I don't follow her. I can see exactly how she looks at him, and I smile.

I search for Claire and Tobias but guess they must have felt too intimidated to venture into this chaos. At the drinks table I take a whisky and it burns down my throat. When I've made my way back to the wall, I spot Luke entering. And damn. He looks good in his buttoned linen shirt. He *always* looks good. I think he does it just to make life hard for me.

That first night we met I thought he seemed unquiet, that there was something restless and wild beneath his surface. Well it's not beneath the surface now. It's the only thing you see when you look at Luke. He bristles, his eyes darting around the room. He looks angry. But when his gaze lands on me I see a smile curl his lips and I know the anger's morphed into something else entirely.

Raven makes a beeline for him and says something that makes him frown. He deliberates a second, then follows her to the drinks table. They look gorgeous together. Of course.

A fight breaks out in the corner and a bunch of people start yelling and hurting each other, but it's so normal here that no one else pays it much attention. At the drinks table Raven gives Luke a lingering kiss on the cheek and then moves to dance with Quinn, who is busting a move or two on the dance floor. He's actually a really good dancer, which is quite charming. Raven's smile when she looks at him is different. I think it's less guarded, somehow. And I think that, even if she doesn't know it, Quinn is good for her.

I decide to find someone with whom to start this new, impossible pact: seeing other people. I imagine applying for permission to have sex with someone and can't help laughing under my breath, it's so absurd. Scanning the room, a few men catch my eye. It's difficult because I have never in my life scoped a room for desirables.

On the edge of the dance floor is a tall man who looks about thirty, which makes him a fair bit older than me, but he has red hair and red freckles and I like that about him, so I cross the room. "Hello," I greet him a bit awkwardly.

He turns to me, surprised, and looks a little lost for words. "Hi."

"I'm Dual."

"Eric."

I nod and we turn to watch the dancers together.

"I know who you are," he admits.

"Oh no. The brat who doesn't work?"

"The Iron Queen. I watched you take a thousand punches and keep getting back up."

"Yeah well, I can only blame delirious idiocy."

"I thought it was pretty great."

"How long have you been here?"

"Fifteen years."

"Wow."

He folds his arms, which are freckled and quite muscly, I now notice. And he has a very nice smile.

"Have you ever thought about leaving?" I ask Eric.

"To go where?"

I shrug. "Good point."

I catch sight of Luke and oh god it hurts. But his eyes cut through the dance floor and find me on the other side and I know that he's as unhappy as I am. Eric is saying something but I can't hear him, because I'm watching Luke round the dance floor toward me, pushing through people to reach my side. He takes my hand and leads me away from Eric, even though the poor man is mid-sentence. Raven is watching us, and Quinn is watching us, and actually a whole lot of people are watching us, but foolishly I don't much care.

Luke draws me into a quiet corner. I feel so flushed I can barely string a thought together. He leans his mouth close to my ear. What is he doing? "Nice slacks."

The tension dissolves and I burst into laughter. I can't help it. "Go away," I wheeze. "I was having a conversation."

"Intolerable," he comments. "I wish I had Will's moves."

Will is breakdancing, and he is spectacular. Everyone has formed a circle around him. He spins on his head, and I laugh with delight. Luke chuckles softly; I can feel his breath too close to my face.

"Wanna dance?" I ask, even though I'm terrible at it.

"Screw dancing. Let's go hunting."

I turn and look at his face. There's something very much alive in his eyes and his mouth. So we finish our drinks and we go hunting.

*

Luke

"What happened between you and Raven?" she asks me.

The question hangs in the quiet air between us. The dead forest is lit by the waxing gibbous moon as it moves higher in the sky. Bark and twigs crunch under Josephine's heavy footfall. She's extremely loud and it's quite stressful. "Hey, girl, hold up. Try walking on the balls of your feet."

"I know how to walk."

"Yeah and tread earthquakes as you go."

"Are you saying I'm fat?"

I can't help but laugh, which was her intention.

"Are you going to answer the question?"

"Nothing happened." She obviously doesn't believe me, and I can't stop thinking about Shadow's words. "She kissed me."

"Is that all? What about last year?"

"She got naked in front of me once. I sent her home."

"A woman as beautiful as Raven presents her naked body to you and you say no?"

I spread my hands, feeling a bit annoyed. "I was with *you*."

"Not really."

"Yes, really. I had no interest in her. I'm not some insatiable beast who has to fuck anything that presents itself." I pause, and when she doesn't reply I add, "I'm not gonna beg you to believe me. I hope you know me well enough by now to see how much Raven repulses me."

"I don't know you at all," she says automatically.

"Bullshit."

A long silence. We keep to the cover of trees as much as we can, constantly on the lookout. "Clearly Raven wasn't all that worried about the law against 'procreation'," Josi mutters. "How gross is that, by the way."

"Very. And I don't think Raven believes the rules apply to her."

"How nice for her." Josi pauses, then concedes, "I shouldn't have asked, anyway. It's none of my business."

"Of course it's your business."

"Shadow climbs trees and waits for them to come. Wanna climb a tree?"

"Okay."

We pick the largest one we can find and I hoist myself up into the branches, then turn to haul Josi up after me, which is a tad tricky with one of her hands out of action. She's put on a bit of weight since her Skeletor days, thank god. She looks so much healthier with some meat on her bones.

We settle in branches with good views of the ground. I have my bow and arrow ready; Josi has knives she doesn't know how to use and a broken wrist. Bring on the cannibals.

"How often do you and Shadow come out?" I ask.

"Fair bit."

"But how do you hunt?"

"I don't. I watch him. We mostly just sit together."

It's dangerous to take someone into the beyond who isn't equipped to protect herself. Shadow should know better, but I can't really talk. It's strange, too, because he hates being around people, so I can't imagine him lugging a novice along with him. I don't know how he managed to get clearance from Quinn. I was lucky enough to find the leader of The Inferno in an obscenely good mood tonight, so he let us go with a wave of his hand. I think he was smug that I'd learned my lesson and asked him at all.

After a while Josi says, "Hey, Luke? I've got my question for today."

"Okay."

"Can you tell me about it?" She hesitates, then murmurs, "Your job. Me as your job."

My heart clenches. "Now?"

She nods. "How did it start?"

I crack the knuckles in my hands. "I got shot on a mission. I was out for several months. When I got back I was assigned to you as punishment. I was pretty annoyed about it. You were classified as a watch op and I was a Gray. Which meant it had been a long time since I'd had to do watch ops."

"Because they're less important?"

"Classified lower. I surveyed you for several months before the blood moon happened that year – "

"Surveyed me? How?"

"I set up on the roof opposite your building and watched you with binoculars. I bugged your apartment. Followed you to and from work."

"Oh my *god*."

"I reported back to the Bloods that you weren't involved in any illegal activity, but I also specified that I was uncertain where your loyalties lay because I wanted to make sure they'd keep me on your watch."

"Why?"

"I was obsessed with you," I say bluntly. "Or something. I dunno. I couldn't stop watching you."

"Jesus." There is horror in her voice.

"I also didn't want anyone else taking over."

"Why?"

"Because I didn't know if you'd eventually be ordered for erasure."

"Is that the polite term for murder?"

I don't reply.

"Did I do anything embarrassing?"

I snort. "That's what you're worried about?"

"It's one of the things," she snaps. "How would you feel if your privacy had been profoundly violated?"

"Like crap," I agree. "Well ... you danced around in your undies a lot. That weird, pseudo ballet."

"That was elegant," she sniffs.

"You played George Michael on your cello and sang loudly to it. Your voice is, in my opinion, horrific."

"I'm well aware of how you feel about my voice."

And then I say, because I vowed to tell her the truth, always, "You looked at your bruises a lot, and you looked lonely every time you shut your eyes, and you had the worst night terrors I've ever heard. I nearly broke into your apartment to wake you from them about a hundred times."

She doesn't reply.

"Truth is," I tell her softly, "those were the things that made me love you, even before we'd met."

"Stop," she says abruptly. "I don't want to hear any more things about me that you know."

"Okay. Sorry."

"Tell me things about you."

"What things?"

"Real things. Embarrassing things. So we're even. Not that that's possible."

I take a breath and search around in the darkness for something to tell her. "Before you brought them with us I missed my parents so much I could barely breathe," I admit. "Which is weird, because I never used to miss them. The waste of Dave's life keeps me awake at night. It makes me sick to imagine how he must have seen me, having the job I did. He's in the mirror when I look at myself. It'll be with me for the rest of my life, that shame." I take a breath, pondering a while. "Uh ... I once ate so much pasta I threw up all over the living room floor. I liked the things on my desk to be in perfect order. If someone moved something, I wouldn't be able to do any work. I like country music about dogs and trucks and lovey-crap. And, um … fuck, for a long time I was totally scarred by this one sexual experience I had with Lou. She started crying in the middle of it, when I was … And after that for ages I thought I was terrible – or, like, that there was something wrong with me. It really messed with my head."

It feels like a blockage in my chest has been released and everything is gushing out of me. It's relieving and horrifying at the same time. Like being vulnerable always is, I suppose.

"Thank you," she says. "It's a drop to my ocean, but thank you."

I can't quite dredge up any sounds, so I stay quiet.

"And there's not," Josi adds.

"Not what?"

"Anything wrong with you."

Oh.

"Drones," she mutters with an air of dignified scorn. Then thinks better of it. "Or maybe she just knew you didn't love her."

I nod.

"Did you? Love her?"

"Not really. I don't think so."

"But you made love to her?"

"Uh … this feels like a trap," I point out. "I already told you that – "

"I wasn't with anyone before you," she declares. She sounds kind of angry and I have no idea what's going on.

"I know." We talked about this a million times.

I guess we never talked about it post-her-knowing-who-I-am. Maybe there are lots of conversations we will have to redo now that she has an entirely different perspective of me. And I'll just have to wear that and hope she doesn't come out the other side of them disliking me.

But all this talk is sending my mind to bad places. My eyes are resting on the long line of her pale leg and I'm remembering the first time I kissed that leg. I'm remembering a whole lot of things that are not cooperating with my self-preservation.

"Can we talk about the whipping?" I ask her, to distract myself. "Why you got so angry?"

Josi falls quiet. "I don't really want to," she says eventually.

"Don't you think I deserve an explanation? Or are the random bursts of fury part of the ongoing punishment you'll dole out to me over the rest of our lives?"

"Don't make out like I'm the one to blame for this situation. I loved you without limits or boundaries or caveats. I loved you honestly. You betrayed that."

I rub my eyes, feeling my heart grow sluggish. We're moving around in circles.

And then, giving me the barest shred of hope, Josi says, "I was *so* angry that day, Luke. When you took my lashings. Because everything inside me turns into either anger or sadness, one way or another."

"I ..." I clear my throat. "What was inside you, then ... before it turned to anger?"

A long hesitation. I don't know if she'll answer me. "Terror," she murmurs finally. "The terror of losing you. Watching you suffer was unendurable."

My heart skips like a stone thrown over the smoothest of all lakes. A hundred times, a thousand.

"Then you still ... ?" My voice breaks.

"Yes, I still," she replies calmly. "But it means nothing without trust, and I won't trust you ever again, Luke Townsend."

It sounds like a vow, not a fact.

✳

That's when we notice the Furies emerging beneath us, drawn undoubtedly by our voices. I curse myself for being idiotic enough to lose concentration.

I'm startled by how many there are. It has to be over a dozen. They move quietly, walking to the bottom of our tree and surrounding it. I can see their eyes as they stare up at us, their red, red eyes. A chill races across my skin as I meet one of those bloodied gazes. The Fury snarls with rage and starts climbing the tree.

I shoot an arrow into his head. But when he drops, more move to the trunk and try to scale it. A lot more than a dozen, now. Flocking to us from all sides. *Shit*.

"Maybe the tree wasn't such a good idea," Josi ventures.

"Get further up."

I'm firing as many arrows as I can and taking down Furies with each, but I have never seen so many together before. I'm about to run out of arrows.

"Damn it," I hear Josi mutter and look up to see her tear the cast off her arm and fling it impatiently to the ground. She starts climbing, even with her broken wrist, and then leaps from our tree into the one beside it. She scrambles around the branches and looks like she's about to jump to the next. "Come on," she hisses to me.

But if I follow her the Furies will too. They haven't realized she's moving yet. So I climb lower, drawing the long hunting knife I carry with me. Reaching down, I start swinging at the Furies, hacking them as well as I can from such an awkward angle. My knife slashes through a throat and a skull and an eye socket, downing the creatures even as they surge over each other to reach me.

When Josi is three trees away, I shout, "Run your damn butt off, girl. I'm behind you."

And bless her, she knows there's only a split second to do it – to go – now that I've shouted it and the Furies have heard. There's no hesitating, no sentimental looks or words. She swings from a branch, drops to the ground, staggers a few steps and then is up and sprinting, black hair streaming behind her.

I launch myself into the fray and hack the shit out of the bastards. Teeth and nails scrape at me but I'm cutting and shoving my way through with blunt force until I'm free enough to dash after Josi.

The Furies follow us, feet pelting over the hard, dead earth. They're full of rage and hungry for flesh. I hear screams leave their mouths and the wet sound of their heavy breathing, and then I feel hands at my back – they're *fast*. I swing backwards and take a hand off, pressing myself forward.

Josi is up ahead. The girl can run. She shouts to alert the guards on duty and the gate swings open just a little. I see her rush inside.

I head into the mad final sprint, just as the gates are shutting. But as I reach them I feel hands grab at my feet and trip me hard to the ground. Several Furies crash onto me, weighing me down.

I hear Josi shout my name from inside the wall, and then I hear her yelling for the gates to be opened again. Several of the guards are firing rifles down into the fray, trying to help me, but there are a hell of a lot of the monsters now, and pain slices through my arms and shoulders as the creatures bite into me. I use my knife to stab upwards into any of the flesh I can find. Blood splashes onto my face but I keep slashing and hacking until I feel some of the pressure lift and I can bodily shove the rest off me. Scrambling to my feet, I lunge through the narrow gap in the gates and turn to guard it.

Two Furies are too quick, slipping in behind me before the gates slam shut. They both surge not at me, but at Josephine. I twist to intercept them and cut each of their throats with two slashes of my knife.

The world slows again and I try to regain my breath. The bodies look pale in the moonlight, and their blood is pooling all over the sandy ground.

Josi winces at a stitch in her side. "God*damn*. Are you okay? Is that blood yours?"

"Not much of it," I assure her, taking a quick look at my wounds. None seem deep.

"You two alright?" one of the boys on watch calls down to us from the top of the roof. It's Batch, and I realize I haven't spoken to him since my return.

"Yeah, thanks, mate," I call. "Don't let anyone else out tonight."

"Hell no – I've never seen so many at once. We'll get as many as we can from here." He pauses. "Good to see you back, Luke."

I smile up at Batch, glad that whatever animosity he felt toward me last year is now gone. I like the guy, and determine to go and visit him tomorrow.

Another couple of guards come down to deal with the Fury corpses – they'll have to be dropped over the wall. I can hear the rest of them out there, scratching to get in. Only that one gate stands between us and certain death. The sound of rifles launching their second attack explodes through the night. We'll need to put double the guards on the wall and refortify the gate.

For now I look at Josi. We're both still a bit breathless. She says, "Screw hunting. Let's go dancing."

So I grin, and we go dancing. I don't even bother to get changed – no one cares about blood stains in the west, after all.

*

February 13th, 2066

Josephine

I wake at the crack of dawn because I'm queasy and thirsty. I'd bet good money that the entire settlement is as hung-over as I am this morning. I stumble to the bathroom to get some water, and that's how I see it. Through the bathroom window.

Something goes very cold inside me and I am moving without being aware of the decision to do so. Barefoot, dressed only in a t-shirt and undies, I walk right out of the house and onto the main road. Fog has rolled in from the sea this morning, and walking through it is like a dream.

I stop, because I have seen this before, and I am sick sick sick to my very guts and my heart is thundering in fear before my brain says *no. This was not you. You are not this anymore.*

On the ground is a body, and its head has been ripped off.

Chapter 15

Luke

I have no idea why his name was Batch. It was an odd name, but I never asked him about it. Thirty years old. Ambitious and full of ideas. He made a mean vegetable curry and he threw a great right hook. I can't get the look of him out of my head, as he called down from the wall to us just last night.

The story goes that Hal was doing the walk of shame from Pace's room when he came across Josephine half dressed and standing silently over Batch's decapitated body in the quiet of dawn.

Which means that she is now, of course, our number-one murder suspect.

Quinn had her put in the interrogation room. I asked to be the one to question her, but there was a resounding *no* to that. Raven took the lead, and now she and Josi are in there together. Quinn, Shadow and I are waiting outside. It's a lovely little parody of a legal system. Except that there are no trials here – if Quinn judges someone guilty of a crime, it's bye-bye to the criminal.

"We can't question everyone," Quinn frowns. "They were all drunk. It'll be impossible to get a reliable answer."

"We can ask the others on watch," I suggest.

Shadow heads out to find whoever that was. Quinn and I wait, and I'm feeling extremely anxious that Raven is in there doing god knows what to Josi.

Eventually the dark-eyed woman emerges. "Says she doesn't know a thing about it. Spotted him from her bathroom window."

"There's no reason to believe she's lying," I remind them.

"She's new," Quinn says bluntly.

"So she's automatically a murderer? Don't let this turn into a witch hunt, Quinn."

"Nobody was ever murdered before she showed up," Raven says. "So we keep an eye on her until we know more."

They nod and leave. I open the door to find Josi sitting calmly in the chair I was tortured in upon my arrival. She has a pink, swollen cheek and a split lip. I don't comment on them.

"Come on, girl," I murmur and she stands with as much dignity as possible when dressed in only underwear. I pass her a jumper so she can wrap it around her waist. "Bad luck, huh?"

"Uh-huh." She doesn't look at me, just walks past, spine iron straight. I escort her back to her house. A few people look at us weirdly as we walk by.

At the door she pauses. "I didn't do it."

"I know that."

"I couldn't have – "

"Josi, I know that."

She nods, then closes the door in my face. I go back to the infirmary where I woke up this morning to find blood underneath my fingernails.

*

Josephine

I stand under the shower for way longer than allowed. I can't get the water hot enough to scald away the sight of poor Batch. I hadn't even known his name yesterday. Now I'll never forget it. I keep telling myself that it wasn't me. It wasn't me. I'm free of the blood moon. And even if I wasn't, I wouldn't be due to change for another eight months. Still, it is chillingly familiar, this feeling of waking up to a crime scene without any memories of it.

I even have a pounding headache like I used to. But that's just the hangover, I assure myself. I drink a gallon of water and sit on my couch, staring at the wall and wondering what will happen now.

They think I did it. And I can't prove that I didn't. Unless we find out who did. Which could turn out to be impossible, given we have none of the technology used in the city for solving crimes, and we have no detectives. The closest we have is Luke – I guess they'll want him on the case. And if he can't find the real killer, I'm in trouble.

Maybe I should be in trouble. Maybe it's time I was punished for my crimes, even if this was not one of them.

*

We don't have training today, so I spend the morning collecting potatoes from the garden, carrying them in a sack to the kitchen, then washing and peeling them for tonight's meal. There are about thirty-eight thousand of the things, so it takes a long time, and it's menial enough that my mind is a million miles away.

I don't hear Luke come in. When he finally clears his throat I yelp in fright and clutch at my heart. "You are such a freak."

"You were the one completely lost to the world for a solid eight minutes there."

I glance at him over my shoulder, but keep peeling.

"Hit me."

"With what?"

"Whatever thoughts you've come up with."

I push a strand of sweaty hair away with the back of my hand. "Either it's a coincidence, or someone put that body outside my house. So they wanted to make a connection to me, or make sure I found it first. Which could mean either I'm being set up, or someone wanted to scare me with the body."

"Pace lives in that house too."

"Are you implying that not everything in the world revolves around me?"

Luke smiles and then bites loudly into an apple.

"He was also decapitated elsewhere, which supports theory number one."

Luke swallows. "Yeah, not enough blood at the scene to have been killed there. So what's theory number two?"

"I don't have a theory number two yet."

"Who in this place doesn't like you? You pissed anyone off?"

"I'm pretty sure I piss off every second person I come across." I look at him pointedly. "Raven hates me."

He doesn't reply, just keeps crunching away. When the apple is done, he even eats the core – I watch in disbelief. "Waste not, want not," he shrugs. Then gives me one of his serious looks. "You're not going down for this, Josi."

"I don't think you're going to have a say in that, Luke."

*

At home I find Pace lying on her bed. I stand in her doorway and wait for her to notice me. "Hey, Killer."

"Is that meant to be funny?"

She immediately looks contrite. "Sorry."

I peer at her. "How was your night?"

245

No response. I know Hal spent the night here, because he was on his way out this morning when he found me and dumped me in the doghouse. But if Pace doesn't want to talk about it, I'm not going to make her.

"Come to dinner," I say.

"Not hungry."

So I go to the Den on my own and sit with Hal and Will. I don't spot Luke or Raven anywhere, but Quinn is in his usual spot at the head of the room. He calls for a minute of silence for Batch, and the entire hall is dead quiet, except for the soft weeping of a woman I can't see.

When the minute is over I feel all eyes on me. Rumours spread quickly in a confined space.

"Sorry," Hal says. "I shouldn't have … I didn't think about what it would mean to tell them how I found you …"

"Don't worry about it," I say. "There was no need to lie."

His big shoulders are hunched with guilt. He looks wretched actually. There are deep hollows under his eyes and a pallid tinge to his skin. Wearily he asks, "Where's Pace?"

"She wasn't hungry."

"Still hung-over, probably." Will smiles, and we nod.

Love is difficult. Unrequited love is even worse.

I think of the unknown woman whose tears I can still hear, even over the din of two-hundred-odd people eating.

*

Raven

Hal has big, hairy knuckles for a kid his age. They are nice hands. He has a nice face, too. If a bit soft. The tattoos on his arms and the mohawk haircut are meant to make him look tougher, I think. Though he doesn't really need them, given his size. Maybe he just likes them.

"Tell me again," I say.

The boy sighs. "I walked out of the house and saw her straight away. I thought about going past but it was weird that she was in her underwear so I walked over to see if she was okay. She was staring at the body. I asked her if she was alright, and she didn't say anything. She seemed like she was in shock. I asked her what had happened, if she'd seen anything, but still she didn't talk. So I came to your house. That's it."

"Why were you in Dual's house?"

"I crashed there. I was drunk."

"Where did you sleep?"

"On the couch."

"And who can verify this?"

He swallows. Idiot. It's so obvious he's lying. "Pace can. I didn't see Dual so she wouldn't have known."

"If she walked out of her house to see the dead body, wouldn't she have walked past you sleeping on the couch?"

He blinks. Pauses. "I guess so."

"But she didn't wake you up when she walked past?"

He shakes his head.

"So you have no way to tell how long Dual was with the body?"

"She was in her underwear. Why would she have ... done anything criminal in her underwear?"

"That's not what I asked you."

"No. I have no way to tell. She's not that kind of person though."

"Why did you get up and leave so early, Hal? It was barely dawn."

"I was uncomfortable on the couch."

"Your house is closer to the Den than Dual and Pace's house, isn't it?"

Hal doesn't answer.

"So why would you end up further away if you were so drunk? Why wouldn't you just stumble home to your own bed?"

"We were hanging out. They're my friends."

"We? Who's 'we'?"

"Me and Pace and Dual – "

"You just said Dual didn't know you were there."

He flushes. "I meant we're all friends. But it was just me and Pace hanging out."

"Would you like to know what I think?" I sit back in my chair and eye him. I'm enjoying watching him squirm. "I think you stayed in Pace's room. You had sex without clearing it with us first, so now you're trying to lie about it. And what I don't think you realize is that the lying is a worse crime than the sex."

The kid looks like he's about to self-combust. I lean forward. "Tell me you at least used protection."

"Yes, of course."

A smile curls my lips. It's too easy. "We're done here."

As he stumbles out I sit a moment longer, formulating a plan.

*

Quinn is already in bed when I get home. I pull the sheet off him and climb onto his lap. "Hello," he smiles.

"Hal's been a naughty boy. I think we can pin the murder on him."

Quinn's eyebrows arch. "He's an excellent hunter, and the only one who knows how to keep the train running."

"So have him teach someone else, and when they're competent, set his punishment."

"I'd rather find the real killer."

"Do you honestly think that's going to happen? We've got nothing. No one on watch saw anything. Batch finished his shift, went home to his wife, they fell asleep, and when she woke he was gone."

"So why don't we pin it on Dual? She's useless – and she's more likely to have actually done the murder."

"Because I think Dual is hiding something, and I don't want her to die before I know what it is."

Quinn considers this for a while, then mutters, "If Luke can't figure out who actually did it before Hal's finished teaching someone the running of the train, then Hal goes down for it."

"Agreed."

I run my hands over him, but he just says, "Not tonight."

*

February 14th 2066

Josephine

My fist throbs and I've barely moved the punching bag. I glance at Luke, who is watching me expressionlessly. It's just after dawn and I'm still half-asleep as I hit the bag again, hard as I can.

"Stop," he says. "It's wrong."

"What is?"

"Everything."

I sigh. Regardless of – or maybe because of – what's happened, Luke and I have started our training classes. He's explained that I'm going to need to be proficient at both a striking technique and a grappling technique. Striking includes styles like karate, boxing, kick-boxing and that type of thing, while grappling is stuff like jiu jitsu and wrestling – on the floor as opposed to upright. I asked him what he uses and he called it krav maga, an Israeli form of mixed martial arts, which he said was a brutal combination of striking and grappling. He said it'd be good for me to learn eventually because it's perfect for allowing females to overpower much larger opponents. It inflicts the maximum amount of physical harm with minimal effort, but I'm obviously nowhere near ready for that.

The first thing he said we'd be working on is my 'blink instinct'.

"What's my blink instinct?" I asked.

Luke threw a punch at my head and I recoiled, squeezing my eyes shut. "That's your blink instinct," he smiled, fist mere millimeters from my nose. "You can't flinch or wince or close your eyes when someone goes to hit you. We'll work on that during sparring."

That was when he started me on the bag, but now apparently I'm too shit even for that.

"Place your feet shoulder-width apart," he directs me now. "Your left side tilts forward. Your hands go here, over your cheeks. Keep them here. Elbows in. Bend your knees."

I do as he says.

"Your left fist is your jab. You throw this to gauge the distance of your target, and to get him going a bit, keep him on his toes. Your right is your cross, and this is the one you're gonna hurt him with."

I throw a couple of quick practice jabs and follow them with a right cross toward Luke's face.

"Thumbs on the outside of your fist."

"Aren't I supposed to be wearing gloves?"

"Gloves teach you to be soft. You're not gonna be wearing gloves if you have to fight a Blood in the city, or a Fury outside that wall."

I get my stance right, trying to do as he says.

"Stronger," he orders.

"What does that mean? I'm not doing anything yet."

He looks at me like I'm a total moron. "Hold your core stronger, your stance, muscles, balance."

I try to do what he's telling me but think I just wind up looking constipated.

"Stop thinking about it so hard," he admonishes.

"You're telling me weird stuff that forces me to think hard!"

"Just feel your body."

I don't like my body. It betrays me. "How?"

He frowns, scrutinizing me. At last he says, "*Ah*. We've found our problem. Okay, get in your stance."

I do so. Luke places his hand on my belly. He hits it lightly, then moves his hand firmly up my abdomen, over my breast and up into my shoulder. I blush bright red – what the hell is he doing? – until I realize how unsexual it is. He is touching me like a physio might, or a doctor. He pinches and I wince.

"Focus."

I focus on where his hand is, and which muscles he's touching. He pinches the skin through my shoulder and back and chest, identifying the muscles I need to use.

"Keep your mind in these muscles," he tells me. "And punch through the bag, not at it."

I swing, hitting the bag way harder than I have before. It swings back. I turn to Luke, grinning happily.

"Your homework is to spend half an hour every night before you go to sleep meditating."

"Not my thing."

He is unimpressed. "You do it, or I don't train you."

"But why?"

"Because if you don't get in touch with your body and its capabilities then you're never gonna be able to use it properly."

"I don't even know *how* to meditate," I mutter.

"I'll give you a lesson later. I gotta head out and do something." He turns for the door.

"Where are you going? That was the shortest training session in history!"

"I have to talk to Batch's wife."

I start after him and he gives me a look. "I need to figure out who killed him more than anyone."

*

Luke knocks on the door of one of the larger houses. Batch and his wife, Lace, shared it with Lace's parents, one of whom answers the door. Her mother is in her sixties with sun-weathered skin and a long white braid.

"Hi, May," Luke greets her, giving her a big hug.

"Hi, kid."

"How is she?"

"Not good."

"Reckon I can talk to her?"

May looks at me, her eyes cold.

"I'm Dual," I say quickly.

"I know who you are."

I hesitate. "It's nice to meet you."

May gestures us inside. The living room looks exactly like a slightly larger version of the one in my house. It's a bit weird, actually – a bit disorienting.

"She's in bed."

"Do you think she'd mind if I went in and saw her?" Luke asks.

"I'm here," a voice says from a doorway and we look over to see presumably, Lace. She looks about thirty and pretty as a button, with a pixie nose and big eyes. Her blond hair is greasy and her skin is breaking out, probably from stress.

In her arms is a baby, and the little creature is beautiful. I can't help but stare at the child as she passes it to May. I am so distracted by it that I don't realize that Lace is crossing the room to me.

But I realize when she slaps me hard across the face. Shocked, I lift my hand to the stinging cheek, staring at the woman.

"How dare you come into my home?" she snarls.

"Woah, steady on," Luke tries, but Lace spits in my face.

I reel backwards. "I'm sorry," I manage to utter, before I turn and dash outside.

I feel dizzy as I wipe the spittle from my chin and neck. The sun is glaringly hot and sends an ache into my skull.

I am a thoughtless, cruel idiot. To come here and not think how it would make her feel, given the whole settlement thinks I murdered her husband. I sit on the ground, in the dust, because I'm not sure what else to do with myself.

*

Luke

The room is strangely still after Josi has gone.

"I'm so sorry, Lace," I say.

The baby squirms, breaking the tension that's permeated the air. May takes the child – I don't know her name as she was born while I was in a coma – into another room and I am left alone with Lace. I should have come to see her and Batch when I woke up. I should have at least congratulated them.

"Dual didn't kill him," I tell her simply.

Lace slumps onto the couch. "I don't think I care."

"I'm sorry," I say again, sitting opposite. "He was a good man."

"What does that mean?"

I'm not sure what to say.

"What if he was a bad man? Would that make it better that he'd died?"

"No. Sorry. I don't know why I said that."

Her expression softens a little. "What do you want, Luke?"

"I'm in charge of the case."

"The case." Her lips twist into a humorless smile. "As though any one of us knows what to do in a 'murder case'."

"I do." Sort of.

"Go on, explain it then."

"Basically I have to determine how Batch was killed, what weapon was used and where the murder took place. I've gotta gather the evidence. Then I have to start talking to people and working out who might be a suspect. I work out who has alibis for the night Batch was killed, which is tricky in this case because of the party. I need to work out who knew Batch well, if he had any altercations with anyone, if there might be a reason someone wanted him dead. Motive, means, opportunity."

"So am I a suspect?"

"That's what I'm here to determine. And to pay my respects."

"Isn't it usually the spouse who's guilty?"

"Sometimes." Often, actually.

Lace leans her head back against the couch and stares at the ceiling. She starts ticking things off on her fingers. "I didn't go to the party that night because I was here with Eve, so I didn't have the opportunity. The only weapon I know how to use is a gun – I don't even know how someone could cut off a man's head – so I didn't have the means. And as for motive, my husband and I just had a baby, so I'd say my motive to keep him alive is stronger, don't you think?" Her voice is drenched with bitterness.

"I know you didn't do it, Lace," I tell her gently. "But I will find out who did. Can I ask you a few questions?"

She nods.

"What time did you go to bed that night?"

"I'm not sure. I've been trying to sleep when Eve does. So probably around seven. Then I woke up a few hours later to feed her. Maybe around one."

"Was Batch home then?"

"No."

"So he didn't come home at all that night?"

"Not to my knowledge."

"You told Quinn yesterday that Batch came home and went to bed, then you woke to find him gone. Didn't you?"

She frowns. "I don't even remember having a conversation with him. I don't remember what happened two minutes ago. I haven't slept more than an hour or two in months."

"Okay, can anyone verify that you were here with Eve all night?"

"No, I guess not. Unless you want to interrogate my two-month-old daughter."

"When was the last time you saw Batch?"

"Before he started his shift on the wall."

"Can you think of anyone who might have a grudge against him?"

"No."

"Did you notice anything strange before that night? Anything that seemed out of place? Any unusual interactions?"

"No."

"What about Batch's behavior? Was he acting strangely?"

"No."

"Okay." I straighten up. This is getting nowhere. She doesn't have a clue what happened, that much is obvious, and her new-mother brain is addled with sleep deprivation. It could be possible, as Josi suggested, that the kill was random – that Batch was in the wrong place at the wrong time and was used in some other plot. Which means there are no clues to be found here. "Thanks, Lace, I'm sorry I had to ask this stuff."

"You're playing the part of the detective," she points out. "You have to say your lines."

"I'll figure it out," I promise. I hesitate awkwardly for a moment. "Can you do me a favor?"

She glares at me.

"Not say anything to Dual about what happened between us last year?"

Lace shakes her head with exasperation. Then without any warning she moans with deep, gut-wrenching despair.

I lurch to my feet, unsure what to do, but May is already rushing to take her daughter in her arms.

"Batch didn't come home," May tells me over the sobbing. "I would have heard him. Now go."

So I do. As the door shuts behind me the terrible sound of weeping is dimmed. Josi is sitting on the edge of the road, arms folded over her knees. She looks up miserably. "Is she okay?"

I shake my head.

"I'm sorry. I didn't mean to upset her."

"She was upset anyway." I reach for her hand and pull her up. She brushes the dust from her pants and we head toward the infirmary. "She probably needed to give someone a good slap."

"Glad I could help then." She sounds sincere. "Did you get any clues?"

"No clues. Which might be a clue in itself. She said that nothing out of the ordinary had happened, he'd been acting normally, and I believe she didn't have anything to do with it."

"So are you thinking I might be right about the kill being a message or a statement or something? Rather than a personal gripe with Batch?"

"Well I've spoken to the guys on guard duty with him, as well as his closest friends. They knew nothing, and said he'd been totally normal. Apparently he finished his shift on watch at midnight and then no one saw him again until you did."

"So we have a chunk of his time that's unaccounted for – from midnight until about 5:30 am."

"And you didn't go home until after 2, which means he wasn't placed at the crime scene until after then, or you would have seen him."

"So where the hell was he between 12 and 5:30?"

I shrug. "He wasn't at home with his wife, according to both Lace and May. Yesterday Lace said he did come home, but I honestly don't think she was lying – I reckon it's more likely she got confused about the days. So it's possible Batch could have been accosted on his way home and kept somewhere for a few hours, either dead or alive."

"Any idea where the killing took place?"

I shake my head. "Had to be a hell of a lot of blood."

"So you have to either clean it or hide it somehow."

"Might be time for me to start searching houses for any remnants."

"That'll make you popular." We head inside Dodge's lab to find him, Ranya and Mom all standing around Batch's body laid out on a table. The three of them are peering closely, talking animatedly, despite the fact that Ben is hammering repeatedly on his glass cage.

Meredith is cuffed, once again, to a nearby chair.

"What do we reckon, gang?" I ask and they all look up.

"Come here," Mom says, ushering Josi and I closer. The body is losing some of its stiffness – yesterday the rigor mortis was at its worse, but it's begun to lessen, making him easier to move. Batch's head sits a little apart from the body. "See this bruising around the sever line?"

Josi and I lean in close. The skin beneath where the head's been chopped off is indeed dark blue. "Yeah."

"We think the cause of death might not have been the decapitation, but strangulation."

"So someone choked him to death and then cut his head off," Josi surmises. "Would that explain why there wasn't much blood at the site?"

"It could."

"So he could have been killed where he was found?" I ask.

"Yes, or he could have been killed elsewhere and carried to that spot, where the killer then chopped his head off."

"Is anyone else finding this very weird?" Josi asks.

We all nod.

"There's no way this was a crime of passion," I sigh. "You don't take pains to set out a confusing crime scene like this unless it's all premeditated."

"Unless you kill someone in a fit of passion, realize the mistake and then try to cover it up by making it look like a completely different crime," Josi points out.

"True. But by the sounds of it no one would have cause to kill Batch in a fit of passion."

"How do we know?" she argues. "Nobody really knows anyone. Just because his wife didn't think there was anything weird going on doesn't mean there wasn't."

I look sideways at Josi. "Not everyone lies," I tell her softly.

"Sure they do," she replies calmly.

"The body wasn't at the crime scene for long before it was discovered," Meredith says abruptly and we all turn to stare at her.

"How do you know?" I ask.

"If a body remains undisturbed for hours after death, a process called livor mortis occurs. This means that the parts of the body touching the ground develop a discoloration, usually red or purple from blood accumulation. This body hasn't suffered that, which means it's been moved too often since death for it to have occurred. Is it also true that the body had yet to develop rigor mortis when you first moved it here?"

Ranya and Claire both nod.

"Then it was within the first three hours of death."

"So he was killed not long before I found him," Josi says. "It's looking more and more like I did it."

"We know you didn't do it," I try to console her.

"This is a bit gruesome for me. I gotta get to my shift in the fields," she says, heading out into the midday sun.

"Dodge," I sigh, "can you do any DNA magic?"

He shakes his head. "I don't have the means to get external DNA off his body, I only know how to analyze his."

"Don't bury the body," I tell them. "I want it kept as long as possible."

258

"We don't have the power to refrigerate it," Ranya protests.

"I'll speak to Quinn about having some rerouted. He doesn't get buried until this case is solved, alright?"

"And where will you put him?"

"I don't know. I'll sort something out."

Ranya throws up her hands and starts fussing about with things as though I have put her out personally.

"You alright, Mom?" I ask.

She nods and walks me to the door. "I know it's a horrible thing to say given the circumstances, but I'm glad to have something to do."

I kiss her on the cheek.

Meredith is watching us all very closely and there's something creepy about it. She and Mom are both drones, but under the lab lights they don't seem anything alike.

*

I spend the afternoon on a cooking shift in the kitchen with Eric, Rina and Grace, trying to come up with innovative recipes for potatoes, potatoes and more potatoes. And bread. There's a shitload of bread.

For once, my mind's not on food. It's stuck on Batch.

"Any idea who did it?" Eric asks me when it's clear I don't have any input about dinner.

Rina and Grace are both lean, hard women in their forties, and they watch me expectantly.

"I shouldn't talk about it," I say. "But I'm close, and it's definitely an isolated incident." A big fat lie.

"It's pretty obvious who did it," Grace snaps as she kneads dough.

"Was it her?" Rina asks in her soft, high voice. Both women, I have good cause to know, are excellent fighters, and both are raising children in The Inferno.

"Who?"

"Don't play dumb, Luke."

"It wasn't Dual," I tell them. "And I can tell you that for a fact." Another big fat lie.

"Never been a murder inside The Inferno before," Grace says shortly.

"And there won't be another one," I assure her.

"Better not be, Luke. Else why should we raise our kids here?"

I don't know how it became *my* responsibility to stop them from killing each other, as the second newest member of the compound, but okay. I don't point out that there isn't anywhere else to raise kids, either. I just nod.

"Get off your bum and grab me some herbs."

I do as I'm told, entering the big walk-in refrigerator. The air is cool in a direct contrast to the hot weather outside, so I hurry for the herbs, grabbing rosemary and mint. But at the door I pause with an idea. And I know immediately that it is *not* going to be a popular one.

Chapter 16

Josephine

I sit between Hal and Pace, with Will hanging from my neck like a monkey. The Den is full, but we're not here for a meal tonight. Quinn has called a community meeting, which is apparently pretty rare.

"Sure you don't know what this is about?" Pace asks me for the fifth time.

"Yes!" I exclaim. "Why do you assume I get told what's going on?"

"Because your lover boy is on the council table."

"He's not my lover boy, and he hasn't told me anything."

Will makes mushy kissing noises in my ear and I push him away as Hal and Pace giggle.

Quinn, Raven, Shadow, Ranya and Luke sit on a long table up the front of the hall, facing the rest of us who are perched around the place in no particular order. I find it amusing that they call it a council table, and can't help feeling as though we are all children playing at grown-up games. Or maybe that's just me.

I'm of the opinion that Shadow shouldn't be out of bed so soon, but he ignored me completely when I whinged at him to get back to the infirmary. He still looks pale from his gunshot wound, but he's tough as guts like everyone out here, and determined to suffer in silence.

"Okay, let's get started," Quinn calls over the din of two-hundred-and-sixty voices chattering curiously. Everyone settles down and there's a general hush. "We have a simple matter at hand tonight, a decision to be made. I don't feel comfortable making it myself, so we'll explain the situation and put it to a vote. Luke?"

Luke sits forward. "As you all know there's been a murder in The Inferno. The day Batch died was a very sad one for all of us, because he was a member of our family. I've been made responsible for the case, and I promise that I will find out who committed this crime. In order to do that I need access to Batch's body before he can be laid to rest."

"This isn't a matter for public vote!" someone shouts. I crane my neck to see an old man I don't know. "What happens to Batch's body is a decision for Lace to make."

"I have already discussed it with Lace and she's refrained from being involved in the decision. It concerns all of you because the only way I can think of to keep Batch's body from decomposing is to convert one of the fridges into a kind of morgue and keep him there for the duration of the case. The kitchen is a public space, and you all need to agree to it before I'll go ahead."

There is a general ruckus of outrage through the crowd.

I sit back in my seat, admiring Luke for trying, but knowing this is only going to end one way.

"This is unconscionable disrespect," May says loudly. "A man should be laid to rest, not kept in a kitchen fridge in the middle of a public area!"

"What about the health risks?" another woman says. "We can't be having a decomposing body around our food!"

"We would of course remove all the food and block off the area – " Luke starts.

"And the practicalities – we need the space," the woman goes on. "Have you ever tried to feed more than two-hundred mouths with only one fridge full of food? It's not gonna happen."

"Oh for god's sake, Grace," someone else groans. "It's not about the practicalities – have a scrap of empathy for once. This is about a man's death, and disrespecting his body and his wife."

"And keeping the body where the kids might see it!"

I watch as Luke slumps in his seat, rubbing his eyes wearily. "It would only be temporary – "

"How do you know? What makes you think you're ever gonna solve it?" a man asks.

"Well he certainly isn't going to solve it if he doesn't have access to the only piece of available evidence," I snap, and everyone turns to stare at me. I feel my cheeks flare, but hold my ground. "It's protocol in murder investigations to legally hold the body as evidence in the case and trial. It's not disrespect – it's correct practice and common sense. Sentimentality needs to be saved for later, when the killer has been brought to justice. Either that, or we leave a murderer walking among us."

Oh crap. I shouldn't have said the thing about the common sense or the sentimentality. Or the murderer walking among us. A ripple of anger and unease moves through the crowd.

"And what gives you the right to open your mouth?" someone asks. I can't see who.

"Oh, sorry, are we living in a fascist regime now?" I reply.

As the hall erupts into voices, Pace cracks up beside me, thoroughly tickled. I meet Luke's eyes and see the hint of a smile tug the corner of his lips.

I shrug, silently telling him *I tried.*

His expression replies *thanks anyway.*

"Alright, alright, settle down," Quinn barks over the hubbub. "Let's call it to a vote. All those who vote to keep the body refrigerated as evidence until the case is solved, raise your hand."

The three musketeers and I all raise our hands. On the stage Luke, Shadow and Raven raise their hands. Dodge does too and, surprisingly, my red-haired failed conquest, Eric. Luke's parents raise their hands, much to the disgust of several people around them. All up, it's only about thirty people out of more than two-hundred.

I can't believe Ranya hasn't raised her hand and, by the look of it, neither can Luke. It occurs to me that this could be a clue, and I start looking around the room at all the people who vote to bury the body. I commit their faces to memory; they've just become suspects. But the problem remains: it's still basically everybody.

*

I go with Luke to the lab to take a final look at Batch before he's put in the ground. Meredith is toiling away, so focused on whatever she's doing that she doesn't even look up at our arrival.

"Can you take one of your mental picture thingies for me?" Luke sighs.

"Yeah, but I can only see so much, and I can't remember things don't know."

He sighs again.

"Those are some awfully big sighs," I murmur, rubbing his back without thinking. It comes to me belatedly that this is probably too intimate a gesture, and I remove my hand quickly. Do friends rub each other's backs?

"It's idiocy," Luke says.

"It's crowd mentality, superstition and grief."

"Don't they want to know the truth?" he snaps, frustrated.

264

I shrug. "Don't take it on. We got what we could from the body and now we have to look elsewhere."

Luke looks at my face. "I get more emotional and you get more rational."

"It's a strange world," I agree.

"Meredith, you got any other little gems of information you want to share with us before it's too late?" Luke asks the scientist.

She looks up, distracted by her work. "I could have gone over him for DNA evidence if I'd had another day or two. Skin particles under the fingernails or in the wounds, hair follicles, blood or sperm residue ..."

"Why the fuck didn't you tell me that yesterday?"

"You didn't ask yesterday."

He looks about ready to hit her. "Is there anything you could do before the morning?"

"Why would I?"

"Because if you don't, I'll see to it that you're punished," he threatens.

I take his wrist and pull him away. "Let's go punch a bag for a few hours," I suggest.

"Josi – "

"This isn't a detention center," I tell him. "We don't 'punish' people for enacting their own human rights."

He tugs his wrist out of my hand and stalks away furiously. I watch him go, thinking him a very different man to the one I lived with.

After a few moments I turn back to Meredith. "You've done some really bad stuff," I say softly. "If it weighs on your conscience at all, feel free to lighten it a tad by helping us out. We'd appreciate it."

"I'm already helping you," she points out calmly. "I'm working on the Zetemaphine blocker to keep that brute alive. I can't do two things at once."

"Well could you please pause that job for the night and try to find us any clue at all to who killed this man?"

She considers me. Something seems to gentle in her eyes slightly and she nods.

"Thank you."

*

Luke

Blood fills my fingernails and pours from my gums, my ears, my nose, my eyes. My hands are around a neck, squeezing squeezing squeezing. All of my strength goes into stealing the breath of the body before me. My hands slip, though; there is too much blood. My feet slip next, and I land heavily on my hip, splashing the thick crimson liquid all over my face –

I jerk awake, sharp pain slicing through my side.

It takes me long seconds to orient myself. My bedroom in The Inferno. Dry, bloodless, just like my fingernails and gums are. I have fallen out of bed and landed on my hip.

Alone, I peer through the dark to the window, beyond which I can see a glowing silver moon. It is almost full.

Or, no. It was full a couple of nights ago. When Batch was murdered.

My skin crawls and even though I know there is no blood, I can taste it in my mouth.

Something under my bed catches my eye, a glint of metal, and I look more closely. Reaching curiously, I feel the cool sharpness of a blade. My blade, I see, as I pull it out.

Except that the knife is covered in dried blood. And I don't remember putting it under my bed.

*

February 16th, 2066

Josephine

Batch is buried at dawn as the sun rises over The Inferno. We are on the very north side of the compound, and the funeral might be beautiful if not for the dreadful sounds of the Furies beyond the wall, still trying to get in.

Lace's daughter cries during the whole service, though Lace remains stony-faced. Eric, who it turns out was Batch's best friend, says a few words, eyes streaming with tears.

I spend the funeral watching the faces of the people around me, trying to work it out. Various forms of grief are patent here on this clear morning. Some look uncomfortable, some look weary. Most look sad, a few angry.

It is a puzzle indeed, and Luke isn't the only one who wants to put the pieces together.

*

Luke

"Oh god."

"What's wrong?" Dad plonks himself down on the couch next to me.

"I think I've bitten off more than I can chew." I hand him the tablet and let him scan the instruction book I've been perusing. It's the only file I kept from the tablet I stole from John Smith and then gave to Josi.

It's the end of a very long day. I've been speaking to just about everyone I can, getting statements about their whereabouts during the hours unaccounted for, during which Batch was murdered. There's no way to prove any of it, of course, so it's all a bit pointless. But it still has to be done. I haven't told anyone about the knife under my bed, which was undoubtedly the weapon used to cut off Batch's head, because frankly it looks bad enough to implicate me. I need to work out who put it there before I tell anyone.

Dad's thick eyebrows furrow as he reads, scrolling through the pages. "Aren't you supposed to be working on the case? This is a big project."

"I'm working the case," I promise him, then gesture to the instructions. "But this is important. I'll work on it through the night if I need to, just do little bits at a time."

Eventually Dad looks up. "You want some help with it?"

I breathe out in relief. "I thought you'd never ask."

*

Dad and I head to the toolshed and have a look around. There's always someone here, no matter the time of day – a guy called Blue is currently repairing one of the dining tables from the Den. He hates me for some reason I don't know, so gives me a few hard looks before pushing off and leaving us to potter.

It's a blessing that this toolshed is impeccably well stocked. Living in a completely self-sufficient community means people have been building and maintaining everything for the last twenty years, so they've stolen a whole heap of building material and tools from the city. I find two big pieces of wood that have obviously come from one of the trees beyond the wall. Dad grabs a few tools and starts piling them together on the bench. We go back to the instructions to make sure we have most of the stuff we need, and have to put our heads together to come up with ways to improvise the rest.

"We don't have delicate enough tools for the bridge," I point out, scratching my cheek.

"We can hand-carve that bit," Dad says.

"Maybe you can, but I can't."

"I'll show you."

I start measuring the wood and making the pencil markings where it'll need to be cut. "You and Mom going alright?"

Dad's gathering a straightedge, a plane and a jig in order to start the fingerboard. He starts looking around for the right bit of wood. "Sure."

"Do you … wish you were still at home?"

"No, son," he says. "It's just an adjustment. Your mom and I have lived in that house for thirty years. And all our things …"

Christ. The house will be reclaimed by the bank and all their things will be discarded. Including all my stuff from childhood, everything they own, and everything that once belonged to Dave.

My hands stop and I am utterly horrified. "I didn't think – "

"It's alright," he tells me gently. "They're just things. It matters, to be here with you."

"But Dave – "

"Wouldn't have cared about all that stuff."

"But we do. We care about it." There's a wooziness in my heart. I can't believe I brought them here without thinking about what they'd be losing.

"No, Luke," Dad says firmly. "Possessions don't connect us with Dave. Love does. Longing does."

I swallow, barely holding it together. I nod. "Sorry, Dad. For leaving you guys when it happened. I shouldn't have … I was a coward."

"I'm sorry too."

"What are *you* sorry about?"

"For not being me anymore."

I look up, struck by the words. He's concentrating on his measuring, tongue poking out the side of his moustached mouth. "You are you."

"No, mate," Dad murmurs. "I don't think I am."

We work quietly for the rest of the afternoon because I don't know what to say to such words. The longing he spoke of is palpable in the air between us – longing for his dead son and longing for the man he used to be. But what I'm not sure he realizes is that the longing itself is new for him, since the cure. And to me, the longing seems like life itself.

*

February 20th, 2066

Josephine

Hal's been ordered to teach someone to keep the train running. There's always meant to be a couple of people at the one time who know how to maintain it, but at the moment there's just him. He asked a bunch of people who said no, and since there were no volunteers, I decided to put myself forward. Truth is, the books Luke got me are great, but they're all fiction, and my brain feels like it's shriveling to the size of a pea without anything new to learn. It's an awful feeling, worse than physical starvation. It makes me dream of being trapped, the cage around me shrinking so that I must shrink with it or be crushed.

I don't, however, look forward to spending extra time with Hal, even though he's become one of my best friends. Pace has spent the last several nights crying. She would gut me if I admitted to having heard her, and she'd hate for me to act any differently around Hal but still. I feel awkward being in the middle of whatever it is.

I follow him down into the train tunnel. It's instantly cooler than the hot air above. "This train was built in the 2020s so she's getting on a bit," Hal tells me fondly. "We took control of her back when we started The Inferno – it's easily the biggest victory we've ever had."

"Where is it now?" I ask, peering into the pitch black.

"On a circuit. Currently she'll be about sixty-seven miles away. Today's operational speed is two-hundred-and-ninety-eight miles per hour, which means she'll arrive in approximately thirteen and a half minutes."

"Oh. Approximately."

"She runs on a magnetic levitation line, which was first used in Shanghai in 2004, at lower speeds than this, of course. The technology's pretty geriatric at this point, but she still runs beautifully."

"How does it know where to stop?"

"She doesn't stop – she's in perpetual motion and has been since the day she was built. The algorithm makes her run at different speeds each day, so her exact location can't be predicted by the Bloods."

"But they could just put constant surveillance on the city stations."

"She runs on a line that hasn't been operational in the city for over thirty years. The Bloods didn't have a clue how we were moving in and out of the city without detection. Until they did know. But Luke destroyed their intel before he came out here the first time."

"Yeah but if Jean whatshername knew the information, then she still knows it, regardless of what's on her computer." I know her name. I know it very well: Jean Gueye. She's a woman I think about a lot. Because she's the person who ordered my death.

"Yeah," Hal agrees.

"So ... what?"

"So we have to be really careful."

"But what if the Bloods just jumped on the train? It would lead them straight to us."

"They're not allowed to leave the walls."

"One of them did." The one I shot.

Hal shrugs. "How would they find us? The line is so long and covers such an expansive area that they'd never know where to get off."

I shake my head. Someone will figure it out, one day. Or they'll set up a permanent watch of the stations and wait for us to come to them. Especially after our latest attack on the Collingsworth lab. They're going to want Meredith back. And then we're screwed.

"She's the only transportation we have," he says. "And we're lucky to have her. We can't move above ground because of the Furies and they don't have access to the tunnels. The risk of the train is one of the reasons we don't make too many attacks and turn ourselves into too much of a priority target – we can't afford to lose her."

"Yeah, I know," I sigh. "It just seems, like, *outrageously* risky."

"I thought you liked taking risks." He smiles.

"What gave you that impression?"

Hal shrugs, blushing a little. "Your boyfriend was a Blood."

I freeze.

"He used to talk about you all the time, Josephine."

"Don't call me Josephine. Raven and Quinn still have no idea who I am."

He spreads his hands quickly. "Okay. Sorry."

"Mouthing off like that can get people hurt."

Hal stares at me, looking mortified. "Is this ... Are you angry because ... Did Pace say something ... ?"

"Not a word."

"I hardly remember what happened!" he tries helplessly. "I was so drunk – "

"Oh *please*. Just grow a pair and talk to her, Hal."

The rest of the lesson is awkward after that. When we're done I hesitate, asking, "Do I have to start referring to the train as a female now?"

It breaks the tension and Hal grins. "It's a requirement."

I head gratefully back up into the settlement for my next lot of training.

Luke is waiting for me on the mats. There are other people sparring, but he concentrates on me, pushing me harder than anyone else and not giving me any breaks. He's in a foul mood, snapping at me constantly and pacing around in annoyance.

I decide to keep my mouth shut, not wanting to get into a shouting match with him in front of the other trainees. They all thought I was lucky to have personal training with him, but after his last roar of disgust at my inept kicking, I think they have now reconsidered.

When we're finished I storm out. He jogs after me. "What are you doing?" I hiss. "Don't follow me."

"Why?"

"That was humiliating!"

"Fine." He changes direction.

After dinner I find a note on my bed. It is written on the torn-out page of a book, as paper is scarce. It's sacrilegious to ruin a book, in my opinion, and I can't believe he's done it.

I can't go to your house, but we need to talk. Meet me at our spot.

Our spot? I definitely was not under the impression that we have a *spot*.

When I find him in the dark I can't help but laugh. "You've got a good sense of humor, Luke Townsend. I'll give you that much."

His smile flashes in the moonlight. We're at the edge of the settlement under the only copse of trees, in the spot where we had our 'break-up' and said we hated each other.

"I'm nothing if not sentimental," he agrees.

"Why aren't you allowed to come to my house?"

"I'm allowed to, I just don't think I should at night unless we want Raven and Quinn to think there's something going on between us."

"What's up?" I sigh.

"Sorry about today." He runs a hand through his hair. "Although I'm not really that sorry."

"Good apology."

"You need serious training," he insists. "I can't be going easy on you, and I'm surprised you would want me to."

"I don't want you to!"

"Okay," he laughs. "So we're agreed." Luke hesitates. "I'm still sorry. I wasn't myself."

"You were angry."

"I'm always angry." He meets my eyes. "It's getting worse."

"Luke," I murmur. "Don't … do anything rash. Don't tell anyone."

"It's dangerous, me being like this."

"Your change won't happen until the blood moon. Meredith has months to work it out."

"You were normal every other day of the year," he points out. "But I feel … I'm not normal."

Ben said he had no idea how the virus would react in an adult subject. Which means that Luke could have completely different symptoms to me, having been injected as an adult instead of a child. Looking at him now, he looks a lot like he did the night he injected himself. Aggressive, restless … His mood swings have been pretty wild over the last few days.

"You have all of your cognitive functions," I insist. "You're aware of your actions. You're still *you*."

"For how long? I have to tell them."

"Tell who? Quinn and Raven?"

He nods.

"No. No *way*."

"Josi – "

"If they know you have a virus that makes you aggressive and violent, they're going to think you murdered Batch."

"Better me than you."

"Better they just find the *actual* killer," I say.

There is a moment of silence, and then Luke asks, "But what if I did do it?"

Cold shears through my heart, but I say, steady as iron, "Then we'll make sure nobody ever knows."

Chapter 17

February 20th, 2066

Josephine

I am making my way home from my secret meeting with Luke when it happens. I am feeling like a bit of an idiot, creeping around in the dark for no reason, when I see someone move behind a nearby building. I pause, something about the movement piquing my curiosity. There's nothing behind that building – it's just an equipment shed, with only a few yards of space between it and the wall.

I hesitate. Maybe if someone hadn't just been murdered I might not be so nosy. Or maybe I would. Who cares. I walk closer, keeping to the shadows.

Flattening myself against the side of the building, I listen. The soft scuffle of footfall reaches me, and then two male voices. They're too soft for me to distinguish the words. I peer around the corner as carefully as I can until I can make them out.

Both big men, their silhouettes roughly the same height. One is slimmer than the other. They are speaking with urgency and jerk

276

hand movements. There is a long silence, and then they move, falling into each other's arms.

And as they do they catch a shaft of moonlight, and I can see perfectly who it is, kissing as though their lungs don't work.

Hal and Eric.

*

I dawdle home, not wanting to see Pace. My stomach is in knots. What am I going to tell her? Nothing – it isn't my place. But how can I look at her and *not* tell her she's in love with a guy who is clearly in love with someone else?

If it wasn't so horrible for her, it would almost be funny that I tried to pick up a gay guy. I clearly have zero ability to detect sexual chemistry.

Pace is crying again in her room when I get home. "Oh god," I mutter. Taking a breath, I knock on her door.

"Go away!"

"I'm coming in."

"Dual, I swear to – "

I barge in and sit down on the bed, despite her groan of annoyance. She buries her face back in her pillow so I won't see her tear-streaked cheeks.

"This is insanity," I tell her. "He's not worth so many tears! No guy is!"

She looks at me over the pillow. "Now I just feel sad for *you*."

"Huh?"

"You don't let yourself feel anything for anyone."

"That's not ... true," I say faintly.

"You just pity yourself."

My mouth falls open in outrage. "I'm feeling something for you right now and it ain't good!"

"Go away," she moans.

"Just please promise me you'll either talk to him or stop this moping. You slept with the guy. It's awkward now. It's not the end of the world."

"I hate you."

I head for the door.

"I'm not crying because it's awkward, you idiot," she sniffs. "I'm crying because I'm in love with my best friend and he doesn't love me back. And that's, like, the worst thing ever."

I sigh, because it's not the worst thing ever, but I guess it is pretty bad.

*

February 27th, 2066

Luke

"We're never gonna finish it," I sigh morosely.

"Still got four days," Dad disagrees.

"I don't have enough hours in the day."

"We'll work through the night then."

I am sanding a piece of wood that I've cut into a rounded shape. Dad's drilling holes in his, using a battery-operated drill that isn't really big enough for the job, but he's making a heroic effort to ignore that fact.

"Wanna come to training with me and Josi?" I ask him. It's late, and we've been in the shed for a few hours now.

Dad smiles slightly. I notice it because he rarely smiles anymore. "Think I'm a bit beyond training, mate."

"Rubbish. You could help me with her."

"What's the problem?"

I shrug. "She can't connect with it. Can't focus. Her head's a million miles away all the time."

He considers this for a while, working away. Eventually he suggests, "Put some music on while you train."

I stare at him, and then I smile. "You're a brilliant man, Dad."

"I am," he agrees.

*

February 28th, 2066

Josephine

Tonight Luke shows up to the training room looking excited about something. He's holding the old stereo from Raven and Quinn's house, and he's got a long extension lead, obviously connected to the generator.

"What are we doing?" I ask curiously.

He puts the music on and it pounds loudly through the room. Everyone turns in surprise to stare at him as he starts dancing.

I watch, astonished.

"Today's lesson," he says over the thumping, sexy bass, "is to get out of that damn head of yours."

I start laughing; I can't help it. Everyone does.

And then Luke runs a training session with all the trainees where we basically just dance while we punch, and it's actually really fun.

*

March 1st, 2066

Josephine

I have been studying with Hal every day for the last fortnight. He's taught me a bunch about how the train runs, the mechanics of the engine, the algorithm and programming that determine the train's movement patterns, and how to reprogram, override, maintain and repair the basics.

I haven't talked to him about The Thing I Saw. And despite the fact that my discomfort with his dishonesty is making things a tad awkward between us, I am still enjoying myself immensely. There's loads more to learn, but he says I could get by at a pinch now.

Today he spoke at length about the elasticity and damping properties of the rail bed, plus the equation of motion for the interaction system, and I ate it all up. He loves having someone to tell this stuff to, as he's pointed out that no one else in The Inferno could care less about how the train works, just as long as it does.

"You have an engineer's mind," he tells me.

I don't tell him that it just seems that way because I can remember every word he says. Instead I smile and say that maybe one day I'll be an engineer as good as he is.

It's an odd prospect. Certainly not something I ever imagined myself doing. I mean, I was never going to be able to get a proper job in the city – not with the Bloods watching me, and not with people's aversion to me. But here ... I guess in a way I can do whatever I want, as long as it's needed by the settlement. No chance of ever being a concert cellist, of course, as I imagine in my most secret of hearts.

"How did you learn all this?" I ask Hal.

"My dad. We came here together."

"Not your mom though?"

"She died from the injection."

"From the *cure*?"

He nods.

"God."

"You don't hear about all the people it kills when it's administered," he says. "They hide it well."

I rub my eyes. *Why do they keep using it?* It is bewildering. "I'm constantly amazed at people's capacity to hurt each other," I say.

On that topic, we have made no progress in the murder case. Meredith said she 'might' have found something on Batch's body, but has been taking *ages* to analyze it and won't even tell us what it is.

"That's true," Hal says. "But we're very good at caring for each other, too."

"Are we?"

He looks at me but I drop my eyes, not wanting the intimacy of his blue gaze. "You haven't been cared for?"

I shrug. "Yeah, sure, I know what you mean. Guess I'm just a pessimist."

"But have you?" he presses.

I frown. I don't want to talk about this. Two people have taken care of me in the course of my life. One of them is dead. One of them is not, but his method of taking care of me was to lie to me and report my behavior to the people I hate most.

"Being taken care of is overrated," I say shortly. "Taking care of yourself is better all round."

"Pace takes care of me," Hal admits. "She's one of the few. It feels good."

"And yet you lie to her." It's out of my mouth before I can stop it. But now that it's out there, I can't help wanting his response.

"What are you talking about?"

"I saw you," I confess. "You and Eric."

Hal freezes.

"Why do you keep it a secret? Why not just be open about it, and then you wouldn't have to lie to your best friend who also happens to be in love with you?"

He says nothing – too shocked, I think.

"Also, while we're on the subject – why did you sleep with her if you're gay? It seems cruel to me."

Hal closes his eyes, mortified beyond belief. "Sexuality can be fluid, Dual. I wanted to want her, and every now and then I kind of did. I love her. I'm just not – "

"In love with her," I finish. "If you were upfront from the start there wouldn't be a problem."

"I couldn't be!"

"Why not?"

"It's a long story," Hal says, shaking his head.

I watch him for a while. I don't have much sympathy for lies. But I do feel sorry for the guy. He looks so thoroughly miserable right now that my anger ebbs away and I simply wonder at the difficulty he must go through, keeping his true feelings a secret from the people he cares most about.

My heart jerks painfully in my chest as I realize that this is exactly what Luke did for the last three years and I can't forgive him for it, can't even find space in my heart to feel compassion for what he went through. It's a burden, keeping secrets and telling lies. But surely it's also cowardice.

"I hope you can be honest with her," I tell Hal, and then I start climbing back up the steps out of the tunnel.

"*You're* not honest," he points out.

"Yes I am."

"You're the most dishonest person I've ever met."

It hits me like a blow, like a mortal wound. I don't know if he's just trying to hurt me or if it's true.

When I emerge into the afternoon sunshine it's to the sound of screaming.

The horde of Furies beyond the wall hasn't lessened or abated. It's impossible to ignore, as they have now surrounded the entire settlement and spend all day and night screaming to get in.

I shudder as I walk. Keep walking. Not even sure where I'm going. I would go onto the wall but I don't want to see the Furies

They're too frightening, their gazes too cold and too human and too savage. They have never flocked like this, according to the resistors – they have always roamed, which was how we were able to hunt them. Something has changed. Now they're trying to get in.

So I go for a run. The circuit around the wall is twelve and a half miles and takes me about an hour. I do it in fifty-five minutes today, and as I run I feel myself start to calm. I think of all the things I should have said to Hal. I wish I had encouraged him more, instead of berating him. I wish I had asked about Eric, given him some hint that it's a wonderful thing to have found mutual love.

Because Pace and Hal haven't been speaking much lately, it's been down to me and Will to make the conversations happen, which means we inevitably start talking about weird stuff like the wingspans of bats or the names of constellations or the height of the ocean tide in relation to the type of moon in the sky. He also really likes it when I tell him stories like the one Luke told me about the Seaborn. He knows a few of his own Celtic myths. There was one about a kelpie – a dark-spirited water horse – whose sole purpose is to drown humans in the watery depths, and one about fey creatures who are physically incapable of telling lies, but are very good at cunning tricks. I love that one, and think I will tell Luke. And now, after so much talk, I think I've decided I like Will better than the other two idiots. They can stay silent and surly forever as far as I'm concerned.

A bird calls as I run past the gate. There's a sudden gust of shock and hope in my chest and I career around, looking for its source, but it's only Shadow, whistling to me. Of course it's Shadow. I wave to him and he motions for me to come up, but I shake my head and go past.

At home I find another note on my bed. This one is on the back of a page from *Brave New World*. *I want to know what passion is. I want to feel something strongly.*

Instead of writing on it he has circled letters and words that I have to piece together like a proper detective. It's not for any reason except that he knows it will tickle me. *Dodge's lab at midnight.*

*

March 2nd, 2066

Josephine

So I sneak over to our midnight rendezvous, feeling very clandestine. Luke is already there when I arrive, down the end in the single orb of lamplight with Dodge and Meredith.

"Two things," Meredith says. "First, I have managed to identify the Zetemaphine in Luke's blood, and work out how it's affecting him."

"Didn't you already know that?"

"No. I've identified the strain of virus, which is no easy thing to do when it works so seamlessly to transform the rest of his cells. Your real name is Josephine Luquet, isn't it?"

I blink. "Uh … yep."

"Then you've been infected with the Zetemaphine. Which means you are the sole survivor of the tests, which in turn means you're the subject that Dr Collingsworth managed to inoculate, correct?"

"Correct."

"I will need your blood – lots of it – tissue samples, bone marrow, urine and stool samples, spinal fluid and brain fluid."

I stare at her. "Jesus. Why don't you go ahead and just take my bones and organs too?"

"I would if I could," she assures me. "A brain scan would make this a lot simpler, but, alas – "

"Hell *no*," Luke exclaims. "Ben didn't need any of that stuff when he made the blocker!"

"I am not Ben Collingsworth," Meredith replies simply.

284

As one we all turn to look at the man in question. Tonight he is crouched in a corner of his cell, staring at us with chilling awareness.

"I need to identify the drug in your system, understand how it works against the Zetemaphine and synthesize it into something I can inject Luke with. I have no confidence that I can do this, because I have no test subjects and because the rapid rate of his cell degeneration means he has very little time left."

I feel cold cold cold in my heart. "Yes," I say. "Do it, of course do it."

"Josi – " Luke starts, but I hold up a hand for silence.

To Meredith I say, "Take whatever you need."

"Excellent. Second, I have the results of the tests I did on the extra fluid I found on the victim's body."

"Extra fluid?" I repeat. "That sounds gross."

"What is it?" Luke asks.

"It's semen. Not his own."

We stare at her, then at each other, our minds suddenly alive with what this could mean, if anything. It could definitely point to the fact that he was having an affair with a man, which could give us a new suspect for the murder. As Dodge and Meredith take as many of the samples as they can tonight, Luke and I talk and talk it around in circles, trying to work out who Batch might have been sleeping with.

When we're done, hours have passed and I'm feeling thoroughly poked and prodded. Dawn is nearing.

"Do you think it means anything?" I ask Luke as we enter the blue-gray dark outside the lab.

"I don't know. It could." But I can hear in his voice that he doesn't believe it.

I feel frightened, suddenly. Because I can see something fading in his eyes.

"I deny it to myself every second I'm awake," he tells me very softly. "But at night the truth creeps out."

And the worst part is that I understand completely. I remember the denial, the disbelief, and I remember how under the moon the nightmares couldn't be held at bay any longer.

"You didn't do it. We're going to find who did." But the promise sounds hollow to my own ears.

"Can I come home with you?" he asks, his voice breaking just as my heart does.

I close my eyes, willing every ounce of strength I have to the surface, every piece of coldness I possess. It's so cruel, this coldness, for the hours he sheltered me from night terrors are too many to count. But if I spend the night with him I will spend every night with him, and to be with a man I don't trust and haven't forgiven would be the cruelest thing of all. It would poison the love between us, suffocate it from our lungs until we were both broken and spent. I can't do that to him, or to myself. I am barely managing our new friendship as it is.

"No," I murmur. "I can't."

So we part.

I creep to my house, and Luke goes to his. I can't help but watch him move down the road, his gait tall and strong as always, but slower now, as though he wishes to walk all night and never dream again.

My treacherous heart is calling to him. Begging him to turn around and come after me, come to my house, my room, my bed. It is begging him to try harder, to fight harder, to ignore every word I've ever spoken about us being apart. The treachery of this heart knows no bounds, and I don't know what I'm going to do with it.

∗

The sun sinks and I stay in the field. Everyone leaves for the Den, but I stay and I don't know why. I haven't slept a second in thirty-two hours, not since well before the lab session I came from this morning.

I feel dazed. And all I can think about is *can I come home with you* and *you have very little time left.*

Tilting my face to the night sky, I breathe in the smell of salt. I run my fingertips over the wheat; it reaches as high as my head and I feel invisible. I feel I am vanishing.

A rustle behind me. So soft I barely hear it. Turning a little, I see him. He's moving slowly through the tall stalks, eyes on me.

He circles me, and I move with him. We walk silently through the field, hands reaching to brush the scratchy edges around us.

He draws closer and circles me again. Watching me, always watching me. It feels like a dance. I look up at the moon. Feel his breath on the back of my neck as he passes close behind.

I imagine a bird flying over the moon and my heart leaps with a fantasy of delight. I know they are dead, all of them. But the one in my mind's eye is so real, and its dark shape holds within it the impossible pursuit of freedom. It is wistful and melancholy, and I go with it.

When finally I come back down, down to the earth and to my body, there is a gaze on my skin. Under the gaze I can feel my body, really feel it, for the first time.

Slowly I look at Luke.

"Maybe you're the kind of creature everyone wants to have," he says, so softly, "But no one ever can."

Chapter 18

March 3rd, 2066

Luke

Dad and I have worked our fingers to the bone, cutting, sawing sanding, drilling, joining, gluing, painting. I've spent all evening negotiating with Rina – she plays the violin but hasn't been particularly forthcoming about giving up her strings. For the bow, I've accumulated a whole bunch of hair from the ladies willing to help out. And it's nearly done. The only problem is varnishing, which will take at least a month, but I figure I can do that after today and it won't matter too much.

Building something over these last few weeks has been a surprising pleasure; building it with my father an incomparable sweetness.

The sun is rising as we finish and stand back to look at our creation. Morning light strikes it through the window, and dust dances through the beam above it.

"I'm proud of you," Dad tells me. "And not just for this."

"I'm proud of you too," I reply, voice rough.

"What on earth for?"

"For still being you even though you've had pieces stolen. For coming here."

He claps me on the shoulder. "I gotta say. It's really something, isn't it?"

"It is," I agree, looking at the beautiful cello we have just built.

*

Josephine

Today is a dreamless nightmare. Today is worse than I imagined a day could be. Today is my twenty-first birthday, but that's beside the point.

Yesterday was strange. I was delirious with exhaustion after the night of testing, delirious with heartache and worry for Luke. The moment in the field with him seems like a dream, and to be honest I'm not entirely sure it wasn't.

We came up with a plan to talk to Eric, who was close enough to Batch that he might be the only who knows about the affair. I haven't told Luke about Hal and Eric, because it isn't my secret to tell, and there's no reason yet to suspect it has anything to do with the case.

That's the plan, anyway. To keep going with the hunt for clues, hoping against all better judgment that we stumble upon a miracle, something that means we have not stepped back in time to the days of the blood moon and its deadly clutches.

But before I can find Luke and head over to Eric's house, Quinn calls a public announcement. We all go to the main stretch of road, which leads to the gate beyond the wall. People have been called off work duty and training, which means that something serious is happening.

I stand with Pace and Will. Hal was on watch duty with Shadow this morning, so he'll probably still be on the wall.

Raven stands with Quinn before the gate. They both look grim. Behind them the disturbing sounds of the Furies drift in, unruly and desperate as ever.

"A dark day, friends," Quinn says to us. "The murderer among us has been found."

A quicksilver rustle goes through us.

What?

I look desperately for Luke. But I can't see him anywhere. My pulse explodes in terror. *Where is he where is he where is he –*

"Indisputable proof and a confession seal it. The culprit is to be exiled today. All who wish to witness may climb the wall. We are not a dictatorship, though. You are permitted to leave and not think of this ugliness again. We, your leaders, are here to ensure your protection, your prosperity, and most of all your freedom."

There is a general rush to the wall. Everyone wants to know who it is. But I think it's more than that. I think there's a sense that, for something of this nature, there must be witnesses.

I feel queasy, my mind rushing to work out how I can stop it. This can't happen. It can't. I'll die first.

The gate opens and shuts below us, and a figure stumbles out into the beyond, straight towards the waiting crowd of monsters.

But it is not Luke.

It is Hal.

I feel everything in my body go numb with a different kind of horror, and to my shame, a deep measure of relief.

Beside me Pace goes rigid and a strangled, almost inhuman sound tears from her mouth. I catch her as she falls and hold her upright. Her legs have utterly given out and her breathing is ragged like a dying person's.

"Oh god," she whispers. "Oh no."

Hal is desperately hammering on the gate as the Furies move in. "I didn't do it!" he screams. "It wasn't me, I swear!"

"He didn't do it!" I shout to Raven and Quinn, but they are stony-faced and they don't even glance at me. I don't understand what's going on. Luke and I haven't found any indication that Hal had anything to do with the murder.

There are dozens of the ferocious creatures descending on Hal as he sobs to be let back in. But the gates don't open, and he is forced to face them.

"Let him back in!" I scream desperately. My mind knows there will be no letting him in, but my heart can't stop shouting. "Please, Quinn – he's innocent!"

"Hal!" Pace shouts suddenly. "Hal! *Hal*!" And she keeps shouting his name, over and over again, her throat hoarse.

Below, Hal is fighting for his life with a horrible urgency, an image I will carry with me to my grave.

I motion for Will to take hold of Pace as she is catatonic with shock, and then I sprint to the nearest guard and wrench his bow from him. I don't know how to shoot a bow. I can't even get to his arrows. But I try anyway, try to at least kill one of the beasts attacking Hal, pointless as it may be.

The guard shoves me away, reclaiming his bow.

"Help him," I implore.

The man is as full of despair as I am, but he doesn't fire any arrows.

We watch as Hal is overcome by Furies who tear at him, devouring him alive. The sick tear and rip of flesh reaches us, along with Hal's screams that seem to go on for so much longer than they should.

"Hal! Hal! Hal!" Pace keeps shouting, over and over.

And then a shot does fire. A single arrow.

It sinks straight into Hal's head, killing him instantly and cutting off his horrible shrieks.

I look to my right and see Luke lowering his bow. His hands tremble. But his expression is cold, brutally cold.

There is a woozy horror in my head, but also an overwhelming gratitude for what he did. The Furies keep eating Hal's dead body. It's so gruesome I don't know how any of us can witness this and still remain human.

I stumble back to Pace, who is frozen like a corpse herself. I don't know what to do. I don't know how to help her.

Will is curled into a ball, sobbing violently. I don't have enough arms to try to hold them both. Luke comes to us, lifting Pace and carrying her down the steps. She curls into him, burying her face in his neck. I try to support Will beneath the arms, and several people reach to help me before Shadow pushes through them and lifts the small boy, carrying him after Luke.

I stop a moment. Everyone is flooding down the wall to the ground. They have seen enough, witnessed enough. Some cry, most are silent. But I turn, dazed, to see that several yards along the wall stands Eric.

He is so straight it's as though there is iron around his spine. I go to his side and stand with him, and he doesn't look at me once. He simply gazes at the mess on the ground, something completely empty in his face.

The monsters keep at it for hours. And we stay for hours, the two of us alone on the wall except for the guards, who have all turned their backs on the horror.

We're very good at caring for each other, too.

Oh, god, the *waste* of it. He was such a gentle, kind young man.

I need to be with Pace and Will now. But I can't leave Eric. And I can't leave Hal. Some twisted part of me can't leave him.

Eric moves at long last, sees me as though only just realizing I'm here. "Dual," he says.

"Eric." My voice aches.

He walks, dazed, from the wall.

I stand alone now, and don't know what to do. The sun sets and through the dead trees it looks golden. Someone moves behind me and I see Raven appear from the steps. She stares expressionlessly down at the macabre execution.

"How could you do this?" I manage to whisper. "You *know* he didn't do it."

"I don't know any such thing."

"But even a quick death," I sigh, tears spilling down my face. I never used to cry. Never. Now I have more tears than I can fit in my body.

"He was not sentenced to death," she tells me. "But exile."

"Exile?" I exclaim. "Exile into the arms of dozens of waiting Furies?"

"We gave him a chance at survival," she says, and that's when I hear it. The abrupt vulnerability in her voice. She's upset.

"There was never a chance," I tell her. "Don't lie to yourself."

"Do you know who did it?" she asks softly.

I turn to look at her dark, dark eyes. The red of her hair is glinting in the sunset. I can't speak, I am so angry.

"He would have died, no matter what."

"Why?"

"He slept with Pace."

It makes me stop. "So?"

"So it's forbidden, unless we sanction it. I made sure he took with him the fear that permeates this settlement."

I am too dazed to understand it. It is too absurd. I feel as though I am back in the city, abuse of power and invasion of privacy running rampant. There is so much space here. Infinite space. We need *more* people. We should be growing our numbers, not murdering them. But I can't speak, can't argue. I am too shell-shocked, too weary by far.

"You could have stopped it from happening like this, though," Raven tells me. "It could have been quick and silent and private. An overdose of something in his sleep. If only you had been honest about who really murdered Batch."

Then she leaves me to anxiously worry that she knows the truth. *What if I did kill him?*

Then we will make sure no one ever knows.

Yes, I could have changed this. I could have stopped it, if I had spoken out. But I wouldn't have. And I wouldn't speak now, given the chance.

I would stay quiet through the nightmare, over and over again, no matter how many times I had to witness it. Because to speak meant condemning Luke, who I know deep down is the real killer, and I will never be capable of such words. I woner if this makes me as corrupt as Raven. I wonder if it makes me as dishonest.

Chapter 19

Raven

I leave Dual and walk around the wall until I am on the opposite side of the compound, staring out at the sea beyond. The Furies have all gone to Hal, so the sand of the beach is empty.

My skin feels unclean.

I thought this would feel the opposite. That it would be like tying up loose ends, like a baptism of fire for The Inferno. A way to move forward with a scorched-clear slate. But actually it feels like dirtying my very soul.

I come here most nights. To watch the ocean.

It is the only thing, without exception, that gives me peace. The counterweight to the hatred, which is what sustains me.

I decided many years ago that I would like to drown. One day, when I am ready.

*

Luke

Pace and Will have become mad creatures. She is raging around the house breaking things, while Will is curled on the couch sobbing like a maniac. Shadow is sitting on a chair, watching. Meanwhile I say stupid things designed to comfort that don't.

"Where the fuck is Josi?" I hiss, panicked.

I am not equipped to handle this. I don't understand grief. I am not good with it. I couldn't deal with my mother's grief, or my father's, so I left them and didn't go back. I cannot deal with my own, so I put it in a very small, locked box. I don't know how to fix this. I don't know how to make it stop.

The pain in the room feels magnificent and throbbing. It feels too big to fit within the walls.

Will eventually cries himself to sleep but Pace keeps moving. She breaks more stuff, and cries and kicks the couch. She even punches through a window, and I can't make her stop for long enough to bandage her hand. It seems so strange to me that her feelings should be so ... overt. I have only ever known dark things to exist within, in tight little corners, but this is like a pantomime. I think it's her unselfconscious expression of her grief that is making me so uncomfortable.

As night falls, Josephine finally comes. She takes one look at the absolute chaos that Shadow and I have been unable to prevent, and she deals with it. She crosses to Pace and grabs her, shoving her against the wall to get her to pause long enough to look into Josi's eyes. She takes Pace's face and says, "You will survive this. Soon it will ease, and you'll come out the other side of it, and you'll still be alive, and you'll still be you. You're strong enough to bear it. You just have to make space in yourself for it."

"I can't," Pace sobs.

"You *can*. You can."

"It hurts."

"I know." Josi moves her gently into the bedroom and lays her down, holding her tightly. "Sleep. When you wake it will feel a little better. I promise."

In the living room I feel sick to my stomach.

"I tried to get there in time," I tell Shadow. It feels pathetic to speak, but I can't stop myself. He is silent as always, but he's listening to me. "I didn't know it was happening. I was in the lab. I ran. I fucking ran, when I heard. But he was already being *eaten*."

"You couldn't have stopped it."

But I could have. I could have, and would have. That boy died for me. And I'll carry it always.

*

We wait. I sit with my hand on Will's back, rubbing it gently while he sleeps. I can feel his heartbeat and it calms me. Shadow doesn't say anything, but he leaves briefly and returns with a flask of home-brew whisky, which we make our way through. When Josephine finally emerges, looking ghostly, I pour her a glass and she drinks the whole thing before reaching for a refill.

"She's asleep." She stands behind the couch, looking down at Will. I don't tell her happy birthday. Of course I don't. It would be like a nasty joke.

"You should sleep too, love," Shadow tells her.

Josi nods. Looks at him for a long moment. "Did you know this was what it was like here?"

Shadow nods.

"It's not right." And it's such a helpless, obvious statement that somehow it manages to fill the room with an aching kind of innocence, a certain awareness – long since forgotten – of what life is *meant* to be like.

There are so many *meants* and *shoulds* and *if onlys* that they take up all the air and I can hardly breathe.

All I know to say is, "We can't take it back, but we'll make sure it never happens again."

If I have to take control of this entire settlement to do it, I will. I will do it so that no more innocent people are slaughtered like beasts. So that a life that is meant to be lived in freedom is, truly, lived in freedom.

*

Josephine

They leave and I sit in the living room with Will for a long time. Hours pass. I feel wrung out to dry. Every inch of me has been squeezed of its hope.

But now I am filled with something else.

Certainty.

I am not a good enough person to just exist. Too much violence lies in my past. I have to earn my life. Earn the beats of my heart, and be worthy of them.

To do that, I will give my life new purpose.

I will find a way to change the rules of The Inferno so that Quinn's power is not absolute and people cannot be wrongly condemned for crimes they didn't commit.

I will find a way to stop the sadness cures and save the poor, destitute drones from a fate they had no choice in.

I will make sure that Luke is rid of the virus I caused him to contract.

And I will make sure that Raven is punished for what she's done, even if I have to do it myself.

Chapter 20

March 4th, 2066

Josephine

As I make these decisions the moon in the sky reaches its apex and a new kind of power comes into my veins. Something entirely other. Something undeniable. I am twenty-one years old and I feel a thousand.

I rise from the couch and I walk from the house, through the dark, dusty street to another house, and I knock on its door.

Quinn answers, looking surprised to see me. He rubs his eyes as though he has been peacefully sleeping. How nice for him. "Dual. What brings you here at this hour – "

"I have something to say. Where's Raven? She should hear this too."

He blinks, but Raven appears behind him in a long t-shirt, her legs bare. "I'm here."

I look at them both in turn. I say, "My name is Josephine Luquet. I was injected with a drug that would later evolve into what we know as the cure. It has made me immune to most other drugs, including the immunization against anger. I was given an antidote, which means I may have in my veins the answer to stopping the sadness cures. I may even have the answer to reversing the anger cure. I tell you this freely, but the study and research of my blood will be entirely dictated by me. Neither of you will have any say in it, because I am a free person. You can disagree with this, but you should know that there's enough blood on my hands to drown the ocean. And after what I saw today – after the appalling misuse of power you displayed – you've woken a creature inside me that I thought was dead, and she's hungry for the two of you."

They stare at me, utterly stunned.

"The walls around us are for protection. But you remake them a prison." And I turn and leave, because for my whole life I have been weak and afraid, and I'm tired of it.

Trained Bloods haven't been able to kill me. A deadly virus that killed all its other test subjects was not able to kill me. So let Quinn and Raven kill me – let them try.

*

My footsteps lead me to a second doorway that isn't mine. Because I've realized something else. The trauma of Hal's death has shed light on so many things, and now I understand.

Forgiveness isn't shameful. Selfishly, I made what Luke did about me. I was arrogant enough to be humiliated. But it isn't about me. It's about a mistake – and who am *I* to ever judge someone for a mistake? For making an impossible choice in the only way he – a brave, generous man – knew how?

To hold onto a stupid grudge seems incredibly childish to me in this moment, given what else I know about Luke Townsend, and what I know about myself.

I hesitate before knocking and instead skirt around the small house to the window. Rapping on the glass with my knuckles, I hear the thump of footfalls from within.

The curtain is thrown aside and I am looking up at Luke.

He's not wearing a shirt, only boxers, and he has white scars on his sun-browned chest. They are nothing compared to the terrible scars he bears on his back, the ones he endured for me. He gazes down at me, startled by my presence.

My heart is trembling in my chest. It's beating its wings to get free. I am so frightened, but I must be brave. I reach up, placing my palm flat against the glass. Our eyes meet.

The moment stretches out indefinitely. And I feel in this moment the presence of our children. Once upon a time, Luke Townsend told me in a supermarket that he imagined us living on a houseboat with three children. I don't think he has any idea how much that moment and those words changed my life. I don't think he understands that by doing that – by giving me the idea of a family – he was indelibly scarring himself on my insides. He is a brand on my heart. A tattoo on my bones. And the children are here now, in my mind, an impossible possibility.

I say, "I love you." And even though he can't hear me through the glass, he can see the words on my lips, and he lets his eyes fall shut. A great ache is in his shoulders as he opens the window and helps me to climb in. His gaze looks incredibly green.

"Luke."

"Josi." He reaches to touch my cheek and his hand is so warm.

"I wanted to punish you for hurting me," I say softly, and there are tears slipping from my eyes. "I just wanted to hurt you, and I'm so sorry. I don't want to do that anymore."

Both his hands take my face and he leans close.

"Luke. I thought it was you. I thought you were being executed."

"I'm sorry," he whispers.

"It doesn't matter. It made everything so obvious. Forgiveness is the easiest thing in the world. We're supposed to take care of each other, and we can't do that by lying, and I don't want to lie anymore, and I don't want to hold onto the lies. They mean nothing, less than nothing because I know you never lied about anything that mattered, I *know* you love me – I *feel* it, I feel the truth of it."

His hands are trembling. My heart is flying away.

"I love you so much," I whisper.

And he kisses me. And it is our first kiss.

It is being reborn.

It is an aching, trembling thing.

It's the whole future.

It is my life in a kiss, the meaning of it.

It is truth.

That's when the door bursts open and several men aim guns straight at our heads.

"Easy," Luke says.

"Luke. We gotta take her," one of them says.

"It's okay, I'll go." I was expecting this.

"What's the order?" Luke asks.

"To take her to the holding room."

"Do you want me to stop this?" he asks me as I'm being taken hold of.

"No. I did this. It might get bad, but I can handle it." And then I smile at him. "I make them nervous."

Luke gazes at me and grins. "I'm not surprised." Then, "I love you."

As they pull me out of the room I say to him, "Even if there were a thousand worlds better than this one, I'd still choose your world every time, crème brûlée boy."

He laughs a little, and our eyes hold until I am dragged from view.

Chapter 21

March 4th, 2066

Luke

The first thing I say when I wind up on Quinn's doorstep is, "It doesn't have to happen like this."

He ushers me in and I take a seat in his living room. He's not the problem – his girlfriend is.

"She threatened us," he says. "She lied about her identity, repeatedly."

"She's scared," I lie. "You don't have to come at this with guns blazing. She and I will both help you, as long as things remain peaceful. If things go bad ..." I hold his gaze. "Life's going to get ugly."

"You understand what threats like that can mean for you?"

"And what's going to happen when you kill us? You think you'd even be *able* to?"

Quinn looks nervous. He glances at the door.

"Don't push it to that," I implore him. "Let Josi go. She'll help you figure out what's in her blood. And I'll help you do everything I said I would. There doesn't need to be any animosity here. We want the same things."

"Raven's furious."

"So what? She causes enough pain without you obeying her every command."

"She's damaged."

I sigh. "I sympathize, mate. But aren't we all?"

He doesn't reply.

"Josi hasn't done anything."

"She lied."

"We all lie. It's human nature."

His jaw clenches. Finally he says, "This isn't over. I just need to think. Make sure she doesn't cause any unrest, Luke, or she really will be dead on her feet."

I shake his hand, thank him and head for the door.

He says, "The same goes for you. They love you and you're a good fighter, but you're not above the law."

I meet his eyes. "Neither are you, Quinn, and you should remember that."

When I arrive at the holding cell Raven is inside with Josi. I open the door in time to witness Raven backhanding Josi across the face.

"Enough," I snap.

Josi's eye is swollen and her lip is bleeding. She's been badly worked over. "Let her go for it, Luke. It makes her feel strong."

Raven is livid. She glances at me, then spins and hits Josi again. I have to stop myself from intervening. It's not fair, and it's brutal, but Josi can't have me trying to save her if she's to earn any respect.

"You think you just decide to have power and then it's yours?" Raven snarls. "That's not how it works. You aren't strong enough for that."

Another hard smack to the face, and then Raven strides out. To me she says, "It would be the easiest thing in the world to find a reason for the two of you to be exiled. You have not been and *will* not be cleared for procreation. They may love *you* here, but they certainly don't love the girl. So you'd better start treading very, very carefully, Luke."

*

Josephine and I go past the infirmary. Ranya's used to seeing battered faces, but we all know this wasn't from training or tournaments. She sits Josi on a bed and starts cleaning her face. "I want Claire," Josi says, a little woozily.

Mom is here in an instant and I shoot her a grateful look as she takes over Josi's care with soothing murmurs. Josi needs stitches in her forehead and she'll have a nice gruesome scar, but she doesn't mind – she's quite out of it.

When I take her home Pace is sitting on the couch, staring off into space. She sees Josi and does a double take. "Who did that to you?"

"One guess."

"That bitch is out of control."

The three of us look at each other. Then Josi murmurs, "We're going to have to do something about her." She sinks onto the couch and the two girls seem content to sit quietly. Josi's eyes move to me, and she looks at me. Really *looks* at me.

I am sick with guilt and worry and grief.

But.

I am also vibrating with a fierce and heady excitement. Bubbles of joy keep rising, and I keep having to force them back down. I am woozy with the sheer, outrageous, mad, desperate *love* inside me – and the ludicrously dangerous relief that has surged. God, the *relief*. To have had to completely recalibrate the point of my life to account for the sudden absence of Josephine Luquet was too strange to fully comprehend. An agony of shifting perspectives, of denying a soul the thing that had only very recently sustained it – this had been telling my mind and my heart that it could no longer have Josi. And the response was a resounding *non comprende*.

But. It seems those dark, dark days are over. They were the universe's way of telling me never, *ever* to take for granted the incredible privilege of being loved. And not only loved, but loved by Josephine Luquet. There is magic in that, and I can feel it in her gaze now. The magic of the world that exists for those who are lucky enough to be loved by her. How sweet, how rare. How perfect.

I am shown the strength in her heart, and the far reaches of a human's capacity. In this look. In her forgiveness of all my cruelties. In her ability to be beaten down again and again and to always get back up. It's the quiet resilience I awoke to see had risen inside her. She is new, remade, but also exactly as she always was.

In this simple look she gives me all of herself, and a promise that we have come to a place where life is shared, forever.

I lift a hand to my heart. I give her the same promise in return. She smiles with love and we allow the moment to stretch out around us, allow ourselves to stand within it forever and for the blink of an eye. And then I turn to leave, sturdier on my feet than I have ever been.

*

On my way to the Den I check on Will, who slept the second half of the night at Shadow's place. The pair is fashioning arrows when I poke my head through the door.

"Alright, you two?"

They both nod. Will gives me a salute.

"Eaten yet?"

The three of us go to the Den and scarf down as much as we can force ourselves to, then gather a few plates to take back for Josi and Pace. They haven't moved when we return, both lost in thought maybe slipping in and out of dozes.

"What happened to your face?" Shadow asks immediately.

Josi blinks, then touches her swollen cheek as if to remember. "You should see the other guy." She winks at me and I smile. "They know everything about me, but they don't know about you, Luke," she says.

"What do you mean?" Pace asks as she takes the plate of food but doesn't eat.

"They don't know that Luke has the virus. And it's going to stay that way."

"Josi, no more lies," I sigh. "I'm coming clean."

She meets my eyes. "No, you aren't."

I search her face, but she doesn't elaborate.

"Will there be a funeral?" Josi asks Pace.

The girl shakes her head mutely.

"Not if someone dies by punishment," Will explains morosely.

"That's ... No, that's not happening. We'll have something private for Hal. Just invite people he loved." She meets my eyes and murmurs, "We remember our loved ones. We grieve for them, because we are still able to."

And I remember Anthony Harwood, whose ability to grieve for his daughter was stolen from him.

*

I do the rounds, inviting all those who Hal had personal relationships with. There are many – he was a well-loved young man, despite the accusation of his crime. Josi was adamant that I make sure Eric comes, so I stop by his place last. It takes him a long time to answer the door, and when he does it looks like he's come straight from bed, despite it being sunset.

"Hi, mate. Sorry."

He swallows. "What's up?"

"We're having a memorial for Hal."

"But he murdered Batch."

I take a breath. It's a very dangerous game to play, but I say, "No, he didn't."

Eric stares at me, his pale cheeks flushed pink. Without a word he follows, barefoot, blanket still around his shoulders despite the heat.

We all gather at Josi and Pace's place. There's about a dozen of us. Each person brings a memory of Hal and shares it with the rest of us, and we take a drink each time. Most of us are sprawled on the floor, squashed onto the couch or perched on the bench. I sit beside Josi but am careful not to touch her, Raven's warning all too vivid in my mind.

When it gets to my turn, I lift my glass, not sure what I will say until my mouth opens and words come out. "He saved my life. When I first came here I hardly knew how to fire an arrow. He laughed, afterwards, saying he felt privileged to have taught me. That was what I remember about him – his unwavering generosity of spirit."

We say cheers and drink.

Josi says, "He taught me about the train. Gave me new purpose to my life. I remember him making me feel welcome, and safe, and most of all I remember the way his voice sounded when he talked about the people he loved. His family."

We all turn to look at Pace, who is leaning against the doorway to her room. Her face crumples, but she swallows hard and gives a small, shaky nod.

I take Josephine's hand, not caring who is here to report it.

Someone clears his throat, and we look to see Eric, who has been sitting apart and hasn't had a turn yet. He raises his glass and says, "Hal taught me that love is kindness. He will live in my heart, always."

We drink with Eric and I realize the truth, as I think we all do, in the wake of such loving words. My eyes go to Pace, who is bone-white. She turns and shuts her bedroom door.

A murmur comes from the front entrance and people move aside to reveal Quinn. He looks at me and Josi, and then at Will, last of all. There are, I see with a start, unshed tears in his eyes.

Someone passes him a cup and he raises it. "A son of The Inferno," he says softly. "Two sons. Two young men brave enough to fight in a world too broken for it to seem possible. We will remember this, and not the crimes that came in the end. We will mourn the courage, not the mistakes." And then even more softly, as though an afterthought, "*I* will mourn this."

We drink, and I am struck but the enormity of the burden that comes with being a leader. The burden and the privilege of loving every one of the people you lead. The impossible nature of having to punish them and guide them and choose for them. It is too much, it seems to me now, looking at Quinn. And I am glad that my life has never required me to lead.

*

While everyone else is leaving, I take a moment to pull Josi aside. We don't touch, we just look. I was going to say something about Raven not clearing us for 'procreation' and me having to leave, having to keep us a secret, but I see now that it doesn't need to be said. She knows and I know and even here, in the sudden bliss of love returned, there is still a measure of bitterness.

"Do they get to decide who we love now?" Josi asks quietly, her voice bleak. I understand, in that one question of hers, that she no longer wants to be here. She has begun to see the walls that protect us as a cage. Maybe she always did, but decisions are being made.

"No. Never." There are eyes on us; I can feel them. I take a step back but hold that blue and brown gaze of hers. "I don't want them to own a single piece of this. We'll find a place one day where it can belong only to us. Until then, we wait."

She shakes her head. "What a waste. A waste of time. Of living."

Quinn is watching us and I don't want to leave her, not now when those words have come loose, but there is no other choice.

"Sleep well, Miss Luquet," I murmur.

She says nothing. I think she is disappointed in me. In what she perceives as cowardice. Her defiance wants freedom. She screams against the roof of the world at the injustice of not being allowed to choose who she loves. But I know when care is needed; I have made an art form of being careful and precise. So I will be careful enough for the both of us, to ensure that one day there is a world in which she and I can have everything we want and room for more.

*

Raven

"Where have you been?" I demand when Quinn returns.

"At Hal's memorial."

"*How could you*? Don't you know how weak that makes us look? He's supposed to be a murderer!"

"But he isn't."

I throw a glass at the wall and it shatters noisily. I feel sick and panicked and horrified – why am I suddenly the villain, when it was Quinn's decision as much as mine?

"Take a breath," Quinn tells me.

I give a scream of rage. "She's a lying bitch," I snarl. "I knew she was lying to us. I fucking *knew* it."

"Calm down, love." He crosses to me and takes my face in his hands. "Calm down."

"I don't want calm," I hiss. "I want to kill her. I can't believe you let her go. I can't."

"*Think*," he urges. "The compound doesn't need another death right now. Hal was necessary because we needed to stem the panic of the murder. Killing the girl will freak everyone out, because we don't have a crime to pin on her."

"She *lied*!"

"And you think they'll give a shit? It's not enough. We have to do this cleverly, Raven."

"So then punish her! Give her fifty lashings!"

"You think she'd survive that? She's weak." He shakes his head. "We need her healthy enough to start testing on – she's got answers in her blood."

I shake my head, unable to quell the rage throbbing through me.

"The bigger issue is Luke," Quinn points out. "Everyone loves him and he's necessary if we want to stop the sadness cures. We kill Josephine and we start a war with a Gray Blood."

"Who gives a shit about the sadness cures? Let them further ruin the already ruined."

"And if they're not ruined?" he asks. "If Josephine really does have the answer in her veins?"

"The answer to what?"

"To remaking the world as it once was!"

"We have our own world. We don't need theirs."

He breathes out, watching me with a calculating look.

I kiss him hard, biting his lip and drawing blood. It is the way we find each other, no matter what. It is the agreement between us. No matter what happens, we will always have this. He lifts me onto the bench and takes my clothes off but then he stops because he can't do it, hasn't been able to since Luke woke from his coma, and I hate him a little for it because I feel humiliated and powerless and ugly, and he has taken away the one thing that eases the fury inside me even for a moment.

*

March 5th, 2066

Josephine

I want Luke to be mine, and I want everyone in this place to know it. I spent the night planning the perfect way in which to declare it to Raven and Quinn. The defiance of telling them who I am is an addictive drug – I want more of it, and I want it now.

But with dawn comes new perspective. I am suddenly aware of how precariously close I am walking to the edge of the abyss. It is more important now than ever for the two of us to call no attention to ourselves and to ensure that Luke's virus is never discovered.

Because with dawn I wake to find another body.

Batch's young wife, Lace, her throat torn open, eyes glassy.

And this time when I hurry out of the house it's to find Luke lying beside her, naked and covered in the woman's blood.

My heart explodes and I look around swiftly. We are alone, but it won't be long before the dawn watch returns home and the workers leave for the day. I crouch to shake Luke awake.

"Luke!" I hiss, but he doesn't respond. "Wake up *now*."

He has a pulse and is still breathing, but he's completely out of it. There's blood all around his *mouth*, as though he has … I close my eyes, breathing through the nausea and the heavy, familiar scent of fresh blood.

The same place. The exact same fucking place. As though he's bringing his kills to my doorstep like a fucking cat dropping a dead bird at its master's feet.

"Shit shit shit *shit*."

I take him beneath the arms and drag him back toward my house. He is incredibly heavy, and the coarse sandy road is putting up resistance, scraping at the skin of his poor, scarred back.

It takes me too long to get him the few feet to my door, and inside we make so much noise I'm certain Pace will come out at any moment. Miraculously she doesn't, and I manage to get him into my room.

I return to the woman's dead body and clear away all traces of Luke's presence – my footprints and the tracks of him being dragged. It's so, so horrible, but I use my thumbnail beneath the thin fabric of my t-shirt to clean beneath her fingernails in case there was a struggle and any of Luke's skin got caught there. Now that Meredith is here, I can't take the chance that Luke's DNA could be found on Lace's body. There is nothing in her mouth, nothing caught in any of her clothing or shoes, so I wipe my footprints away as I backtrack to my place and shut the door.

Breathing heavily, I lock myself in my room and stare at Luke. He's on the floor as I don't have the strength to get him onto the bed, plus he's covered in blood and I need to be careful not to stain the sheets.

This is very, very bad.

It is not the blood moon. Not the anniversary of the day he was injected.

There were no physical signs leading to this like there always were for me – none of the illness, the bruising on the body, the bleeding gums and nails. If anything, he has been getting stronger, more energetic, his body the picture of health. But there were emotional signs.

I go to the bathroom, take a towel and wet it under the shower. I use it to wipe Luke's body, cleaning the blood as best I can. He's shivering slightly as I scrub at the skin around his mouth – the blood's clearly been here for a while, which means he killed the woman several hours ago, probably closer to yesterday's side of midnight. Unlike with Batch, he did kill his victim outside my house, instead of taking her there posthumously. The blood from her neck was all over the ground and it was undisturbed. She also had the discoloration marks that Meredith was talking about, from the accumulation of blood that happens over a few hours.

Which means he went from tearing her throat out with his teeth to almost immediately losing consciousness. Oddly, it's like something just switched off in his brain, whereas during my changes I made my kills and then wandered for hours after, some part of me unable to stop moving.

It's also curious that nobody heard anything – wouldn't Lace have screamed as she was being attacked?

Frankly, none of it makes any difference. The only thing worth knowing at this point is that I can't let anyone find out who killed her. And it strikes me as really, really awful that I just cleaned her fingernails and looked inside her ripped trachea while the one and only interaction we ever had was her slapping and then spitting on me.

I get out my largest pair of pants and drag them up over Luke's hips – they're way too tight to do up, but they'll do for now. I can't get a sweater over his shoulders or chest so I just cover him with a blanket. I don't want him to wake up naked and not knowing where he is. It is the worst, most emotionally disorienting feeling there is.

A knock comes from the door. "I'm naked!" I shout quickly.

"Why?"

"I'm getting changed."

"Well I'm hungry. Meet you at the Den?"

I can't let Pace be the one to walk outside and discover the body. She doesn't deserve to see that, nor do I want her implicated like I was.

I duck through the door and close it behind me. "Pace, hold up."

She turns and waits.

"I've been really lightheaded," I say. "Do I have a fever?"

She frowns, but crosses to press her hand to my forehead. "You feel okay," she murmurs. "But you've been giving a lot of blood lately, so you might feel fatigued. Do you want to stop by Ranya to check on it?"

"Guess so."

"I'll go with you now. Get dressed."

I make sure she doesn't get a look at my room, pull some clothes on and duck back out, locking the door behind me.

We walk in silence toward the infirmary, which is in the opposite direction to the body. Ranya is just opening up for the morning when we arrive. Before we have a chance to say anything a shriek cracks through the air behind us. Ranya is running toward it, and we follow her. I brace myself, moving more quickly so that I can beat Pace. Someone I don't know – an older woman – was the one to discover the body, and now more people are following the scream.

I grab Pace, pulling her away from the body.

"Don't, Dual!"

"You don't need to see it," I implore, trying to shield her.

"I'm not a child – " She catches sight of the mangled corpse. Slow breaths move in and out of her lungs, and I can't work out what she's thinking. Then she says, "It wasn't Hal. Batch wasn't murdered by Hal." And wanders away to the Den for breakfast. My eyes fall shut with a whole-body weariness.

Quinn and Raven arrive and start sending everybody away. The sounds of sobs and wails follow them.

"I bet you guys feel good about yourselves," I say coldly. The leaders of The Inferno look at me, and I look at them, not backing down. "And before you get any ideas, I wasn't even here," I forestall. "Ask Ranya."

"She wasn't," the doctor agrees. "She was with me when we heard Kristin's scream."

They start questioning poor Kristin, and all the while the body just gazes up at us with sightless, milky eyes. We stay with Ranya as she examines it. "She's been here for about five hours," the doctor says as she feels the rigor mortis that has set into the limbs. So that's around 1 am.

"Your house is closest," Raven says to me. "Did you hear anything?"

"Nothing," I say honestly.

"Could she have been brought here after the attack like Batch was?" Quinn asks.

Ranya shakes her head. "All the blood's here – that's where her throat was ripped, and then she wasn't touched again."

"Start asking everyone in the vicinity if they heard anything," Quinn tells Raven, who nods and heads off, for once without argument.

"The killer might have been able to incapacitate her before doing this," Ranya suggests. "It would explain why she didn't scream."

"If the vocal cord was the first thing to go, she could have been alive for who knows how long without being able to make a sound," I say.

"How do you know that?" Quinn asks me sharply.

I shrug. "A basic understanding of human anatomy. You might try reading a book some time, Quinn."

"So whoever did it was strong and fast and probably very quiet," Ranya surmises.

"Or known to her," I say. "If it was a friend, she wouldn't be on her guard."

"We're all friends," Quinn points out, and I realize it's essentially true. Inside the wall it's safe. It is meant to be safe.

"What would she have been doing walking around in the middle of the night?" I ask, trying to ask questions that will take their minds off the kinds of people who are strong and skilled and fast.

"No idea," Quinn says. "She's been unwell, since Batch. Maybe she was …"

"Grief-stricken," Ranya supplies and Quinn nods.

I shake my head. "Let me know if I can help at all, but it's not really my area."

"What *is* your area?" Quinn asks.

"I guess it's trains now," I say calmly, not reacting to the barb. "Can I go?"

Quinn waves me away and I head into my house, making sure all the curtains are open so it doesn't look like I have anything to hide. I would have loved to annihilate them for the gross misjudgement they made in killing Hal, but I don't have time. In my bedroom Luke is thankfully still out cold.

A major problem occurs to me now though. Quinn will go straight to Luke's house, if Raven hasn't already, as he's their point man on all things murder. When they find the man of the house not in, it's going to look very suspicious.

"Luke," I try again, bending to shake him gently. This time he stirs. He licks his dry lips and groans. Slowly he winces and opens his eyes. They are badly bloodshot, but thankfully the blood vessels haven't all ruptured, leaving him with terrifying demon eyes like I used to get.

"Easy," I murmur. "You're okay."

He tries to sit up, groaning again in pain. "What – " He blinks a few times, notices where he is, looks down at the pants I put him in. "What the fuck? What's – " Another wince as he reaches for his head. "Jesus, my skull feels cracked."

He swallows a few times, takes a few breaths through his nose, and I watch as his skin is literally sapped of all color. I lurch into action just in time to grab a hat for him to vomit into. As he heaves, I gently stroke his back, avoiding the skin scraped raw by gravel.

"This is my favorite hat."

"Sorry," he pants.

"You okay?"

He's not, but he manages to sit on the bed. "What the hell is going on?"

I don't want to tell him. I really, really want to spare him. But in a way I suppose it's better to have someone who loves you explain it than to have to wake up and work it out for yourself, alone. "I found you beside Lace's body this morning."

He frowns, not understanding. I watch his hazy mind tick over and clarity come to his eyes. Along with panicked horror.

"They have no idea it was you," I say softly. "I brought you straight here and destroyed any evidence."

"*What the fuck*?" he demands hoarsely. "It's not even the blood moon!" Despite his raging headache, torn skin and obvious nausea, he starts pacing the room. It's scary, watching him. This isn't the despair or guilt I expected. This is fury. He slams his fist into the wall, breathing through the pain, then does it again and again until I try to stop him. "Don't touch me!"

I raise my hands quickly. And watch him keep punching the wall. Hurting himself. The pain, I realize, is grounding him.

Luke eventually stops in exhaustion. His hand is bleeding.

I see something in his gaze that fills me with more fear than I have ever known. It's an apology. For the goodbye he is about to make.

"I'll confess," Luke says quietly.

"And be killed," I manage to utter.

"Yes."

I lick my lips and stay very calm. I *try* to stay very calm. But in his eyes there is a world of regret and pain and love and sorrow and it is making it very hard for my heart to keep beating as it should.

"Luke Townsend," I say. "I told you once that I was going to kill myself. Do you remember how that made you feel?"

"Of course. But you also told me that I didn't get to control when you died," he replies. "That it was the only choice you had left. You were right."

"And then I learned about Dave. And I realized that the cruelty of it, the selfishness, wasn't worth the relief of my own guilt. Hurting you wasn't worth anything."

He doesn't answer, just watches me and there's that horrible apology still there, no shift at all of the sadness in his farewell.

"I wanted to die," I admit desperately, "and sometimes I still do, but most of the time I'm very glad to be alive. It will change, what you feel now. It won't always hurt this much."

"Josi," he murmurs. "Two innocent people who couldn't escape me. A third, who took the blame and died for it. I don't know when I could change next. The people in here are like caged prey."

I cross to take his face in my hands. I struggle to keep them from trembling. But he feels far away. I reach for him but can't find him. There is so much fear in his eyes. "You are not dying for them. For what they did to you, in the city."

"I did this to myself," he says, low and rough. His eyes glitter and I have a resounding sense of *animal* sliding over my skin. "I injected myself."

"Because they backed you into a corner!"

He shakes his head, but I hold him more firmly.

"Listen to me. There's no use pretending. It is the worst thing in the world to have to live through – being responsible for the deaths of innocent people. But you are going to live through it, Luke Townsend. Because I do, every day, and I need you to help me save what's left of humanity. I can't do it on my own." I swallow, unable to help the tears that are forming in my throat. "Please," I whisper, voice breaking. "Don't make me do it on my own."

Luke's jaw is clenched so tightly it feels like his teeth will shatter in my hands.

But something gives way inside him. I see a guilty kind of relief bow his shoulders. The succumbing to all of life's wants. He has plans for us, I know. And a desperate need to fulfill them. I am begging him to do so, despite the anvil of weight dragging him in the opposite direction.

Luke nods, moving into some place between. As we skirt the grounds of the camp and rush to reach his house before anyone else can, a kind of limbo stretches out around us. A limbo in which we will wait for our lives together to begin. Wait for the day when we can start the fight. And wait, as will be the real difficulty from now on, for the day when he kills again.

Chapter 22

March 12th, 2066

Josephine

The second murder has left The Inferno sick with horror. I can feel it all the time, throbbing in the air. A week since Lace's death, and I've finally managed to convince Luke that we must keep going with the case. If we stop searching for the murderer, people might start looking at us instead.

It is sickening, of course. Beyond sickening. Luke is barely keeping his head above water. So I push him and prod him and sometimes I guilt him – I do anything and everything to make sure he lives a little longer, one day at a time.

We don't meet in secret. We can't. Raven is watching us too closely.

This evening after dinner Luke and I go to Eric's house. He looks like a walking ghost. I've brought him a plate of food because he wasn't at the Den. He takes it and puts it untouched on the table, then motions for us to sit on the couch.

"I'm sorry," I say. "Sorry for everything. It's unbearable."
He nods.

"We're still trying to work out what happened. And I need to tell you that I know you and Hal were involved with each other. I knew before he died."

Eric blinks. "He told you?"

"I saw the two of you one night. I didn't say anything."

He sighs. "Yes. We were involved."

"I'm so sorry," I say again, and it sounds pathetic. Luke is silent beside me, going through his own personal torture of guilt. "Look, I have an awkward question to ask you. You were Batch's best friend."

Eric nods.

"Do you know if he was seeing anyone? Besides his wife?"

Eric frowns. "What?"

"We have some forensic results that lead us to believe he was."

"Oh, Jesus," he sighs, resting his head in his hands. "Yes. It was me."

I'm confused.

Eric takes a breath. "Hal and I have been together for a few years. *Had* been. He … broke up with me recently because he wanted to try to make it work with Pace." He stops, shaking his head in disbelief. "The kid was seriously messed up. So I let him. I fucking *knew* he'd come back. But sometimes people have to try stuff. They need to know. So whatever, he went and had his little fling with his best friend, and I waited around feeling like a bit of an idiot. Batch and I … We'd been best friends since we were kids. He came over and we slept together. It was a bit stupid and it surprised us both. He left my place late and he was murdered that same night. Hal and I got back together, briefly, and then he was murdered too."

I breathe out in a rush. I don't know how to take it in, the amount of grief he must be enduring. I don't know if *he* even knows how to take it in. He seems numb and lost and utterly dazed.

"Eric, I … Fuck."

"Yeah, fuck," he agrees.

"Do you ..." I take a breath and try to gather my thoughts. "Do you remember what time Batch left here that night?"

Eric shrugs vacantly. "Maybe like four or five?"

So he left this house and was killed on his way home. It makes sense, suddenly, all that time we couldn't account for after Batch's shift on the wall had ended.

"Why are you doing this?" Luke asks suddenly, looking at me.

"What?"

He stands thunderously and heads out the door.

I look at Eric awkwardly. "Sorry. He's ... a bit unwell."

"Hal told me about the two of you."

My mouth opens but nothing comes out.

"He was really fascinated by the story. I was too. By the man who was so ... loyal to this woman he'd left behind. We knew about you long before you got here, Josephine."

I meet Eric's eyes. Smile a little helplessly. "I could never live up to the story."

"You have," he says. "You have surpassed any story."

Something catches in my chest and I don't understand. "Why?"

He thinks about it, considering me with that face I really like, and really liked even the first time I saw him. "You're resilient," he says eventually.

And I am so close to tears that I have to stand and make my way to the door. He follows me. "I know it probably doesn't mean anything, but I'm here for you, any time you need *anything*," I tell him.

Eric nods. "You're the only one who knows the truth," he admits. "I mean they probably guessed after my toast, but I feel ... I might need to keep seeing you."

"Please do."

He kisses me on the cheek and I hug him tight for a few seconds.

Outside Luke is standing with his back to me, looking out over the veggie garden. "Luke."

He turns to look at me with such disappointment that for a second I can't believe he is the same person. He has *never* looked at me like that. "Why were you doing that?" he asks. "Putting him through that?"

I don't know how to answer, filled abruptly with shame.

"Why are you forcing us through this fucking charade, Josi?"

I swallow. "Because we have to chase the leads. If Quinn and Raven find out what we know about Batch and Eric, and then see that we haven't been following it up, then they're sure as shit going to know we're hiding something."

It's beyond belief that someone like Quinn, who seems so nice, could be capable of punishing his people with death. Luke is his *friend*, for god's sake, but there is no doubt in my mind that it doesn't exclude him from the rules. Quinn is obsessed with the rules.

I take Luke's hands. "We have to build some sort of case. Something to show him. He has to know that we've at least been trying or he'll start snooping around."

"It just feels so awful, making Eric drudge up all that shit about Batch and Hal while the whole time I just sit there in front of him ..."

"I know. But I think it helped him to know that we know. That *someone* knows."

"It's awful being the only person to hold a secret."

I touch his cheek. The first touch we've allowed ourselves in a week. "Will you come with me to check on Lace and Batch's daughter?" he asks me.

I nod, and we walk to their house.

May answers the door again. But this time she smiles in relief to see us, and the expression builds knots of confusion in my chest. "Come in," she implores. "Do you have questions?"

"We ..." Luke falters. "No. We just wanted to see how you and Eve are."

"Thank you, sweetheart. I wanted to say sorry for how obstinate we all were about Batch's body." May has a steady stream of tears sliding down her face. "Maybe if we'd let you take him there wouldn't have been such a terrible mistake and sweet Hal would still be with us. Maybe you could have even saved my Lace."

"No," Luke says emphatically. "That's not on you, May. It's not. There was no ... No way to stop the mistake. It was ..."

"There's no explaining violence," I say. Her daughter. She had to bury her daughter four days ago. And now she's raising her grandchild. "We can just try to make the world a little less violent for Eve."

*

After we've left, Luke and I look at each other in the evening light.

"I never know what to say," he mutters. "Why don't I ever know what to say?"

"No one ever knows what to say. Or what to feel."

"You're always so sure of your feelings." This surprises me, because it doesn't seem true at all. "I'm just reaching around in the dark for something to grab hold of," he adds with a wry smile.

"Is this the right place for that child?" I ask abruptly, thoughts still with Eve. Because I'm listening to the sound we here at The Inferno have forced ourselves to become accustomed to – I'm listening to the scratch and scrape and growl and moan of the Furies beyond the wall.

I walk to this wall, tracing it around to the gate. The guards are up there, firing what few arrows we can make into the fray below. It doesn't seem to be slowing the creatures. The gate trembles a little; they are even now trying to open it.

"One gate."

"With reinforced locks and hinges."

"How long can we keep them out?" I press. "It's not safe here, Luke."

"There's nowhere else, Josi."

I can't help my jaw clenching as I listen to the chilling sounds. One gate, and one wall, and who knows how many ravenous monsters. "Well we'd better start thinking of a real way to solve this problem," I mutter, "'cause I've got a bad feeling about this."

It's simple. Locks can be unlocked from the inside. And there's a man beside me who is not in total control of his actions.

*

April 1st, 2066

Josephine

We train, night and day. Luke plays classical music during our sessions, and it helps me to concentrate. He tells me it'll help even more to meditate and I try, but I don't know *how* and it's now too dangerous for him to come over and teach me. Raven watches us with alarming attentiveness.

"Maybe we could find somewhere else to practice the meditation stuff?" I suggest breathlessly, finishing my round of squats.

"Like where?" Luke's in training gear and has been working out alongside me, giving me orders in between lifting his own weights.

I've spent the last two hours doing lunges and squats and push-ups. My muscles feel like jelly. According to Luke I'm still very 'out of touch' with my body.

"I dunno," I sigh. "Raven can't watch us constantly, can she?"

"She has just about everyone on the alert to notify her if we're spotted alone."

"*Gross!* This is *so* messed up."

"Uh-huh."

I am distracted by his push-ups. I'm pretty sure he's moved beyond the hundred mark now, and doesn't seem to be slowing. "Do you know that the record for most non-stop push-ups is 10,507?"

He pauses, looking at me. "Bullshit."

I shake my head, smiling. "Sorry, pal. That's fact."

He immediately starts doing as many push-ups as he can, as fast as he can, and I laugh as I watch him. After he reaches two hundred I get bored. "Okay. I get it – you're strong. Can we do something else now?"

He jumps up, full of energy and dripping with sweat. He grins and shakes himself off like a dog – all over me. "*Ew*, Luke."

"Don't you like sweat being sprayed all over you?"

"Can we make me a good fighter now?" I ask. "Seriously. All these exercises aren't helping me punch anyone."

"Haven't you ever seen *Karate Kid*? We have to build your strength, flexibility and agility with seemingly unrelated tasks, and then when we start the combat training you'll have all these miraculous new skills."

"It's a lot of work."

"Yes, baby, it is."

"If only we could montage it. Did you do this much work?"

He grins. "I've been training every day for the last nineteen years."

"Ew."

"I have an idea where we can go. Come on."

*

We wind up outside Shadow's place. "No," I hiss as Luke knocks on the door. "I don't want to meditate in Shadow's house!"

"Why not?"

"It's weird."

The door opens and Shadow frowns. "Hey, man," Luke greets him. "We have a favor to ask as part of your ex-student's training regimen."

Shadow stares at us.

"Can we use your house to meditate?"

He looks at us like we're both freaks.

"It's his idea," I say quickly, pointing to Luke.

We wait as Shadow peers at us, then finally gestures us inside. His house is the same as Luke's, a tiny one-bedroom studio. It's awkward – I don't want Shadow watching me meditate. He seems to intuit as much, for he makes some excuse about being on watch duty and leaves the house.

"Sit down and cross your legs," Luke orders me, so I sit in the middle of the room. "Close your eyes."

I do so. Luke starts telling me, in his soft, calming voice, to let my mind move through all the parts of my body. I do as he says as well as I can but I can't really feel anything and mostly I just sit here and think about how we're alone in a private residence for the first time in ages. I also think about the case, and I think about the cures, and Raven and Quinn and Hal –

"Look," Luke says, abruptly bringing me back to the room. "You need to be present. Focus, Josephine."

I focus, knowing I'm in trouble if he calls me Josephine. He talks me through feeling all the nerve endings in every part of my body but I'm just listening to his voice and how lovely it is –

Until he starts to touch me.

My heart jackhammers in my chest. "Woah, what are you doing?"

His fingers touch my toes very lightly. "Can you feel that?"

"Is that a trick question?"

"Concentrate."

I concentrate. He's touching my feet, and now my calves. His fingers are moving up and under my knees. Over my thighs and inside them. I'm breathing very quickly and suspect he might be trying to kill me. The nerve endings in my skin are on fire.

But I am existing, abruptly, within my body. Within each part of it. As I never have before. The sensation is electricity through every one of my muscles.

Luke moves his touch to my hands, tracing my fingers. Up my wrists, my inner arms, to my shoulders and my collarbones and my neck and jaw and cheek and lips …

"Luke, stop," I breathe.

I feel him pull away.

"You're torturing me. We can't do this in Shadow's house."

"I think I'm dying," he agrees, and I open my eyes with a breathless laugh.

"You're a very good teacher. I can feel every inch of my body."

"Not every inch. Not like I could make you feel it."

We stare at each other. My skin is scalding, almost painful in its need to be touched. Why did I stop him? "It's not fair," I mutter.

"It's criminal."

And that's when the door opens to admit Shadow. Luke and I jerk away from each other even though we haven't been doing anything.

"Good session," he tells me loudly. "Thanks, Shadow."

Shadow stares at us as we rush past him.

We circle around behind my place, on the lookout for spies. It's so absurd that I can't stop laughing. Luke opens my window for me. "Uh-oh. You're hysterical."

"Who could possibly know if you stay the night?" I ask.

"I don't know, but I won't risk it."

I reach for his face, running my fingers over his lips and –

– and then he's kissing me. Hard and fast. His mouth is open and I can feel his tongue against mine and he's pushing me up against the wall of the house. His hands slide beneath my t-shirt and along my spine, circling around to my breasts. His fingers trace my nipples and pinch them gently and I can feel it everywhere.

"I thought it wasn't worth the risk," I breathe against his mouth.

"I never said it wasn't *worth* the risk," he replies fervently, kissing me again, pushing me harder against the wall. "I just said I wouldn't. But we're not technically *procreating*."

I laugh, shoving him away. "Killed the mood."

His shoulders slump and he looks at me. I feel the gaze as if it's a touch and it burns.

"Go home," I tell him. "We're not animal enough to die for it."

He smiles. "I think *I* am."

"Go home," I smile.

"Love you."

"Love you too."

*

April 6th, 2066

Josephine

Ben looks like a wraith. He is fading fast. His skin is so thin it looks translucent – I can see the spider-veins running like black tar beneath his surface. He no longer paces, despite the restlessness in his body. I don't think he has the strength for it. He's starving to death.

"We have to feed him," I say.

"And how are we meant to do that?" Raven asks.

Quinn, Luke, Raven and I stand on the other side of the glass and watch Ben. Meredith works nearby, ignoring us. Dodge isn't here today, and it's funny to think of him having any life outside this lab.

"People die here."

They all look at me.

I spread my hands. "They're dead. They won't know they're being eaten."

"You want to feed our dead family members to a cannibal?" Raven asks incredulously. She bursts into laughter. "Oh my god they're going to hate you even more than they already do."

"You really are incredibly unsentimental, aren't you?" Quinn muses. "It'll never happen. They wouldn't even let us postpone a burial, let alone dig someone up and feed them to a Fury."

I sigh. "Well when I die, I want it known that my body goes to science. Cut it into a million pieces for all I care. Let monsters feast upon it."

"Morbid chick," Luke mutters.

"You," Quinn says bluntly to the scientist.

"Her name's Meredith," I point out.

Meredith looks up.

"Is there any work being done on this creature?"

"I believe Dodge has been working on him."

"Doing what?"

"You'd have to ask him."

"So you have no idea if the creature is even worth keeping around."

"We can't just let him starve to death!" I protest.

"And we can't feed our people to him!" Raven snaps.

"If it's possible," Meredith interjects, "I'd like to start testing him. If this one cannot be kept alive, I'd like another, please."

"For what?" Quinn asks.

"You've got me synthesizing the chemicals in Miss Luquet's blood," she says. "I need test subjects if you ever want to inject healthy humans."

And if we ever want to use it on Luke. I look over at him but he's not listening. His eyes are locked on Ben and he's lost in a dark world I know all too well.

*

April 8th, 2066

Raven

I wake from a dream of Luke with an idea. But before I can throw off the covers and dash to the shower, Quinn draws me to him and I remember the role I am here to play instead.

His kisses burn me in a way I like. Sometimes I am a doll in his arms, sometimes I am more alive than I have ever been. This morning as he kisses me, pretending he will be able to get an erection, I think of the dream I just had. Luke and I were walking through a building made of glass windows, which caused the two of us to seem fractured and multiplied. Everywhere I turned, there had been a piece of him, the back of his shoulder or the side of his ear. I'd been running through the twisting halls of glass, trying to find the real Luke, but instead I'd been faced with the real me. And she was very ugly.

As the dream reveals itself to me I feel sick and shove Quinn away from me.

"What's wrong?"

"Nothing. I have work to do."

"It's barely six."

"It's not like there's any point in me staying in bed with you anyway." It wounds him, I see, but I don't really care.

*

On the wall I fire my gun into the Furies, one after the other. The explosions of sound hit my ears and numb my head in a throbbing, whining way. *Bang bang bang bang bang.* The Furies surge toward the fallen and as I continue to fire I watch them lunge at their own dead, tearing into the flesh hungrily.

I kill more. I fire all the rounds in my clip and then I load a second and a third, watching the feeding frenzy I have started below.

"Raven!" a voice shouts and I turn to see Luke on the wall, raising his hands to me in a way that suggests I am a deranged lunatic.

"What?"

"*Stop!*"

I blink, looking around to realize that half the compound has come out to see what the gunshots are about, and now stare up at me with unease. I start firing again, angrily this time. Screw them all. More Furies fall under my hail.

Luke is upon me, wrestling the gun from my hand.

"Don't!" I snarl, shoving at him, but he unloads the weapon and slips it into the back of his track pants.

"What the hell are you doing?" he demands.

"Killing Furies."

"With a gun? At 6 am?"

I shrug.

"You know better. It's a huge waste of ammunition and it freaked everybody out. Fire arrows if you want to go on a killing spree. Shitload quieter."

I meet his green eyes. "You are not above me, Luke Townsend."

"I didn't say I was!"

"You say it every day, with every look and every action."

He shakes his head, walking away along the wall. "This is getting really dull, Raven. Grow up."

My heart hammers. "There's a reason, you know."

"For what?"

"For why I'm up here killing Furies."

Luke turns around. "Okay."

I fold my arms. "Take a look."

He peers over at the bloodbath below. Thinks about it for a while, then looks back at me. There's a light in his eyes, something new. "They eat their own dead."

Smugly I nod.

"How haven't we noticed this earlier?"

"We don't kill enough at once for it to be obvious," I shrug. "But kill a dozen and it's a feast."

*

Josephine

Before I head off to training this morning I check on Pace. She hates that I do this every morning and every night. But instead of the stream of insults I usually receive for my nosiness, this morning she is in the bathroom before me, and won't come out.

"What's going on?" I call through the door.

"Piss off, Dual."

"Are you sick? It's been forty-five minutes."

"Why are you monitoring my bathroom time, you freak?"

"I'm opening the door."

"Good luck. It's locked."

I sigh. "Fine, if you swear you're not in there dying of some revolting illness then I'll go."

"I swear."

At the training room Luke has left me a message to meet him on the wall.

Sweat immediately starts creeping down my spine as I take the steps two at a time.

One of the guys on duty points me east so I make my way around the wall until I spot Raven, Luke and Shadow bent over something.

"What's up?"

Luke glances at me, then nods down at the ground. "Specimen collection."

I peer over to where the Furies have swarmed. Raven is dangling a noose toward what looks to be a dead Fury, trying to hook its neck. "Is it dead?"

"Tranquilized."

"You're kidding. You're bringing a live Fury inside the walls?" I stare at the three of them. "You're out of your minds."

"We've been trying to bring dead ones in, but they were all eaten before we could hook them," Raven replies impatiently.

"What do you want with it?"

"Really, sweetheart," she murmurs. "I thought you were supposed to be smart."

"Whoever promised you that?"

Raven looks at me briefly, and I actually see a hint of amusement in her eyes. She must be in a good mood. "Why do scientists study anything? To learn what they are, and figure out how to destroy them."

"Oh, lovely. I'm sure species destruction is at the forefront of every good scientist's motives."

"They're human," Shadow says abruptly. "Not a different species."

We look down at the creatures. Their snarls and barks sound through the quiet, still morning air. But he isn't wrong.

Something catches my eye and I realize it is a female Fury who stands a few paces back from the wall, more still than the others. She's watching me. The whites of her eyes are blood red, and when my gaze accidentally catches hers, she gives a very slow, very cold smile. It chills my core because in that expression there is calculation and worse – there is cunning.

That's when she scares the shit out of us all by taking a long breath of air through her nose and saying in a rasping growl, "Pure flesh."

"Christ!" Luke exclaims.

"Did you know they could talk?" Raven demands.

"We heard them once in the city," he admits. "I'm not sure they all can."

I lean out over the wall, keeping my eyes on her. "What do you want?" I ask.

"Einstein's really proving her worth this morning," Raven mutters. "She wants to eat you, dumbass."

I'm not convinced. Not about this one.

Human indeed.

*

Luke has set up a pulley system so that when Raven finally manages to hook the Fury's head with the noose, they can pull him up without any trouble. It is a shocking sight, for it looks like a hanged corpse dangling in the air like that. I am hoping fervently that it doesn't decide to wake up before we can get it in a cage. Raven's idea is to kill it here where it won't be gobbled up, and then feed it to Ben. It's all very disturbing.

Once it's on this side of the wall, Luke slings the creature over his shoulder and walks through the street with it. I follow closely, thinking him a reckless idiot to leave himself so vulnerable, but he is a man who doesn't seem to know fear anymore. I've heard people talk in the Den of how he's more than a man, and I pity them – and him – because he is more fallible at the moment than the lot of them put together.

We watch as he puts the Fury on the floor of the lab. We stare at it. Raven draws her gun and squats beside its head.

"Wait," I say quickly.

"What?"

"'S'alright," Luke murmurs, placing a hand on the back of my neck. Raven eyes it coldly, then turns and shoots the Fury in the head.

"God, Raven," I exclaim. "We could have given it an injection or something a bit more humane."

She glances at me as though I am a child and doesn't bother responding.

Inside the cage Ben begins to scream. It's awful because it doesn't seem like he cares if he shreds his voice completely. I wonder if they feel pain anymore. It occurs to me that we are about to feed a person to another human being. We've become barbarous, out here in the west. It's full on *Lord of the Flies. Maybe there is a beast ... maybe it's only us.*

Raven and Luke roll the body to the door. I open it carefully and they try to shove the Fury in, but Ben is hurling himself at the opening and it's all very chaotic for a moment as they try to push the corpse inside against the blunt force of a savage beast. They manage to get it in and re-lock the door.

It's only after Ben has determined that he can't get out that he sets upon the other Fury, tearing at it with teeth and hands.

I look away, nauseous.

"Did you see that?" Luke asks.

"Uh – *yeah*," I reply.

"No, Ben didn't want the dead body as much as he wanted what's outside the cage."

"Why is that surprising?" Raven asks.

"Because animals go for the kill that's closest and easiest. He was having food delivered to him on a platter and he didn't want it."

I think of the female Fury and the look in her eyes. "I don't think he is an animal," I say. "At least, I think he's a lot smarter than one. I think they all are."

*

I go to the training room and punch the bag. The meditation has been helping, so Luke's finally started teaching me combat. The lessons are all about how to use my size and weight and speed against an opponent, most of whom will inevitably be bigger and stronger than me.

Luke appears silently to watch. He's all hopped up on testosterone – I can feel it in the air, in the way he's watching me. The virus is making him mindless, someone who wants to fight and hunt and break stuff all the time. The speed at which he's changing is really scaring me and I've taken to hassling Meredith night and day about her progress on the antidote for him. She is tight-lipped, and it's driving me up the wall.

"What?" I ask.

"Lazy," he accuses my punches.

So I turn and punch him. He's too quick, so my fist sails straight by his head. Luke grins and launches himself into the fight, jabbing at me swiftly. I manage to block him but I'm on the back foot now, and he has the advantage. Who am I kidding? He would have the advantage against me even if he had no arms and legs.

I track back, blocking his heavy blows. I step into the punch like he taught me and go for his sternum. I'm blocked so I go for his face with two quick right crosses. Blocked again, and again. But at least I'm managing to refrain from being hit.

He catches my arm and pulls me in close so he can send a blow into my kidneys. It's embarrassingly light. I sweep out with my legs to try to knock him off his feet but I just kick hard shinbone and it hurts my foot.

Dropping suddenly, I manage to wriggle out of his grip and scramble out of the way of his next attack.

We have an audience now. Several trainees and a few of the soldiers are watching us delightedly.

I'm not strong, and I don't think I ever will be, but I've learned over the last couple of months that I'm fast. I force my mind to stay in my body and I dodge out of the way of a massive head kick Luke sends at me. I try my luck at ducking in close to him and hitting him in the guts. The punch doesn't land – he blocks it, but I hear him breathe, "Nice one."

Mostly what I've discovered from boxing is that you get really sore forearms. Luke gives mine a hammering today, but he doesn't land too many body blows, and by the time he finishes with a flourish and slams me onto my back, I feel positively proud. Despite the complete lack of air in my lungs.

Until someone shouts, "Ever landed a punch, Dual?"

My good mood evaporates and I shove Luke off me.

"Take a knee," he orders. Every time we have a sparring session he finishes it with a rule or two. I crouch on the mats, and he crouches before me. "Stop hesitating," he tells me. "You hesitate and you lose."

"It doesn't feel real," I admit. "When we spar. I can't believe it enough."

"Then find a way to make it real. It *is* real. Don't worry about me – respect me enough to come at me as hard as you can. It'll mean the difference between life and death for you one day." He leans forward. There's a trickle of sweat moving down the side of his temple. "You're still protecting yourself more than anything. You can't be concerned about protecting yourself."

"Isn't that half the fight? Blocking and stuff?"

"The fight isn't about your pain," he says firmly. "It's about his pain. You're going to get hurt. It doesn't matter, because the only purpose of your existence in those minutes is to hurt him more than he hurts you." He holds my eyes. "Are you hearing me?"

"Yes."

"Sometimes you have to take a terrible wound to inflict an even worse one. That's an important thing to remember. You can't be afraid of it."

"I'm not," I tell him softly. I've been hurt. I've taken wounds. I've known a lot of pain. It shouldn't scare me anymore – I should be free of it by now. I don't think Luke believes me, though.

"I want to go back to the city," I tell him, my voice low. His eyes narrow and he leans in. "I don't give a shit about Raven's rule anymore – come to my place tonight so we can make a plan."

Luke cracks his knuckles and then nods.

*

I don't know how I get through the afternoon of work. I am so distracted that I move at half my usual speed along the planting rows. My mind is eighty percent focused on a mission to the city, twenty percent focused on my complete sexual frustration. I never imagined that if Luke and I got back together we would basically have to not be together. He and I haven't had sex since last year before the last blood moon, and that's feeling like a very, very long time ago.

"You're really grossing me out," Pace observes at one stage, and I realize I have been daydreaming and washing my hands under the tap with slow, sensual movements. Maybe it's not quite eighty/twenty.

Cheeks flaming, I jerk away from the tap and let her wash.

"Why don't you just apply for breeding permission?"

"*Breeding* permission? Because I'm not a cow."

"Cows don't apply for permission," she points out mildly.

"You're right," I agree. "Applying for permission to have sex is so disgusting that not a single species on the planet does it, except for, of course, the poor freaks who live in The Inferno."

"At least you're not out there, struggling to survive," she says. "Or in the city."

"You know what? The city was better than here."

She stares at me, her mouth falling open. "That is such bullshit, Dual," she snarls, and I realize I've really offended her. "*The city steals pieces of you!*"

The people in the garden behind us all look over to see what the shouting is about.

"Okay," I murmur carefully. "Sorry. I didn't mean it."

Pace shakes her head.

"But it's not perfect here either."

"Of course it's not perfect! We don't get to have everything!"

"Why not?" I ask and she stops. Frowns. Doesn't understand me. "Why shouldn't we get to feel everything and have everything? Like, basic human rights."

"It's a basic human right to have sex?"

"*Hell yes!*"

Our eyes hold and then she drops hers to the ground. It can't be a good feeling to have had your one and only sexual experience be with a man you love who didn't feel the same and is now dead. In fact, it must be complete anguish.

"You and Hal – " I start.

"Had sex once, when he was drunk and I wasn't, and I have no way to tell if it was horrible or not."

I pick at the dirt under my nails. "Well. Did you enjoy it?"

"What do you mean?"

"It's not a trick question, Pace."

"Yes," she says slowly. "Sort of."

"Did he enjoy it?"

"How should I know? He was gay so probably not."

I fall silent. A taut moment stretches out.

"Did you know?" she asks me, the one question I've been dreading.

"Yes," I answer.

"For how long?"

"Not long."

"Did he tell you?"

"No. I saw him."

"After … he and I … ?"

"Yes, after. And only a day before he was killed. I … It wasn't my truth to tell."

Pace looks ready to vomit, she is so pale. "I feel so humiliated," she whispers. "To not know something like that – "

"Nobody knew."

She shakes her head. "I was his best friend. I should have. So that I could support him."

"We don't …" I clear my throat. "We can't know people absolutely. There will always be pieces of us that we keep from each other. But do you know what my last conversation with him was about?"

Pace watches me mutely.

"He said we needed to take care of each other. He said you were the only person who he felt truly took care of him, and that it was a lifeline for him. He said he loved you. And that was the last conversation I had with him."

Pace moves a hand to her chest and sinks to the ground. She is trying so hard not to cry. It's agonizing to watch. When she looks up at me she says, "Dual, I'm pregnant."

*

I forego the lab and the training and I stay home with Pace. She has been completely uncommunicative ever since telling me. But I can't help feeling awash with excitement. While she does push-ups in the living room, I take inventory of both our bedrooms, and all the space in the house. It is more than big enough to house a baby.

"What are you doing?" she finally asks when she sees me peering at her cupboard space.

"Just working out what will go where."

"Huh?"

"With the baby."

Pace squints at me suspiciously.

"I'm just daydreaming," I admit. "I wanted to imagine where it would go, and what we'd do with the house …"

Luke arrives at the door. "Hey …" He stops when he sees Pace and I watching each other like hawks.

"Was that wrong?" I ask my roommate.

Luke stalls awkwardly near the door.

"Josi," Pace says, and it strikes me that it's the first time she's used my real name, and it worries me. "I'm not keeping it."

I take a slow breath. "Why?" I ask.

"I can't."

"Why?"

"Are you one of those pro-lifers?" she snaps.

"No. Really, not at all." I shake my head. "I'm just asking you why."

"Because Hal's dead," she says. "And I'm alone."

"You're not alone."

"Don't. It's not the same and you know it. I don't want a child. I've *never* wanted a child. I'm too young."

"But it's so rare to be able to bring a baby into the world without fearing it will be cured," I say. My heart is beating in panic. She doesn't understand the magnitude of this. "This is precious," I utter. "This baby is a *treasure*."

"I don't know if I'd be able to love it," she exclaims. "That's not a treasure. Bringing a child into a home that doesn't want it. That's a tragedy."

I swallow. My chest feels enormous. "I'll raise it," I whisper. "I'll do it." Because the truth is that when she told me she was pregnant, the reality of how much I want a child of my own hit with painful clarity.

Pace stares at me.

I feel shattered on the inside, destroyed with hope. A moment takes me, a big moment, and in it I turn to look at Luke. Even though I would want the baby alone, there is also a part of me that knows the decision is not only mine, but his as well.

Luke Townsend looks at me across the room. He holds my eyes, and I know he understands, and then he nods.

I have no space in my heart for the gratitude I feel for him, for the love.

I turn back to Pace. "We'll take the baby, if you want. We'll love it."

Pace shakes her head desperately. "You're not thinking straight," she says. "We didn't have clearance for procreation. Hal was killed for it. *I'll* be killed for it. They'll let me have the baby and then they'll punish me with exile."

Oh fuck. I didn't even think. The air leaves my chest in a rush.

"You have no idea what you're actually asking me," Pace says and goes to bed with a slam of her door.

I close my eyes. Try to get a hold of the ridiculous floundering hope inside me. It isn't fair, and it isn't realistic. I *know* this.

Hands brush my cheeks, my jaw, my neck. Hands I know very well. I tilt into his touch and open my eyes.

"I love you, Josephine Luquet," Luke says, "And whether it is this baby or not, you and I will have children."

I kiss him.

*

Luke

I lie on Josi's bed with her. We face each other, hands touching.

"We're not permitted to breed," she says with a smile.

"I'm a rebel."

"That's why I like you."

"Oh yeah? How much do you like me?"

"Medium."

I laugh, tracing my hand over the curve of her hip.

"Luke," she says. "Can you tell me about your parents?"

"You've met my parents. You have dinner with them every night."

"I want you to tell me secret things about them. Things from your childhood. Real things. Things from before the cure."

I lie still for a while, thinking about the question and the answer. About how uncomfortable it makes me, about how thoroughly I would have avoided it had this been during our first relationship. But that was the relationship full of lies, and I need to build something else. My hand moves up to gently thread through her thick, dark hair.

"Mom has pink cheeks. They're pink no matter what. She made eighteen cups of tea a day. Every problem in the world was solved by cups of tea. But she was smart, too. She knew how to talk stuff through, and I always had this sense that everything she said was inherently true. She could deal with anything – usually injuries. Her laugh was very high-pitched. And unexpected. She loved listening to Motown music and blues. She had great stories from her childhood, which she relished telling us. Dave and I always got sick of them, but they were good. I drove her nuts 'cause I was always pulling things apart so I could figure out how they worked and then never putting them back together." I smile, thinking about all the times she threatened to punish me and then never did.

"She was an excellent woman," I say simply. "She's only a few hundred yards away but I miss her terribly."

Josi's hand moves to my cheek, her thumb stroking gently. "And your dad?"

"He was a philosopher in worker's clothes. Had all the best sayings for every occasion. I have absolutely no idea how he came up with them because I never once saw him crack a book. But he was a perfectionist. Good at everything with his hands. God, the stuff he used to build was so beautiful I didn't understand how it was possible. His hands were dry and perpetually covered in dirt. It gets under his fingernails and you can't get it out – I'm not kidding. That dirt is there forever. I tried to scrape it out once when I was a kid but there was no moving it. He said he wished his hands were as soft as mine. He also paid me a dime to scratch his feet." I start to laugh. "Man, he loved it. My fingernails weren't sharp enough so he made me use bottle caps. I really used to dig in."

Josi is laughing too, imagining the gross picture I paint.

But then she says, "Tell me about Dave."

"I can't."

"You can. I'm right here."

The ache of it. I have never imagined such an ache could exist. I close my eyes.

"He was good at everything," I say softly. I'm not sure if Josi can even hear me, but she doesn't ask me to repeat it. "He was surly about being good at everything. He didn't want to be good at things, but unfortunately he was. He was brave, but it annoyed him. A stray cat used to bring dead rats to our doorstep every day and we told Dave he was the man-of-the-house-in-training so he had to get rid of the entrails every morning with a shovel. He *hated* it, which I thought was hilarious. But he did it, and none of us doubted for a second that he would do it. He could just do stuff. He fixed stuff. He was the person you knew would come through for you. Always." I stop, drawing a breath. "He was so funny," I whisper finally. I think it's the worst bit of all, that he used to make everyone laugh so much.

Josi's hands move over the lines and shapes of my face; I can feel her fingers tremble, but her voice when she speaks is strong. "The only wisdom I have comes from books," she admits, and I give a breathless laugh until she says, "but Thornton Wilder said *'There is a land of the living and a land of the dead and the bridge is love'*."

It's just like what Dad said, and I feel it suddenly and intensely; I feel it as a great, gaping ocean, and me slipping into it. Her melancholy has found me, for the first time. Her yearning.

She holds me as I weep for my brother, for the loss of him.

An ancient, tight thing within starts to loosen. I do not feel any better; you can't cry away grief. And you can't cry away the knowledge that your brother was a far better man than you. He would have killed himself, rather than leave the people in this compound in danger. He would have ended this madness because he was selfless. But the girl in my arms makes me selfish; secretly I know that I'd let the whole world burn down if it meant she and I would live in the remains alone, just as we did the first time we fell in love.

*

It's very late when I whisper to her, not knowing if she's still awake or not.

"What did it feel like for you?"

She doesn't move, or open her eyes. I think she must be asleep until she says, "A shadow. One I could see only when I didn't look directly at her."

Josephine's eyes move to mine, and for just a moment I have the most vivid memory I have ever experienced, like a vision or a hallucination or something far too real. Her eyes, in the space between blinks, are bleeding red like they were on the night of the blood moon.

My heart lurches and I have to slam my eyelids shut; her soullessness on that night is a foretelling of my own and I can't shake the dread of it.

"How does it feel for you?" she asks.

I'm unable to speak, at first. Josi traces her fingers over my lips; she touches me now as though she will never have enough touch, as though she has wasted so much time not pressing her skin to mine. I clear my throat. "I've spent most of my life learning to inflict harm. Control means *everything* to me. It has to, when you know how to kill someone." I swallow; there is so much fear uncurling in my heart. "This is like … long, crooked fingers reaching through the dark to tug at the edges of me, gentle and sinister. And they'll keep slowly tugging until control unravels, and me with it."

Chapter 23

April 9th, 2066

Josephine

Luke has nightmares all night. Terrible, violent things. I try to hold him, but it's too much of a hazard as I get hit in the face and knocked off the bed twice, so eventually I just sleep on the floor.

I wake him before dawn. We need to work out a plan before he has to sneak home. He lurches loudly awake, then spots me and calms down. "You okay?" he mumbles.

"I'm good. Are you? How do you feel?"

"Bit sore."

I sink onto the bed. It's still pitch black outside, but we don't have time to waste. "Here are my thoughts."

"About what?"

"Everything."

"Woah. Can I, like, wake up a bit first?"

"No time. Objectives: stop the cures. Reverse the cures. Get Raven out of power. To do the first two we have to change the hierarchy of power in the city. Do you agree?"

He blinks. Nods.

"If we don't change the power structure the cures will never stop. We can destroy the labs and the factories but they'll just start again and keep going. So to shift the power we need to attack the circle of Ministers, starting with Falon Shay."

"Hang on," Luke says. He rubs his eyes. "We make a void and then what fills it?"

I hesitate. "You do."

"*Me?*"

"You're a born leader."

"Fuck no. I was not born to lead the last remaining humans on the earth."

"We don't know we're the last – there could be other cities left."

"Whatever. I'm not a leader."

"Actually," I reply calmly, "you are."

I move us past it – he's nowhere near ready to agree to anything like that. "So this means we have twelve people to either incapacitate, turn to our cause or kill."

"Not gonna happen before the cures are administered."

"No. So first we take out the lab and the factory. We delay, while we work out how to kill the fuckers."

His eyebrows arch. "Ruthless."

"Yes."

"Alright," he says sleepily. "To do all of that we're going to need – for *starters* – a proper team. Not rag-tag, feral resistance fighters. I need Bloods."

"Can you turn any of the Bloods you knew?"

"Too risky. They don't have loyalty to anything except their jobs."

"Can you train new Bloods out of us?"

"I can try."

"Good. Now to Raven."

"We can't just remove her from power, Jose. Unless several people were to take her down in combat, and then her hierarchical spot would automatically drop. But even that wouldn't work, because she's in Quinn's ear constantly."

"Well we have to do something – she's the reason this place is so messed up."

"No, she's a product of how messed up this place is."

"But she perpetuates it."

"Yes." He rubs my back. "Raven's not a problem to be solved. She's a person we happen to not like."

"So what do we do?"

"I don't know yet."

*

Raven

I'm watching the window when he climbs out. It is too early for anyone to be around, but I knew, I knew there was something wrong when I didn't see him arrive home last night. So I came here to be met with this.

It's a volcano in my heart, seeing him come from her room.

I don't know what to do. I want to make him hurt as much as I do. I know it's simple, this desire. Childish. *Mad*, even.

But if we exist for a reason, it's to be driven by our passions. And that is one thing that both Luke Townsend and Josephine Luquet will never disagree with.

*

May 1st, 2066

Josephine

"Pace?" I push into my housemate's room to find her lifting weights that are so heavy I doubt I could pick up even one of them using the strength of both arms and legs. "Good to see you're not pushing yourself too hard."

"Good to see you obeying the knock-first rule," she replies.

Will ambles in behind me. The kid has been going through a serious growth spurt lately, and is now taller than me in that gangly, hasn't-quite-grown-into-his-limbs-yet way. Which means the poor guy looks clumsy and awkward ninety-nine percent of the time, the other one percent being when he breakdances.

"Do you plan on hiding in here forever?" he asks her, sprawling onto the bed.

"I'm not hiding."

"Bah!" Will and I both say at the same time, then, "Jinx."

"First of May, girl," I say to Pace. "We're coming up on three months."

Pace nosedives onto the bed and covers her head with a pillow.

"I have a plan," I announce.

"For what?" Her voice is very muffled.

"For if you want to keep it."

"But I don't."

"But I think you do."

"I think you do, too," Will says. "If it helps." Will sniffed out that something was wrong and wouldn't stop hounding Pace until she caved and told him everything.

"See?" I grin.

A muffled scream of frustration leaves the pillow area. After a minute, though, she says, "What's the plan?"

"At the moment you see it as a ticking time bomb, right? So what if you knew you wouldn't be punished for the whole having-sex-without-permission thing?"

"How would I know that?"

"You apply now."

"A) you can't apply retroactively. And B) do I need to remind you that there's usually a second person involved in 'breeding'?"

"No, you do not, my wise-cracking little incubator."

"So then who?"

"Here's where it gets interesting," I warn her. "Please welcome our new best friend into the fold." Popping my head out of the door, I look at the guy sitting nervously on the couch. "Come on in, Eric. But beware of flying pillows."

"Or weights!" Pace snaps, sitting up in a fluster of mortification.

Eric plods in uncomfortably, giving Pace an awkward wave.

"What's going on?" she demands.

"Try to have an open mind," I forestall. "Here's my plan. I spoke to Eric and in an overwhelming act of generosity he's climbed aboard. I think you and he should apply for procreation permission – " I can't help but shudder " – and you can report the pregnancy after."

Pace's neck and face go so red it looks like she's about to spontaneously combust. "You want us to pretend to be a *couple*? I don't … No. No way."

"Why not?"

"How awkward is that?" she hisses.

"Very," I agree cheerfully.

Pace folds her arms and shakes her head like an obstinate teenager. Oh wait, she *is* a teenager. I have to keep reminding myself that she's only eighteen.

"Pace," I say as gently as I can manage. "It's awkwardness, or you getting exiled into the Furies."

"Or I could just end the pregnancy," she points out. "Ranya has stuff you can drink."

We consider it, glancing around at each other. "It's your choice and we support you either way," I tell her, thinking about me at eighteen, which wasn't all that long ago, and how I was a million light years away from being ready to have a child.

"Look, I don't relish the thought of pretending either," Eric says, breaking the long silence. "But if it means that a baby of

Hal's gets brought into the world, it would be my privilege to help. No pressure."

Pace rubs her face wearily. "I'm three months along already."

"It's not like we have an OB-GYN to give you an exact date," I remind her. "We can fudge it a bit and say it's premature. Plus by the time this kid is born I'm hoping none of these rules will matter anyway."

"Have you thought about this?" Pace asks Eric. "It means you have to actually be this child's dad. And me its mother. Obviously. But, like, that's you and me being parents together forever. It'll be weird."

"Yep," he agrees.

"Don't you hate me?" she presses.

"I did. But only briefly. Do you hate me?"

"No more than I hate most people."

I clap my hands excitedly. "Oh my god, this is really going to happen!"

"Don't get carried away," Pace says sternly. "I haven't agreed yet."

But she does agree, and I do get carried away, because I can see that she's secretly excited about the decision, which means there's going to be a baby, and this is the whole point of it all, I think.

*

I find Raven doing a guard shift on the wall. As I approach I'm in time to see her release an arrow with a calm exhale and take a Fury straight through the eye.

"Nice shot."

She glances at me, red hair glinting under the setting sun. "What do you want?"

"To ask you something. About permission for ... procreating." I forcibly stop myself from shuddering.

"I've told you – "

"Not for me. For Pace and Eric."

Raven looks at me properly. "Isn't he gay?"

I blink, startled.

A smile twists her lips. "You think I don't know what's going on in my own camp?"

Oh. "Relationships are complex," I shrug. "They've connected over the brutal murder of their best friend – unsurprisingly. They want permission to be a couple."

Raven knocks an arrow and takes sight. "And why don't they ask me themselves?" She lets loose the string of the bow and takes down another Fury with ease. They're getting riled up down there, feasting on their fallen.

"They're embarrassed."

"And they thought it would help their case to have *you* ask me?" She laughs, drawing another arrow. "Why would I give them permission?"

"Raven …" I shake my head. "Why *wouldn't* you?"

"Because, Josephine," she says seriously, "relationships make us weak. Children make us vulnerable. Change disrupts survival patterns, just as you've done. And Pace is one of our best soldiers."

I find the words interesting, and slot them away to ponder later. For now I point out, "You're in a relationship."

"Not one that makes me weak," she mutters, as she kills another monster.

"Have some empathy!" I exclaim. I'm trying to be civil with her, even to connect with her a little, but she makes it so damn hard.

"You think I don't care about them?" Raven asks coldly. "You think I don't care about this settlement? Then you're more stupid than you look."

"If you could just show some kindness, they'd be loyal," I try.

"I don't care if they're loyal. I care only that they're hard and strong." She meets my eyes. "And I'll do whatever I have to, to make them that way – that's how we survive, Dual eyes."

*

May 25th, 2066

Josephine

I am standing at the end of a line of men and women. There are twelve of us. Will and Shadow are here, as well as Eric. Pace is not. Luke and I talked about it for hours, but in the end we both decided we couldn't put a pregnant woman in harm's way, despite the fact that she has the potential to make an excellent Blood. Despite Raven's words to me, she surprised us by permitting Pace and Eric to be together, so it's full steam ahead for this baby.

Now Luke Townsend walks slowly along the line, looking at each of us and then walking back again. His eyes, this evening, are sharp. His movements are precise. He is sizing us up.

I have not been alone with him for weeks, and I'm going a bit batty.

"I've been watching each of you over the last months," Luke finally says. "You show potential. Which is why you've been selected."

An excited rustle moves through the line.

"Do not move or speak unless I order you to," Luke barks and we all freeze.

I am, clearly, witnessing Luke the Gray. And it's a very interesting thing to behold.

"I need a team. If you're on this team you will eat, sleep and breathe it. My training will be the worst thing you've ever experienced. But at the end of it you will be agents capable of taking on a Blood and winning."

He lets this sit as he walks up and down. His gaze doesn't change when he comes to me – he appraises me in the same cold manner he does the others. "The sadness cures are scheduled to be administered in October. I will be taking my team into the city to stop this. It will be dangerous and we are likely to die in

355

the process. Anyone who doesn't wish to be a part of that may leave now."

Nobody moves.

"Good," Luke says. "Let's get started."

"No offence or anything," says a man down the end of the line. His name is Blue and he's always in the middle of a fight. "But ... why is Dual here? I'm not gonna feel very confident beside a chick who couldn't fight my one-year-old son."

I blush bright red but remain expressionless. What a scumbag.

Luke looks at the man with this long, slow look, and I would hate to be that guy right now. "How many buildings make up The Inferno?"

"Thirty-four."

"How many doors are there in this camp?"

"Doors?"

"Yes."

Blue opens his mouth but nothing comes out.

"How about windows? Can you tell me how many windows there are in The Inferno?"

"What's that got to do with anything?"

"Can you tell me how many weapons are in the armory?"

"Lots."

"How many bows hang on the wall? How many guns are in the safe?" He moves closer and though his voice remains steady, Luke seems incredibly menacing. "Rows of wheat? Potatoes harvested?"

Silence.

Without taking his eyes from the man, Luke barks, "Dual."

I swallow. "137 doors, 272 windows, 188 weapons in the armory, 65 bows on the wall, 91 guns in the safe, 100 rows of wheat and 15,785 potatoes harvested."

Another silence, a deeper one this time. I risk a glance down at Blue. He looks livid.

"It takes more than fighting ability to make a good agent," Luke says. "The necessities and skills are many and varied. Dual has more of them than you do, Blue. Keep that in mind before you shoot your mouth off. As punishment you can do five laps around the perimeter. I'll know if you take any shortcuts. Go."

Blue shakes his head furiously, but jogs off to get started on the five hours of running. He'll never do it. Not without stopping. But I guess that's a good way to learn a lesson. I am feeling immensely satisfied.

Luke takes us into the armory and unlocks the safe, passing us each a handgun. "You all know how to use these."

Uh … wait. I don't. I've cleaned the hell out of them, but I've only fired one, once, and it was a debacle.

"But you're nowhere near up to scratch. While Blue runs, you will disassemble, clean and reassemble your weapon. And you'll keep doing it until you can do it in under a minute."

"Just for a change," I mutter.

"What was that?" Luke demands.

"Nothing," I assure him quickly.

We sit down and get started. For the first time I have an advantage because I've already been part of one of Luke's weaponry sweatshops. I watch Will's movements beside mine and consider that I might have been doing it wrong to begin with –

"Luquet," Luke snaps. "Do you want to run laps too or do you want to get your hands out of your ass and start working?"

I start working.

My hands are clumsy as I pull my gun apart, copying Will's actions. The weapon feels heavy and awkward in my hands. I'm the slowest in the class for a few goes, but then I decide to just use the method I came up with on the train, and pretty soon I look up to realize that I'm nailing it way faster than the others.

When Blue returns we move on to shooting. This goes on and on until I have a pounding headache and blisters all over my hands.

Luke finally dismisses us for bed – it's well and truly past midnight – with a lesson.

"Count your bullets and your shots, every time. If you fire your gun without a bullet, it will make a particular sound and the Bloods will know they have at least a ten-second window to kill you – which they will."

Ha! Something I already know, suckers.

I sink into bed, utterly exhausted, and sleep finds me immediately.

*

May 31st, 2066

Josephine

On day two those of us in Luke's team are woken with the task of standing still – all day – without a single movement. If we move, we accrue more time standing still. Luke places us in a line beneath the wall, the screams of the Furies fresh in our ears. It is so hot I can feel sweat pouring off me, and my skin burns to a painful crisp. I'm convinced it is torture, but it definitely instills within us the difficulty of being patient and still.

On day three life gets worse. Luke blindfolds us and sends us into the wheat fields to fight each other with big sticks. I get whacked so many times I can't count, and on top of the sunburn it feels like getting raw flesh grated off. I can only imagine that this lovely little activity is designed to get us to use senses other than sight, and I take comfort in the fact that everyone is finally as crappy at fighting as I am. Luke then makes us take turns shadowing each other. If we get spotted we're punished. If we can't spot our tail we're punished.

Day four is different again. Luke has us solving logic puzzles. He says we need to learn how to deduce facts. It's about taking one piece of knowledge and using it to infer something else. *If that, then that.*

Anytime we get one wrong, we are punished with more physical hell. He goes on to test our intuition, which he defines as knowledge plus experience, and then last come the lateral thinking tests, which are a bunch of really cool riddles. I have to say, I thoroughly enjoy day four. Day five is all about memory and observation. Needless to say, I am queen of these. We are put into pairs and have to question each other extensively, then be able to report all the information in perfect detail. There is stuff on observation, which Luke alluded to on day one. We have to take notice of everything surrounding us and be able to identify things like exits, possible dangers, weapons, allies and enemies, all in a matter of seconds.

Day six is set in Dodge's lab, which he does not appreciate, and consists of Luke teaching us – on the only three computers – coding, firewalls, digital security, cracking passwords and a whole lot of other nerdy stuff. This leads into a discussion of codes and cyphers, which is a world of complexity that Luke promises we will come to understand like learning a new language. Will is hands down the best at this kind of technical stuff – he's even better than Luke.

And now, finally, on day seven of our 'week of enlightenment', as Luke has taken to calling it, he's throwing us into a bunch of dangerous training situations designed to test our ability to make difficult, quick decisions and analyze risks. Stuff like 'if you're faced with two paths, and you can see that one of them is dangerous, but you're blind to the other and know it could be either dangerous or completely safe, which path do you take?' This last part he calls the 'Gambler's Edge' and he says it's one of the most important skills an agent can have.

Everyone chooses to take the unknown path, weighing up the risk factor as fifty/fifty, given there's a chance it could be safe. But I take the first path.

"Why?" Luke demands when we're through the makeshift course. Everyone's watching me as though I'm a dumbass for having made the wrong decision.

I shrug. "The known is always less of a risk than the unknown. I'd prefer to face the danger I can prepare myself for."

Luke watches me for a moment, then nods once before throwing another scenario at us. I *think* it's his way of praising my explanation, but who the hell knows? It goes on like this for the whole day. He gives us scenarios and makes us choose courses of action, and at one point I decide I'm not happy with either of the paths he's offering us, so I make my own path, decide on a completely different option. Luke doesn't say anything when I start doing this, so I don't know if I'm in trouble or not. Every time we take a risk Luke blows a whistle. I get three times the amount of whistles as the others, and by the time we've finished, Luke says I would have been dead at least half a dozen times. Which isn't particularly encouraging. Blue sniggers at this point. But then Luke says that I also would have completed more than double the amount of missions of anyone else, so I shoot Blue a really mature smirk.

*

When it's over we line up, exhausted, battered, mentally fried, waiting to be handed whatever punishment comes next. We've all had enough. Luke is doing his pacing-up-and-down-the-line thing that he does to look all serious and impressive. Or maybe he just is serious and impressive. There's one thing I'm sure about after this week: despite the cruel and unusual punishment that has made me sort of hate him, I am also more in love with him than ever.

I can't even imagine what he has been through in order to do or know the things he does. It occurs to me that I am glad, for the first time, that Luke is a Blood. I want to know this side of him, all the ins and outs of his time as the highest-ranking agent in the country.

For the first time this week, Luke's face breaks into a grin. "You guys killed it."

We give a wild cheer of relief. I hug Shadow, who went through this hell alongside those he's spent the last years training. He's older than all of us, higher in rank and skill, but he did it with humility and without a single complaint.

"I'm so fucking proud," Luke goes on. "As a reward you get tomorrow off. Go get drunk, get rowdy, spend tomorrow sleeping and then get your asses back here on Monday."

We stare at him, the excitement dying.

"Monday?" Blue asks with a wince.

Luke looks at us. His smile this time is very slow, very knowing. "You didn't think this was over?"

He cracks up, and the laugh is definitely evil. "It takes *years* of this kind of training to be a passable Blood. The twelve of you aren't even close. Which means you're mine for the foreseeable future, so you better get used to it. Go on, piss off."

*

I have had two glasses of whisky by the time I head to bed. I've never been so bone-weary. But the instant I hear the knock on my window I am alive with humming energy and excitement.

Luke climbs in with a grace I am newly appreciative of. He opens his mouth to say something but I lunge at him, kissing him hungrily.

"Josi, wait – "

"No, enough. I'm not waiting anymore."

"But – "

"I want to make love to my boyfriend. *Now*. Is that going to be a problem?"

Luke breathes out, his pupils dilating. "Fuck no."

He lifts me and shoves me against the wall. I feel the impact and find his lips breathlessly. Our hands are trembling as he makes love to me, fast and hard and wild. I am barely breathing as it all builds and explodes inside me, and he has to hold his hand over my mouth as we come together, so hard my mind goes black for a few seconds.

We breathe raggedly and slump against each other.

"Holy shit," he breathes. His shaking hands thread through my hair and he looks at me, at my face, my swollen lips, my dazed eyes. "You were so good this week," he says.

I kiss him again, more slowly. There is so much heat in it I think we are about to be lost again. I can't contain the heart in my chest; it is beating so hard and with so much.

"Take me to the bed," I tell him and he does, and I realize I just don't give a shit about the rules anymore. I undress him and straddle his lap, removing my own clothing so he can watch, and then we make love a second time, slow and gentle and aching and we don't stop looking at each other the whole time and I think I will die when this ends and I can't stand the thought of losing him or not having him or any world at all in which there are people who tell us that we can't do this whenever we want.

Each time I think the love between us cannot grow bigger or deeper, I am wrong. It does, again and again, and I am scared that I can't possibly be big enough or strong enough to bear it, can't possibly be good enough to be worthy of so much. But I try to remind myself that if I am not enough, then I have only to grow, and become enough.

Afterwards we lie for a few minutes, letting our pulses return to normal.

"That was different," Luke says.

Different?

"You were different," he amends.

Oh my god. Isn't different code for bad? "Different how?" I ask warily.

He scratches the stubble on his chin as he thinks about it. "Much, *much* better."

"Jeez, how bad was I before?"

He gives a breath of laughter. "That's not what I meant. Thing is … You were never quite … with me, before. I never felt like you were completely present. Which sometimes made it a bit … lonely."

I swallow, mortified. I can't believe I did that to him without even realizing it. And why didn't he tell me he felt that way?

He rolls over and cups my face. "You're really here with me now. And *damn* it feels good. Without implying that I had anything to do with it, I want you to know that I'm proud of you."

I smile as our lips touch. Truth is I wouldn't have been able to do anything about it even if he had said something. I was way too messed up back then, way too abhorrent of my body. It's no surprise I was crap in bed, really. What matters, I guess, is that I got from then to now, made it from those moments to this one, and I refuse to look back.

We are getting dressed when I find myself gazing at him as he pulls his jeans and shirt back on. "I'm proud of you, to," I tell him without warning, because in this moment it is a bursting, undeniable thing. "*So* proud. You're the best person I've ever met."

Luke's hands fall to his sides and he looks at me. "You haven't met many people," he says with a faint blush.

"Don't do that," I say firmly. "I made you feel ashamed of the man you are, of the job you did and the choices you made, and I'll *always* be sorry for that, because you should be proud of yourself and what you can do. You were fifteen years old. Getting recruited meant money and stability, and it meant not being cured. I would have done the exact same thing had I been given the choice. So don't regret it anymore. Be proud of the person you are, because he's an incredible man."

We cross to each other and hug for a long while.

"Even though you're a total jerk when you're training people," I add.

"We're not gonna become one of those gross mushy couples who just compliment each other all the time now, are we?" he asks.

"Ew, no way." My nose crinkles in distaste.

"Okay then. You're so bad at brushing your hair that you often look like the bride of Frankenstein," he tells me.

"You have the most disgusting layer of dirt under your toenails that the thought of them touching me makes me want to gag."

"Ah, that feels better," he sighs in relief.

We both crack up. "I think we're the only people who find each other funny," I point out, making us laugh even more. I think we're overtired.

"Okay, okay," he says. "So before you seduced me I came to give you the inside track."

"Naughty," I grin. "What about the others?"

"Who cares about them?"

"Oh, nice leadership. Okay, let me have it."

"Ten rules of being an agent," he says as we sit on the end of the bed. "Be offensive. Be observant. Honor your skills. Own the streets. Do your research. Don't be parochial. Use logic, not emotion. Stand your ground. Know when to get out. And don't ever give up."

I feel the rules lodge eternally in my brain. "Are you going to tell the others this?"

"When they're ready for it."

"So why am I ready for it?"

Luke smiles. "Do you know what lateral thinking really means? Seeing infinite choices. You made your own paths instead of choosing from the ones you were presented with."

I flush, lips curling.

"And if I'm not around – "

"Luke – "

"*If I'm not around*, I need to trust that my team has someone with great instincts to follow."

Chapter 24

Luke

Beneath my feet is a wall made of stone. Below me, down in the dusty, dead earth, stands a sea of monsters. And above, littering the sky like a thousand flower petals on a current of wind, are birds.

As I watch them I see that they are not only ravens, but hawks and eagles and finches and parrots and magpies and owls and swallows ... Swirling around each other in one perfectly choreographed dance of feathers.

The sight is too glorious to believe, too magnificent.

A sound of astonishment leaves me; I feel absurdly close to tears.

"Luke?" Shadow stands beside me, staring at my face. I blink, dazed. "What are you looking at?"

"The *birds*," I say, as if he's an idiot.

Shadow follows my gesture and peers into the sky. And as I see his confusion, I realize.

There are no birds in the sky.

But I continue to watch them anyhow.

*

Josephine

My back aches from planting vegetables all afternoon, and cracks like an old woman's as I straighten. Luke's waiting at the edge of the garden for me, and I give him a wave. His skin is brown from having spent so much time in the sun lately, and as the evening light turns golden I see him tilt his face to enjoy the sky.

As I draw nearer, however, I realize he's not enjoying anything. He's staring too hard and his jaw is clenched as though in pain.

"You okay?"

He looks at me and there's something weird in his eyes. Something ... distant. Without a word he turns for the Den, and I follow. His hands are trembling, I see, and there is blood beneath his fingernails.

In the Den we head for our usual table at the back, but something's not right. A disturbance is unfolding. Several men are grouped around our table, where Claire and Tobias sit quietly. One of the guys – it's Blue, I now see – is pouring ale on Tobias' head, trickling it slowly down his neck and laughing as he does so.

"Doesn't this annoy you?" Blue asks him. "Doesn't it make you even a *little* bit shitty?"

"Fucking freak," someone else mutters.

"How about you?" Blue asks Claire. "Doesn't it piss you off to see me humiliate your man this way?"

Claire and Tobias are both miserably trying to ignore the men.

Blue leans close to Claire's face, making it impossible for her to look anywhere else. "Where's your fire, love?"

I realize too slowly, way too slowly, that Luke is no longer at my side. I start forward in a rush, but he's much quicker than me. He is through the crowd, bowling people over, and he has Blue by the throat. He lifts the large man off the ground until his feet dangle helplessly. His strength is ludicrous – no one is that strong.

Everyone around us scatters back, startled and excited. People fight all the time, every night, but not Luke. Luke never fights. And at the very idea a kind of hush falls over the Den.

"You want fire?" Luke asks Blue softly, while the man chokes. "You want *rage*?"

Luke slams the man down heavily – it's a serious body blow from such a height. Crouching over him to make sure his whole body is pinned, Luke punches Blue in the face. Over and over again. Blood spills and I see teeth fly.

I run and slide, shoving myself as far between them as I can and forcing Luke to stop. He meets my eyes, milliseconds away from hitting me by mistake. His gaze is an eruption of cold, brutal fury.

"You'll kill him," I warn.

It takes him several long moments to come back to reality. "Breathe," I murmur, and he does so with difficulty.

Blue is groaning beneath us, but I don't rise until I'm sure Luke is with me.

"Outside," I order him. "Run it off."

"My parents ..." he manages.

"I've got them."

Luke disappears through the crowd of awed observers; they shift nervously out of his way.

"Psycho," Blue spits through a mouth of blood. He's trying to rise, but he looks barely conscious.

"How idiotic can you get?" I demand of him. "Taunting an elderly man with *Parkinson's* in front of his Blood son? Be thankful you're not dead."

"Get him to Ranya," Quinn interrupts and a few people help Blue out.

I meet the leader of The Infernno's gaze. He doesn't look impressed. He looks like he is starting to understand that a rabid dog must be muzzled.

Before Quinn can say anything I turn to help Tobias out of his seat. The man is shaking quite badly, so Claire and I both take an elbow and support him into the cool air.

"I'm so sorry," I say.

"Cruelty is much easier than kindness," Tobias replies placidly.

Claire giggles. She sounds like a madwoman, and the sound follows us through the quiet, moonless night.

*

August 1st, 2066

Luke

Josi is sitting on the floorboards in front of the couch. Behind her, Mom is combing through the knots in her long dark hair. Dad is reclined with his feet up nearby; he was reading the tablet, but his hands started to shake too much so now Josi is reading aloud. *"The world to me was a secret, which I desired to divine; to her it was a vacancy, which she sought to people with imaginations of her own."*

Frankenstein, by Mary Shelley. Demanded by Dad. A curious thing to me, but then I guess I always wondered how he had so many annoying pearls of wisdom. He must have read the classics in secret, careful to make sure we never caught him.

I sit apart, nursing a glass of wine and watching my family. I have a peculiar ache in my chest as I do. There's a yearning in the frame of Josi's shoulders, as there is in the tender touches of Claire's fingers. A yearning for mother, a yearning for daughter. It hurts to think of all the things Josi has missed in her life, all the tiny pieces of childhood. I took safety for granted, and love. I had so much of both. Josi had neither. And now here she fits, as neatly as a puzzle piece, with her hair in my mom's fingers, reading my dad a story.

I have been stealing moments to lacquer her cello nearly every night for the last two months. Rina gave me her violin strings, but they weren't thick enough so I stripped an extension cord, took the copper wiring inside it and twisted it around the strings to give them a deeper *twang*. The instrument is as ready as it will ever be, but I don't know when to give it to her. No moment seems right. I feel strangely nervous about it. *All* of me has gone into those panels of wood, those carvings and bridges and strings. I don't know what I'll do if she doesn't like it, or if it doesn't work.

I remember words, and they haunt me. *Yes, I still. But it means nothing without trust, and I won't ever trust you again, Luke Townsend.*

Will she see the cello as a means to win her trust? I don't want it to be about that. I want only her enjoyment of it, because I can see how she fades a little each day without her music. Perhaps I'll leave it for her anonymously, or find someone to give it to her instead of me.

Mum looks up at me as she braids Josi's hair. She smiles a soft smile, one I remember from many years ago. But it is edged, as it will be forever, with sadness. Where will Dave exist, if we have no sadness with which to remember him? What connection will remain between him and us if we can't grieve his loss? The thought causes a revolt in my chest.

I realize that Josi is not looking at the tablet as she reads, but at me, the words drifting from her absent mind. She's read this one before, then. I meet her eyes and she pauses. Then says, still not looking at the book, "*How mutable are our feelings, and how strange it is, that clinging love we have of life, even in the excess of misery.*"

I smile. We look at each other, lost in thought, until Dad says loudly, "Hey? Which bit is that? Read it in order, kid!"

"Sorry." Josi curbs her laughter and goes back to reading.

*

"When?" she asks me, later tonight when we are alone.

"When it's over."

"What if it's never over?"

"It will be."

"But what if it's not?"

I consider her. She is taking off her cardigan and hanging it over the knob of my bedroom door. I move to lift her t-shirt over her head, revealing the ravens on her back. I run my fingers over them, one at a time.

"Now, then," I say softly.

Surprised, Josi tilts her neck to look at me. Her eyes spark and glow. "Now?"

I nod, and kiss her. Her mouth opens to mine and I push her to the bed. "Tell me again how many."

"Three," I say against her lips. "I dreamed of three. Two boys and a girl."

Out of the corner of my eye I can see three black crows perched on the windowsill, watching me.

*

September 7th, 2066

Josephine

I have my hands pressed against Pace's swollen belly. I can't feel anything moving, but I'm determined to sit here until I do.

Right now, in this moment, I feel happy. Despite everything. Despite the cures and murders and Raven hating me and the looming death of us all, which seems imminent at the best of times. I am reminded of something I read once. That happiness is not a perpetual state, but a fleeting moment, a thought, the lick of an ice-cream. So in this fleeting moment, in this thought, I am happy. And I want to lick an ice-cream.

"I'm not enjoying this," she warns me.

"Shhh." I lean closer so my mouth is near her skin. "You are wanted and so loved, my little darling," I tell the fetus.

"Wanted and loved!" Will yells loudly, like a football referee upon the final goal of a match. He's bouncing a soccer ball on his feet and keeps accidentally breaking stuff with it. Half the furniture in this house has been smashed several times by that ball.

Pace groans and pushes me away. "This thing is the reason I'm not part of Luke's team!"

I dismiss the statement with a wave. "Oh, Luke's team is awful. You're lucky you got pregnant before he recruited you. I wish *I* had."

"Me too," Will adds.

She rolls her eyes. "When do you leave?"

"Next month. Cures are getting administered at the end of October."

"You'll wind up getting yourselves into a complete mess without Hal and me," she sniffs.

"Probably," I agree, watching her face as she in turn watches her belly. Hal's here in the room with us – he's in every room with Pace, I know.

"But not likely!" Will grins. "Luke's turned us into a well-oiled machine."

It's true, actually. I'm constantly astonished at how far we've come in a few short months.

Maybe it's the baby, or my general thawed-out state lately, but I feel a pang. Clearing my throat, I murmur, "Either way, you two have really wormed your way inside me."

"*Gross!*" Pace exclaims.

"Figuratively," I amend quickly. "Not literally, of course. I just mean I …"

"We love you too," Will says with that complete emotional ease of his.

The baby moves and I squeal in delight. "It kicked!"

"Goal!" Will shouts, then kicks the ball straight through the window. Glass shatters and all three of us scream. In the wake of the mess Will turns to us with a sheepish grimace. "My bad."

*

I head for Dodge's lab. Tonight there is almost no moon at all, and the weather's cooled off substantially. Yesterday Luke and I presented all our findings to Quinn and Raven, basically telling them that after months of searching and interviewing and collecting evidence, we don't know who killed Batch and Lace. There is no motive that we can find, and no plausible story about how either of the murders could have happened. The only connection between the two – and it's a big one – is the fact that the victims were married, but this only seems to confuse things further. Of course, if one was to be told that a man was made beast for a night, there might be some conclusions to draw. But of course one is not told that. One will never be told that.

Quinn said that he and Raven would take over the case themselves while we prepare for the city mission. I feel confident they'll come to as many dead-ends as we did. The main concern is that they'll once again choose someone innocent to blame.

Beyond that it nags at me, though. Something about it.

I run all the pieces of evidence over in my mind as I walk the dusty road. The case should be open and shut. I know what happened. I know that Luke was responsible. Man made beast. But … it just doesn't *quite* fit, and I'm not sure why.

"Josi, what a nice surprise," Dodge greets me as I enter the lab.

"A real shocker," I reply, given we have a standing appointment.

Meredith isn't here tonight. She's been given proper living quarters, since she's been so cooperative and well behaved. She's practically a girl scout, and I don't know if it's my general suspicion of everyone that makes me wary of this fact, or the knowledge that no one, not even a cured drone, is a girl scout. Except for, you know, girl scouts.

Dodge takes a blood sample and swabs my mouth and skin.

"Yo!" Luke bounds in, flinging himself into the chair next to mine. He is buzzing with energy.

"You're in a good mood," I point out.

"So are you," he grins. "I can smell it."

"Huh?"

"Superpowers, baby."

Dodge and I both look at him. I'm sure the concern is patent.

"My synesthesia," Luke supplies. This seems to satisfy Dodge, but not me.

"Your so-called superpowers are hallucinations," I remind him.

"Au contraire, mi amore."

"Are you also hallucinating that you know how to speak French?" I mutter.

Luke laughs as Dodge takes his blood. "What's the diagnosis? Am I still a zombie?"

"Yes."

"I'm a medical marvel," Luke informs me happily.

"Are you drunk?"

He laughs again, and that's when Meredith enters at a bit of a rush. She goes to her workbench and starts fussing around.

"You okay, Doc?" Luke asks her.

"I couldn't sleep. I want to inject him now."

"Who?" I ask.

"Dr Collingsworth."

I blink. "Inject him with what?"

"An amphetamine I've been working on. The first I feel confident might work. I was going to wait until tomorrow, but – "

"But instead you decided to get all shaky and urgent," Luke finishes.

Meredith takes a syringe over to the glass cage where Ben is stock-still and watchful. "Mr Townsend? Your assistance, please?"

Luke walks straight up to the cage and opens it. Without any kind of preparation. Ben attacks, snarling. But I needn't worry, because Luke gracefully sidesteps the old guy, taking him in a headlock that sends him straight to sleep.

Meredith injects Ben in the neck and then locks the cage once more.

"It'll take at least twenty-four hours before we see any possible results," Meredith informs us.

"Results of what?" I ask. "What's the drug for?"

"To make him human again," she replies, and heads off back to bed. Luke and I look at each other in astonishment.

Dodge watches Ben's sleeping form for quite a long time. I can imagine he must feel intimidated by Meredith.

"Can we hurry this along, Harley?" Luke asks. "I'm missing dinner."

There's a silence.

Luke realizes what he's said and goes abruptly still. "Sorry," he murmurs, good mood evaporating. "Sorry, Dodge. I – "

"It's fine, Luke," Dodge says quickly.

My heart aches. I reach to take Luke's hand and squeeze it. He sighs wearily and rests his head against the back of the chair. "Remember his wasps?"

"I remember his wasps." I move my hand up to smooth his hair. "What's the prognosis?" I ask Dodge.

"Both still the same, by the looks of it."

"Degenerating and healthy?" Luke asks.

"She's not healthy," Dodge says, alarmed at the idea. "Josephine, you're not healthy. You know that, right?"

"Impossibly fast healing? If anyone has superpowers, it's me," I tell him.

"Jesus – not at all! Don't you remember what I told you?"

"Of course I remember – "

"You're precariously balanced. Anything could destabilize you."

"Yeah, but everything's anything," I say with a breezy wave of my hand.

"Exactly!" he exclaims.

I roll my eyes. Luke is watching me worriedly. "I'm *fine*!" I assure them.

"I don't know if you're quite understanding the predicament – " Dodge tries.

"I get it," I say, growing irritated. "I'll be careful. I won't put anything in my system that could destabilize the drugs already there."

Dodge looks at me, standing. He looks at Luke, too. And it's in that moment that an alarm goes off inside my mind. It's the way he keeps looking *between* us. That damn pity is back.

"That includes all number of things," he tells me carefully. "It's *any* bodily change. Including hormones."

I swallow. But no. He doesn't mean ...

"You can't get pregnant, Josephine," Dodge specifies clearly. "Your body has undergone too much damage."

"What – *ever*?" Luke asks.

"The spike in hormones would kill her."

I am frozen.

"Oh ..." I manage faintly. "Shit." The room is spinning slightly. I squeeze the armrest. "Sorry, I ... didn't realize. Sorry." I look at Luke. "Sorry."

There is agony in his eyes. "Josi ..."

I feel a bit like I haven't taken it in. I think it's one of the worst things I've been told in my entire, miserable life, and I don't want to take it in. I breathe out. "Sorry." I keep saying sorry and I'm not sure why. "Can you take me home?"

Luke leads me out of the lab even though our session isn't over. We walk quietly through the night until we reach his house.

Waiting outside is Raven and two guys. Carlos and Kim.

"What?" Luke asks rudely.

"You haven't been cleared for procreation, and you've been spotted spending the night together several times."

Luke groans. "Raven, don't."

"You're to be put into holding until your punishments are decided." Raven sounds so cold, so angry. I am abruptly sad for her. She clearly loves Luke, in her own twisted, sicko way.

"You can put us in holding in the morning," Luke tells her.

"What did you think would happen?" she asks. "You flagrantly break the rules and expect no punishment?"

"In the morning," he repeats flatly. I can hear the danger in his tone. She's an idiot if she can't.

"No – " Raven replies, and that's when he moves.

He steps forward and flattens Carlos with a punch to the jaw. The big man goes down silently, and Luke is already twisting Kim's arm tightly behind his back.

"If you don't go home now, I break his arm."

"You think I care about his arm?" Raven asks.

Luke shoves Carlos away and advances on Raven. He is brutal, and she evades him for only a few moves before he takes out her legs and pins her to the ground.

"I could kill you so easily," he murmurs. "And who the hell would care?"

Raven gives a feeble struggle, and I can see the hurt in her eyes.

"If you come back before morning I will fucking annihilate the lot of you." He lets her up and she scrambles away with a grimace of hatred.

I watch emotionlessly. Luke is completely out of control these days, but I feel nothing about any of it right now, except mild envy that he can punch his feelings away and I have no outlet for anything anymore.

He opens his front door and gestures me inside. I walk in, a bit dazed.

"I have to go somewhere," Luke tells me. "Don't move. I'll be thirty seconds."

I blink as he sprints away into the night. It is very odd, but I'm having trouble fathoming or caring about anything. I wander listlessly into the middle of the room and look around. It is empty of any personal possessions. It looks nothing like the house Luke was raised in, full of mess and chaos and memories.

Where did I imagine these children of mine would be raised? Surely I didn't think I could have them *here*? In The Inferno? The two of us are under constant scrutiny, enemies in the place that's meant to be our refuge from the enemy. And then there's the death that seems to follow the two of us around – the corpses that stretch between us won't stop growing in number.

Me as a mother. What a joke. I am broken and have always been broken. Of course my body wouldn't be fit to conceive children – I've spent my life as a danger to everything around me. What was I *thinking*? I actually allowed myself to fall in love with three completely fictional children. I am standing here pondering my own lunacy when Luke returns.

And in his hands he carries an object. An impossible object.

The breath is stolen from my lungs. I stare at what he holds, struck dumb. My eyes flick up to his face. He looks vulnerable and hopeful.

I feel my heart break and mend and break and mend.

It's a cello.

An imperfect, mismatched cello, and it's the most beautiful thing I've ever seen in my life.

"You built me a cello?" I whisper.

He nods. "Me and Dad."

"You built me a cello." Tears spill from my eyes. "Oh my god."

"*I'm* your family," Luke says. "Always."

I start crying and he puts the cello down to take me in his arms, holding me against his chest and pressing his lips to my temple. His hands are in my hair, along my spine.

This: the sweetness of being loved by Luke Townsend. The *generosity* of it. From the very beginning. From those first days when all he cared about was my safety and my happiness, when he gave me a place to live and he spent his days helping me to find an answer. He came here, to the west, for me. He went back to the city for me. He has done *everything* for me. I am the luckiest woman in the world, because something conspired to have him take a job that would one day lead him to me.

"Thank you," I tell him.

"Play," he murmurs against my ear. So I do.

I cross to take the cello in my hands, feeling electrified at the sensation of the wood. I carry it, measuring its weight like an old lover – no, it's more intimate even than that. A part of me. A shadow of my own soul, here in its shape and its weight.

I sit on the edge of the couch and move the instrument between my legs. I trace my fingers over it, over every beautifully sanded edge and lovingly glued join. It's remarkable, what he and Tobias have created.

I feel the bow in my hand and run my fingers over the strings, plucking them lightly. They're rough but it doesn't matter. I tune the instrument carefully, twisting the awkwardly shaped pegs and plucking until I hear the right notes.

I lift the bow to the strings.

"I'm nervous," Luke says.

I meet his eyes and smile. "You don't ever have to be nervous again, darling. This is, in my opinion, the best thing that's ever been made."

He blushes.

And I play.

I am wildly, effortlessly in flight. On fire and tingling and electrified. The notes explode gorgeously into the room and I feel ancient and newborn. I am come back to myself. A person once more. Alive once more.

My fingers tremble and the notes aren't perfect but it doesn't matter, they exist. There are notes coming from my hands and the bow and this miraculous instrument. And I think I love it more than I love myself. I love this cello like it is a child of mine.

In the notes I exist, abruptly. Here is the nameless thing I have been yearning for; here is one of them, at least.

*

September 8th, 2066

Josephine

Luke listens as I play for hours. And then he says, as we crash to the bed for an hour or two of sleep before they come to take us into holding, "Best night ever."

I smile. There will never be any children. And it's a tragedy. A profound reshaping of my place in this broken world. But there is sweetness and beauty in the same broken world, even without my two boys and girl, and I must try, I must *try* to be happy, because no one has stolen the ability from me.

Not yet.

*

I wake alone. I blink slowly, still exhausted. My hands reach out and find only empty bed. Struggling to rise, I feel it. A veil descending upon me. Something is wrong. My skin prickles. Dawn is only just breaking through the window; he should be here, where he fell asleep beside me.

I pull on yesterday's t-shirt and jeans and go looking for him. My feet move slowly at first, and I have to force them to walk at a normal pace.

Stop being an idiot. He probably just went to the bathroom. But he isn't there, and when I reach the living room I see that the front door is wide open.

I pause. I'm not sure my body is working of its own volition right now.

I walk to the door.

Stop.

There before me, strewn along the ground, are human body parts. A leg here, an arm there. A torso. A head.

Two people, I think. A woman and a man, scattered over the dusty road. I can't tell who they are.

But there at the end of the trail lies Luke, covered in their blood.

I vomit violently onto the ground beside the door. I can't cover this one up, there's no way.

As I straighten I close my eyes and draw a breath. I block the sight from my mind. I breathe deeply and force myself to place walls around the horror. I have to be focused, or Luke will die for this.

Opening my eyes, I run to his side. He's out cold, so I shake him hard. I don't want him to see this – he has never seen the remnants of his murders before – but I can't drag him inside without pulling him through the body parts.

He stirs groggily. Squints up at me. Groans. "Ugh, Jose, I feel like shit – "

"Get up now."

Luke blinks, starts struggling up. "What?" And that's when he sees it. The tableau of death.

It's also when I realize we are no longer alone. Standing a few feet away, mouth agape, is Raven. She gazes at me and Luke, and at the dead bodies.

I meet her eyes. "Raven …"

But she is already dashing away, and I know it's too late. It's way too late. I sit back on my haunches and look at Luke. His face is pale green with shock and horror.

"Get to my parents," he says abruptly. "They won't be safe. You'll have to get them out of here, once I'm dead."

I recoil. "Woah. Don't even – "

"Promise me!" he yells.

I stare at him in shock. There is iron in his eyes, an ocean of steel. He's preparing himself to die.

"*Promise me.*"

"I promise," I tell him.

"Go now, or you're implicated in this too."

"Raven's already seen me!"

Luke stands with a burst of energy and I can see that whatever phantom passed through him during the night has gone – he is restless and powerful and bursting out of his skin. This was never how I woke, on the morning after the blood moon.

I remain crouching; I don't seem to be able to move. This isn't right. It isn't. There's something … I look at my watch. It's 5:23. My mind pulls a thousand pieces together, tries to make them fit. There wasn't enough time.

Quinn arrives at a run, followed by Raven. Shadow is with them. They all stop and stare in horror.

And in the silence Luke says, "I'm so sorry."

Chapter 25

August 9th, 2065

Luke

Hal waves me over to his table. Surprisingly, tonight Will and Pace are elsewhere, so he's sitting with three people I haven't met yet. Hal introduces the guys as Batch and Eric, both big, solid-looking men. The woman, who is young and pretty enough to catch my attention, is Lace.

"We're finally graced with the Mighty One's presence," she grins.

"Sorry – I've been meaning to get around to meet everyone, but there aren't enough hours in the day," I reply.

"All good," Batch tells me, passing me a mug of homebrew and a bowl of curry.

"I wonder if the man will live up to his legend," Lace says. She's either mocking me or flirting with me – I'm not yet sure which.

I take a mouthful of the vegetable curry and blink in astonishment. "Damn! This is good."

"Lucky," Batch points out. "If you'd said otherwise I would have had to kill you."

"Did you make this?"

Batch nods.

"And if anyone ever insults The Vegetable Curry, he goes all Hulk on them," Eric smiles fondly.

"Luke's a great cook too," Hal offers.

"I'll give you the recipe then," Batch tells me.

"Ooh, he never gives anyone the recipe," Lace points out. She winks cheekily at me, and I realize she's definitely flirting. I glance between the four of them, wondering about the dynamics of the group.

"Your place for poker?" Eric asks her.

Lace shakes her head. "My parents'll be up. Your place."

"I share with Old Bat," Eric points out morosely.

"Old Bat?" I ask around a mouthful.

"We call him Old Bat 'cause he's old as shit and batty enough to be committed," Batch explains.

"We can go to my place," I offer. "I don't share with anyone."

"Why would royalty deign to share his abode?" Lace asks.

I roll my eyes and we head to my place.

*

Several hours later all four of them are drunk as skunks and virtually passed out around me. I haven't been drinking, so it's been highly amusing to watch them wipe themselves out. I've also cleaned up in the poker game.

What I have gathered so far: Lace and Batch are married. Surprisingly, since she keeps looking at me as though she'd like to eat me. She's got a very deadpan sense of humor that reminds me, painfully, of Josi's. Batch is boisterous and full of ideas that he has no shame about announcing in pseudo-poetic fashion. Eric and Batch are best friends from years ago – they escaped from the city together. Eric is gentler than Batch and Lace, and finds them both hilarious. Hal slots into the edge of the threesome with easy grace because he's Hal and everyone likes Hal. I suspect Eric likes Hal a little more than the others do – in fact, I suspect he likes Hal more than he likes anyone.

And I like them all. I wish it hadn't taken me so long to meet them.

I leave them curled up on the couch or splayed over the floor and creep outside. Sitting on the front step, I spend a moment enjoying the fresh air and thinking about Josi. One month until the blood moon. I leave for the city in a couple of weeks – I have to make sure Ben has the antidote ready, and then I have to bust my girlfriend out of the asylum.

"You hustled us," says a voice from the doorway and I see Lace emerging to sit beside me.

"No, you got yourself drunk," I argue. "I won fair and square."

She sighs dramatically. "We do tend to do that."

"How long have you and Batch been together?"

"Three years."

"You met here?"

"Yep. He swept me off my feet with a mended hoe and gardening gloves."

"Just what every girl dreams of."

She laughs a little. "Is this how you imagined your life?"

"Not once."

"Me neither."

We sit in comfortable silence for a while, until she asks, "I've heard you have a girlfriend in the city."

My eyebrows arch.

"Josephine, immune to the cure."

"God, everyone knows, don't they?"

"Word travels fast when you live in a rat cage."

I glance at her, surprised by the sudden bitterness. "You don't like it here."

"Not particularly, no. Do you miss her?"

I am asked this often. Asked about Josi often. It is as though no one can quite grasp the concept of leaving a loved one behind in the city. I'm not sure I even understand it. What if I had brought her here with me? Would she have been better off?

No, I decide. It would have been like putting a snake in with the rats; she would have eaten them one by one, and then perished herself with the weight of all those wriggling bodies inside her own.

"Yes," I say simply.

"I miss Batch," Lace murmurs. "I miss him even when he's with me."

"Why?"

"Because he loves those two idiots in there more than he loves me."

And then she kisses me. Just leans right over and plants her mouth on mine. I jerk away, startled. "Woah. Lace, no – "

"Sorry," she breathes, standing up quickly. "But now I don't have to lie."

I watch her go back inside, not knowing what she means but knowing it's bad.

*

September 1st, 2065

Luke

I get what she means now, and yep, it's bad. Apparently Lace toddled off drunkenly to bed and told her husband that I'd just kissed her. So Batch came around and started yelling that he wanted to fight me. When I asked Lace about the large man who seemed to think I'd grievously insulted him, she simply said she wanted to make him jealous to see if he still loved her. Needless to say, I got pretty pissed. But when I looked at her pleading face I couldn't help but pity her, so I agreed to go along with it.

Now instead of being on my way to the city, I'm forced to face Batch in the ring for the honor of a woman I have no interest in.

"Private bout!" Quinn announces. "As you all know, Batch wouldn't normally be eligible to fight Luke without having won several bouts prior, but because an insult to his honor has been made – namely, Luke having kissed his wife – Batch has the right to challenge Luke directly. If Batch wins, he takes Luke's place in the hierarchy."

Great. Now I sound like a philanderer. The whole bloody crowd is abuzz with it. I glare at Lace but she just gives me an apologetic shrug.

Batch moves into the circle, looking extremely aggressive.

I sigh and move to meet him.

*

September 8th, 2066

Luke

Josi sits; I pace. I can't stop. I am bursting out of my skin. I have more energy than I've ever had. Josi looks the opposite. There are dark hollows under her eyes.

"They better hurry this up," she snaps. I can hear her rage and I like it. It stirs something inside me, something primal. I've already compartmentalized the grotesque sight of my violence so that it can't yet touch me.

The door opens to admit Shadow. His eyes dart between us and I can see quicksilver fear in them. It makes me cold. "They think you did all the murders."

I am awash with the most intense relief I have ever felt.

Josi stands so quickly the chair goes flying behind her with a slam. "*No*," she snarls. A she-wolf. She would have made a great mother.

"They know about the virus in his system," Shadow says. "Ranya's been spying for Quinn and she's told him everything about

Dodge's tests. They pieced it all together – they knew even before this morning."

"*Fuck*," Josi whispers. She starts pacing now, while I remain still. "They don't have any proof. There's not a single scrap of evidence."

"He was at the scene this morning."

"So was I!" Josi says. "Being at a scene first means nothing."

"Josephine had nothing to do with any of it," I tell Shadow woodenly.

"They think she did. They know someone's been covering things up."

"They're wrong." They're right.

"It doesn't make sense," she mutters to herself. She's still trying to find a way out of this.

"What doesn't?" Shadow asks.

But the door opens again and this time it's Quinn. "Out, Josephine," he orders her. "But don't go too far."

"What about Luke?"

"He stays." Quinn folds his arms.

"Go," I tell Josi. "Do what you promised me."

I can see her wanting to cross to me, but instead she strides out. Shadow goes with her, and I am alone in the cell to contemplate what I've done.

*

Josephine

I have to move fast, before word spreads. Quinn let me out because he underestimates me. He thinks Luke's the only dangerous one. So I'm going to take advantage of that.

But before I have a chance to get going, Shadow grabs my arm.

"What?"

"The plan?"

I eye him up and down, not trusting him anymore. All he does is exactly what Quinn and Raven tell him to. Actually I'm not sure I trust anyone right now.

Just Luke.

"Let me help," Shadow says, and there's something in his voice that surprises me. It's desperation. What does *Shadow* have to be desperate about?

I breathe out. "We get Luke's parents out of here. Round up the team. Move the start date of our mission forward."

He doesn't say anything.

"Will you help me, or are you gonna run and tell Quinn and Raven?"

Shadow gives me this look that says I'm supremely stupid for even asking.

That's when we hear Quinn start his interrogation. Even though there's no time, we both return to the small window, unable to help ourselves.

"This is a right mess you've got yourself into," Quinn says.

Luke doesn't reply. I can't help feeling like he needs a lawyer, if only there was one. And if only there was an actual legal system. I recall, abruptly, the lie he told me about his past job as a state prosecutor, and I give a burst of laughter.

Shadow looks at me like I've completely lost it, which is very possible.

Raven arrives, moving to watch the interrogation, too. She looks me up and down and says with a sneer, "Dead woman walking." There are bruises around her neck from where Luke held her last night, and even though she's a complete bitch I still can't help feeling a bit concerned for her. She just seems so ... lonely. Even when she hurts people, it's kinda like she's just trying to be around them. It seems incredibly pitiful to me, suddenly.

"Here's what we have," Quinn sighs. He places a tablet on the table to record the conversation. "Four murders. Reports from

Ranya, our doctor, stating that she's witnessed several interactions between you and Dodge, our scientist, revealing that on your last visit to the city you were injected with a drug called Zetemaphine, which was an early form of the drug used to cure anger. The same drug that made your girlfriend Josephine act violently to the point of multiple murders."

I can feel the stares of both Shadow and Raven burning holes into my skin.

"The first two murders in The Inferno were committed directly outside this same woman's house, and she was first to find Batch's dead body. If you had committed the murders, it would make sense that Josephine might want to cover that fact up," Quinn goes on. He pauses briefly, seeming at pains to go on. "You laid it out nicely for me, Luke, when you explained that to convict someone we need means, motive and opportunity. Your drugged state would imply you had means. Even without it, you had means. We all know your combat capabilities. You had ample opportunity to make the kills. Your drug-induced states would explain why you didn't hide the bodies – you didn't know you were killing anyone until it was too late. As for motive ... It all seems very obvious, with a bit of perspective."

"What's he talking about?" I demand. My face is so close to the glass my breath makes condensation and I have to wipe it away.

"Last year you admitted to having kissed Lace," Quinn says.

I freeze.

Luke says nothing.

"You were challenged by Batch to a fight in her honor. So we now have motive for you to have killed both Lace and Batch."

Luke clears his throat. "And what would that be?"

"You killed Batch because you were in love with his wife. You then killed her in a lover's quarrel."

"And the two this morning?" he asks, strained.

"Lace's parents."

"Oh god," I whisper. I hadn't known who they were. By the look on his face neither had Luke. His lips are pale as chalk.

"Isn't it true that May and Ronan went to your house last year and threatened you for having endangered the relationship between their daughter and son-in-law?"

Luke swallows. He looks like he's about to be ill. "Yes. They told me to stay clear of their family. But it was all fine after Batch and I fought. We sorted it out. There was no ... animosity between any of us."

"Maybe that's what you thought. But it was clearly otherwise. We have motive, means and opportunity, and we have statements from our doctor. And we have common sense. There were no murders in this place before you came along, Blood."

And with that, he stands and leaves the room.

Quinn and Raven start discussing something but I can't hear them. I am lost in Luke's expression, in his eyes. My hands press against the glass and everything around me disappears except the sight of him. He looks to his left, then his right, as though he has heard something but isn't sure what. His neck cranes until he's gazing at the wall behind him. A deep terror enters his gaze. Slowly he stands, staring at this one spot.

"What's wrong with him?" I whisper, barely aware that I've said it aloud.

Shadow takes my hand.

In the room, Luke punches himself in the jaw. He does it again harder and harder. Then he walks to the wall and smashes his head straight into it.

I scream.

He does it again, and I can see blood smeared on the concrete.

Shadow flings the door open and charges in, tackling Luke to the ground before he can smash his head a third time. He tackles the much younger man to the ground and Quinn races in to tie Luke's hands with rope. Luke is screaming and he sounds just like the Furies. Shadow and Quinn manage to tie him to the chair.

I try to go to him, but my feet won't move. I am too shocked, or too scared. I can't bear to see him like this.

Raven watches too; instead of looking at Luke I look at her. There is no sympathy in her gaze. I stop feeling anything at all for her except hatred.

*

Raven

I wanted this, didn't I? I wanted his complete destruction. For not loving me, but for more than that. For looking at me and seeing something to be pitied, something to scorn, something to laugh about. He was above me, somehow, with his looks and his disdain. Always better than me. I wanted him and I couldn't have him, so instead I wanted to destroy him so that he'd always know he *wasn't* above me – not in the ways that count.

I wanted it and now I have it.

The ruin of a beautiful, powerful creature.

And I realize Luke's destruction has absolutely nothing to do with me. Just as his life never did.

*

Luke

There's a bird staring at me. It's just sitting there, on the ledge of the back wall. I move toward it. It doesn't blink, just trains those small, black eyes on me. It tilts its head.

A black crow.

It knows me. It knows me. And I know that I must be mad, because I am the only one who can ever see it.

I want it dead, but I only want that for a moment. Because as I realize that what I really want is my own death, I feel a sense of kinship with the bird. A connection deeper than any I have ever know, as if this creature is aware of everything that I am and have been, everything that I could be or yearn for. I wanted life badly enough to sacrifice the safety of others. Here is my punishment for that.

The crow, I think, is here for me. Just as all the birds are. For my end.

Chapter 26

September 8th, 2066

Josephine

I run as fast as I can to Claire and Tobias' house. They look shocked to see me flustered and speechlessly pushing into their living room.

"Get whatever you need in a bag. We're leaving."

"What? Why?" Claire asks.

I am utterly unprepared to explain what's happened. I am dazed myself. Unmoored. "We just have to go. Luke told me to come and get you so I did. It's not safe here for you anymore." I don't know what I'm saying. I search around for something to bolster this with. "Do you trust me? To look after you?"

"Of course," Claire says simply, and I believe her.

"Then get your stuff ready and wait here for Will. He'll take you to the tunnels and I'll meet you there."

They hesitate only a moment, and to their credit they are as calm calm calm as drones as they run off to gather their meager possessions. I turn for the door and sprint home because I don't have time for *anything* except getting him free.

Pace and Will are in the living room when I burst in.

"Where the hell have you been?" she demands hysterically. "Two more people were murdered – "

"Will, I need you to get Luke's parents to the train," I rasp as I stop for breath. "They're waiting at their house for you."

He nods immediately and heads for the door. I *love* him. "Get weapons and gear!" I call after him and see him nod mid-run.

I dash for my room and start grabbing anything I might need. Which is essentially a couple of changes of underwear and another t-shirt. My heart breaks as I realize I can't bring my cello. I can't.

"What are you doing?" Pace hisses.

I straighten and face her. "Luke's going down for the murders."

Her mouth drops. "*No.*"

"I'm getting him away from here."

"I'm coming."

"No you're not, Pace. It's not safe."

"I don't care," she snarls, and runs out to pack her own bag.

I follow her. "Please, don't. I don't know if we'll survive this."

"You think it's safe for us here?" she demands, and I realize she means her and her child. "We're coming with you."

"No – "

"I'm pregnant!" she snaps. "I'm not an invalid! I can *help*."

I sigh. This is a disaster waiting to happen. "Righto. Come on then."

"Josi?" she says, and I stop at the sound of my real name on her lips. "Did he do it?"

Did Luke commit the crime Hal died for?

"I don't know," I tell her honestly. Because the truth is, I don't. There are pieces that don't fit, but I'm determined to make them.

*

I stand now before ten people. Luke's Bloods in training. Will has gone ahead, Shadow stands by my side and Pace has taken Shadow's place in the line.

"I'm not anyone," I say. "But Luke is someone. He's our person. The one person who's been teaching us to be enough to survive, and to fight. You followed him. And now I'm asking you to free him, so that we can complete the mission we've been training for."

There's a long pause.

"Did he do it?" Blue asks. Shadow brought the bully here, against my wishes.

"I don't know," I say. "But he believed in every one of you. So I'm asking you to believe in him."

It seems to work. Blue meets my eyes. "I'm in, then." And all my animosity toward him seeps away as if through cracked glass.

The rest of them step forward, one at a time, until there are twelve of us.

*

We raid the weapons closet and then head out. Shadow and I came up with a very basic plan, pretty much relying on the element of surprise. As a bound Luke is being led out toward the wall for his 'exile', we'll take weapons and spread out over the square.

We reach the gate where a crowd of people has formed around Quinn, Raven and Luke. There are weapons trained on Luke from all angles so he can't hope to escape.

Before the gate is opened for him, we surround the crowd and aim our weapons straight at them. "Stop!" I yell.

Everyone swivels to see me.

"Let him go, or people die."

"You're not going to shoot innocent people," Raven laughs.

"Watch me."

And there is so much steel in my voice that I see her hesitate. The thing is, I'm not going to kill anyone – I'd rather be mowed down myself. But ironically I'm an excellent liar. I'll do anything to make her think I will. Including shooting a young man in the leg.

Which I do.

The man squeals in shock and Ranya races to help him – she'll be able to treat him easily enough. I hope.

But the gunshot has freaked everyone out. It's obvious this could swiftly become fatal. Quinn waves his hand to the soldiers on the wall. As soon as they stand down we move in, taking Luke and shepherding him toward the train.

"None of you will ever be allowed back in The Inferno if you do this!" Quinn shouts. "It's an affront to everything we stand for!"

I pause while the others take off. Everyone is pretty much just watching us in astonishment – no one really wants to stop us because they love Luke, without exception, and I don't think anyone actually has a clue what's really going on.

I look at Quinn. "What is – resistance?"

He opens his mouth but nothing comes out. I run for the tunnel.

*

Luke

There are birds on the backs of every seat, staring at me, but I ignore them as I walk past and find a spot at the end of the train carriage They turn their heads and watch me; I can feel them even when I'm not looking at them.

Josi sits next to me. I feel boxed in. She's taking up too much space and I can't breathe. She looks at my scalp, inspecting the cuts there. I don't even remember how I got them, but I can feel their sting.

"What are you feeling?" she asks me.

I consider the question; it's somehow better than if she'd asked *how are you?*

The rest of my crew is on this train, further up the carriage. They're all raucous with excited energy, with nerves and general exuberance. I can see them wrestling and checking their weapons and chattering away manically. Shadow stands up the front, silent as usual but casting a grave presence over everyone. Even Pace is here, talking to Will who can't stop moving. They both look hyperactive.

I watch it all through a haze as if I am underwater. My heartbeat is restless.

My parents are not with us. They were waiting at the bottom of the tunnel steps, but wouldn't get on the train. Too much for Dad, Mom said. Too hard on his body. The Parkinson's is getting worse. And then there was no time to convince them because the train was there and we were jumping on, and the last image I have of them is standing on that platform as we sped away. I *have* to believe they won't be harmed. I have to.

My eyes make their way back to Josi. She can see what I'm feeling. I want to run run run run run run run run –

"Go," she says. So I do. I run up and down the train carriages for eight hours straight without stopping.

*

September 10th, 2066

Luke

What the virus made Josi feel: angry. Sick. Guilty.

What the virus makes me feel: bat-shit crazy.

And *goooooooooooooooood.*

There's power in my muscles. And I am used to power, but not like this. I like knowing exactly what my body can do, what I can demand of it. Now it does more.

I hit a punching bag and it bursts. I run faster than I ever have with zero effort. I win fights, and want more fights. I want to kill Furies, and Bloods, and I want to show anyone who gets in my way that I can destroy them and it's not even hard.

I want Josephine. I want her every second of every day, I want her right now, and I'm not dealing well with the fact that I can't have her. I'd stop this train if I wasn't so intent on killing the people we find when it arrives. Death and sex fill me, drench me.

A distant memory of the man I was tells me to be careful. He is caution and discipline and he is made of iron. He's spent a *lifetime* being precise. But he grows more silent with every passing day. The man now taking his place is loud and brash and he knows exactly what he wants. He doesn't care about hurting people; he takes what's his. He's a Viking.

I stop running after eight hours. Everyone is staring at me. I don't want to talk to any of them.

Josi moved down the train so she can be alone. I take a breath and follow her, knowing I will have to face this conversation at some point. She has her legs up on the seat, staring out the window.

I sit opposite, then can't even manage to sit, so stand again.

"What are you feeling?" she repeats.

I crack my knuckles. Realize she actually needs to know. Alright, here goes. "Restless. Pissed off. A bit numb. I have too much energy. I want to smash stuff and break things. I can barely think straight. I'm ... *angry*. Obviously whatever the hell is in this drug is ramping up my testosterone levels. And my adrenalin."

"Yeah, no shit," she agrees. She watches me and I can't read her expression.

"I want you," I blurt out. "I want you *now*, and all the time, and I want to have you whenever I want. I want you to be mine to have.

I'm tired of this *bullshit* pretending. I ..." I struggle to form words and my hands start shaking. "I can't think of anything else."

"Take a deep breath and try to calm down."

I draw a breath, a deep one.

"Close your eyes," she orders, so I do. I breathe as slowly as I can, and feel my heart calm infinitesimally. My blood seems to cool a little, enough perhaps to have a normal, human conversation.

"Drink this," Josi bids me, and I realize she's offering me whisky from a sack. Whoever thought to bring this is a genius; I drink the whole thing and feel myself mellow somewhat. I slump onto the seat opposite.

After a while I am able to focus on her. "You look tired," I murmur.

"I am tired."

"Thank you for trying to get my parents out."

"Of course."

We look at each other for a while. I feel relaxed, but I know it won't last long.

"You kissed Lace," she says abruptly.

Oh, god. "No," I reply. "She kissed me."

"Your standard answer these days."

"Yeah, well it keeps fucking happening."

"I believe you," she tells me. "But I was humiliated, having to hear about it from the other side of a holding cell, after you and I had been over every inch of that case. You don't think it would have been kinder to tell me about this before I had to hear it from Quinn in your murder investigation?"

"I wanted to spare you," I say. "I'd caused you so much pain already."

"Because of the lies," she specifies. "The lies are what hurt. And then you lied again."

I stare at her helplessly. There is a red-breasted finch sitting on the seat behind her, watching me. It's beautiful. It makes my toes curl and my teeth ache.

"Yes," I say simply. "Yes."

Something smashes against the train window. I jerk in fright, looking to see a smatter of blood. There is a second impact, a mighty crack, and I realize there are birds flying straight into the glass, one after the other.

I stand, deeply unnerved. My heart explodes. I can feel sweat trickling down my spine. My skin is two sizes too small. "You still don't trust me," I snap, "Because you're so fucking irrational I can't even talk to you anymore. *I haven't done anything wrong!* You won't believe me no matter what I say because you let your own shit rule you – all those people who hurt you as a kid rule your whole damn life and you just *let* them – "

"Stop," she says.

I clench my hands to stop them shaking.

"You've never been cruel. This isn't you."

"You said you didn't know me," I rasp.

"I lied."

Something collapses inside me. I sit down again. "I'm losing my mind," I whisper.

Another bird slams into the window and I jerk backwards. The impact shocks something deep within me. My nerves are shattered. I can't take it anymore.

"What do you keep seeing?" Josi asks me worriedly.

Tears spill onto my cheeks. "Birds."

She closes her eyes. For her there are no birds and no cracked windows, but she can see the fear in my face. "Why?"

"I don't know. Anthony. You. The world being extinct of them. I don't know."

I'm about to get up and leave her, run and run and run, when she says, "I guess you don't yet understand, so I'll explain it to you."

One of her eyes looks very blue and one of her eyes looks very brown. They're strange, disorienting things, Josephine Luquet's eyes.

Smash, smash, smash go the birds into the glass around us.

"You and I are it," she says. "We're it. So you don't lie to me, *ever*. You can tell me anything – even the very worst things about you. The things you can't even tell yourself – you can tell me those. If you fall in love with someone else, you can tell me that. If you do something terrible, you can tell me that. If you see birds where there are none, you can tell me. Because I'll help you bear it. I'll hear it and I'll love you regardless. What will make me fall out of love with you is if you lie."

I stare at her and the birds stop. They stop flying at the windows, and they vanish from the chairs around us. They are gone for the first time in days, and I am overwhelmed by Josephine.

"I'm not going to fall in love with someone else," I tell her.

She nods slightly.

"And I'm not going to lie."

"Okay." She moves, sliding onto my lap. My heart ruptures.

"I don't know what's happening to me," I utter.

Against my lips she says, "I'm not going to let anything happen to you. I promise."

And in her arms it's easy to believe her, even if she has no way to make it true.

Chapter 27

Josephine

Sun beats down on my face. I focus on keeping my expression utterly neutral. There's a collective rustle of discomfort from the heat making its way through the crowd around me. We have been waiting here for some time now.

I glance over to the opposite corner of the city square to see the familiar faces of Will and Pace. North behind the stage is Shadow. Up in one of the windows to the west is Blue. And to my left, about a hundred yards away, stands Luke, blending into the crowd as I am.

"Hot, isn't it?" says the woman next to me. She looks tired, but pleasantly relaxed. She looks like she's quite enjoying the sun, actually. She has tiny, elegant lines around her eyes and mouth, and pretty red hair.

"Yeah," I agree. I can't think of anything else to say so she drops her eyes. "Are you missing work?" I blurt, for some reason wanting to continue the conversation.

She nods. "I feel naughty. I quite like feeling naughty. Don't tell anyone."

It makes me smile. "I won't."

The screens all around us blink on and everyone relaxes.

The time has come, they read. *Peace is upon us. Happiness. Safety.*

Falon Shay's magnified face appears to give the address. "Good morning, citizens. It gives me very great pleasure to announce that a breakthrough has been made, and it is finally time to step into the future of mankind. Ten years ago we changed the world. We cured anger. This time we are going to save you from a disease that is just as dangerous in its malignance. Sadness."

It is in this moment that the connection skews and the screens all blink out. A rustle moves through the crowd, but it's only a second before a new image blinks onto all the screens, citywide.

It's video footage of Dr Meredith Shaw, taken in the interrogation room at the bottom of The Inferno by one Mr Luke Townsend.

"So let's talk about the other ten percent," says a man's voice from the other side of the camera. Luke's voice. "What happens to them?"

Meredith sighs. "They can have unpredictable emotional responses to stress and stimuli."

"And do you think that's also a likely result of the sadness cure?"

"It isn't yet finished."

"But the test subjects have all shown such symptoms, haven't they?"

No response.

"How many have you tested so far?"

No response.

"I'm pretty sure I heard you say there were sixty-six, right?' And then, 'How many of these children died?"

"Forty."

Around me there is a communal gasp. I can see police running along the sides of the squares, but they won't be able to do anything.

Onscreen a hand reaches out to tilt Meredith's chin up. We get a close-up of her face, wretched as it is. "Did you and Collingsworth create the Furies and then blame them on the plague?" Luke's voice asks.

"Yes."

The woman beside me covers her mouth in horror.

"Does the current version of the cure also cause certain patients to become Furies?"

"Yes."

"Is that what happened to Collingsworth?"

"Yes."

"Does Falon Shay know about this?"

"Yes. It was his idea to put them beyond the wall so no one would ever be able to leave the city."

"Is the land beyond the wall diseased at all?"

"No. It's perfectly habitable. It's regenerating as we speak."

Chaos erupts. People are scared and confused. They're not sure what to do or how to respond.

The image changes once more to one of the many images automatically captured by my earpiece when Luke and I broke into the labs. It shows the children in their glass cages, dying of various side-effects.

Words flash up. *Your government is murdering children and damaging your brains. It wants to control you. It stole your anger so you would be quiet. Quiet like the dead. And now it wants to steal your sadness so you will forget how to grieve your losses.*

A new image flashes up. It's a picture we took yesterday of all twelve of us on the train. We're wearing eye masks so we can't be recognized and we're armed to the teeth. We might look scary, except that we're all smiling, grouped together like a family.

But you are not alone, the words read.

We haven't forgotten you.

We're out here, and we will fight for you.

The screens go black and the cacophony of panicked voices washes over me. I look at Luke, who returns my stare through the moving crowd. I can only glimpse his eyes briefly, but he smiles.

I feel a touch and see that the woman beside me has taken my hand. Astonished, I look at her face. There are tears streaming down her cheeks, but she's smiling as though she's alive for the first time in years.

*

September 12th, 2066

Josephine

It's late. Or early. I'm so tired I can't think straight. Shadow is studying blueprints with bloodshot eyes – I can't imagine how frustrating it must be not to just remember what you see. "We need to sleep," I tell him.

The abandoned garage basement we're squatting in for the night is filled with the sleeping bodies of our team. Luke remains on watch, the only one of us who doesn't seem to need rest. While Pace and Will are doing a low-risk recon sweep.

"We've done as much as we can," I add, when Shadow looks reluctant. "Anything else is beyond our control." These sound like the words of a person who is far more reasonable than I am. I have become, abruptly, the responsible one. The worrier. It's gross.

Shadow nods and takes a place in the corner to try to get some sleep, impossible though it seems on cold concrete. We have a month until the sadness cures are administered, which should give us enough time to set up the operation to take out the factories.

Luke barely speaks. His muscles keep freezing up and his jaw is clenched so tightly it looks as though his teeth will shatter. He grunts. Moves with abrupt, jerking power. Seems inclined to want to attack anyone who goes within a twenty-foot radius of him. He runs a fever, bleeds from fingernails and gums, and has trouble focusing his eyes. I am frightened, but I don't let anyone know that.

He can't make plans – he is too distracted – so it falls to Shadow and me. If Luke grunts his approval, we move forward. I don't know if he's going to be able to help us, and the thought of heading into something so dangerous without Luke's skill is very scary. I try to focus on everything he has taught me over the last few months.

In my pocket is a vial. In this vial is Meredith's experimental drug, the one she injected into Ben. The one she hasn't tested or trialed or checked. The only thing that might save Luke from this nightmare. Or the thing that could kill him more quickly.

The date of his very own blood moon draws near. And if he has already caused this much damage without the moon, I can't imagine what he might do when it rises. Before that happens, I will inject him, no matter what. Even though it might kill him. This is my vow.

I climb the stairwell of the abandoned building to look for him. My footsteps echo. He's on the roof, and I pause to watch him pace around its edge, keeping his eyes peeled both above and below. His long sniper rifle rests comfortably over his muscular shoulder, and to my shame, it makes me nervous to see him with a weapon. I keep telling myself he's okay, but actually – he's not. He has snapped and murdered before. There's nothing stopping him from doing it now. All the pieces of him look slightly different – stronger, sharper, bigger, more athletic. I wonder if he can see birds at this very moment. It's a curse that is cruel in its beauty, one that a part of me longs to experience.

I remove the vial from my pocket and cross to him. He continues on his patrol, so I fall into step beside him. "Let me inject you," I plead.

A shake of his head.

"You're not well – "

"I feel *good*," he snaps. The most he's said in days.

"Well you look like shit." I try to moderate my frustration. It isn't his fault he's like this. It's mine. And I know better than anyone how awful it is to lack control of your actions and feelings. "I'm worried you won't get through the op tomorrow. We're blowing up a factory, for Christ's sake – you would never have made me do something so dangerous right before the blood moon."

No response, so I change tactics. "It's scaring me, watching you like this."

"I thought this was what you always wanted." He rounds on me. "Me to be angry."

"I just want you to be you. With nothing added or removed, without tweaks or enhancements or modifications – just *you*."

I stop talking, because he is pushing me against the stone balustrade. And he's dropping to his knees and undoing my jeans, and he's pulling them over my hips, along with my undies, and he's pressing his face to me and slipping his tongue inside me and I gasp because *what the hell is he doing* but then I stop questioning all together and instead I look up at a black night sky and the only thought I have is for the missing stars, lost to all the lights of the city.

*

It must be close to dawn when I hear the walkie-talkie crackle and Will's voice comes through. "*Base, come in ... Dual?*"

I scramble over to it, annoyed with myself for falling asleep when Will and his team are out on a recon trip. Luke is still up on the roof but everyone else is asleep around me in the garage. "I'm here, Will. What's up?"

"*We're at the crest of the hill, and there's definitely something going on down there.*"

"What is it?"

"*A whole lot of movement,*" Pace's voice interrupts – she's taken hold of the walkie. The only things we let her partake in are surveillance operations, where she is a *long* way from any danger. "*Bloods are crawling all over the place, trucks going in and out. Started about an hour ago.*"

407

"Stay there and keep watch," I tell them. "Look out for any recognizable faces."

"*We're not close enough for that.*"

"Then get closer. But be *careful.*"

"*Aye aye, cap'n. Incubator out.*"

I almost smile. We started using Incubator as Pace's codename, much to her horror, but it stuck and now even she uses it, albeit begrudgingly. I think she secretly likes it.

But a whole lot of movement at the factory can mean only one thing.

*

"They've moved the administration date forward," Shadow agrees after we've received another report from Pace and Will at the site. Apparently Falon Shay has been in there this morning, along with a couple of the other Ministers and the Blood leader, Jean Gueye. Which is big – the Ministers don't often leave the safety of their guarded compounds.

Luke grunts, pacing furiously.

"Shit. What do we do now?" I ask.

There's a silence. Showing our video was meant to sow the seeds of doubt in the minds of the drones, and give them hope for a different future. It was meant to scare those in charge. None of that has a chance to work, now, because the prick of a prime minister has moved the date forward.

"We can't blow up the factory if there's nothing in it," I answer my own question. "So we have to destroy the drug some other way."

"Only other place is on the road, which we've missed our window for, or at the clinics," Shadow says.

"So we destroy the clinics," I say.

"And murder a whole lot of people?"

"No. We get them cleared out somehow." I think fast, glancing at Luke. "Okay. Okay. New plan."

*

By sundown we're in place. I've had about an hour of sleep in three days, but I'm wired as hell and ready for action. The sadness cures have been distributed to twelve different clinics for their injection. The announcement went out this morning on a repeated national bulletin that every citizen is to report for administration at 8 am tomorrow morning at their nearest clinic. They'll then either be injected in the first wave, or scheduled for one of the next several waves of injections, depending on the 'importance of their contribution to society'. Whatever the fuck that means.

We have a massive night ahead of us. Because there are only a dozen of us, and we need three people per clinic, we have to do this in stages – four teams to take out four clinics at a time, instead of all twelve simultaneously, which would have been a thousand times quicker and therefore safer. But *c'est la vie*, as Will said earlier. Pace corrected him with a *c'est la merde vie*, which didn't quite make sense but was generally appreciated by the team as some very weak comedy.

Shadow leads one group. Rina another. Blue has control of the third, and me the last. *Me.* For some blatantly ludicrous reason the resistance fighters have all started looking to me for instruction, and flat out refused the idea that I wouldn't be leading one of the teams. Which I guess is flattering, but won't be great when I stuff something up and get a bunch of people made dead.

Luke is coming with me, which was my one stipulation, and no one argued. No one asked why he isn't leading a team. They can see why. He's sick. Or mad. Or something just very wrong. And it's scary, and none of them want to do this without him really being *him*, but we have to.

Shadow, Blue and Rina are already in place in the field. I'll take my team out once we've set up a few things first. Will and Pace will remain here on the ground to deal with the inundation of technical stuff.

Pace, Eric, Luke and I sit surrounded by the open hoods of three stolen cars. Will's equipment is all hooked up to the car batteries for power. I gaze at my watch. "Okay. Let's do this. Trigger it."

Will taps quickly on his laptop. He's just wirelessly triggered the bomb alarm of the most central clinic in the city. This alarm is immediately sent through to both the prime minister's office and the Blood headquarters, but Will patches the Blood's alert straight to us instead. We then respond to the clinic.

"Yes, hello?"

"Emergency services, please hold for an operator," Will says calmly.

"What's going on?" a voice says on the other end of the line. There's a wailing alarm in the building there.

Will passes the mouthpiece to me. "Emergency services explosives unit, please respond," I say.

"Yes, I'm here."

"Your name and position, ma'am?"

"Dr Jill Martin, I'm the head of the Brunswick Clinic."

"Are you aware that your explosives alarm has just been triggered, Dr Martin?" I ask her.

"Yes – I have no idea why."

"You didn't trigger it yourself, Doctor?"

"No."

"Do you have any knowledge of who might have?"

"No, I – "

"That's fine, Doctor. I'll need you to start your evacuation procedures immediately. A team is already on their way to you."

"But is there a bomb?"

"There could be any number of reasons this alarm was triggered, so all you need to concern yourself with is remaining calm, following your procedure and using your security team to evacuate the building. Can you hear the sirens?"

"It's hard with the alarm on as well – "

"That's okay, it's the emergency services on their way to you now. They're very close. A team will be arriving to help you any minute."

I gesture for Pace to give Shadow's team the go-ahead to enter the clinic. They'll pose as three Blue-level Bloods working as a bomb squad, and then they'll plant the bombs once everyone's out of the building.

"I want you to hang up the phone now, Dr Martin. Start your procedure."

"Yes, thank you." She hangs up and we move on to the next clinic, going through the same process so that Blue's team can get started on clinic number two. This time Pace takes over the job of fielding the emergency calls, following my lead, because I have to take the much scarier call that comes in from Falon Shay's home office.

His head secretary connects me to him directly, thinking I'm currently sitting in the headquarters of the Blood offices. Luke watches me closely, having managed to briefly run me through the procedures so I'll know what to say.

"Who am I speaking to?" Shay asks curtly. His voice, for some reason, chills something inside me and I feel my guts turn to liquid.

"Agent Slater, Blue status, in Jean Gueye's office, sir," I reply calmly.

"Where's Jean?"

"Agent Gueye is currently on active duty in the field, responding to the multiple explosive alarms that were set off three and four minutes ago."

"Where are the bombs?"

"No bombs have as yet been confirmed, sir. The alarms were triggered at the Brunswick and Masters clinics. Teams are already arriving at those locations now and every procedure is being followed. Protocol is to evacuate all twelve clinics – "

"There've only been threats at two," he interrupts. "I can't afford disruptions at all of them."

"Protocol is to evacuate all twelve clinics," I repeat smoothly, robotically, just as Luke coached me. "Your own guards have been notified and you will be required to remain within the safety of your home until the threat level is ascertained and nullified."

"Tell Jean to contact me immediately," he says shortly and hangs up.

Will disconnects us and I sag in trembling relief. "Holy shit," I gasp.

"You nailed it," Eric assures me.

I look to Luke, who gives a single nod of approval.

"Okay," I stand. "Time for us to tackle our own clinics. Will, keep intercepting any calls to the Bloods. Don't let Shay or his men connect with anyone but you. You know the drill." The longer we can keep Shay in the dark and withhold information from the Bloods, the better. They'll get a whiff of the commotion at some point soon, though, so we need to be quick.

"Good luck!" Will calls, then gets back to doing four million things at once. He's a genius. Pace is still busy on the phone, so she just gives us a distracted wave. Eric bends over and kisses her tummy, which I find adorable and can't help grinning over.

Our first clinic is close. Eric drives, while Luke and I check our weapons and gear. We look impressively like Bloods after having broken into one of their armories to kit ourselves out. The clinic is still open this early in the evening, but foot traffic has dwindled and the staff inside are getting everything ready for the morning's rush of injections.

If Luke was normal right now, this would be the easiest thing in the world. No one knows better how to act like a Blood than an actual Blood. Obviously. But since he's all jerky and angry, he can't waltz into the clinic and charm the pants off everyone within earshot like he would have. And since Eric is the nicest guy on the planet and is incapable of being anything but sweet as pie, the acting falls to me.

I lead the team inside and straight to the front desk. I move with as much grace as I can muster, and an arrogant tilt to my shoulders. I catch sight of a security guard and motion for him to join us with a cool flick of my wrist.

The thing is, I know exactly what a Blood is like. I lived with one for a year. Now I just have to channel what I saw in him but never recognized. And since we have no form of official identification, we have to make the notion of us being anything but Bloods seem preposterous.

"Evening," I greet the secretary at the desk. "Could you notify Dr Mahatmi to make his way here immediately, please."

The woman blinks, then grabs her phone to make the call.

"What's going on?" the security guard asks me.

I raise my hand in a gesture for him to be patient. I do it coolly, calmly. I am mostly expressionless, except for the flicker of disdain I allow to pass through my gaze as I turn away from him. Out of the corner of my eye I see him blush and take a minute step backwards.

He needs to fear us. They all do.

We stand patiently as the head of the clinic makes his way downstairs. When he arrives, Dr Mahatmi looks flustered and very tired. He is slim, with a thick white beard. I don't shake his hand when he offers it; I leave mine clasped loosely behind my back. He appraises all three of us and settles on me. "Are we still going ahead?" he asks. "You said the last load would be here by now – "

"We're with the emergency services explosives squad," I inform him. "Alarms have been set off at several clinics and due to a widespread security threat you are required to start your evacuation protocol immediately."

He stares at me. The secretary covers her mouth in fear.

"Our last orders were to leave six guards within sight of the product at all times," the security guard tells me. Which means upstairs is probably crawling with security. "And to keep everything locked down," he adds.

I meet his eyes and repeat, very clearly, "*Immediately*. Or those six guards, and everyone else in this building, might well be blown to pieces before you can blink those big brown eyes of yours."

The guard swallows and Mahatmi rushes to the front desk to set off a loud tone throughout the clinic. People begin to move, mostly staff.

I step toward the security guard. I try to make myself bigger than him, even though he towers over me. I've seen Luke do it a thousand times. The bone-deep knowledge that he could destroy you – it's that certainty that makes you big even if you are small. "Are you in charge of security?" I ask the man, allowing my eyes to skim him up and down briefly.

He clears his throat. "Yes."

"Have you run an evacuation procedure before?"

"Once."

"Good. Record time for an evacuation of a building this size is three minutes. I expect you to do it in half that."

He jerks into action, running with sudden speed to a stairwell and screeching into his radio.

"Three minutes?" Luke asks me.

"He looks like he could use the exercise." I am absurdly happy to see the edge of Luke's mouth relax into a faint smile.

I wait with Eric and Luke, holding our stances, until everyone is out of the building and security has done several sweeps to ensure that.

"You are not permitted to enter the building, or allow anyone else to enter, until you have specific clearance from me. Do you understand?" I ask Mahatmi and the security guard, who are the last to evacuate.

They nod.

"You will remain at a distance of at least one hundred yards from the building at all times. We will now do our own sweep of the building and ascertain the existence of any explosive material. Do you understand?"

They nod once more, looking pretty freaked.

My team and I make our way swiftly upstairs.

"You are scarily good at being a Blood," Eric mutters.

"I'm just glad they didn't question why there aren't a bunch of police and a whole host of emergency services people to set up perimeters," I reply.

"Too stupid to," Eric shrugs.

"Not stupid," Luke grunts. "Scared."

Hurrying to the storerooms, we check the mountains of boxes to see thousands of vials of the drug. "Yep, this is it," I breathe, holding one of them in my fingers and looking at the yellow-colored liquid. When the boys aren't looking, I slip the vial into my left pocket.

We set up the homemade bombs, which are wirelessly connected to Will's command computer and will be triggered when each team has given the all-clear. We place more explosives in the loading bay, enough to ensure the whole building will come down. I do feel bad about destroying a place designed to help sick people, but seriously – don't fry people's brains and we won't blow you up.

Without exiting through the front where the staff waits for us, we head straight out the back and on to the second clinic on our roster. We'll let Mahatmi and his people wait a safe distance away for us, and when the bomb blows they'll think we were killed inside, removing any trail.

The second clinic goes pretty much the same way, although the head security guard isn't as nervous around me so I have to work harder to get him to back off on the questions. Soon it too has been evacuated and planted with bombs.

On our way to the third and last clinic I check in with the other teams and find that their evacuations have all gone smoothly. Blue's team has one more to get through, but the rest are finished. I instruct them to head home to the garage.

As soon as we enter the last clinic, I know we're going to have a serious problem. We left the largest until last, not wanting it rigged with explosives for too long before detonation because they'd be more likely to be discovered. And in this riskiest of all clinics, right here in the main reception, stand five Bloods. Real ones.

I panic, my footsteps faltering. I can't bullshit these guys. I won't even get close.

And that's when Luke finally finds some measure of control over his poor body, and steps up to help me. He walks straight over to the Bloods. "Status?"

They turn, this group of cold, detached young men, all sleek and dangerous like the cool touch of a gun or the soulless ruthlessness of a great white shark. They are terrifying, and they scare me more than the Furies. They are dead-eyed and still, and there was so much of this in Luke when I first met him – I just didn't recognize it until this moment.

"ID?" one asks. He has red hair and freckles, and it occurs to me that he would have been an adorable child before he was emptied of his humanity. It's a different curse, being a Blood, but a curse nonetheless.

"Explosives squad sent from headquarters," Luke replies flatly. "They haven't updated you yet?"

A headshake. Those calculating eyes trace Luke shrewdly.

"Connect in," Luke orders with blunt impatience.

The red-haired guy, who is clearly ranking officer, touches his earpiece and radios in to headquarters, where I'm praying Will will intercept the call.

"Update status for the Leeds clinic," the Blood requests and then listens.

I hold my breath.

"Copy that." He turns to Luke with a different expression, this one more curious than anything else. "Evacuation protocol."

Two of his Bloods move to alert the clinic.

"We haven't met," he says, offering a hand to Luke. "Knox, Blue."

Luke shakes it, doing a good job of looking bored. Apparently the same intimidation techniques apply *within* the Bloods too.

"Been on explosives long?"

"No one's on explosives long," Luke says.

Knox grins, and there's a savage edge to it. They are all ultra-aware of death, these men. Luke's been training us to be able to kill them, but I realize now that we haven't even come close to their level of ruthlessness. The difference between us and them is that they don't care if they die – I can see it in every dart of their eyes, every empty twist of their lips.

Luke's fists start clenching and unclenching of their own accord. I don't know if he's noticed, but Knox sure has. The Blood's eyes go to the unusual movement and then dart back up to Luke's tight jaw. That gaze narrows.

"You didn't tell me your name," Knox points out softly.

"I didn't," Luke agrees.

Come on, I urge the staff as they evacuate. This place is so much bigger than the others though, and there are so many more people to move. I can feel Eric fidgeting nervously beside me and give him a reassuring look. My heart is thumping painfully.

"I asked you a question," Knox says.

"No, you didn't."

The Blood smiles, but there's zero humor in it. "Alright. I'll specify the implied question for you. What is your name and rank, soldier? Or would you prefer me to contact headquarters to verify it?"

Luke turns to look at Knox properly for the first time. I watch, my breath catching in my throat, as the coldest expression I have ever seen passes his eyes.

"You're going to feel very foolish," Luke warns quietly, emotionlessly. "And you're going to feel small. Better you just leave it, Agent Knox."

Knox hesitates for a fraction of a second, thrown by the words. "I'll be the judge of that."

Luke murmurs, "Agent Luke Townsend, Gray."

I freeze in horror.

And I watch as Knox looks ashen. All words are stolen from his white lips and he looks like he might either faint or vomit. "Forgive me," he manages to blurt. "I had no idea ... You ... Why are you on *explosives*, sir?"

"The rest of the world grew too boring for me," Luke replies lazily.

Knox flushes beet red and gives an awkward laugh. He is utterly awestruck, and opens his mouth to say something.

"Stop speaking," Luke orders him without so much as a glance, and Knox's mouth snaps shut.

My heart is pounding. It's patently clear that Knox doesn't know of Luke's rogue status, but Jesus – pretty big gamble.

The evacuation finishes at last. Luke orders Knox to form a perimeter outside and make sure everyone stays well behind it. He, Eric and I then make our way upstairs.

"I think I just had a stroke," Eric admits when we're alone in the first storeroom.

"You're out of your mind!" I exclaim.

Luke is busy setting up the explosives. "There's no way in hell Jean will have informed anyone except other Grays about my status," Luke says. "Disloyalty within the Bloods can't exist."

"I thought there weren't any other Grays," I say.

"Exactly."

I shake my head, nerves too fried to argue further. *We're fine*, I tell myself. *It worked.*

My radio crackles and Will's urgent voice sounds. "*Dual. There are too many calls coming through. I can't field them all – the server's about to crash.*"

"Calm down, Will," I tell him. "Have the others all reported the okay to detonate?"

"*Yes.*"

"Great. We're very close, we just need a few more minutes to get clear of the building."

"*You don't have a few minutes – Oh fuck.*"

"What?"

No response.

"Will!" I shout.

"*The Bloods know. They know the clinics have all been evacuated. They're being dispatched as we speak.*"

Which means we have to blow the buildings *now*.

The only way Will could rig the detonation wirelessly was to have all the bombs in all the clinics connected to the same detonator, meaning they all go together, or none of them do.

We scramble to finish connecting the bombs and turning them on, then dart out of the room and back into the corridor.

"We have to do the ground floor!" I shout, knowing that the whole clinic needs to go. No loose ends.

"*The Bloods in your building know!*" Will shouts into the walkie. "*They have orders to kill you on sight!*"

We draw our guns. My instinct is to split up – it would be quicker – but one of Luke's rules reappears in my head. *Never split from designated team members. The team exists to protect each other, or you wouldn't bother having one in the first place.*

We sprint through corridors and down the stairwell. We'll never make it across the clinic and out the back without being spotted. I run through the blueprints of the building in my mind, making a swift decision.

"This way," I pant, veering into a service elevator. We take it down two floors, below ground-level, then emerge into the parking lot. Which isn't a parking lot anymore. It's a storage space.

All three of us skid to a halt, eyes widening.

"Oh my *god*," Eric breathes.

It is thousands and thousands of crates full of the sadness cures. The garage is enormous, spanning what must be the next few city blocks.

"We would never have got it all," I whisper.

Luke grabs us and urgently shoves us behind a huge wall of crates, covering our mouths. The sound of several sets of feet passes by us and I catch sight of at least four Bloods, weapons raised. They sweep into the rows of crates and disappear.

"This whole space will be crawling soon," Luke whispers. "Teams will have already been stationed down here."

"We can't let this much of the drug survive," I say.

Luke nods, too quickly. We bend our knees, lower our heads and start creeping our way through the rows of crates. Every few feet we stop and listen as more Bloods pass by on their patrols. Several times we have to duck around to the other side to keep from being spotted.

We make it to where we can see the second stairwell, which will take us up and into a patient area. This will then lead us outside, but we are forced to pause as two Bloods emerge a few rows in front of us. Peering around the crate, we wait for them to move, but they don't.

One of them is speaking into his earpiece. "… is all clear."

We don't have silencers on our guns, which means if we were to fire at them, the whole clinic would know exactly where we are. I turn to Luke to whisper something – I don't even know what – but realize as I do so that he's moved around the row to come at the Bloods from an angle.

He moves forward silently, superhumanly fast, and snaps the first Blood's neck. The man falls in a crumpled heap without a sound. Luke has already jabbed his fingers into the second man's throat, stopping the shout of alarm. Moving more carefully, he looks into the Blood's eyes as he twists his neck sharply, and then both of them are dead and it wasn't even hard, it was easy easy easy.

As Luke motions to us, I swallow the churning horror in my gut.

Up we go. Straight into another Blood, who dies with Luke's dagger in his heart. Past the body. Down the hallway and into the cafeteria.

"Freeze!" a voice booms from behind us.

Half a dozen Bloods this time, all with guns raised.

We dive beneath tables and start scrambling across the ground. Shots fire, a storm of them. The table above my head explodes as I skid along the cool linoleum floor. I manage to roll onto my back and fire up at the Blood towering over me. It takes him by surprise and my shot lands in his chest. I keep firing in utter panic, letting loose bullets and unable to release my finger.

Abruptly my gun stops firing at all, and instead makes an empty clicking sound.

Oh my god. I have just done the one thing I was warned not to do on multiple occasions. What a complete idiot. As I scramble for a new magazine cartridge, a Blood arrives and would have undoubtedly killed me if not for Eric's shot taking him through the cheek. Blood sprays me but I have time only to keep moving, sliding awkwardly behind another table for cover and getting my gun reloaded.

Luke and Eric have found their own tables and are firing around them, as quick and sharp as they can. Three of the Bloods are down, so the other three have stopped advancing, taking their own cover. We're in a shootout, I realize. An actual gun battle. Jesus, my hands are shaking.

Remembering Luke's words, I will myself to calm down. *Don't ever do anything while you're panicked.*

There's only about twenty yards between us and the door, but there's no more cover on the way.

"I've got you," Luke barks. "On my count, you both run."

Another breath, a shared glance with Eric, and then Luke shouts, "Go!" and we go. I hurl myself forward, certain that any one of the shots I can hear is going to collide with my body. But I keep moving, keeping running, until I have launched myself behind the door and out of the line of fire.

Eric skids into me and I pull him to safety.

We draw our guns and start firing around the door to cover Luke. We aren't as efficient at it as he is – as he turns to run I see a bullet slam into his back and a savage gasp is torn from me. But he keeps going, barely faltering at all. It's hit his vest, I realize with woozy relief.

Luke doesn't even stop when he reaches us, but hauls us forward and along the hallway.

"Left!" I shout when we hit a turn, and we follow it around and into the patient area. Dozens of beds are lined up on either side, all thankfully empty. It's dark in here, and I can only just see the shapes of Luke and Eric ahead of me.

"Get to the controls," I tell Luke. "On the wall – there's a quarantine button that'll stop them following us."

My hip cracks into the edge of a bed or something and I hit the ground hard, wincing.

"Josi – " Luke yells.

"I'm fine! Hit the button!" I struggle to my feet and run after them. As he finds the controls the lights flood on and glass walls begin to slide out of the roof on either end of the room. Four inches thick, this glass was developed a decade or so ago, after the walls went up and containment became the government's top priority. It's all over the city, throughout government buildings and facilities, and there is no record of it ever having been breached.

This is what runs through my head in the split second my eyes catch sight of something glinting on the floor in the middle of the room.

A vial.

My hands dart to my pockets – *please please please* – to find that my left still contains the sadness cure I stole, which means the one I dropped when I fell must be Luke's antidote. *No.*

I don't think. I just move.

"Josi!"

My body bullets across the room and lunges for the vial, feeling it between my sweat-slippery fingers. I am turning back when Knox arrives, ducking beneath the lowering glass and coming at me.

I hurl myself toward Luke and Eric, but that glass is coming down way too fast.

I'm not going to make it.

I throw myself along the floor, extending my hand and letting the vial skid beneath the glass a second before it seals us off.

Everything goes quiet.

Slowly I rise to my feet. Luke is staring at me in horror. At his feet, the vial has rolled to a safe stop. Eric jabs at the control buttons frantically, but he won't be able to get it open, not without the code, which none of us knows.

"Go," I tell them bluntly, unsure whether they can hear me. "Go detonate the bombs, or I'll never forgive either of you."

I turn around without waiting for their responses.

In the sealed quarantine section with me is a Blue-level Blood, his soulless eyes appraising me. I can feel him noting my small stature, my exhaustion, each one of my weapons. I try to do the same to him, but I'm so unfocused, my mind darting around in panic and weariness. A rush of adrenalin strikes and I grab my gun, firing wildly at him.

Knox ducks behind a bed, but the bullets ricochet off the glass, pinging around the room unpredictably. Beds are hit, trays explode, screens smash and glass sprays the ground. I yelp and take cover behind a chair.

"Not too wise, kid," Knox calls to me. I hear something clatter and peek out to see that he's thrown both his guns to the ground.

Oh god. I don't want to face him without a weapon. But I sure as hell can't fire a gun again. The bullet could just as easily bounce into my skull as hit him. With trembling hands I return my gun to its holster.

I can hear him walking toward me but I can't move.

"Stand up," I hear Luke's faint voice say, and look through the glass at him. Eric is gone, I hope to safety.

"Josephine," he orders. "*Stand up*."

I take a breath and lurch to my feet. Knox is upon me, hands reaching for my neck – he must think he can snap it like Luke did to the other guys. Then terror spikes and rushes my body, making me *fast*. I duck beneath his hands and shove my shoulder into his solar plexus with enough force, so that I can get around him, find the middle of the floor and turn to lift my fists.

Knox faces me, astonishment in his eyes. "You wanna *fight* me, kid?"

"Do I have a choice?"

"Guess not," he shrugs, lunging at me with a swift right jab to my head. I only just manage to dodge it – he's too quick – and as I jerk backwards my hands come up to protect my head with a wild gasp of panic.

Knox's punch flies toward me and I duck low into a huddled crouch, trying to cover my head again. He stops. I wince, looking up to see that he's just staring at me with *pity* in his eyes. Pity and scorn.

What am I doing what the fuck am I doing –

"Stand up!" Luke roars at me.

I rise unsteadily, ashamed but unable to do anything about it.

Knox shakes his head. "This is ridiculous." He turns to Luke and yells. "I'm not gonna fight a *little girl*, Townsend. Tell her to stand down and I'll take her in gently." Knox removes handcuffs from his belt.

Luke looks only at me.

All this training and this is what I've turned out to be: a coward.

His voice reaches me faintly through the glass, but I hear every word. "He's going to hurt you," Luke tells me, holding my eyes. "*It doesn't matter. All you have to do is hurt him more.*"

A chill travels down my spine, and something unlocks itself inside me.

There have been moments in my life when I have been savage. I remember only fragments of these moments, but I can feel them, somehow. They live in my heart, where the monstrous one dwells.

It was me who always cared about pain. She never did. So in this moment I let her icy fingers reach out to clutch at my heart and squeeze. The pieces of her coil into the pieces of me until I am not sure where I end and she begins. She is colder than any Blood, and she is screaming to get free, and for the first time in my life I will let her.

Knox approaches me with his handcuffs.

Everything in my body tingles; I can feel it all, every inch of it. I open my eyes. Hold my wrists out to him.

As Knox reaches for one, I snatch the metal of the cuffs and wrench him toward me, sending my knee into his groin.

A shocked breath of air escapes him and I use the split second to curl behind him, the cuffs cinching around his neck. I put all my weight into dragging him to the ground by the throat, choking the air out of him.

He swings me sideways, slamming me to the floor and crawling on top – *No, don't let him on top of you.* If he pins me it's all over. I roll out of his way and grab the edge of a bed, pulling myself awkwardly to my feet and just managing to avoid his clutches.

I'm about to attack him while he's still rising but he's too quick, launching to his feet in less than a second. I raise my fists, and this time I do it properly. No fear, only concentration. *Spot his weakness.*

His blows hit me hard in the arms and body and it *hurts*, but I'm watching him. He fights like Luke does, and also not. I can see the edges of his blows, can see the dart of his eyes before he throws a punch, and I can see how much more certain he is with his right side.

I attack his left with a quick jab, wanting to see.

Sure enough, he dodges it, but there's a slight shift in his stance. It doesn't look right to me.

Knox jabs me twice in the guts and as I lower my arms to block him he hits me in the chin with a heavy uppercut that sends me reeling. I let the momentum take me backwards until I feel a metal tray against my spine. Ducking low beneath another incoming blow, I twist and grab the tray, propelling myself around in a wide arc to smash the metal straight into his face.

Blood spurts and I do it again, twice more until he catches the tray and pulls me in close to his body. His knee jams up into my guts and the air leaves my lungs with an *oomph*.

I hit the floor on all fours and he kicks me in the ribs, breaking at least three by the feel of it.

I am dizzy with pain. My brain stops working. My limbs feel liquid.

But it's only pain. As long as I'm conscious, it's only pain.

As his next kick connects with my abdomen I curl myself around the impact of it, sending him off balance and falling forward. I draw the knife from my belt and lunge up at him with it. He twists and the blade takes a thin slice off the fabric on his shoulder.

We rise, facing each other. He draws his own knife.

Great. I don't have a clue how to be in a knife-fight.

He lunges and I jump backwards, narrowly avoiding a blade to the guts. *Focus*.

We jab and slash, neither one of us able to land a cut, both too protective. I have to change tactics. On the next jab of his knife, I allow it to slash through my cheek. I immediately swing my own blade, not toward his body but up and into his extended right arm. It slices through his flesh and his blade flies free. Before he can react I dart forward and slash my knife through his right hip.

Knox twists back and away, shielding himself. Unfortunately the movement catches my knife and tugs it from my sweaty fingers. I punch him in the back of the head instead, but the blow isn't hard enough.

His arm snaps up, fist taking me in the face before I can try again.

Spots dance before my eyes and he's coming at me, hitting me in the chest, the guts, the face. I can't breathe. There's blood in my mouth and the room is spinning. I remember to get my arms up to take the blows.

Through the delirium I can see again the weakness I spotted. He's still favoring his right side, even after I slashed it with my knife. It's his left knee – he's protective of it, like he might be if he's had a recent injury.

I can't last much longer like this. I have to finish it before I lose consciousness.

I turn and run – as though my tail is between my legs – and hear him give a breath of victorious laughter. But I reach the other end of the room where I know there's a chair, because it was the chair I hid behind. And when I hid, I saw that the chair has metal legs that click out of the base.

And I know a lot about using metal chair legs as weapons. I know too much.

Sliding to the floor, I grab the chair and twist one of the legs free. I barely scramble under the bed before Knox reaches me, his knife reclaimed and swiping through my ear.

I haul myself up onto the bed, using the spring of the mattress to launch me. I twist mid-air, kicking out with my leg and taking Knox heavily in the head. It stuns him, and as I land I swing that chair leg as hard as I can into Knox's left knee.

A scream leaves him and his legs buckle.

I hammer his knee again and again until I feel the bones smash beneath the metal of my pole.

The pain of it causes him to faint dead away.

I am breathing heavily, the adrenalin leaving me in a steady rush. The room slows to a stop, the details of it coming back into focus. I blink, returning to my mind. Everything goes quiet and still.

"Josephine."

I look up, so dazed I can barely see him.

"Kill him," Luke tells me.

I swallow. Shake my head.

"He's going to wake up and manage his pain. You can't let that happen."

My mouth is full of blood. "I don't want to be this," I manage through it.

Luke's expression is hard. "You don't have a choice. He wakes up and you're dead. Take everything inside you, every tiny piece of rage and hurt and all the fucked-up shit you've been through, and shoot him in the head."

I start crying.

"Don't cry," Luke orders me. "Draw your gun."

My hand is shaking badly as I pull out the pistol. My eyes are swimming with tears. "He's like you," I plead. "He's just like you."

"Doesn't matter. Go closer. Put the barrel against his forehead."

This is sick.

Clenching my jaw, I hold the barrel against Knox's forehead.

"He's about to wake up. Do it now."

Knox stirs, and I don't think about it – I pull the trigger.

*

Luke

I watch it all, and understand when the knowing of something becomes the *knowing* of something. I knew she was strong. I knew she had an incredible strength of will. But I didn't *know*. Not until this moment, as I watch her defeat a Blood twice her size. I feel the closest I have felt to normal in weeks. It's as though watching all of this has scorched the drugs from my system.

As I see her kill him I realize the price of this victory. The price of her *survival*. She has become like me, and I wouldn't wish that upon anyone.

I sent Eric with the radio and instructions for Will to detonate. It will be any second now. I can feel the steady rush of an ocean tide ripping all the moments of our life from us.

Josi straightens, the gun falling from her hand. She is splattered in Knox's blood and her own.

"Come here," I say, heart pounding.

She crosses to me, in shock. I press my hands to the glass, look into her eyes. "Put it in a box, and lock that box, and then put the box away. It's a part of you, but it doesn't rule you. You decide where it goes."

Josi wipes her mouth with the back of her hand, smearing the blood further. "What was the point? I'm dead anyway."

I shake my head.

"Why are you still here?" She is suddenly very cold. The result of putting it in a box. This is what happens, what has to happen. "I told you to go. Get out of here and tell Will to blow the place. Or all of this was pointless."

I don't move.

"Go!" she shouts furiously. "I don't *want* you here."

"Josi – "

"You think you're being noble or something but you're not. The resistance needs you, Luke Townsend. The world does. *Leave and finish what we started.*"

I take a breath, hold her eyes. My words, when they come, are simple and sure. A tide rushing out. "There is no world in which I would ever leave you to die alone."

She stares at me. Her shoulders finally sag and her face presses against the glass. I want to hold her, reach through this glass and melt into her. Instead I rest my forehead to hers.

I don't care about the world. I am a selfish creature. Ruled by love and violence. If I must watch her die, I will die with her, and that's the end.

Chapter 28

Luke

Movement in the corner of my eye. I straighten to see figures enter the other side of the room and stand behind the glass. Four Bloods, Jean Gueye and Falon Shay.

Josi turns to face them too. Knox's body lies in the space between.

The Minister taps the control panel and the glass starts to rise. My heart explodes with hope and then shatters the second I realize that only their side of the glass is moving. I am still separated from Josi.

They enter the patient area with her.

"Miss Luquet," Shay says. "I've heard a lot about you." His eyes dart up to me. "And you, Townsend. Nice to see you again. You've been busy since we last met. Think I might revoke that medal of honor of yours after this business."

I don't feel very human as I look at the man. I turn my eyes from him without a word, which I know will get under his skin more than anything. "Jean. I've missed you."

She looks *really* pissed. "Well haven't you turned out to be the biggest mistake of my life."

"I reckon a lot of people feel that way about me." I smile darkly.

"You surprise me, Prime Minister," Josi interrupts the reunion calmly. "I sort of pictured you as a cockroach."

Shay smiles. "And why is that, dear?"

"You're the one man who manages to survive through everything because you hide out of sight and avoid danger. And yet here you stand. In a building seconds away from being blown up."

"They won't blow up their leaders," he says, unbothered.

It's Josi's turn to smile now, just a slight tilt to her lips. "Oh dear. You thought we were in charge? Not at all. We're soldiers, easily replaced and sacrificed if need be. You understand that, don't you?" Her eyes move to the dead Blood on the ground.

Shay watches her. He's not amused anymore. I can see him weighing it up. He's itching to get the hell out of here. But he's also smart, and thinks she's bluffing. She and I are big gets, now that we've openly waged war on the cure. He wants to string up our corpses as examples for all to see.

He gestures and the four Bloods take hold of Josi. She struggles with a wild snarl of rage, but they hold her firm and there's no way out of it.

Something strange uncurls within me. Something dark.

The drug inside surges back to life with a vengeance, but I think it's carried by a wave of my own fury, a beast of a thing that has lain in wait for a very long time, yearning to rise.

Thoughts go. Logic and rationale go. Control goes. Fear with it.

I am animal. I'm a brain that has flushed my limbs with grunt guts blood fists balls teeth *fight*. My amygdala explodes, flooding me with the primal screaming shrieking need to survive and to kill.

The glass separating her from me must go.

I slam my fist into it. Pain slices up my arm. But there's power there, too, unnatural power. I punch the glass a second time

432

Blood smears it. I punch it again and again and again and again and again and again –

My hand breaks, the bones within splintering. Ravens fly around my head, hundreds of them. They make me strong.

I punch again.

The glass cracks.

Josi is screaming at me to stop, please stop, but they are dragging her away and I know that if I don't get to her now I'll never find her and I must kill Shay now now *now* –

A roar leaves my mouth as I smash through the unbreakable glass.

Shards slice through my skin and blood pools to the ground. I feel nothing. Nothing but rage. It overwhelms, drowns. I am saturated in it.

*

Josephine

I can't get free, even as I struggle with all I have. The hands on my arms are too strong, too tight. Shay and Jean lead me down an empty corridor, fast like they finally believe the building could blow at any second.

They'll put me in a prison I can never escape from.

Luke will die trying to break through my glass cage.

We reach the front reception. Through the front doors I can see what looks like hundreds of people all flocked behind a partition. Police sirens wail. Cameras flash. Loudspeakers bark at people to remain back.

I've lost my radio so I have no idea why the hell Will hasn't blown the place yet.

Four more Bloods enter from the front to meet us.

It takes me several seconds to realize. They are *mine*. My soldiers. Not Bloods at all. Shadow, Eric, Blue and Rina.

They move smoothly to flank us as though they have been ordered to. "All clear, sir," Eric reports.

Jean and Shay don't bat an eyelid, but continue their path to the doors.

Until the prime minister's feet falter. He slows, frowning. And then he spins, drawing his gun. I am pulled hard against his chest, his weapon shoved to my temple. The second he moves, everyone else is moving. The resistance fighters point their guns at the Bloods, who point theirs straight back.

"Stop," Shay shouts before anyone can fire. "Nobody move or she dies!"

Everyone freezes mid-standoff.

"You thought I wouldn't recognize you," Shay breathes. "But I've looked at your file a thousand times. A million. I know your face better than any in the world." He pauses, draws a breath that I can feel tremble. "It's not every day a man steals your wife and then murders her, after all."

What? It's well known that the Minister's beautiful, young wife disappeared twenty years ago and was never found.

I pull against Shay's arms, but he jams the gun harder into my head. I scan the faces of my friends, but I can't see any –

Oh, *shit.*

Shadow. There's death in his eyes, and hatred. I've never seen such hatred. He's staring at Falon Shay as though he was born to destroy him.

"How have you survived this long?" Shay asks him.

Shadow says nothing.

"We don't have time for this," Jean snaps, but Shay doesn't move. I can feel his heartbeat against my back and it's *pounding.*

"Let her go," Shadow orders softly.

Shay laughs, this sick sound hot against the back of my neck. My skin crawls.

"How did you do it?" Shay hisses. "How did you murder my wife?"

"Let. Her. Go."

"You think I wouldn't kill her in front of you? You think I haven't dreamed of this moment for the last two decades?"

Shadow steps forward and Shay cocks the gun, that familiar click sounding throughout the eerily quiet reception area. "Come closer," the Minister says. "I dare you."

I can see agitation in Shadow's face.

And then Falon Shay says, "You and all of your people are under arrest, Philippe Luquet."

I blink.

Shadow's eyes meet mine.

The air goes from my chest.

"Josi – " he whispers.

But that's when Jean gasps and we all turn to witness her slump bonelessly to the ground. Behind her stands Luke, his knife dripping with her blood.

But it isn't Luke. Not really. I can see that he's gone from his body and the blood moon has come early for him. He's monstrous as he kneels over his former boss. She is squirming, trying to get up.

"You always knew it'd be me, didn't you?" he asks, and he sounds nothing like the man I know. His hand is shattered and bleeding but he holds the knife without any concern, and he slices it straight through her throat.

It breaks the trance the rest of us are in. Guns explode as both sides fire at the other. Shay yanks me backward toward the exit, but Shadow appears and cracks him over the head.

The Minister loosens his hold on me and I manage to wriggle away.

He has already facing Shadow in a brutal fight, decades in the making.

I turn to see the Bloods fighting the resisters, but really, Eric, Blue and Rina aren't working all that hard because Luke has gone full Hulk, and is smashing his way through the four Blood soldiers.

I circle him, knowing that he'll turn on his friends as soon as the closest bodies are out of his way – there's no control when the virus takes hold. No choosing who to kill and who to save.

And that's when it hits me.

There's no choosing.

All the pieces suddenly fall into place and I am awash with a relief so fierce it blinds me.

But there isn't time now to deal with any of that, or to dwell on it – Luke is killing the last Blood, and next in line are the resistance fighters. I continue on my path, moving to edge in behind him –

He looks quizzically at me over his shoulder. "What are you doing?"

I frown. "Oh. Shit. I thought you were, like, turned."

"Still here."

I feel like an idiot. But I'm also relieved. Until a whole bunch of Bloods burst through the door.

And goddamn Falon Shay grabs hold of me. "Again?" I snap. Out of the corner of my eye I can see Shadow rising woozily from the ground.

Every single person in the room then hears the crackle of Eric's radio and Will's voice echoing through the reception. *"The goddamn failsafe just activated! Thirty seconds until detonation! If anyone is still in that building then get the hell out!"*

We freeze for half a second, and then everyone launches for the front doors, not caring which team anyone is fighting for, just scrambling like mad to get out.

Except for me. Because Shay is dragging me further into the building. A yelp of horror takes me and I thrash against him. "Stop, you freak!"

"He'll watch you die," he breathes against my ear. The man has totally lost it.

Abruptly his weight pitches on top of me and I hit the ground hard. Wriggling from under him, I see Shadow wrestling Shay off me.

"Run!" he yells at me, struggling to hold the prime minister down.

There is no way I'm running without him. I lunge forward to help, but hands take hold of me, lifting me off the ground.

"Shadow!" I scream.

But it's Luke, and he's carrying me away. "Don't!" I shriek. "*Shadow*!"

Shadow looks up in time for our eyes to meet. He shouts, "*Go*."

And then Luke is hauling me away, sprinting as fast as he can, and we're outside and I'm screaming my throat hoarse and beating at him but he isn't letting me go and we're too far away now –

The building explodes into a mighty inferno.

We are thrown off our feet by a massive burst of energy. My ears explode and everything goes black.

*

When I gain consciousness again the world has descended into chaos. Fire engines roar and sirens wail. People are running all over the place and the clinic is a burning wreck of smoking rubble.

Luke is out cold beside me; I reach urgently to shake him awake. We're in a grassy ditch beside the main road, and have been so far overlooked in the dark and the madness, but that won't last long. My ears are ringing terribly, but I seem to be getting some hearing back.

"Luke!" I hiss, slapping him hard in the face.

He lurches straight up, disoriented but adjusting quickly. We struggle to our feet and take off down the hill, running for all we're worth. I can't see any of the others, but I think they made it out before we did.

We have to get through a dozen streets, past cars and people swarming everywhere, but we manage to reach a residential area and climb over into someone's backyard.

Ducking behind some shrubbery, we peer around in the dark. There's no way we'll make it back to the garage like this, not with so much chaos going on. We'd be just as likely to lead the Bloods straight there.

"We need to find somewhere to hide for the night," I say.

He can't hear me; his hearing hasn't healed as quickly as mine. Loudly, he says, "Gotta find an empty house."

I cover his mouth quickly. "Shhh! Jesus."

We start backyard hopping, searching for anything empty. Several times lights come on and we have to run for it. It seems we're never going to find anywhere and I'm not sure how long I can keep going on pure adrenalin.

*

September 13th, 2066

Josephine

It's 1 in the morning before we manage to find somewhere. It's a guest studio, but thankfully there's no view of its windows from the main house, and it's empty.

Luke can't pick the lock because his hand is broken and swollen to the size of a watermelon, so he has to talk me through it. I fail – my fingers are trembling too much – so we wind up breaking one of the windows as quietly as possible and climbing in.

We don't turn on any lights, but even in the dark I can see it's a studio with a bed, a table, a mini fridge and a sink. It also has a small bathroom to one side. Luke takes one look at me and leads me straight to it. I feel so numb I'm not sure I'll ever feel anything again. I'm in shock, and I know this as if from very far away. My teeth are chattering.

He gently removes my clothes, even though it must hurt his hand. I remove his, and we both move as if in a trance. We are filthy with dirt and soot and blood. Our bodies are bruised and broken. We are ghostlike in the dark bathroom.

He turns the shower on and together we step in, letting the warm water sluice over our bodies.

He runs his good hand over my skin, using his fingers to remove the dirt and blood, moving it through my hair to clean it. I don't have the energy to do the same for him. My legs can't hold me up any longer. I sink to the floor and he sits with me, drawing me into his arms.

I look up into his face. Water runs over the lines of it, dripping onto me. The last time we were in a shower together was the morning before he told me he was a Blood agent. One year ago, I realize.

"It's alright, darling," he whispers to me.

But it's not. "His real name was Philippe Luquet," I say numbly.

Luke frowns, searching my face in the dark. "Who?"

I swallow. "Shadow."

He breathes out, like someone has punched him in the gut. "No."

"Yes."

"Oh, *fuck*."

I press my lips hard against his, wanting quiet and loud and hard and soft and anything at all but this fist of thorns in my chest.

He pulls back. "Josi."

I kiss him again, more firmly. I push him until his back is against the shower wall and then I slide my legs over his hips. My hand reaches down to find his cock, already hard. I slide it inside me, my mouth opening against his.

His hand traces over my collarbone, down over my breasts, resting for a moment against my heartbeat. Then moves to grip my hip, pulling me against him as he moves deeper into me. A soft moan leaves me as he grinds inside, his fingers reaching to stroke my clit at the same time. I gasp, my heart and skin and nerves exploding into wingbeats that thrust up into the sky.

My fingers go to his hair and tug on it, and I lean down and bite his shoulder, hard, until I draw blood. He thrusts harder inside me and I can feel the tingling pressure building. I can't think straight or feel straight and I don't want to. I don't want to think or feel again, except for this, I want this forever.

"Don't stop," I tell him.

He lifts me quickly onto my back and moves much deeper inside me, and muffles my cry with his mouth. His tongue is on mine, against my lips, my teeth, he is biting my lower lip.

He takes my face in his hand so he can look at me as I come. As soon as he sees me dissolve he lets himself do the same, and then he slumps on top of me, the water still running over us both.

I don't realize at first, until he looks at me and this expression of anguish twists his face. He leans down to kiss my eyelids, and that's when I know I've started to cry. It builds in a great big rush of agony in my chest, a heavy weight that belongs to disbelief and anger and absolute unfairness.

Luke carries me to the bed and dries me off before wrapping me in a blanket. Then he wraps himself around me and holds me as I cry. The only thing that keeps me sane is the thought of the vial I stole and put in my pocket, the one that can cure me of this wretched sadness. The minute Luke falls asleep I'm going to inject myself.

*

Hours later I realize I must have dozed off at some point as I stir awake again. The gray light of predawn peeks beneath the curtain above us. Luke is staring at the ceiling, lost in thought. I roll onto my back beside him, keeping my hand laced with his. I've missed my opportunity. It will have to be when we get back to the garage.

Knox's face is in my mind. I'm not sure I'll ever get it out of there. And Philippe.

"We did what we came to do," Luke murmurs, as if responding to my thoughts.

"At what cost?"

"It was always going to be messy. There was *always* going to be cost. It's fresh right now. At least let the dust settle before you start questioning yourself."

"I'm not cut out for this."

"Actually," he replies, "I think you're the only one of us who really is."

I don't know how he means them to sound, but they feel cruel, those words. "People died last night."

"You're losing sight," he says. "Don't lose sight."

"But who are we to decide?" I ask softly. "Why do *we* know best? What right do we have to choose for the rest of the city?"

There's a silence, and finally he replies, "I don't know."

*

Luke's hand is so mangled that it frightens me, and his lips are white with pain as I bandage it. We switch the television on, keeping it low enough that no one will overhear. News bulletins cover every channel, footage of last night's mission that makes it look like a brutal terrorist attack.

I'm not entirely sure it wasn't. It's certainly a fine line between being a terrorist and a savior.

The bulletins all go on to say that despite the terrorists' efforts, Prime Minister Falon Shay made it out alive.

Luke and I look at each other, shocked.

If the Minister got out, then maybe Shadow did too. Giddy longing is born in my heart, and I make a vow. If my father is still alive, I'm going to find him.

*

When Luke and I make it back to the garage the sun is just starting to rise and we find the rest of the crew in a maelstrom of emotions. They're elated that the mission was a success, but they're grieving, too, because Shadow, Blue and Rina didn't make it out. I share my hope for Shadow, but no one looks as though they buy it.

The conversation falls to what comes next and an argument breaks out.

"We can't go back there," Pace points out angrily. "You heard Quinn!"

"It's our home!" Eric replies.

"Not anymore. We're dead if we go back there."

"And how long do you think we can survive here? After what happened last night the whole city's gonna be on red alert."

While they argue, I walk over to the medical supply kit. Will sees me remove a syringe. I nod toward Luke, who's standing stiff like an iron statue at the doorway, muscles locked with tension.

"Has to be done," I tell him softly. "But he won't want it."

"Why?"

"It makes him feel powerful. He thinks he needs it."

I slip the syringe into my pocket and turn to Luke.

*

Luke

Josi has a falcon on her shoulder as she approaches me. I watch it, as it watches me. It's the most beautiful thing I've ever seen; it is silent and majestic, its plumage speckled gray and white. I feel sad that no one else is lucky enough to see it.

"Give me the vial," she orders me.

"I can't," I say.

"You have to."

I meet her eyes and I lie, as I promised her I would never do again. "I already used it. Injected myself while you were sleeping."

She frowns, searching my face. Then a breath of air leaves her, and she clutches her heart in relief. "Thank you," Josi says fervently.

I nod. And I don't feel guilty about it. Because the truth is that Falon Shay is still alive, and I'll need to be more than a man to destroy him.

The moment shifts, twists. The falcon screeches and flies at me, its talons clawing at my face, its beak pecking at my heart. Through the chaos of it I hear Josi interrupt the others.

"We're going back to The Inferno," she says. "Luke didn't kill anyone. But I know who did, and we have to set it right."

Chapter 29

Raven

I wake with a feeling. It is not a good feeling. It is heavy and prickly and completely unnameable. I turn my head and look at Quinn, still sleeping beside me. I think, inexplicably, of a tidal wave.

"What's going on?" I ask as we enter Dodge's lab at his behest. He and Meredith are peering into the glass cage. Quinn and I cross to do the same.

My mouth falls open. Because Dr Ben Collingsworth is Dr Ben Collingsworth again. I don't know how I know it, but I do. It's the thing in his eyes that wasn't there before, the sudden appearance of something all too human.

The old man is sitting with one arm over his heart, as though it is causing him pain, and he's looking up at us wearily. "Could I have some water?" he rasps, throat raw. He sounds vulnerable.

Dodge rushes to get him a drink.

"What happened?" Quinn demands.

"I injected him with an experimental counteractive amphetamine," Meredith replies.

"So he's *normal* again?"

She shrugs. "In a manner of speaking."

"Then you can cure the Furies," I say, astonished.

"Theoretically."

"And practically?"

"How do you expect us to be able to inject every one of them?"

"What about the drones, then?"

"Theoretically," she repeats. I feel like throttling the woman.

We keep Ben in the cage a little longer, just to be sure. He doesn't argue or complain. He just sits quietly, but instead of the eerie restlessness he used to have, he now exudes sad contemplation. His clothes are dirty and torn, he has blood smeared all over his hands and face, and the stench of his cell must be of death – because though we removed the eaten carcass of the second Fury, we could not clean the remnants away.

I stay and watch him even after the others have gone to get lunch. I feel inexplicably compelled by him.

"How much do you remember, Old Man Fury?" I ask him, sitting on the edge of a bench with my legs swinging beneath me.

His milky eyes find me with a bit of a squint. "All of it. All the things I've seen, and all the things I've done."

"What did it feel like?"

Ben doesn't reply.

"I don't feel sorry for you," I tell him bluntly. "It's right that you should go through what you did to the others."

"Karma," he comments with a faint, empty smile.

"Justice. And it's unfair, in fact, that you were the one to get turned back."

Ben looks at me properly. And he says, "I think it's fair."

On impulse, I open the glass door and step inside with him. I crouch and help him to his feet. He shakes a little, that old-age sort of shaking. It's incredibly strange to see a feeble geriatric in place of the strong, savage predator who sat in here yesterday. I help him to the seat in the lab and get him some more water.

"You in any pain?" I ask.

"Wouldn't I deserve it?"

"Yes."

"What's your name, young lady?"

"Raven."

"What's your real name?"

"Raven." I fold my arms. "I was born here and I'll die here. Free."

"But why were you named for dead creatures?"

I swallow, unsettled by the question. "What were you named for?"

"Nothing." He finishes his water and hands me the cup. I turn to refill it for him. "Remembering things lost is a fool's game," he says softly.

When I turn back he is taking the scalpel from the bench.

And he is slicing it straight through his own throat.

The cup drops from my hand and smashes onto the floor. I lurch forward in shock to press my palms against the gaping wound in his neck, but there's way too much blood and it's too slippery to even keep any pressure there. The color drains quickly from his face and he slumps onto me. Together we slide to the floor and I feel his life pour out of him and we are trapped in a macabre sort of embrace as Ben Collingsworth dies atop me.

It is Quinn who finds me and helps to drag me out from beneath the dead body. I am shaking and covered in Ben's thick blood, so pungent that I gag violently.

"What happened?" Quinn keeps asking me, and I blink, trying to wrap my mind around the question.

"I don't know," I answer honestly. "I ... He remembered too much."

*

There's a tidal wave and it's coming for me. Didn't I always wish to drown?

I wake, disoriented. Ben's blood is still all over me; I'm choking on the stench of it. I throw off the sheet but it gets tangled in my feet and I trip clumsily to the ground. Blinking, I look down at myself. There is no blood. I'm washed and clean.

Footsteps sound and I look up to see Quinn appearing in the doorway. He sits on the edge of the bed and runs his hand through my red hair.

"Did you kill him?" he asks me.

And I hate him for it.

I *hate* him.

I hate him for his weakness and his lies, and for this pathetic, empty relationship of ours. I hate that he has always pitied me and patronized me, I hate that he doesn't trust me or believe me, but most of all I hate that he doesn't *know* me, not even a little. I am a stranger to him because he doesn't look at me. I am invisible. I am invisible to everyone in this whole fucking compound and I hate them all, I hate the whole world and I hate myself most of all.

A little piece of poison was born on the day I slipped out of my mother's womb and killed her in the process.

I rise to my feet. I don't look at Quinn; I will never look at him again. He's dead to me. I get dressed and walk out into the scorching hot sun, and as I walk down the main street of our compound I see people emerging from the steps to the tunnel.

She's at the front. Josephine Luquet. She doesn't look like she did when she first got here. Not plain or sullen or weak or sickly. Or perhaps she does, and it is me who looks at her with different eyes. Either way, as she walks toward me now I see something entirely different.

At the back of the group is Luke Townsend, and my heart is splintering with longing. It hurts so much and I don't know where to put it or how to get it *out* of me – I think I'm drowning after all, drowning not in love, but in the scorching *shame* of love.

"I told you what would happen if you came back here," Quinn's hard voice speaks from behind me.

The bedraggled group faces us. I count them quickly and see that three haven't returned with them. One of them is Shadow.

"We took out all stock of the sadness cure," Josephine says. She looks tired, but there's a clarity to her incredible eyes, a sharp kind of certainty that makes her seem very strong. "It'll take them a while to manufacture more, so it buys us some time."

"Some time to do what?" Quinn asks.

"Take out the Ministers," she replies simply.

We stare at her. I feel a thrill over my skin, under my bones. It's the audacity of it. The sheer, courageous lunacy. For the first time since she arrived in my home I think I like Josephine Luquet. I think I like her a hell of a lot more than I like my coward of a boyfriend.

Until she says, "We came back because this is our home, and because Luke is innocent of the murder charges. It was Raven who killed four people."

I freeze. "What?"

"What are you talking about?" Quinn snaps.

A few resisters have crowded around, excited to see the returned. At Josi's words, suspicion fills their eyes. They'll want to believe this. They hate me and they love Luke.

"Can we go somewhere and discuss this?" Josi asks.

"Say your piece before I have you all put through the gate," Quinn orders.

I watch her eyes search for and find Luke. He gives her a small, simple look, but it crystallizes everything for me because it is *intimate*. He will never look at me that way. Just as Quinn will never.

Josephine takes a breath. "Fine. It's simple. The whole premise of your case against Luke doesn't make sense. You condemned him because you were convinced he had motivation. That there was this old feud between him, Batch and Lace. You then said he had means because of the drug in his system that caused him to have violent blackouts. But the two cancel each other out. The very nature of those blackouts is the complete loss of your own personality, all your memories, all the thoughts and feelings that make you *you*. You don't care who you kill – the bloodlust is blind. Luke wouldn't have been in the right mind to recall a conflict, search out those people and kill them. On top of that, the drug doesn't make you turn any old time. It takes years to build in your system to the point of a complete blackout."

"You said it works differently for adults and children," Quinn argues.

"Not that differently." She shakes her head. "Luke's had symptoms, sure. But he wouldn't have been likely to turn for a couple of years. Beyond all of that, the third and fourth murders can't have been him, because Luke and I went to bed only fifteen minutes before I woke up and found the bodies. It wasn't enough time. *Besides which*, if he had turned that morning, I'd be the one who was dead, as I was lying right next to him in bed."

"So you were sleeping together without permission!" I accuse desperately. I am ignored.

"So then what? What are you saying happened?" Quinn presses.

"Luke's disoriented state and lack of memory is conducive with him having been drugged. It would have been easy for someone to set it all up to look like it was Luke. The link between the people who were murdered proves, if anything, that someone was trying to frame him. The only people who knew about the drug in his system were the two of you, plus Dodge and Ranya. Ranya's a treacherous bitch, as we have already established. But Raven's the only one with real motive."

"What motive?" Quinn snarls.

Josephine meets my eyes. "She's in love with him." Her hands squeeze my insides and my heart jackhammers. *No.* "And we all know how Raven handles rejection."

You bitch.

They're all staring at me with outrage and scorn. I am mortified.

"Is that true?" Quinn asks me. In front of the whole compound. I stare at him with more hatred than I know what to do with. I can see in his face that he already believes them. There's not even a scrap of loyalty in the man.

So I say nothing. Why do I say nothing?

Because fuck them all, that's why.

Quinn motions for a couple of guys to march me to the holding cell to await my punishment.

"I challenge you!" I say abruptly, wrenching my arms from their rough grips. "I have a right to challenge my accuser! Josephine Luquet, I challenge you to a bout."

There's silence in the hot, dusty afternoon.

It's Josi who replies, surprisingly. "She's right," the girl says. "I accept."

I am escorted home to wait until the fight. They aren't watching for it, so it's easy. Easy to ask for permission to go to the toilet, and while I'm in there to remove the blade from my leg razor and slip it into my sock.

*

Josephine

"That was too easy," I mutter. I am pacing my old living room. It's weird to be back here after I never thought I would be. Pace, Will, Eric and Luke sit squeezed together on the couch, watching me.

"Why does everything have to be *too* easy?" Will moans. "Why can't anything just be easy?"

"Quinn believed it too easily."

"That's because it's obvious she's guilty," Pace points out.

I shake my head. Something still feels off. After all this time, I finally figured out the truth, and I thought it would put an end to the nagging frustration at the back of my mind. But it's still there, still nagging away. A piece I missed.

"It's not your concern. Focus on the fight," Luke orders me. Claire's already put his broken hand in a cast, which he reaches inside to itch. She and Tobias were fine, thank god. They pretty much holed up in their house, and it was Raven, surprisingly, who took them food.

Luke hasn't asked me to step aside and let him fight her. I know he won't – we've moved beyond him trying to protect me from stuff. He knows what'll happen if he takes a flogging for me again. I made the accusation, and we should have been smarter about letting him do it, but we weren't, so I'm the one who was challenged. No way around it. This is my fight.

It feels right, anyway. It feels like facing Raven was always going to be my fight. I have to beat her, or she walks free for the murders. So I will. I'm not sure what we'll do with her after that – I don't want to kill anyone ever again, frankly, and no matter what she's done I don't believe sending her out to the Furies is right.

"Time to go," Eric announces, before I can come to any conclusions.

*

Every member of The Inferno has come to watch. They are crowded around the combat ring as I push through them to the middle. Their eyes don't belie much confidence in me. Raven is already here, readiness in every muscle.

She smiles and it looks brittle. "I haven't forgotten our last fight. It was a joke, Josephine. You can accuse me all you want, but you'll never be able to face me with any real strength, in any way that matters."

There's a nervous shuffle moving through the onlookers. They know she's right. They know I'm about to have my ass handed to me on a platter, and that the murderess will go free.

But what they don't know is that I'm not the woman I was a year ago.

"You challenged me. I'm here."

"Fine," Raven says with a bitter, hopeless laugh of regret. She believes to her bones that she's going to win.

I walk to meet her. My eyes find Luke's. I feel his power, and I feel my own.

"Begin," Quinn says.

She comes at me, hard and fast. But what I once thought was fast is now … not. She *is* fast, but she is not as fast as I am.

Cello music begins in my mind and it centers me in my body, in every single inch of it. I can feel it, feel every movement, every flinch and tense and stretch.

I run at her and slide beneath her blow, arching backwards and spinning to slash out with my right arm. I take out her knees and I am already sliding up to hammer my elbow into her neck as she falls, slamming her heavily to the ground. Twisting to drop with her, I land with my knee on her chest, pinning her. Blood spurts from her mouth and she is so shocked I decide to give her a moment to regain herself.

Rising, I stand back.

I become aware of the absolute incredulity of our audience. I don't let it breach my walls. I have to stay present. Raven's a formidable opponent.

She coughs and manages to get to her feet. She's woozy, I can see.

This time when she comes at me it's with wariness, and far more concentration. A left jab, followed by a right. I block them and when she's overextended I swing a deep left hook into her unprotected kidneys. The pain shocks her and I take the moment to hit her twice in the nose, two fast right jabs.

I duck low and hit her in the solar plexus, and as she stumbles back I smash her in the side of the head.

Raven hits the ground. I straighten, waiting for her to tap out.

But she rises to her feet. Faces me. Wipes blood from her eyes so that she can look into mine. "You got back up," Raven says. "You got back up every time. The least I can do is the same."

And it hurts. The sudden appearance of her humanity, her *grace*. I long for life to have been different, for the world to have been different. I long for her to have known love and kindness, instead of whatever cruelty drove her to such hatred. I regret that I must do this. I regret.

Raven attacks me, and this time her blows are harder, faster, as though she has found some reserve within her.

I block and block, my right coming up to guard, my left staying low to guard; we move so swiftly together it's a blur, a dance, a thing I never imagined I'd be capable of. I feel her fist sweep by my jaw, only just missing.

Sometimes you have to get hit.

She's holding herself tight now, aware of any attacks I might make. She's being careful. So I feint right, duck in and jab low, knowing it will leave my whole left side wide open to her. She takes the bait, swinging a mighty right blow into my face, but I am waiting for it and I know where her center of gravity will be and I know how unguarded her side will be. I lunge *into* the blow, taking it harder than I would have, but tilting so that I can send my boot into her ribs. I feel them crack beneath my kick.

Raven gasps in pain, stumbling backwards.

I don't give her any respite; I want this to be over. I follow, hitting her in the side of the head, and again as she goes down. I jam my arm beneath her chin, pinning her.

"Yield," I order her. "Or I'll kill you."

Her eyes are struggling to focus. "You won't kill me."

"Once upon a time I wouldn't have. A lot's changed." The truth is in my eyes.

Raven gives a feral scream of rage and taps out. I rise from her body. My cheek stings from her blow, but it was the only one she landed.

I feel cold, and older than I am. The crowd converges on us. Several people lift Raven and carry her to the holding cell. Quinn hasn't moved from his spot; he appears ghostly.

People are looking at me differently, I realize. There is furtive awe in their glances now and it stirs something discomforting in me. I think I'd prefer them to think me the bratty girl they disregarded once upon a time.

Luke joins me. "Welcome to the other side," he says grimly. "They'll never look at you the same way again."

"Can we go home?"

He nods. "I'm proud of you. It was a thankless task but someone had to do it."

I shake my head wearily. "Don't be proud. This was ugly."

"Most things are."

Chapter 30

September 16th, 2066

Luke

After the bout Josi sleeps while I sit beside her, contemplating the red, red moon in the sky.

The drug works in cycles. Just as the body does. Its effects will be bad again soon, and then not so bad, and so on. Now that I know I haven't been turning all year, I guess it's safe to assume the effects are more like what happened to Josi than we initially thought – and maybe, like her, I'll only change on the blood moon. For her it took a couple of years to progress to the point of a proper blackout, but I can feel it building. My skin itches and my teeth ache.

I know precisely what it feels like to believe you've murdered someone without any memory of it, and it's not a feeling I wish to endure again. And if I am to assume it'll only happen once a year, then it means, basically, that I have twelve months to destroy Falon Shay before I use the antidote to make myself normal again.

And now I just have to get through tonight.

I'm not sure what time it is when I climb from bed and make my way to the holding cell. Still early in the night, from the feel of the moon tugging at my insides.

Raven's sitting in the corner of the room, face swollen and bloody. I don't know why I'm here, but I enter and sit in the opposite corner.

"Why?" I ask her. "I'm struggling to believe you could be broken enough to do this simply because I didn't want you."

She watches me with her black eyes, but she says nothing.

"What *happened* to you?" I murmur. "You grew up here, free of all the madness. You're supposed to be one of the healthy ones."

Raven licks the blood off her bottom lip.

"I really thought I'd done it," I say with a hard laugh. "I've had nightmares, every single night, of killing those poor people. You did a thorough job of sending me mad. Even down to the blade beneath my bed."

Still she refuses to talk.

"Why aren't you saying anything?" I demand, frustrated. "Don't you want to at least explain yourself?"

"What's the point? I'm the villain, aren't I?"

I shake my head and stand up. The cast on my hand itches like crazy and I'm feeling claustrophobic in a box with a madwoman. I need sky and moon *now*. "Bye, Raven. Thanks for trying to get me executed."

"Bye, Luke. Thanks for making sure you weren't."

My feet falter momentarily, because she sounds sincere. I leave before she can mess with my head any further.

The night is quiet. I watch the stars above me as I walk home. And the red, red moon. When I look down I see the shadow of a figure passing across the road I'm on.

"Meredith," I call softly, and she pauses to wait for me. "Whatcha doing?"

"I'm on my way home for the night," she replies.

"Josi gave me the antidote you made."

"It's not an antidote. It's a blocker."

"Right. Well thanks."

She nods. "It worked very well on Dr Collingsworth, before Raven murdered him."

"*What?*" I exclaim. "Ben's dead? Why would she do that?"

"I don't know," Meredith replies. "By the sounds of it she has violent tendencies and a lack of empathy that suggest she might be clinically psychopathic."

"Jesus Christ," I breathe, rubbing my eyes wearily. "I'll come by in the morning and you can run me through it. I can't deal with it right now. 'Night, Meredith."

"Goodnight, Mr Townsend." She carries on, and I do the same. She's a weird lady, but it ain't her fault, I guess.

A sound drifts out to me as I draw nearer to home. The deep notes of a cello being plucked. I listen to them and let them wrap me in melancholy; it's not a bad feeling. It's quite beautiful, actually, and something I'd never experienced before I met Josephine. I realize it's the first time I've felt anything other than anger in weeks. In a strange way, it's a welcome feeling. Like sinking into a soft mattress or through a gentle ocean.

I think sadly of Ben; in my heart he joins the other casualties of this war. And I thank god we have Meredith.

The cello notes stop abruptly, and there's something about the way they cut off mid-song that alerts me. Quickly I head inside to find Josi standing in the middle of the room, her bow in hand, staring at the wall with a look of such deep concentration that I know she's doing some serious mental acrobatics.

Without looking at me she says, "Batch didn't die of decapitation."

"What?"

"The bruising, remember. He was strangled to death, decapitated after."

"Yeah, so?" I watch her, trying to work out what she's telling me. A faint tingle of dread is uncurling in my stomach.

"How big is your neck?" she demands, dropping the bow and striding to me. She puts her hands around my neck as though to strangle me. "Batch was bigger than you. We went over every inch of that body. I remember his neck – it was thicker. There's no way I'd be able to strangle you to death. I don't have the strength, and Raven's hands are smaller than mine. There was also no sign that he'd been beaten into submission first."

"So how could she have strangled a bigger, stronger man?" I agree.

"And how could she have carried you both to the crime scenes? You would have had to be drugged and unconscious, and you weren't dragged because there weren't any marks. I know firsthand how heavy you are. Batch was even heavier. It's *possible* she could have carried you, but pretty damn unlikely. And particularly unlikely in the time frame of those last kills."

"Which leaves us with – "

"The killer being a man."

We stare at each other.

"*You go down a second time and you irreparably damage the respect they have for their leader,*" she intones. The words I spoke to Quinn before my flogging. "He was so humiliated, Luke," she breathes. "I didn't get it at the time. But he was furious. You undermined his power when you publicly beat him the first time. He tried to humiliate you in return with the flogging but you only earned more respect by staying silent. He knew he had to take you out without looking like he was the bad guy."

Horror curls inside me, and then we take off in a sprint to get Raven free.

*

Raven

I wanted to drown, and so I shall. A tidal wave. I felt it coming. It called to me as it approached. *I'm coming as fast as I can. Wait for me.*

After Luke goes I ready myself.

But Quinn arrives first. That's alright. It's good, I suppose. A rounding out of it all. The end of the circle meeting the beginning.

"Hello, dear," I greet him sweetly. "Beloved apple of my eye. Light of my life."

"You worked it out then."

"Well, it wasn't *moi*. So who's the most duplicitous, two-faced rat in this whole place?"

He clasps his hands and gazes down at me. Jesus, how did I ever let him touch me with those pudgy hands of his? "It was never meant to be you who took the fall. The whole fucking point of it has now been blown to shit."

"The point being to get rid of the one person who posed any threat to your power."

Quinn nods. "But this would have had to happen anyway. For Ben."

"The murder I didn't commit."

"He was old as shit. As if he would have been strong enough to drag a scalpel through his own neck. You admitted it too – you told me you killed him because he remembered too much."

I gaze at him in disgust. "I don't know if it's worse if you actually believe that's what happened, or if you're lying about it."

"Doesn't matter either way," he shrugs. "That's what they'll all be told."

"I used to like that about you," I tell him. "The mask of kindness you wear over the cruel truth. I liked that only I could see beneath it." I laugh, shaking my head. "I thought it was dangerous and thrilling. How childish."

"We understand each other," he argues. "I see beneath your mask and you see beneath mine."

"I guess that's true," I nod slowly. I meet his eyes. "Here's the truth I know about you, Quinn. Your power is part of that mask. Underneath it you're weak and impotent and scared. You haven't even been able to get a fucking *erection* since he woke from his coma. The Inferno won't be yours for long. There are people here now with true power."

He is livid. I think he's about to attack me, but he restrains himself. "And I'm going to destroy them both, starting with his parents."

I stare at him. "Bullshit. Even you aren't that sick."

"How else am I meant to take him down?" Quinn asks coldly. "I thought you'd get that, being the mistrustful, heinous bitch you are."

"If I don't trust, it's to keep this place safe. *Everything* I do is for the settlement."

"Well, now you can be eaten alive for the settlement." He turns for the door with a smile and my heart ruptures because *shit* he's really going to do it – he's going to murder Luke's parents just to hurt him and I can't let him, I *won't* let him.

"Quinn," I say, and as he turns I attack him with a ferocious blow to the temple. He hits the ground but rolls swiftly, kicking me so hard in the stomach that I hit the wall. He crawls to me, taking my chin so he can smash my skull against the stone. Things go black for a second. I can taste steel.

I've never been able to beat him. I certainly can't beat him now, so recently brutalized by Josephine. But no matter what he does to me, I will not let him leave this room.

He smashes my head again. But with hands that are steadier than rock I reach into my sock and pull out the razor blade.

Quinn holds my chin and leans right in close to say, "You're worthless, Raven. The only thing you've ever been good for is looking at."

I drag the razor through his throat and hold his eyes as he dies.

Luke

We are sprinting along the road I travelled only minutes ago when I pause at the spot at which I ran into Meredith.

"What?" Josi asks.

I frown. "Where does Meredith sleep?"

Josi nods behind me, in the opposite direction to the one Meredith took. "Couple of houses that way."

"Shit … I think …" I shake my head. "I gotta check something. You go get Raven out and I'll meet you there."

I sprint off after Meredith. I'm only a few minutes behind her. The lab is in this direction, but she specifically said she was going home for the night. I check inside but it's empty. All that's left over this way is the Den, the fields and the wall. The second I see the empty hall and kitchens, I know, and launch myself into a sprint.

The wall looms, and up ahead I can see the east gate. There are guards up there, but they're focused, of course, on this perpetual need to kill the beasts outside. They aren't looking for any danger within.

And so I see, with horror, the gate being unlocked.

By Meredith Shaw.

"Meredith!" I shout, knowing it won't do any good. I'm too slow, I'm tragically slow, I can't push myself fast enough, even with this monstrously fast body of mine, a body Meredith created herself with that first damn cure for anger.

The guards have turned at the sound of the shouted name. "Take her down!" I roar, and they fire wildly at Meredith, but she has already unlocked the gate. *Why?* I ask myself desperately. *Why has she done this? To kill herself? To kill us?* I'm not sure I'll ever know, because as the guards are shouting in panic and rushing to sound the alarm, and as the bell tolls over the compound in a foretelling of doom, I see Meredith swarmed and eaten alive.

461

I am unarmed and I have a very broken hand. Shattered, in fact. But I keep running straight toward that open gate, and the flood of Furies swarming inside the wall.

*

Josephine

The bell rings so loudly and suddenly that I get a fright. I peer around in the dark, wondering what it means.

Something's wrong, that's for sure.

I start running for the steps to the holding cell, a sense of urgency propelling me.

*

Raven

I think of Ben as I slice my wrists open. He destroyed himself before his memories could. There was a lot of guilt in his past. There's a lot of cruelty in mine. I have never been a nice person. I took pleasure in the fear and discomfort of others. I liked hurting people, and that's the sign of a truly weak human being.

There's too much hate in my heart. I don't know where it came from or how to come back from it. I'm drowning in it. And in the blood slipping from my arteries. I always wanted to drown.

The door bursts open and someone gasps.

It is Josephine Luquet. I start laughing. Because of course it is.

She takes in Quinn's dead body and my bleeding wrists, and then she stumbles to me. Her hands try to grip the wounds, but she's too late, way too late. I am seeping away with the gentle lapping of waves.

"No, Raven, no no no," she utters, and I see that she's crying. I'm in her arms and it feels warm.

"I used to think you ruined my life," I tell her. At least I think I do. I feel hardly here anymore, hardly tethered to the lips of my body. "But it was me who did that."

"Don't," Josi cries, then screams, "Help!"

"'S'alright," I mumble. "I've wanted this for a long time."

"Raven," she says. "This is my fault. I'm sorry. I'm so so sorry."

"It was Quinn," I manage.

"I know. I know it was," she sobs.

"Good," I sigh. "He was a prick."

Josi laughs. Her tears are all over me, and my blood, too.

I think of Luke Townsend, who is the reason for this. Not that it's his fault. He was simply the catalyst. It was that glimpse of love that set me on this path, and I was never going to be able to get off it, not even if Quinn hadn't been such a small man. The arrival of Luke was an irreversible rotation of my soul into a new position, one that had seen a pinprick of light and couldn't ever unsee it.

I look up into Josi's beautiful dual eyes.

I think of my mother, in the end, whose life was traded for mine.

Chapter 31

September 16th, 2066

Josephine

I don't think I could have moved if I hadn't heard the screams coming from above. They shatter through the nightmare of this moment. She seems so fragile in my arms. She never seemed like this when she was alive.

I am filled with a surprising grief. It's the timing. The tragedy of the mistakes made and me being five minutes late that meant she died. Five minutes.

Fury engulfs me. There's no place for it to go – just a dead man on the ground. I feel like spitting on him. How fierce she must have been, to kill the man she loved so she could protect the rest of us from him. My hatred has been so misplaced; all along I have been punishing the wrong person.

I emerge from the stairs into chaos. The bell is ringing and ringing, but it's almost drowned out by the screams of running people and the snarls of Furies.

The camp has been overrun.

I'm right by the training room, which means the armory. Dodging through an oncoming rush of hysterical people, I get the door open and scramble for weapons. Two handguns, even though my aim still sucks, several magazines and a huge machete.

Something growls and I whirl to see a Fury lunging at me. I manage to get the blade in between us and the creature impales himself on it, but still scrapes his fingernails through my shoulder. I grunt, stabbing the machete deeper until I see the Fury die, then I shove it to the ground and wrench my blade free.

Dashing outside, I am met with a horrifying sight. The guards on the wall are openly firing, but the Furies have integrated with the people and in the dark it's almost impossible to see who is who. Bullets take out anything that moves. A resistance woman drops dead before me, shot in the chest.

"Get to the tunnel!" I scream as a group rushes past me. I don't know if they listen, and I can't wait to find out.

I plunge into the fray – I have to find Pace and Will. My gut is wrenching me to wherever Luke is, but I know he can take care of himself. As I hack my way through half a dozen Furies, slicing at anything I can, I yell for everyone to take cover in the tunnel, yell it over and over.

It starts getting harder to move forward and I realize there are too many. I can't cut them down fast enough. Drawing my pistols, I start to fire wildly into the mess of snarling teeth and limbs and bloody eyes.

I catch a glimpse of something a few feet away. It is the female Fury, the one who spoke to me. She's just standing there, watching as the creatures attack me. Another Fury moves between us, and by the time I kill it and look up again, the woman is gone.

The guards are still firing into us and they're dropping bodies one after the other, and I'm taking down as many with my guns, but I'm about to run out of bullets and there's not enough time to change the magazine.

So this is it. Honestly, it's not how I thought I'd die. But I guess it's as good a way as any. Better, maybe – I never thought I'd die fighting.

That's when a Fury gets past my guns and reaches for me.

Suddenly a knife slashes its throat and Luke bursts to my side with a wild grin.

"Sorry I'm late," he says, and I remember the first time we said these words to each other, in Anthony Harwood's office last year.

"You're right on time," I tell him.

Luke wields a long knife, and as we lunge forward he uses the blade to cut a path through the monsters. His right hand is useless, the cast hanging half on, half off. But even with only one hand he's too fast for them to stand a chance, even so many of them; he slices through throats and thighs and guts, stabs eyes and skulls, dropping one after another and allowing us to move toward the nearest building.

"Any reason you reckon they're all in love with you?" he asks.

So I wasn't imagining it – they're attacking me more than anyone else. "I have pure flesh, apparently."

"I wouldn't call it pure." Then, "We're nearly at the tunnel, girl. Keep it up a bit longer."

"Did you see Pace and Will?"

"Nope. But hopefully everyone was on their way to the tunnel. Did you see Quinn? My knife has his name on it."

I'm about to tell him when instead a Fury grabs my shoulder and wrenches me backwards. I trip against it but manage to twist and stab it in the neck.

We fight our way to the tunnel, shouting to be let through the trap door. Below ground it's cool and much quieter, but now the sounds that find me are those of people crying and moaning in pain.

Claire and Tobias lunge to Luke gratefully. I run through the crowd, searching for faces.

But the three I'm looking for are not here.

I whirl back to Luke, and he sees my expression. "No."

"They're my family," I say, holding his eyes. "Them and you."

An agonizing second passes between us, and then he nods. We race back to the steps, grabbing more weapons and magazines from people as we pass, then plunge up into the night.

The Furies swarm, their shrieks almost as lacerating as their nails and teeth. Our guns get one hell of a workout as we sprint through the chaos to my house.

They're not here – the place has been smashed open and emptied. "Where the fuck are they?"

"And why wouldn't they have gone to the tunnel with the rest?" Luke asks as he shoots a rushing Fury in the forehead and slams the door shut on the rest.

"Infirmary?" I suggest. But then I see it. My cello. I run over to lift it up, but it's damn heavy.

"Tell me you're joking."

I ignore Luke, grabbing a sheet and twisting it into a sash.

"What the fuck are you doing?" Luke snaps. "You'd die for a goddamn instrument, Josi? I'll build you another one!"

"It's coming," I tell him simply. He built it, but he still doesn't get it.

Luke groans in disbelief, then comes over and snatches it out of my hands. "Strap it to my back. And for the record this is incredibly dumb."

I'm about to argue but we don't have time and Luke is a hell of a lot stronger than me, so I strap the cello to his back. "Extra protection," I offer. And then we charge outside.

Three Furies emerge from the shadows to the side and collide with me before I spot them. We go down in a tangle of limbs and I fire into any flesh I can find. Teeth bite through the fleshy part of my arm and I give a short yelp of pain before Luke gets them off me and hauls me to my feet.

We make it to the infirmary to find about a dozen Furies all trying to get inside. Some have smashed windows and are trying to climb in, but I see one of the creatures blown away from the building, shot in the face. Which means there's someone inside.

Hacking our way through the Furies at the door, Luke roars that it's us. The door unlocks and swings open, and I give a sob of relief to see Will. His eyes are wide as he ushers us in and we slam the door shut against the rush of monsters.

"Thank god you're here," he says, "It's really really bad."

A scream slices through the air, a woman's scream. My insides go cold. We race around the corner into the main room to find Eric rushing around to each of the windows and shooting anything he can. And Pace, lying on one of the beds, wailing as though she's being eaten alive. Or in labor.

"Oh my *god*!" I exclaim.

Pace sees me and moans. "It's too early!"

Luke and Will rush to help guard the windows as I race to Pace's side. "Okay. Okay okay okay. Are you sure this is definitely happening?"

"*Yes!*" she shrieks.

"Holy shit. Okay."

"Stop saying okay!"

I take a deep breath and concentrate. "I need to look."

She moans again. Her cheeks are red and she looks like she's in deep distress. "Whatever, just do it!"

I unbutton her pants and pull them off, then her underpants.

"There's too many windows!" Luke shouts. "We should get her to the Den – we can barricade it better."

"We're not taking her away from the only medical equipment in this whole place," I respond. "So keep guarding those windows."

I've got no idea what a dilated vagina looks like, but there's no baby actually coming out yet.

"It's too early," she says again, sitting up on her elbows, apparently in between contractions.

"It's not too early. Twenty-eight weeks is fine, Pace." I think that may only be true when there's modern medicine and facilities, but I'm definitely not telling her that.

Luke arrives at my side. "I'm not shitting you. We're running out of ammo, and then we won't be able to guard the windows. We *have* to move her."

"Don't look at my vagina!" Pace shouts at him.

Luke's eyes jerk away. "Sorry! Bit hard not to."

I start giggling and have to get a hold of myself. "Oh god."

"And why do you have a cello on your back?" she asks him furiously.

"God only knows, Pace. Josi, what do we need to take?"

"How should I know?"

"Towels," he says, racing to grab some. "Water. Morphine?"

"No! Morphine could kill the baby."

Pace moans. "Don't kill the baby."

"We're not going to," I assure her. I help Luke grab whatever we can, including a few surgical bits and pieces, then we get her gurney to the door.

"You're going to wheel me, half naked, to the other side of a zombie-infested compound?"

"Yes," we say together.

Pace groans and covers her face with her hands.

"Boys!" Luke calls. Eric and Will abandon their posts and run to flank the gurney.

We unlock the door and explode out into the night, firing wildly and pushing that bed for all we're worth. A contraction hits and Pace *screams* and we run and shoot and try to shield her and it's all a brutal blur of go go *go*!

*

Luke

We get to the Den, but I don't know how. Literally. I'm losing chunks of time.

Last thing I remember is pushing out of the infirmary, I blinked and suddenly we're inside the Den, boarding up the doors. And I'm doing this as though in my momentary blackouts I'm still fully active and cognitive. Which is really, really weird.

Hold it together. Just hold it together for this one night, don't let Josi see you wig out, and get these people out safely.

But even with no windows, even unable to see it, I can *feel* the moon. Tugging persistently away at me. It's a sweet, sinister, seductive thing. It's an uncurling of something deep within.

Pace shrieks again, breaking through it all.

And as I turn to see them, the four of them, I make a decision with the moon and the beast and the violence within. *Not tonight.*

I run to help my family.

*

Josephine

The doors are all barricaded. There are no windows. No Furies are getting in here. So now all we have to deal with is this baby.

Will is holding Pace's hand and coaxing her to do that Lamaze breathing thing, which I don't think is helping, but at least it's focusing her rage on him and not me. Eric keeps running around to get more stuff from the kitchens, including strange items of food that Pace does *not* want to ingest right now, while Luke and I try to work out what's going on with the baby.

I feel her stomach, trying to trace the position. "I'm pretty sure it's head first," I mutter. There's a whole lot of stuff that can go wrong if the baby's turned the wrong way, I know that much.

"Feel how dilated she is," Luke tells me. "I can't see and I don't think she wants my hand going up there."

"I do *not*!" Pace snarls.

As gently as I can I press my fingers inside her, then pull them back out to show Luke the width.

"That's like three and a half inches!" he exclaims, and I see a look of terror cross his face. "It's totally coming!"

Pace gives this low moan that sounds sort of like a cow, making us all jump in fright, and I see her really start to *push*.

"Good girl," I tell her, ducking back down to see. I am, in a word, appalled. Because this kid is tearing out of her. The head pushes through and it looks like it's the size of a fucking basketball. "Keep going!" I yell. "I can see it!"

"Push, push, push!" the boys are chanting as if they're at a sports match.

Pace is moaning and screaming and I'm taking hold of the baby's shoulders and helping them to slide out. The tiny person slips the rest of the way free and into my hands, with a lot of blood and mucus and I don't feel the miracle yet because this little boy is not crying or breathing. I try to clean his nose and mouth with my fingers but they're too covered in fluid to help.

"Dual?" Pace is crying out, over and over, wanting to know what the hell is going on, but I don't have time to respond – I duck my mouth to his tiny mouth and I suck all the gunk from his face, and the minute it's clear he takes one mighty breath and lets out a resounding wail.

The boys let rip one hell of a cheer, and I sag, almost falling in my relief. But he's still in my arms, and he opens his eyes and stops crying, and I'm in absolute awe as he looks up at me, my whole soul reaching right into the sky for the sheer, perfect joy of it.

Eric grabs the scissors from the tray we brought and cuts the umbilical cord, and I can see that he's crying as he does so, and I'm crying as I carry the little fella to his mother, and I think everyone is crying as together we watch her hold him and kiss him.

I lean against Luke, and he says, "I'd kiss you right now, but you still have all that gross goop on your mouth." And then we are all laughing and it's perfect, even though there are a bunch of cannibals trying to eat us.

*

After I've used the towels to clean Pace (and my mouth) a bit, we swaddle the baby and tie him in a makeshift sling against Pace's chest. She can't stop staring at him, utterly in love.

"Okay," Luke says, bringing us all back down to Earth. The four of us step away from Pace and her son to speak privately. "A way out."

"Don't look at me," I sigh. "I'm braindead."

"Oil. Matches. Let's light these suckers up," Luke answers his own question. He and I run to the kitchens and gather supplies.

"Pace is amazing," he comments, impressed, as we tear through the pantry.

"Pace is a superhero," I agree.

"You were pretty damn great too."

I check to make sure we're alone and then mutter, "I sure as hell don't want to have a baby anymore. Yeesh."

He laughs.

After dousing a bunch of knotted up tea-towels in cooking oil, we distribute them among the group, along with matches and lighters.

"I need pants," Pace points out. "I'm not streaking naked down into the tunnel where everyone is waiting."

The mental image causes us all to giggle. I think we are hysterical with adrenalin and nervous energy. Eric takes one for the team, removing his pants for Pace to put on. At least he's wearing boxers.

"Here, Dad," Pace says to him, handing him the baby.

He blinks, looking startled.

Pace meets his eyes and nods. We watch Eric's face crease; he is deeply moved as he reaches reverently for the baby.

Luke hauls the cello onto his back again, with a glare at me.

When Pace has put the pants on, with a wadded-up towel for a nappy underneath, the baby is returned to her sling and we all move to the door closest to the tunnel.

"We throw these as we need them and force a path through to the tunnel," Luke instructs. "We don't stop no matter what."

"Even if one of us goes down," I agree. "Except for Pace, obviously."

We're about to break out when – "Wait!" Will shouts. "What's his name?"

We all turn to look at him, our little miracle. Pace gazes into her son's eyes, then smiles and says, "Duh."

And so together we light the doused rags, fling the doors open and send fire straight into the midst of the Furies.

Chapter 32

September 17th, 2066

Luke

It's dark as hell down here. There's a substantial group of us traipsing through the tunnel, but when you take into account how many people lived in The Inferno, it becomes apparent that at least two-thirds of us died at the hands of the Furies.

I move past the survivors in silence, not wanting them to notice me. Past Eric and Will, Pace and baby Hal. What I have to do now needs to happen as invisibly as possible. I feel hungry; it's a disturbing notion, and reminds me all too clearly of the monsters we fled.

I am looking for a man. A man who was once a child who ran from the city, seeking death and solitude but finding instead a life he would not turn out to be worthy of.

Four innocent people, I remind myself. Four people who trusted him, obeyed him, worked tirelessly for him. He was meant to protect them, not slaughter them. I wanted none of this – I wanted power for *him*. I wanted peace. But he let himself be twisted by the ugliest of things: greed. And so.

No pity dwells in my heart, no hesitation.

But as I creep through the tunnel I realize he is not here. And I realize, too, how much I wanted to be the one to kill him. Which frightens me more than anything.

The blood moon still shines, down through the night sky and the dusty earth, down through the rock and steel of this tunnel, right down into my dark heart.

*

Josephine

When Luke joins me at the back of the group I take his unbroken hand and we walk through the tunnel with the rest of our kind, the uncured souls who now have nowhere to go except back underneath the city that would see us destroyed. We have no home, except these tunnels. The Underworld indeed.

But this is what happens when you try to break our spirits: you leave room for only the strongest and the most ruthless to survive. You create an army sad enough to mourn what it's lost and furious enough to destroy those who steal from it. You create a *real* resistance.

There's a lot of despair in this world, a lot of anger, a lot of sadness. Raven let those things burn her to a husk. But all the threads that keep us tied here to our bodies, to our souls and to this big empty, broken planet – they all start and end in the same place. With hope.

Here in the west they know a lot about hope. They know how to ration it. How to squeeze and wring it dry. They know when to let it go; they know when it ends.

But here's a secret I know: it never ends. Not if you don't let it.

I remove a vial from my pocket, one that is filled with a drug that could take away my sadness. But happiness like this wouldn't feel as sweet without sadness. I have believed this always; I simply let grief confuse me. So I smash the vial under my foot and keep walking.

I'm coming for you, Shadow.

A sound whispers through the dark, and I falter. Turning to face the endless black hole behind me, I peer into it, skin prickling. I don't know how I know, but I know. They got through the barricade. The Furies are in the tunnel with us.

"Run!" I scream.

And we run.